I0724366

THE STONE COLD THRILLER SERIES - BOOKS 10-12

A STONE COLD THRILLER BOXSET

J. D. WESTON

STONE FIST

CHAPTER ONE

Sweat dripped from Fraser's swollen brow, collecting blood from the cut above his eye then fell to his knee, ran down his leg and discoloured his white sock. In the one minute break between rounds, Fraser tried to control his heart rate, but all around him was a fear-inducing blur of taunts, shouts, bright lights and abuse. Ahead of him, in the far corner, his opponent, Mackie, sat staring back at him while his trainer held up a water bottle to suck at.

"Let's go, boys," called the ref, a middle-aged man dressed in a white shirt and black trousers that struggled to contain his excessive paunch. "Round five."

There was no bell. The audience didn't fill an arena. The ring was in the basement of a pub in Plaistow where bare-knuckle fighting provided high stakes for every villain worth his salt for miles around. But the bare-knuckle fights at the Golden Ring Pub had one major difference; they were no holds barred fights to the death.

Plaistow was Fraser's home turf. Mackie was the guest fighter, but he was good, and he had got in early with a debilitating blow to Fraser's sight in round two.

"Get a move on," called someone from the crowd behind Mackie.

"Yeah, get up and fight, you pussy," another shouted.

Mackie's red shorts were in the centre of the ring. Fraser could see them, rocking from side to side as his opponent bounced from foot to foot to stay warm and loose.

Fraser pushed off the ropes but held onto the ropes for a second. His vision was returning, or so he thought. He turned his head from side to side trying to focus on something, anything. Movement in the corner of his eye caused him to duck instinctively and Mackie's arm swung across the top of Fraser's head, grazing his shaved scalp. Fraser jabbed at his blurred shape, felt the connection, and followed through with a combination, the last of which glanced off Mackie's sweaty body and sent Fraser stumbling forward.

That was when he knew it was over.

A hook out of nowhere connected with Fraser's head. He raised his arms to block the attack, but it was too late. The blows came fast, hard and with relentless brutality. The gloveless, hammer-like punches finding their mark every time.

Three punches sealed the deal. The first to his temple slowed Fraser's world to a crawl. The second to his nose brought with it the familiar iron taste of his own blood. The third was an uppercut that shook the life from Fraser's mind and turned his world to a dance of swirling lights.

Darkness came as he hit the floor and felt the warm rush of adrenaline fighting a lost cause.

Spinning lights greeted Fraser when he woke. Angry shouts from the wild audience waned and dropped an octave as if someone had slowed time to a crawl.

"Finish him," yelled a man, who had climbed up onto the ropes and leaned into the ring.

But all Fraser could see was a dark silhouette above him that seemed to spin as if Fraser was laying on a turntable. The man's voice was rough and hoarse from shouting but carried authority. The man wasn't just a member of the audience; he was Del Dixon, the renowned South London gangster who managed Mackie.

"Mackie, get in there and finish it or I'll get in there and finish you myself."

More faces appeared at the ropes, keen to see the fight come to its ultimate conclusion.

Two knees dropped down onto Fraser's shoulders, slippery with sweat. The spinning slowed enough for Fraser to make out Mackie's blurred form.

For a moment, the two fighters locked eyes, sharing some kind of kindred understanding.

Fraser understood what Mackie had to do. He was ready.

He nodded once and closed his eyes before Mackie delivered his final blows. The first was a hook that forced Fraser's head to one side, ripping his neck muscle and breaking some teeth. But the pain was short-lived. The second blow crushed Fraser's temple against the canvas floor of the ring, fracturing his skull. The third broke his jaw.

The fourth punch turned the lights out for Fraser, but enough consciousness remained for him to hear the taunting, muffled count of five, six and seven, before Mackie's final punch opened Fraser's fractured skull and consciousness leaked away like bloodied water into a drain.

CHAPTER TWO

"What are you going to do, John?" asked Mick, as he handed John a tumbler of brandy. "You can't pull out now. There's only a few days until the next fight. Dixon will start a bleeding war if you pull out now."

"I'm aware of the time constraints, Mick. I'm thinking. Can't you see I'm bleeding thinking?" replied John Cooper. He loosened the collar of his tailored shirt and ran his hand through his silver brush of short hair.

"I reckon Dixon's boys got to him before the fight," said Mick. He paced the floor of John Cooper's office, swirling his brandy and trying to put the images of Fraser's crushed skull to the back of his mind. "I mean, he was a dead cert. Never lost a fight. Never been knocked down. And in one bleeding fight, the most important of his life, he goes and gets himself killed. It doesn't make sense, John."

"So what do you suggest then, Mick? You seem to have all the answers. What do you suggest we do? I just lost two hundred grand on a dead cert. If I pull out now, I'll lose another three." He fumbled with his silver cufflinks and rolled his sleeves to show an aged but tanned and toned pair of forearms.

John had worked his way up the ranks. He'd done his share of dirty work. Being so close to losing it all over a fight was not part of his master plan.

Mick eyed him above the rim of his brandy glass.

"If you've got a plan, Mick, now's the time to mention it."

"Only one thing we can do, John," he replied, matching John's tone, a trait he knew he respected. He returned to his pacing, a habit John recognised as Mick running scenarios in his head, seeing all angles. "Make sure we don't bleeding lose. If we win the next one, we'll be three hundred grand up."

"Don't give me ifs, Mick. Ifs aren't going to give me a boner. Ifs aren't going to put money in my bleeding pocket, are they?" He sank his drink and held up his glass for Mick to refill. His number two might know how to talk to him, but he still had to be put in his place every now and again. "No. No, what we need is a dead cert."

Mick span back to face him. The long tails of his three-quarter length jacket followed shortly after.

"With all due respect, John, Fraser *was* a dead cert."

"Fraser wasn't a dead cert. He was a loser, Mick. No family. No obligations. And he had more debt than Greece. What do you think he was thinking when the fight started going pear-shaped for him? He wasn't thinking of his wife and kids, was he? No, he wasn't. There was nothing to make him try harder."

"Nothing worth fighting for, you mean?" said Mick.

"Exactly. He knew what he was up for and he knew who he was up against. As far as Fraser was concerned, if he won, he'd have fifty grand in his bin to blow on hookers and coke, or he'd have been killed. Either way, he couldn't care less."

"So we need someone who's married?"

"Not necessarily married, Mick. But someone with a few more scruples. Who have we got?"

"Bill Jackson. He's not married, but he's got a couple of kids."

"No, he's a mincer. He dances about too much. I'm not having three hundred bags of sand sitting on someone who can't keep bleeding still for three seconds, let alone stand in a ring and have the crap beaten out of them."

"How about Fox?"

"Stan Fox?" said John, dismissing the idea before Mick could even make an argument. "When was the last time he fought?"

"I don't know, but word is out that he's training again and in good shape, by all accounts."

"No, Mick, be serious. Stan Fox is an alcoholic. All Dixon would need to do to convince him to go down in the first round would be to tell him there's a bottle of vodka in hell with his name on it, and he'd flop before the bleeding bell rang."

"There must be someone, John," said Mick, handing him another brandy.

"Why haven't we thought about this sooner?" asked John. "I mean, we put five hundred grand on the table, two for the first fight, three for the second. And we haven't got any contingency? Why the bleeding hell not?"

"Well, John, Fraser was a dead cert, right? You even said it yourself once. You wouldn't even enter into the bet if we didn't have Fraser."

"Yes, Mick, but Fraser, in case you hadn't noticed, just had his head caved in by some South London bleeding pikey, and if we don't have a replacement for the fight in two weeks' time and I have to hand over three hundred more of my hard-earned grands, I'll be caving your bleeding head in."

"Alright, John, alright. We'll sort it, okay?"

"No, Mick, it's certainly not alright. Alright is certainly not what it is. Here's what I want you to do."

"Go on, John. Anything. You name them, I'll find them."

"No, Mick. We're not going to use anyone we know. Dixon will be one step ahead. We can't have the slimy little bastard getting to them before the fight, and we don't know who he's already got to, do we? No, we don't."

"So who then, John?"

"Someone new, Mick. Fresh blood."

"Where the bleeding hell am I supposed-"

"On the streets, Mick. Find me someone."

"Someone married, yeah?"

"What I need, Mick, is someone who can stand in the ring with the hardest pikey I've ever seen. Someone who we can offer a carrot to. And someone who might have a thing or two to lose."

"I'm on it, John. I'll talk to Nigel down the gym. He might-"

"You'll talk to no-one, Mick. Take Jack with you."

"Jack's a bit of a loose cannon, John."

"Even more reason to take him with you."

"Got it," said Mick. "I'll go get him now and call you with what we find." He sank his drink, put his glass down and opened the door.

"I'll tell you what you're going to find, Mick," said John.

Mick turned at the door and raised his eyebrows, waiting for John to finish.

"You're going to find me a dead cert."

CHAPTER THREE

The morning dew that clung to the wild grass soaked Harvey's feet and legs with every stride he took. Wispy leaves and branches whipped at his face as he tore through the brush and clean, fresh air filled his lungs with every rhythmic breath.

The early morning fog hung across his neighbour's field, blocking his view of the beach and the sea when he broke free of the forest and ran into the soft mud that stuck to his boots and doubled their weight. The three-hundred metre stretch of dirt that ran alongside the field to the beach road was littered with potholes. Only when Harvey had launched himself over the small hedgerow, run across the old tarmac and reached the sandy beach did he open himself up for the final sprint along the water's edge. A full five-hundred metre sprint.

Harvey passed the old man who swam naked in the cold sea each morning. He waved mid-sprint as he did every day, then slowed for the five-minute jog home. Only when he reached his driveway did Harvey start to walk and warm down. He stretched, kicked the mud off his boots then entered his house by the back door, which opened into the kitchen.

He tossed four small logs into the wood-burner then, from

a metal pail he kept beside the fire, he grabbed a handful of dried kindling and made a small pile inside the stove. He lit a match, waited for the kindling to ignite, and then moved two of the logs either side of the flame. It didn't take long for the oils in the pine to find the flames. He closed the door and stripped off. Before he went to the bathroom, he poured a jug of water into the cast iron kettle that sat on the burner and left it to boil.

With no hot water in the pipes until the wood-burner had been running for thirty minutes, Harvey took his usual cold shower. It was a habit he'd formed from necessity. He'd heard stories of macho characters in films like James Bond who took cold showers because it made them feel alive and woke their senses so they could operate at full efficiency. For Harvey, he'd been for a run and needed a shower, so he took one. It was simple.

He had just stepped in when the door to the bathroom opened. The movement was caught in the corner of his eye, but he turned away, pretending not to see. In the reflection of the chrome shower rail, a shadow passed behind him, slow and stealthy. He continued to rinse the mud from his short, dark hair, counting down all the while and gauging the timing of the attack until he was sure his assailant's hand would be just inches away.

He turned and grabbed a wrist, twisting it up and backwards so their body fell into his, and dragged Melody into the shower screaming from the sharp sting of the freezing cold water. Soaked in her nightdress and with water dripping from her hair, she wrapped herself in a towel, cursing him.

"One day, Harvey Stone," she said. "One day, you won't see me coming."

Harvey didn't reply. He turned his back on her, finished rinsing his body, and switched the water off. Taking the towel that Melody offered him, Harvey stepped out. Melody edged backwards out of the room, smiling at him.

"Go and stand by the fire," said Harvey. "It'll be hot by now."

"I'd rather stand here watching you," she replied. "I missed this."

"You missed what? Launching an unsuccessful attack on me and having your morning ruined by a cold shower?"

"I wouldn't change it for the world. What did you do when..."

"When what, Melody?" asked Harvey. "When we were split up?"

"Yeah. What was life like for you? How was it different?"

"It was the same as it is now," replied Harvey, as he turned to face Melody. "There was only really one major difference to my life."

"Oh," she said, biting her lower lip, "and was it something to do with what we did last night?"

"No," said Harvey, wrapping the towel around his waist and preparing for another attack. "I had to make my own coffee."

As Melody's face dropped and she whipped her towel at him, the kettle on the wood-burner began to whistle.

"Timed to perfection, Mr Stone."

"We've got a long drive ahead of us. We need coffee."

Melody continued the conversation from the open kitchen-lounge area, shouting through to Harvey as he dressed.

"I still can't believe Reg is getting married. After all these years, he's never struck me as the type, you know?"

"He's happy. I think we both owe the guy more credit than he gets. Let him have his moment," he replied, as he walked into the kitchen, pulling a clean t-shirt over his head.

"How many times?" asked Melody, as she handed him a coffee then reached for her own.

"How many times what?"

"How many times do you think he's saved your life?" asked Melody. "I mean, all the dumb things you've done, all the broken bones and nearly getting yourself blown up, and Reg has taken care of us from behind his laptop, sitting in a van."

"Too many times," said Harvey, as he stoked the fire with two more logs. "Too many times."

"Left jab, right jab, hook. Left jab, right jab, hook," said Old Man McGee, leaning into the pads as Tyler followed his commands. "Watch my feet. Watch my feet. Lead with your right. Right jab, left hook. Faster, Tyler. Right jab, left hook. Watch my feet. Watch for the change. Too slow. Back to basics. Left jab, right jab, hook. Left jab, right jab, hook. Good. Watch for my feet to change. Look at my eyes. You don't need to look at my feet to see them move."

Tyler held McGee's eyes and dealt him the required moves, hard and fast.

"Move, Tyler. You're flat-footed. Get me up against the ropes. I'm moving, Tyler. Follow me. Left jab, right jab, hook. Watch my feet. Are you tired?"

Tyler watched the pads dance in front of him. He bounced from foot to foot and landed the three punch combination.

"Get your weight behind it. Come on, Tyler. You're a big boy. Move with it."

Another combination hit the pads. Three successful blows. Three vibrating exhales that matched the dull thuds like a snare drum with a bass.

"Right, good," said McGee. "Let's call it a day. Get washed up."

The old man shook the pads off his hands. Tyler turned to Lloyd, who stood beside the ring to help remove his gloves.

"You did good, Tyler," said Lloyd. His voice hit the lower octaves that seemed to be reserved for men of African descent. "Listen to the old man. Do what he says. He's putting time into you. Respect that. When he says move your feet, move your feet. When he says put your weight behind the punch, he means it. You won't hurt him. I've seen bigger guys than you in here, and the old man would put them all on their arses with a look when they don't do what he says."

"Yeah, I know," said Tyler. He turned and watched McGee pick up a broom and sweep the floor beneath the row of six-foot punch bags that hung from the ceiling joists. "He knows his stuff. Did he train you?"

Lloyd gave a laugh through his nose like a single note on a tuba.

"No, but I've been ringside long enough to know a good one from a bad one," said Lloyd, as he pulled off the first glove.

"A good trainer, you mean?" said Tyler, flexing his hand.

"A good man." He nodded at Old Man McGee. "And that right there is about as good as they get. Do you see anyone else in here tonight?"

"Well, no, but I guess it's late."

"How many gyms have you trained in?" asked Lloyd.

"Enough."

"Were they ever empty?"

"Well, not really. There were always one or two guys there."

"The old man's putting time into you. Right now, you're his focus. You want my advice?"

"Yeah, go on."

"Make the most of it. Don't let him down."

"I don't plan on letting anyone down, Lloyd," replied Tyler. "Did you fight?" He held out his left hand for Lloyd to untie.

"Yeah, I fought. Won some. Lost some. I just like being here."

"I know what you mean," said Tyler. "I've been in gyms since I was a boy. It's the smell that gets me. I don't think I'll ever forget that smell."

"Sweat?" asked Lloyd, as he pulled the glove.

"No, mate. Hard work." He winked at Lloyd who held the ropes open for Tyler to step through. "I'll shower up at home. See you tomorrow, yeah?"

"You sure will," said Lloyd.

The old man leaned on his broom as Tyler walked past.

"Thanks for tonight," said Tyler. "Same time tomorrow, yeah?"

"If you're game," said the old man. "I'll be here. Always am."

The sound of the brush strokes faded as the door closed behind Tyler, giving way to the sound of rain hitting the street. The gym was in the fourth arch along below a railway bridge. Dim street lights lit the road, but the path was dark and immersed in shadows, lit only by the reflection of the city on the surface of the water.

A few cars rolled past, creating small waves as they cut through the deep puddles of water. At the end of the road, Tyler turned left and made his way towards Shadwell. The walk home usually gave Tyler time to think about the things the old man had said about his technique, but it was Lloyd's words that accompanied Tyler that night. The fact that the old man had chosen to focus on him over all the others, it was motivating. It was his chance and he wouldn't let him down.

He passed tyre shops and garages, an old church, and small parks that were tiny pockets of green between rows of blocks of flats. An old factory that had been reclaimed and turned into high-end apartments marked the end of the council housing. A narrow road marked the division where offices took over, climbing higher towards the city. The division also marked Tyler's home, which was a small flat in a two-story high building. He was thankful for the location. Although he would have liked to have been closer to the gym, the council flats were a maze of gang fights, drugs and crime. The last thing Tyler needed was to be mixed up in anything.

"Mum?" he called, when he opened his front door. "Are you awake?"

No reply came. Tyler eased the front door closed, stepped into the kitchen, and flicked on the light.

On the sideboard was a plate with a knife and a mug. He washed them under the tap and turned them upside down on the draining board to dry. The kitchen, which overlooked the road below, had been painted in a sickly yellow. The ceiling had signs of mildew in the corners and the linoleum floor was torn by the door. The council provided the housing. His mother had been taken ill two years previously and had since been unable to work. Tyler took care of her between work and training. Although she was stubborn and determined to cook her own meals and bathe herself, some days the chemo cut her down and reduced her to a fraction of the woman Tyler remembered as a child.

Tyler used a cloth to wipe the sink clean, then folded it, hung it over the tap, and reached over the counter to close the two small curtains.

That was when he saw two men staring up at him from the street below.

CHAPTER FIVE

"Was that the best you've got, John?" Del Dixon's already hoarse voice was like gravel over the mobile connection. "Who are you putting up next? Your old lady?"

"Very witty, Del," replied John. "How did you do it?"

"Do what, John? I hope you're not accusing me of anything."

"There's no way Fraser lost his form overnight, Del."

"Choose your words carefully."

"I'll choose my words how I like, Del."

"So we're still on for the second match then? I mean, you're not going to run away?"

"I've given you two hundred grand, Del. I don't intend on losing any more."

"So tell me. Who are you putting up?"

"Why? What are you going to do? Pay them a visit? Are you going to send the boys round? I don't think so."

"You don't have anyone yet, do you?" said Dixon.

John remained silent.

"I'm right, aren't I? You're not your usual cocky self because right now you don't know who's going in that ring."

"I've been in this game a long time, Del. I can smell when a fighter has been got to. It smells like rotten flesh."

"Maybe you need a break from it all then, John. Maybe you've lost your touch. It's nothing to be ashamed of."

"I haven't lost anything."

"Except two hundred grand."

"I'm too long in the tooth for your games, Del."

"So we're on then, are we?" said Del. "Two weeks' time. Oh, and John?"

John let the silence speak for itself and waited for Del to continue.

"I prefer cash if you don't mind."

The call disconnected. John slid his phone onto his desk, picked up his tumbler of brandy and downed its contents. But Del's words played over in his mind. He imagined the self-righteous smile that accompanied the smug voice. John hurled his glass across the room. It smashed against the wall, sending tiny fragments of crystal glass to the solid oak floor, and left a tear of amber to run down the plaster.

He picked up the phone again and dialled Mick's number, who answered on the first ring.

"Give me good news," said John.

"Nothing confirmed yet. But we have two options, John. We're working on bringing them in."

"I want a name tonight and I want to meet them tomorrow. Make it happen, Mick."

He hung up the call before Mick could respond, then poured a fresh brandy into a new glass from the tray beside his desk. At the forefront of his thoughts was an image of Del handing over three hundred thousand pounds. A profit of one hundred thousand wasn't bad. But in the two-match run, the scores would be equal. One win each. A hundred thousand pounds didn't have the same ring to it as the original five hundred. Taking five hundred grand from Del Dixon would have set John back on top of the food chain. One hundred would just about make them even, once the damage to reputation had been factored in.

He tapped his phone against his lip, letting possibilities run amok like a roulette wheel inside his mind. Ideas were scratched off as they appeared. Having Del taken out was too risky, and he'd be expecting it, just as John was ready for a hit himself. Having Del's family taken out just wasn't how things were done. Families were a no go. It was an unwritten rule between men such as John and Del Dixon. Hitting his business was a possibility. But two weeks wasn't long enough to coordinate such an effort. The wheel span with just a few ideas remaining. It slowed, and the clicking sound slowed with it, until the pointer hung between two final ideas, both as dangerous as the other.

And then the wheel stopped.

With the last of the brandy in John's gullet, he dialled Del's number. He breathed in and savoured the air that cooled the alcohol burn inside his throat while he listened to the ringtone.

"Cooper?" said Del. "You're keen tonight. You've caught me counting my winnings, so make it quick."

"Double it," said John. "Six hundred grand."

A silence followed, broken only by the whisper of the telephone signal.

"Six hundred grand and the Golden Ring," said Dixon.

CHAPTER SIX

With a final glance around the house, Harvey committed the scene to memory. It was a trick he'd learned from his mentor, Julios. Each item, no matter how small or trivial, had been placed in such a way that any differences in position would stand out a mile on Harvey's return.

He pulled the back door closed, locked it, and then walked around to the front of the house, where Melody was waiting in her little sports car. The roof was down and their luggage was in the tiny back seat. She smiled as he approached and started the car. Harvey took a final look at the house then climbed into the passenger seat.

"Are you sure you don't want to drive?" asked Melody. "It's a long way to London."

The seat slid back as far as it would go and Harvey stretched his legs out.

"I'm good," he replied. "It's about time you earned your keep."

"You know what, Harvey Stone?" said Melody. "If I'm not mistaken, I do believe you're developing a sense of humour."

Harvey didn't reply. Instead, he watched the house disappear in the side-view mirror and let Melody ponder on her statement some more.

"Maybe it's just that you're relaxed," she mused. "You love that house, don't you?"

"Have you any idea of the things I had to do to get it?" asked Harvey.

"Yes, I do. I found the bodies, remember?"

"You found some of the bodies, Melody. And yeah, I do love that house. I dreamed about it for years. I just wish I could actually spend some time there to enjoy it."

Keeping her eyes on the road, Melody shuffled in her seat, making herself comfortable for the long drive to London.

"This is the last one, Melody."

"Last what?"

"The last trip. At least for a while. I'm supposed to be retired with my feet up."

"It's Reg's wedding, Harvey. You can't not go. He'd be devastated."

"I know, I know. I'm going, aren't I? But after this, no more. London has a lot of memories for me. Most of them I'd like to leave behind and forget about."

"They can't all be bad."

"No, not all of them. But enough to keep me away. Besides, every time I go there, something happens. I need to keep my head down. Julios would have a fit if he was alive and knew about the things I've done."

"Julios?" said Melody. "Wow, I haven't heard that name for a long time."

"Yeah, well," said Harvey, "it doesn't mean I've forgotten about him. The bloke was like a dad to me."

"Do you ever think about your real dad?" asked Melody, as she pulled out of their lane and onto the main road, a dual carriageway that would link them to the main artery network of French motorways.

"Yeah, of course. But there are no images. Not like Julios. I've got memories of him. As clear as day, most of them."

"What's your favourite?"

"Memory?" asked Harvey. "I don't have a favourite."

"So what one do you remember the most? If I said the name Julios to you, what memory does it invoke?"

"The one of him lying on the ground full of bullet holes."

Melody was silent.

"You asked," said Harvey.

"And I wish I hadn't."

Melody sat for a while, deep in thought and quiet.

"How about you?" asked Harvey.

"Me?" asked Melody. "How about me what?"

"Your favourite memory." He asked the question to break the silence, but waited for the answer, intrigued as to her reply.

"My parents. My dog. No specific memory," said Melody.

"So if I mentioned your parents, what memory does it invoke?"

"The funeral," she replied, then gave him a sideways glance and returned her attention to the road.

"See," said Harvey. "I'm not the only psycho in this car."

"There it is again," said Melody.

"There's what again?"

"That sense of humour," said Melody, as she dropped to third gear, manoeuvred into the outside lane and overtook a lorry. "You should be careful. You might be losing your mean streak."

"See you tomorrow, boss," said Tyler, as he heaved his work bag over his shoulder.

"Are you not coming for a beer, Tyler?" said George. "Come on, son. Dirty Harry had a kid yesterday. We're going to wet the baby's head."

"Not tonight, George. Sorry, mate."

"Tyler, what is it? Don't you like us? Is Frank too hard on you? Don't worry about him. Look at the bleeding size of you. You could knock him over with your little finger." George slammed the door to his van and moved around it to stand beside Tyler.

"No, George, I've got training, that's all, and I need to check on my mum. Another time, yeah?"

"When? Christmas?" said George. "That's a long way off, Tyler. Are you okay, mate?" George lowered his voice. "Are you alright for cash, son? Do you need a bit more work?"

"No, it's fine, George. Honest."

"I can get you on the tools if you want. We'll start you off slow. No more fetching bricks and muck for us lot. You'll have your own labourer."

"No, seriously," said Tyler. He backed away from George. "I'm fine, mate. Honest. I like the graft. It keeps me in shape."

"Yeah, but you can get some serious cash on the tools. Price work, Tyler. That's where the money is."

"Yeah, maybe one day. Listen, I'm running late. I've got to see my mum and get to the gym."

"Alright, son, if you're sure. But listen, if there's something you need, you tell me. Alright?"

"Yeah, no worries," said Tyler, as he moved towards the gate of the construction site. He turned and called back to George. "Hey, George."

"What's up?" said George, as he opened his van door, leaned in and started the engine.

"Thanks," said Tyler. "I'll have a think about getting on the tools."

"You do that, son," said George, and he climbed into his van.

Tyler turned right out of the site, tightened his hooded sweatshirt around his neck, and pulled on his beanie hat. He worked himself into a stride that was just out of his comfort zone, enough to raise his heart rate, but not too much to tire him out on the three-mile walk home.

The winter sky loomed above, dark and foreboding, and although the rain had stopped, the roads still held their sheen, magnifying the lights of passing cars and street lights. Tyler turned onto Commercial Road. It was the easiest route home and a straight line from Poplar to Shadwell. There were faster routes to take, but they meant entering the maze of back streets. The direct route gave Tyler a chance to go over the things that the old man had told him the night before. Lloyd had advised him to listen to the old man; the last thing Tyler wanted to do was make him repeat himself. He needed to prove how good he was and demonstrate his potential.

He opened the front door to find his mum standing in the

kitchen. She was stirring a saucepan of soup and beamed at him as he closed the door.

"You're up and about," said Tyler. "Shouldn't you be resting?"

"Oh, Tyler, I can't lie in bed all day. I get up when I can. Anyway, how was your day, love? Do you want some soup?"

"Here, let me, Mum. Why don't you sit down? I'll bring it through to you."

"Stop fussing. It's only soup. I can manage," she replied. "So? How was your day then? Tell me about the world outside these four walls."

"You're better off inside, Mum. It rained all day."

"Yeah, I know. I heard it on the window. And the wind. I hope you wrap up warm at work."

"Of course, Mum. It's hard work though, up and down ladders. I'm usually stripped down to my t-shirt within twenty minutes."

"Does George make you work in the rain?"

"We all work in the rain, Mum, or else we don't get paid. We do the internal walls when it's wet outside. You can't lay a wet brick, Mum." He talked to his mum from his room as he changed into his gym shorts, a fresh t-shirt and clean socks.

"Are you training tonight?" she asked.

"Yeah," said Tyler, as he pulled the door closed to his bedroom. "The old man's giving me some of his time. Lloyd said I should make the most of it. I reckon I can really show them what I can do, Mum. Now could be the chance I've been waiting for."

"Which one's Lloyd?" his mum asked.

"He helps the old man. He's a really nice bloke. Knows his stuff too."

"Will you be late?"

"I don't know, Mum. If the old man wants to carry on, I'd be stupid not to."

"Oh," she replied, "okay, dear. I don't want to stop you doing what you want to do." Her tone had dropped. The cheerful demeanour had all but gone.

"Why don't we do something special this weekend, Mum? If you're feeling up to it?"

"Yeah. Why not, love?" she replied with a smile as she turned the gas off. "Maybe I'll cook a roast dinner. You'll need to go shopping though."

Tyler picked up his bag and slung it over his shoulder, then stepped into the kitchen to kiss his mum goodbye. But as he did, the saucepan she was using to pour soup slipped in her hand. The hot broth splashed onto the counter, causing his mum to step back in alarm. Her foot kicked a chair, but before she fell, Tyler reached in, pulled the pan from her hands, put his arm around his mum to steady her, and then set the pan down on the stove.

He switched off the gas and wiped the mess.

"It's alright," he said. "You only spilt a bit of it. There's loads left."

"I'm sorry, Tyler, I-"

"Hey," he said, rubbing her arm, "go in the living room and sit down. I'll bring this in for you."

He poured the soup into a bowl and fetched a spoon from the drawer, marvelling at the fact that they didn't have a nice TV, the curtains needed replacing and the carpets needed burning, but they had soup spoons in the cutlery drawer like a fancy restaurant.

Tyler glanced out of the window to the street below. There were no tell-tale signs of exhaust smoke in the cold night air. No interior lights were on in any of the parked cars. But he couldn't shake the feeling that it wouldn't be the last he saw of the two men.

His mum was sat at a little four-seater table by the window in the living room. Tyler set down the bowl and flicked on the TV. He placed the remote beside his mum and gave her a kiss on the cheek.

"Leave all this here when you're done," he said. "I'll clean up when I get back."

"I'm sorry, Tyler," she said.

"What're you sorry for?"

"I'm getting more useless by the day."

The statement saddened Tyler but he couldn't let his mum see. He coughed to clear his throat and then stepped across the room to put his arm around her.

"Your job is to love me, right?" he said. "And my job is to look after you." He looked around the room. It wasn't much but it was clean and tidy. "I think we're doing alright, Mum."

He kissed the top of her head and returned to the front door, giving her a wave as he pulled it closed behind him. Then he took the single flight of stairs to the ground floor two at a time.

A biting wind found his neck and ears as soon as he left the building. He pulled on his beanie hat and wrapped his hooded sweatshirt closer around his neck, then found his pace and got into the rhythm, working through combinations in his head as he walked.

A group of teenagers huddled together outside a block of flats. The smell of weed was thick even in the strong, cool wind. They quietened as he approached. All four heads turned to watch him. Tyler didn't turn away. He kept looking ahead with his fists clenched inside the pockets of his hoodie.

No abuse or taunts came his way, so Tyler kept moving. He'd done well to get through school and avoid much of the trouble. His grades hadn't been great, and aside from one close call with the police, his record was clean. Many kids his age left school on the back foot with records for stealing or abuse or some kind of drugs possession. But Tyler had steered clear, finding solace in the various gyms he frequented. Even the single infraction he'd had with the law had been instigated by others seeing how far they could push him until he snapped.

It was because of his size; he knew it was. But they were soon sorry.

They wouldn't be pushing anybody else around in a hurry. But Tyler would do whatever it took to avoid any more trouble. The policewoman who had spoken to him had been nice. It was as if she'd understood and saw that Tyler was a nice guy deep down. He remembered how she'd sat on the blue plastic mattress in his cell, while Tyler buried his face in his hands. His mind often recalled the memory. Someone on TV had once said that certain events were turning points in life, and that by recognising them, no matter how painful it is, the stronger the lesson will be. At the time, Tyler hadn't even realised how hard he'd hit the boy. He hadn't known the damage he'd caused. It was a blur. But when the officer who sat beside Tyler told him the boy was no longer in critical condition, it was as if something inside Tyler snapped. The very thing that held him upright and gave strength to his bones was gone.

He'd crumpled to a heap on the sticky, blue, plastic mattress and the tears had flowed.

The smell hit him as soon as he opened the door to the gym, causing memories of the police officer and the blue mattress to fade away. It was a close second to smelling his mum's roast dinner from outside the flat. Nothing would ever beat that smell.

"Alright, Lloyd?" said Tyler, as he dumped his bag on a bench to change his shoes.

"All good," said Lloyd. His baritone voice lay beneath the

dull thumps of punch bags and muffled voices from outside the changing room. He waited for Tyler to change his shoes so he could wrap his hands. "Do you work outside?"

"Yeah, labouring for a brickie. We're on a job in Limehouse at the minute. It's not too far. What about you? Do you do anything else?"

"Anything other than getting this lot gloved up?" said Lloyd. "No. I'm too old for much else now."

"As long as you're happy, I guess," said Tyler, holding out his right hand.

"The old man's in a good mood today. Do what he says when he says."

"Yeah, right," said Tyler. "Do you think he'll put me up for a fight soon?"

Lloyd pulled the wrap tight and held Tyler's glove open for him to slide his hand inside.

"Be patient."

Tyler nodded.

Once Lloyd had wrapped and gloved his left hand, Tyler emerged from the changing room in the gym. Two punch bags swung back and forth as two young boys practised jabs and staying on their toes.

"That's good, boys," said Lloyd. "Look light on your feet, Billy. Don't settle."

"I remember all that," said Tyler. "I used to look up to the kids like me thinking they must know it all."

"Nothing changes, Tyler. I've been in this game for forty years and nothing changes but the names and faces. You know that smell you like?"

"The smell of hard work?" said Tyler.

"It smelled the same back then too, just a different name and a different face. Get warmed up on the bags, Tyler. The old man will be with you soon."

Tyler moved his body from side to side as he walked through the centre of the gym, running through combinations in the air. He rolled his neck, waiting for the click of his joints, then threw a few light jabs at the bag.

A breath of fresh, cold air licked at his bare legs, enough for him to turn to see who had opened the door.

Two men, both huge, walked in and let the door close behind them. The first man wore a long, dark, double-breasted jacket, as if he was a city worker, but with smart jeans, a casual shirt and brown leather boots. The second man wore a short bomber jacket, light blue jeans and smart shoes.

The pair looked comfortable in the gym, not intimidated as some people look when they walk in for the first time. They eyed the boys on the bags, and then the teenager that the old man was training in the ring. Then they found Tyler at the far end of the room. Tyler nodded then continued with his jabs, feeling the stretch of his muscles with each punch.

The two men both sat on the small bench beside the door. The smartest of the pair played with his phone. The other watched the old man. But every now and then, Tyler would glance across to find one of them staring at him. Just like they had the night before.

"Tyler, you're up," called the old man.

Lloyd held the ropes for the teenager in the ring to climb out. The boy's arms hung by his sides like lead weights. Tyler smiled. He knew the feeling all too well. It was a feeling that didn't go away the more training he did; it just took longer to tire.

"Let's go," said the old man.

Then he eyed the two men on the bench. They made eye contact but neither spoke.

"You remember what we did yesterday?" asked the old man, slipping back into the pads as Tyler ducked beneath ropes.

"Jab, jab, hook?" said Tyler, punching the air with the combination.

"Not the moves, Tyler," said the old man. "The eyes and the feet. Look at my eyes, watch for my feet, and roll with the punches. Let's go. Right, left, right."

Tyler threw the first punch before the old man had finished, but he was ready with the pad.

"Good, Tyler." The old man sidestepped as Tyler threw the hook, which missed. "Come on. Dance with me. Get me on the ropes, Tyler."

The old man moved around faster than he looked capable of moving. The two men stared up at Tyler as he jabbed at the pads. But Tyler's punches were weak, his feet were flat, and the old man moved before he'd finished one combo.

"Tyler, look at me. Let's go. You think I'm dancing for my health?"

Tyler bounced into action, and let three punches go in quick succession.

"That's better. Again. Watch my feet. Watch my feet."

The old man's footwork changed. His leading arm switched to his left, so Tyler adjusted the combo to left, right, left, and powered them into the pads.

"On your toes, Tyler."

No matter how hard he tried, Tyler couldn't shake the stares of the two men at the door. He threw one punch and the old man shifted the pad to the right then returned the blow to Tyler's head.

"Wake up, Tyler. Let's go." He offered the pads again but caught Tyler's glance at the men by the door.

"Right. Stop," said the old man. He shook the pads from his hands, turned, and leaned on the ropes.

"Can I help you, boys?" he asked. His authority in the gym

quietened the thuds of gloves on bags and skip ropes until all eyes were on him. "I said, can I help you, boys?"

The larger of the two men stood up, followed by his counterpart. Lloyd walked over to them, bridging the gap. He spoke in a quiet voice so as not to antagonise the men. But his deep grumble could be heard by all.

"Are you waiting for anyone?" asked Lloyd.

The bigger of the two men looked as though he was about to say something, but then closed his mouth.

"Can I politely ask you both to leave?" said Lloyd. "We don't want trouble, but the boys need to train."

The lead man shook his head, gestured for his friend to follow, and they left the building.

"Right, the show is over," said the old man to the room. "Let me hear those bags going."

The old man turned back to Tyler.

"Friends of yours?" he asked.

"Never seen them before."

Tyler threw two jabs and a hook at the old man, who blocked them with the pads and returned to his dance around the ring.

CHAPTER EIGHT

The Golden Ring Pub was a Victorian building with heavy brickwork and large windows. It was split into two bars. The first was a saloon with a long bar across the back wall and booths around the edges. There was a small stage area at the front where the landlord hosted a jam night every Thursday evening. A well-reputed local band would play a few hits from the sixties or seventies, mainly classic rock, and then other people could join them. Guitarists, singers, drummers and bass players, mostly bedroom musicians, took the opportunity to get in front of a crowd to perform. It was one thing to play a song note for note in the confines of your own home, but to perform it in front of a crowd was a different game.

The jam night brought in customers from all over the East End. The host band, Double Trouble, was comprised of middle-aged men who had each mastered their instruments but never made the big time. That didn't stop them rocking the Golden Ring for one night a week and showing the wannabes how it was done.

They opened with a Gary Moore number, Still Got The

Blues For You, a steady beat to warm up to with enough of a solo for the guitarist to stretch his fingers. The crowd loved it, and the noise from the saloon raised a notch.

It was for this reason that John Cooper chose to sit in the other half of the pub on Thursdays, the family side. It was decorated with exactly the same red-patterned carpet and textured wallpaper as the saloon, with the same oak bar, but without the screaming Marshall amps and Les Paul guitars or an eight-piece Ludwig drum kit being thrashed by a six-foot pipe-fitter.

John had a wing-back seat beside the large fireplace. It was where he sat every Thursday night. From there, he could see the rest of the pub, whoever entered through the doors, and he had the benefit of having his back to the window.

The family side wasn't busy. Most of the clientele were watching the band perform, so John enjoyed having the place to himself. Two youngsters were playing pool, but they were local boys, probably just turned eighteen, and they knew to keep the noise down. Keeping a few local boys on his side was something he'd always done, and he found the practice worked well. He'd explained his thought process to Mick once when they'd both been sat in that very spot.

"Society works in layers, Mick. Although you might think you've got your ear to the ground, you only know what's going on in the layer in which you reside."

"What, like a sandwich, John? Is that what you're saying?"

"If that's the analogy that works for you, then yeah, Mick. Like a sandwich. A triple-decker club sandwich. The top layer is where the mayo and lettuce is. That's where the politicians are, the top cops, and all the stuffy businessmen who go home to their vanilla wives every night, pleased with their day's work but absolutely ignorant to the rest of society. You see, those in the top layer still have two more layers beneath them, even three sometimes. They might have an inkling of what happens in the layer below, but the next layer? No. They don't have a clue, Mick. Blind to it, they are."

"I get you. So who's in the bottom layer?"

"The bottom layer, Mick, is the one that gets crushed by the weight of the layers above. That's where the tomatoes go. We're talking street gangs, drug dealers, thieves and the lowest rung of society. In the same way that the top brass doesn't have a clue what goes on in the bottom layer of the sandwich, the bottom layer has no clue what goes on in the top of the sandwich. That's why there's so much disconnect in society. The local government makes changes that they think is going to solve a problem and all it does is create new problems, different ones, in the bottom layer. And the cycle starts over."

"So where are we then?" asked Mick.

"We, Mick, are the meat. Crispy bacon and turkey stuffing. We reside in the middle layer. We are neither blind to the tomatoes nor blind to the mayo and salad on top. The trouble is, Mick, in most restaurants, you don't get much meat in a club sandwich. They stuff it with tomatoes and mayo and lettuce when all we really want is meat. The good stuff. In fact, without the crispy bacon and turkey, the lettuce and mayo would be nothing. And likewise for the tomatoes. Nobody needs a tomato on its own, Mick, do they?"

"No, John."

"So we sit strategically in the middle. Of course, we know some lettuces and we use them to understand what's happening above because that's how we don't get caught doing what we do. Right?"

"Right, John."

"And we know a few tomatoes too because that's how we know what's going on below."

"I understand."

"But we need to have some tomatoes on our side, Mick. And we need to have some lettuce watching our backs too. There's far too many tomatoes in this sandwich that need to be controlled. Just as the mayo has far too much power; it needs to be culled every now and then. That's why we have local elections."

Mick looked a little lost.

"See those two boys playing pool?" asked John.

Mick nodded.

"I could quite easily turf them out for being underage. But what's that going to do?"

"I don't know, John."

"Well, they'll come back tonight, when we're all at home, and they'll smash the bleeding windows, won't they? They might even start a little fire that gets out of control. You remember being a kid, right?"

"Right," said Mick.

"So by having a few tomatoes on our side, by keeping them keen, then firstly, we don't get our windows broke or the place burned down, and secondly, we send them in like little soldier tomatoes and pay them a bit of pocket money for any information they feed back to us. It keeps them sweet."

"The same way we pay off the top brass?"

"Exactly, Mick. You see? Being in the middle layer is a great place to be."

"Right," said Mick, and sat back in his chair.

John could see the analogy had blown his mind.

John's phone buzzed on the table and snapped him from his memory.

"Mick," he said, dismissing the greeting, "give me some good news."

"We've got someone for you to talk to. Where shall we bring him?"

"You said you had two options. Is this option one or option two?"

"This is option one, John."

"I'm in the boozer, Mick. Bring him here."

CHAPTER NINE

The lights of London lit the horizon like a distant, hazy, orange dome as Melody and Harvey made their way along the M2 from Dover. During one of the fuel stops, they had pulled the roof back up on the little sports car. As they'd made their way through France, the heater had been turned on, and less than one hundred miles from Reg's house in South London, the temperature was raised another notch. Harvey had removed his jacket and relished the cool breeze that found a gap in the old car's soft top. Melody had kept her jacket on and warmed her hands in the heated air that was pumped through the dashboard vent.

After a fifteen-and-a-half-hour journey, with three stops for fuel, bathroom and food, Melody parked the car in a bay reserved for visitors outside Reg and Jess' flat in Clapham. The engine shuddered to a stop beside a new Volkswagen camper van and Melody sat back in her seat.

"I'm beat," she said.

"You did well," said Harvey, opening the door and stretching his back and neck.

Melody followed suit as Harvey pulled their bags from the

rear seat. A clatter of paws on the tarmac stopped him, and he turned to find his old dog, Boon, tearing across the little car park with his ears flat against his head. Boon slammed into Melody with excitement, ran a few rings around her then settled for her to stroke and dote on him. Then he was off again. He bounced around the car, saw Harvey, then came to a sudden stop. He sat straight like a soldier on parade, looking up at his old master with his tail banging against the ground, as he waited for Harvey's acknowledgement.

Harvey stared him in the eyes and waited a few seconds. The dog was bursting to be welcomed, his front legs twitching with restraint.

"Good boy," said Harvey.

The dog remained still but his tail beat harder.

"Come," said Harvey, and the dog erupted into a frenzy of running rings and nosing Harvey's hand for affection.

"Be careful. He's a trained killer," said a familiar voice. "You'd better watch out."

Harvey straightened and found Reg standing beside Melody on the other side of the car with a smile on his face from ear to ear.

"The dog, I mean," continued Reg. Then he put his arms around Melody and gave her a hug.

Harvey shooed Boon away, grabbed the last bag from the car, and then slammed the door. Reg had walked around the car and Harvey offered him his hand to shake, but Reg pulled him in for a hug, which raised a smile on Melody's face.

"Good to see you, Harvey," said Reg, giving him a last squeeze before letting go.

"Likewise, Reg," said Harvey. "Is Jess inside?"

"She's just had to pop to the office. She'll be back in a few minutes. What do you think of the new van?"

"The camper?" said Melody. "Is that yours?"

"Just got it," replied Reg. "Fully kitted out with beds, a cooker and all the technology I could fit inside."

"So it's a mobile criminal investigation unit?" said Melody. "I thought you'd left all that behind?"

"Ah, well, you can take the nerd out of the crime, Melody, but you can't take the crime out of the nerd. Come on, let's get you guys inside. How was the drive? You must be shattered."

"It wasn't too bad," said Melody. "But I am glad it's over."

Reg's flat was on the first floor of a small but expensive-looking block of two-story-high private flats. Well-maintained lawns encircled the building with two pathways that cut through the grass and a new iron fence that ran the perimeter of the complex.

"This is nice," said Melody, as Reg held the front door open for them to pass through.

"Thanks. We thought we deserved an upgrade when I got the new job."

After stepping inside, Reg poured Melody a glass of wine, then handed Harvey a bottle of water.

"So how about a tour?" asked Melody.

"A tour? Well, what you see is what you get really. You're standing in the kitchen-diner. The lounge is behind you and your bedroom is through the door at the end. Our bedroom is over here. Both of them are en-suite and there's a small wash-room in the hallway."

"It's great, Reg," said Harvey. "Thanks for putting us up."

"No, thank you for coming to our wedding. Without you, I'd have exactly one guest on my side, and he's got bad breath and too much hair," said Reg, looking at Boon who sat by Harvey's feet staring up at him.

"And how has Boon been? Are you guys still happy with him?" asked Melody.

"He's great. Jess adores him. She wouldn't let you take him if you tried."

"I think he's happier here with you, Reg," said Harvey. He put his hand on the dog's head and ran his fingers along his snout. "I couldn't give him the time he deserves."

"So how's the new job going?" asked Melody. She sat down in one of the comfy leather armchairs and rested her wine glass on her knee.

"It's good," said Reg. "I haven't been shot at, blown up or kidnapped, and I haven't had to break any laws or risk imprisonment of any kind."

"Sounds dull," said Harvey, sitting on the armchair opposite Melody. Boon followed and sat beside him so that Harvey could continue stroking his head.

"I'm head of the research department, so I have a few other people in my team and they're all great. Quiet. No fuss. Plus the pay is a lot better and I haven't had to sign the official secrets act. I should have done it years ago."

"No," said Melody, "you'd have missed all the fun we had, and besides, you wouldn't have met Jess."

At the mention of her name, the front door opened and Jess walked in. She didn't bother to close the door. Instead, she ran to Melody and gave her a big hug. Then she approached Harvey and wrapped her arms around him.

"Wow, two hugs in twenty minutes," said Melody. "That must be a record for Harvey."

"It's great to see you two," said Jess, her public school, middle-class accent shining through. "I bet Boon was pleased to see you both."

Boon's head flinched at his name, but he made no effort to move away from Harvey.

"Did you get it?" asked Reg. He raised his eyebrows at Jess, who was pouring herself a glass of wine. She stepped across the room and topped up Melody's glass.

"I did," she said, and pulled a folded piece of paper from her pocket. She handed it to Reg.

"So, Harvey," Reg began, "Melody messaged me a few hours ago with an idea."

Harvey stopped stroking Boon and sat upright in the chair, causing the dog to nuzzle his hand for more attention.

"Jess has been to the office and done some digging around, and well, we thought you might like this."

Reg handed Harvey the folded piece of paper and stepped back.

"What is it?" asked Harvey as he unfolded it.

But he soon saw for himself.

"Is this Julios?" asked Harvey in disbelief.

"Only his family know his whereabouts," said Jess. "I had to pull some strings, but, well, we thought you'd like to visit."

CHAPTER TEN

"Good, Tyler. Get yourself washed up," said the old man as he shook the pads from his hands. "You listened and you've got good energy. Keep that up."

Lloyd leaned over the ropes and untied Tyler's gloves, then began to unravel the wrap. Tyler's right hand was unwrapped first. He loved the tingling sensation as his skin breathed the air after being constrained for so long.

"Your posture is improving. Can you feel it in your back?" asked Lloyd.

It was only once Lloyd had mentioned it that Tyler realised his lower back wasn't aching as much as it had in the past. He rubbed his hand across his back as Lloyd unwrapped his left hand.

"I told you. You need to listen to him. Your feet were faster too," said Lloyd.

"I didn't notice that," replied Tyler.

"That's because you were paying attention. But I saw it well enough."

Lloyd pulled the last of the wrap free then held the ropes open for Tyler to slip through.

"Thanks, Lloyd," said Tyler, as he dropped to the floor.

He picked up his bag and scanned the room for the old man. But he was nowhere to be seen. So Tyler walked past the three punch bags and into the changing room. The old man slammed the door on an old washing machine full of towels, span the dial and hit the power button.

"I just wanted to say thanks," said Tyler. "For staying and helping me. I appreciate the extra time."

"We all need a leg up every now and then," the old man replied without looking at Tyler.

He carried on cleaning the little changing room while he spoke. "You did good. I mean it. But you need to be consistent. You've got a punch like a mule and when you're focused, you're a good boxer. But you need to curb those emotions. They're your weakness. Show your opponent that and you'll spend more time on your back than those hookers on the street."

"I'm not emotional," said Tyler. But he heard his tone turn defensive.

The old man cast him a sideways glance, then continued to wash the shower down with water and squeegee the tiled wall.

"I'll work on it," said Tyler.

"Good. You do that."

"So when do you think I'll be ready?" asked Tyler.

"Ready for what?"

"To fight. When do you think I can get in the ring?"

"You were in the ring tonight, son. Or was you concentrating so hard you missed it?" The old man smiled to himself.

"You know what I mean. I want to fight. Maybe if I had a target to train for-"

"You'll go up against some other dam fool when I say you're ready. Until then, you're just a very big rock that needs a hell of a lot of polishing."

"But how do you know I'm not ready?" asked Tyler.

The old man stood straight, switched off the water and tossed the squeegee into a bucket. He pulled a towel from the slatted wooden bench and dried his hands, then leaned on the washing machine.

He eyed Tyler and sucked at his teeth as if he was choosing his words carefully.

"How many boys out there tonight, son?" the old man asked.

Tyler glanced into the gym but saw only Lloyd pushing around the broom.

"No-one," he replied.

"No-one," repeated the old man. "And what time is it?"

Tyler looked up at the cheap plastic clock on the wall that showed only the twelve, three, six and nine, but had a picture of Frank Bruno's face on it.

"Eleven thirty," said Tyler.

"So do you think I stay here late at night to train you for free for my health? Is that what you think?"

"No, I-"

"I'm giving you years of experience because I believe in you, Tyler. Someone like you could go far. You have the power. You have the dedication. But you need to calm those emotions down. They're your crux. When you show me you can stay in control, I'll think about putting you in the ring with someone other than me or Lloyd."

"Right," said Tyler.

"Don't be disheartened, son. Your time will come. But most importantly, don't let me down."

"I won't, I-"

"If you want to fight in a ring, if you want to have a few hundred people all watch you get your nose smashed flat and your eyes blackened, then be my guest. Join some other gym with some other trainer. But if you want to go places, son, you stick with me. You work hard and you damn well listen."

"I will," said Tyler.

"Who were those two men?" asked the old man.

The positive feedback from the old man and Lloyd had overshadowed the two men who had sat on the bench in the gym earlier that evening.

Tyler shook his head. "I don't know."

But the old man had an air of disbelief. Tyler could see it in the way he threw a shower gel bottle into the little cupboard above the sink, then slammed the door.

"Honest," said Tyler. "I haven't seen them before."

The old man dropped a full black bag outside the changing room, rinsed his hands and dried them on one of the fresh towels he'd piled on the towel rack. He leaned on the door frame.

"If you train with me, you fight with me. Nobody else," said the old man, supporting his statement with a shake of his head. "I'm not spending my evenings training you for some other toe-rag to get you beaten to a pulp. I'm too long in the tooth for all that. Been there. Seen that. Bought the t-shirt."

"Yeah, I know," said Tyler. "Why would I fight for anyone else?"

"Those two men," said the old man, "they're trouble. I can smell it a mile away. If they approach you, I want to know. You can talk to me or Lloyd. And don't think that because I'm old, I don't know people. There isn't one person in this game that I've never heard of. There isn't anyone worth their salt who don't know me. I can tell you this, son. There's some nasty pieces of work out there who prey on kids like you. You come to me, I'll help. But if you go against me, Tyler, you'll make an enemy you wish you hadn't. And trust me, in this game, an enemy is the last thing you need."

"Understood. And thanks again for trusting me. For putting your faith in me."

"Just don't let me down, son," said the old man. "Now scat. I thought you had a sick mum to look after?"

Tyler pushed off the wall and edged around the old man. "See you tomorrow, yeah?"

"Yep. Same time. Same place," said the old man. "Oh, and son?"

Tyler turned in the doorway, his eyebrows raised in anticipation of more words of wisdom from the old man.

"The next time you see an old man cleaning up after a load of young kids, emptying bins and washing towels, do yourself a favour and get stuck in." He offered Tyler a friendly smile. "Go on. Get out of here. We've all got homes to go to."

CHAPTER ELEVEN

A breath of fresh air licked at John Cooper's feet as Jack entered the family side of the pub and held the door open. A stranger walked in. He was cautious and checked either side of him before committing to the room. Mick followed, nodded at John and led the stranger towards the fireplace, while Jack closed and guarded the door.

John remained seated but offered his hand to the young man.

"What's your name, son?" he asked mid-shake.

"Blake," the big man replied.

"Is it just Blake? Or do you have a last name like the rest of us?"

"Green," came the reply.

"Blake Green?" said John, sitting back in his seat and crossing his legs. "Well, Blake Green, why don't you take a seat? Can I get you a drink?"

Blake shook his head.

"Mick, get him a drink, will you? He looks like he needs loosening up."

"I don't drink," said Blake.

Mick raised his eyebrow at John who nodded once.

"Just water, Mick."

"I don't want a water either."

Mick walked behind the bar and poured two brandies for John and himself, and pulled a bottle of sparkling water from the fridge for Blake.

"Tell me, Blake," said John. "What does a man your size have to eat every day to stay that big?"

"Are you going to tell me what this is all about?" said Blake. His tone cut straight through the niceties that John had laid out. "Tell me why I'm here. I don't know you, or your two mates, so tell me what the bleeding hell is going on and I might be able to help you."

"I bet it's eggs," said John. "Eggs and chicken. Am I right?"

"What are you talking about?" said Blake. "Eggs and chicken?"

"And rice. I forgot rice. They all eat rice apparently."

"Who do? Who eats rice, chicken and eggs?"

"You do," said John. "All fighters your size eat rice, chicken and eggs. Do you enjoy fighting, Blake?"

"Listen, mate. Who are you? And why am I here?"

"Mick tells me you're a bailiff. Is that right?" asked John, ignoring Blake's question but enjoying his growing impatience. "You're a debt collector. Is that right?"

"So what if I am?"

"I bet a man like you collects quite a few debts, don't you? I imagine when some low life scumbag opens his front door and sees you on his doorstep, he must drop his lunch. What do you reckon, Mick?"

"I reckon you're right, John," said Mick. "I reckon they hand over everything they own when they see this fellow standing on their doorstep, especially in that lovely leather jacket."

"I don't know who you are, and honestly, I don't care. I need to go," said Blake.

"Do many of them put up a fight, Blake?" asked John. "You know, the offending parties, as it were."

"Some. It's mostly the women that give me the most grief because they know a bloke won't hit them back."

"Ah, most blokes wouldn't. But some men would, and they do, Blakey," said John. "What type are you?"

"What? What do you mean what type am I?" said Blake. "I wouldn't hit a woman ever."

"What if someone paid you?" asked John.

"No, mate. The answer is still no. It's not right."

"Do you think that some women deserve to be hit by a man, Blake?"

Blake paused. It was the answer John was looking for.

"I take it by the pause that yes, you do think some women deserve to be hit by a man."

Blake began to protest, but John held his hand out to quieten him. Controlling the conversation was key to getting the answers he wanted without asking the question that Blake didn't want to hear.

"It's okay. I agree. I've met a few in my time that could have done with being dragged into an alley and taught a lesson. You see, Blake, some women, as you rightly said, prey on men because they know they won't hit them back. It's cowardly, that's what that is. But you know what? Sometimes, just one or two need to be taught a lesson. It's a form of bullying, you know?" said John. "Did you know that a third of all domestic abuse victims in Britain are male?"

"This is a joke," said Blake. "You have about three seconds to explain what's going on before I walk out."

John took his drink from Mick and watched as the water

was placed on the table in front of Blake. He checked his watch to make sure the three seconds were up.

"So?" said John.

"So what?"

"The three seconds are up and I haven't explained what's going on," said John. He slipped his tumbler onto the table and sat back, interlacing his fingers and letting his chin rest on his knuckles. "Have you always been so emotional, Blake?"

"I don't need this," said Blake. He pushed himself out of the chair. "I don't play games, mate. I don't have time for them."

"Jack," called John, as Blake shoved his chair back, "stand aside, will you, and let young Blakey out."

Jack did as requested, and John watched as Blake's hand grabbed the door handle and pulled the cold air into the room once more.

"Oh, one more thing, Blake," he said, taking another sip of his brandy. "Before you go."

The big man turned to face John with the dark, wet night waiting behind his huge frame that filled the doorway. John nodded at Mick who pulled a single photograph from his pocket and handed it to him.

"Your little girl," said John, studying the photograph. He waited until he had Blake's attention and saw the big man moving towards him in his peripheral vision. "She's very pretty. She's the image of her mum, isn't she?"

CHAPTER TWELVE

A blanket of leaves lay on the damp ground in chronological layers of death. Fresh leaves crunched under Harvey's boot, while older generations that had been exposed to the wet turned to pulp and became an unidentifiable part of the environment.

Rows of headstones stood upright like proud sentries guarding their posts while below them, the cycle of life and death rolled on. The deterioration of the leaves on the surface, the unending quarrel of insects below, and below them, the bodies of the dead in their long journey of decay, as piece by piece, their bodies returned to the earth.

The East London Crematorium and Cemetery spanned thirteen acres of hallowed ground. It was a pride of green, a walled-in escape from industry, evolution and the chaos of city life, a pocket of peace for those who rested.

An avenue of trees greeted Harvey along with the calm aura of eternal rest. Beyond the avenue, shrouded by oaks and elms, was the chapel and to the sides of the avenue lay the dead. Some of the headstones had fallen with age. The dark and crumbled stone had cracked or broken. But some fresh graves shone bright white with the gaiety of a freshman, naive to the realm of eternal peace. Slowly, they would too fade and succumb to the cycle of life, as day by day, week by week, and year by year, they perished, as do all things.

Standing tall among the older graves, adorned with great Celtic crosses, the faded, once-cherished names of the dead stood between carved angels, saints and the ever-present Jesus, nailed to a cross, a symbol of sacrifice.

The grave of Julios Saville was not guarded by an angel reaching for the heavens, nor was Harvey's mentor's journey to the afterlife accompanied by an ornate saint, carved in granite by the loving hands of a mason. Instead, a simple plaque, seven inches squared, was fixed to a lump of marble and set in the earth beside identical markers with identical plaques.

It was a government burial ground offering the minimal contribution of memory to lives who, in the eyes of society, deserved less. Although the simple markers were uniform, Julios' grave was unique. Neighbouring graves were overrun with weeds, seeking a place to hold onto and fighting for light to thrive among the memories, and hide the names of the shunned from the honour of the dead. But Julios' grave was clear as if somebody had pulled the imposing weeds from the earth and exposed his name for all to see. It was the work of pride.

No flowers lay across the bare earth, but the contrast of dark soil against the neighbouring battle of plant life honoured Julios' simple and clutter-free life.

In all the years Harvey had known Julios, his mentor had never once shown an affection for possessions. The cars he drove were simple and cheap. The clothes he wore were bland and nondescript. Not once had Harvey ever visited Julios' home. But he'd imagined it hundreds of times as a basic one-room apartment with an armchair, a bed, perhaps a table, and a landlord willing to ask no questions in return for a monthly cash payment.

On his walk through the graveyard, Harvey had tried to picture what the grave might look like. He'd expected nothing grand, knowing that a state burial would offer the minimum viable option. But what had been clear in Harvey's mind had been the name. In his mind's eye, the carved letters portrayed finality and reflected the greatness of the man Harvey had admired and looked up to more than anybody else during his childhood.

But the stark reality hit him hard. The small chunk of synthetic marble with a template plaque punched out in some factory by a cold-hearted machine to form the words 'Julios Saville' and the date of his death offered no sense of the person.

It had been Julios who had trained Harvey to be the man he'd become. Stealth, defence, and attack were at the core of those lessons, as was the power of barely existing until it was time to strike. But when he did strike, he was taught the ability to read an opponent before either man made a move, which added weight to the perfection in every placement of his feet and accuracy in every delivery of a blow. Julios Saville was a dangerous man to stand toe to toe with, and over years of training, Harvey had taken those skills, and added his own blend of prolonged suffering.

Defence and attack were not the only attributes Harvey had gleaned from his mentor. Their work required a state of mind, and a clean life free of the complexities that the average man collated. There could be no routine for anyone to follow. There could be no item out of place. And there could be no emotion.

But it had been emotion that killed Julios in the end. Harvey thought back to the time when he'd found Julios in the mud, his huge face torn apart by the wheels of a Range Rover. His body riddled with bullet holes. It hadn't been Julios' emotion that killed him, it had been Harvey's. He'd added complexities to what was a very simple job, and it had gone wrong. In the blink of an eye, Julios had been torn from Harvey's life.

Ironically, as Harvey stared down at the pressed plaque and Julios' name, emotions stirred somewhere deep inside. It triggered some hidden part of him that barely existed save for two people: Melody and Julios.

A single tear formed in the corner of Harvey's eye. But as it did, a shape, out of place among the surrounding green, moved at the edge of Harvey's vision.

He glanced up but saw no movement. A trick of the tear?

With a final look at the only evidence that Julios Saville ever existed, Harvey whispered his name. He wasn't sure why. Perhaps it was to substantiate the synthetic block and pressed plaque. Perhaps he was sorry. But Julios would scoff at sorrow. Mostly, thought Harvey, he spoke Julios' name for his own closure. The greatest man he had even known would be remembered in Harvey's heart, as alive as if Julios walked beside him every day, but rarely would his existence ever breach Harvey's lips.

Harvey looked back once more at the plaque, but this time he just nodded at his old friend. Then he walked away. He made his way between two rows of headstones. They were new plots and had retained the glossy sheen of machined marble and granite. It would be years before nature wore down the surfaces to a dull matte finish, and the carved epitaphs would outlive the memories of those who lay beneath them.

At the end of the row, at a crossroads of pathways, all silent, solemn and carpeted with the same broad oak leaves, he glanced back once more at Julios' marker three hundred yards behind him. Bent on one knee and using his hands to clear the earth around Julios' grave was a man. He wore a black jacket and a hat. As if he felt Harvey's stare from afar, he slowly turned his head, and they locked gazes.

Harvey turned to face him. He cocked his head and tried to find some kind of recognition. But the man stood up, glanced back once at Harvey, then took to his heels and ran in the opposite direction.

CHAPTER THIRTEEN

The card reader beeped to unlock the door to the two flats, but it was already open. The lock had been forced. But there was no sign of any other damage. The warm smell of home-baking greeted Tyler when he pushed open the security door on the ground floor. The scent still hung in the air as he sprinted up the single staircase and onto the small landing that split into two entrances, his own flat and his neighbour's flat. He'd recognise the smell of his mum's cooking anywhere. He opened the front door and peered around the frame, unsure of what he'd find.

"You're home late, dear," said his mum from the kitchen.

Tyler closed the door behind him and gave his mum a hug and a kiss.

"Mum, you're up again. What's going on? And you're baking. Mum, you should be resting."

"Oh, leave off," replied his mum. "If I can get up, I will get up. Tomorrow could be my last."

"Don't talk like that."

"Well, don't tell me what to do. Besides, I made some cakes. Your favourite, cherry cupcakes."

"Ah, Mum, I'm training."

"You might be training, Tyler, but you still need food inside you. I haven't seen you eat in god knows how long."

"I eat at work, Mum."

"So you don't want the cakes then?" She glanced across at them on the cooling tray.

"How can I refuse? Thanks, Mum. But seriously, you should be resting. You could have had an accident." Tyler took a cupcake from the tray.

"They'll be hot," his mum warned.

"That's when they're the best," said Tyler with a smile. "Next time you want to get out of bed, can you call me at least?"

"At least what? So you can check up on me?"

"No, Mum. But if I know you're up and about, I can try and get home quicker. It's great you're moving, but you know it only takes one fall. I could even ask Sami next door to pop in and make sure you're okay." He swallowed the remainder of the little cake.

"Well, when you put it like that," she said. Then her face brightened. "How is it?"

Speaking with his mouth full to emphasise the point, Tyler mumbled that the cake was fantastic and gave her two thumbs up, then made his way to his room.

"You didn't tell me where you've been anyway," his mum called from the little kitchen. "You're normally home earlier than this, aren't you? Are you training tonight?"

"Yeah, I'm just getting changed and then I'll go," said Tyler. He walked from his room, pulling a clean t-shirt over his head. "Are you going back to bed? Or shall I get you set up in your chair?"

"Well, I might stay up now I'm awake. I might do some cleaning."

"No, Mum. I've done it all. I did it last night when I got home. Please leave it. Just relax and let me take care of you. Here is your blanket. Here's the TV remote. Do you want a cup of tea before I go?" Tyler held out the blanket, waiting for his mum to sit in her armchair. She walked over slowly. She was frail but far more active than he'd seen her in a long time.

"No tea, dear," she said. "I'll be up and down to the loo all night. Are you going already? Why don't you tell me about your day before you go?"

"Ah, Mum, I'm running late," said Tyler. He threw his bag over his shoulder. "The old man will be waiting for me. But if you're up and about when I get home, we can have a chat then. Okay?"

"Okay, dear. I don't want to stop you doing what you need to do," she said. "I might go back to bed in a while."

"Okay, Mum," said Tyler, and he bent to kiss her on her head.

"That's if I don't get disturbed again."

"What do you mean? Who disturbed you?" said Tyler, his hand holding the door catch.

"Oh, I don't know," his mum replied. "Just two men came knocking."

Tyler remembered the broken door downstairs.

"What did they want?"

"You know, the funny thing is, they never said. I let them in, of course, and offered them a tea. But they were more interested in the photos on the wall."

Behind Tyler, fixed to the hallway wall, were three frames. One was of Tyler and his mum at a family wedding a few years before. Another was of Tyler at his first junior fight. The photo was taken before the bell. It showed Tyler with his gloves on the ropes looking down at his mum taking the picture. A nervous but excited boy. He'd been stocky for his age but had still been just a boy. The third photo was of his dad. A three-quarter-length leather jacket, which was old and worn, hung from his huge shoulders and in his arms was baby Tyler.

"Mum, lock the door behind me and don't let anybody in," said Tyler, and he slammed the door closed.

"Is there any news?" said John. He sat back in his office chair and pulled his right foot up onto his left knee. He licked a tissue and wiped a smear from his Oxfords, then tossed the tissue in the bin behind him.

"News, John?" asked Mick.

"News about our new boy Blake. Is he looking good? Is he a winner? Jack, take a seat, mate. You're making the place look untidy," said John. "Sorry, Mick. You were saying?"

"He hasn't lost a fight yet and hasn't seen anything further than round two."

"Knockouts?"

"He's got a punch like a mule, John," said Mick, smiling at the good news.

"But has he got what it takes though, Mick?"

"A few sessions with Jerry, and Blake will be unstoppable, John."

"Good," said John. "Good. That's what I want to hear. When is he meeting Jerry?"

"Tomorrow morning. He'll have the whole day with him."

"And why is he going to do it?" asked John. He left a pause

to allow Mick time to consider his answer, then lowered his voice. "What have we got on him? Tell me his weakness."

Mick smiled once more at the opportunity to deliver favourable news.

"He owes money, John. He can't pay his loans."

"So?" said John. "There's a lot of people out there who owe money without the means to pay."

"Most of them are drunks or have gambling habits. Blake has a wife and a young kid and a little bird tells me they might lose their little flat soon, unless they come up with some rent."

A cruel grin spread across John's face, wrinkling his leather-like skin.

"That's the type of news I like to hear, Mick," said John. The news appeased him, and he relaxed back in his chair. "Tell me about our number two. I want him ready too. I want nothing left to chance. Is that clear?"

"Crystal, John," said Mick. "We paid his mum a visit yesterday."

"His mum?" said John. "What was you doing? Asking permission?"

"She's sick. I get the impression she's terminal."

John understood where Mick was going with the conversation.

"And the boy? How does he feel about that?"

"We haven't caught up with him yet. But she's all he's got. The dad died when he was a kid."

"Right," said John. He rested his chin on his steepled fingers and ran the scenarios through in his head. "And he can fight?"

"He's the size of a bleeding house, John. All muscle."

"Who's training him?"

"Old Man McGee in Limehouse."

"That old bastard?"

"He might be old, John, but he knows his stuff. He's had more of his boys go pro than any other trainer I know."

"Who is this boy?" asked John.

"Tyler."

"Is that his first name or his last name?" asked John.

"It's Tyler Thomson, John."

"Right. So make sure Old Man McGee doesn't get wind of this. He'll know people who know people, and if he finds out we're putting his boy up against Dixon's in a fight to the death, he'll bring the bleeding house down on us, and we'll all be putting wagers on cockroach races in Pentonville bleeding prison."

The phone on John's desk lit up, but the ringer was set to silent. John answered the call but said nothing.

"Boss, you might want to come down here," said Northern Mike, John's pub manager. "You've had a delivery."

John replaced the handset and stood up from his seat. He threw on his jacket then pulled his cuffs and cufflinks down so they showed. His tailor-made shirts and jackets were all cut to show an inch of white cuff, just enough for his diamond cufflinks to make a statement and to offer a glint of his platinum Breitling watch.

"Let's go, boys," he said. "Mike reckons we have a delivery."

The three men, led by John, made their way down the rear stairs of the Golden Ring and through a door that opened out into the family side of the pub. The muffled sounds of men laughing and talking with the percussive chink of pint glasses being washed and stacked came from the bar next door.

At the entrance, Jeff the Plumber, one of the regulars, held the door open, letting in the cold night air. Outside on the pavement, Northern Mike was hunched over a man lying on the ground. He looked up as John approached and shook his head, his face solemn.

The body of Blake Green lay on the wet ground. His lifeless eyes stared up at John.

"Get him inside, boys," said John to Mick and Jack, then he checked the street for nosy passers-by.

They hauled the huge man inside by his arms and dropped his lifeless body on the carpet beside the fruit machine.

"I just found him like it, John," said Jeff, as he shut the doors and slid the bolts to lock them. "I don't know how long he'd been there."

"Did you see anyone else? Any cars?"

"Nothing, John. I swear."

"Alright, mate," replied John. He flicked five twenty pound notes off a roll of cash bound with a silver money clip and stuffed them into Jeff's top pocket. "Do me a favour, yeah?"

"I won't say anything, John. You know me."

"I do, Jeff. Thanks, mate. We'll take it from here. Tell Debbie to put your drinks on my tab."

Jeff slipped past the group of men and through the door, letting the noise of the public bar fill the space for a few seconds. Then it faded as the door closed. Northern Mike locked it and turned to face John.

"Do you know him, John?" he asked.

John nodded.

"Yes, Mike, I do." He thought for a few seconds then verbalised his plan.

"Right, Jack, get this pile of crap out the back and into the motor. Dump him in Epping Forest. Somewhere he'll be found by a dog walker. Mick, as soon as you see the discovery on the news, pay his wife a visit. Slip her five grand in an envelope."

He turned to the pub manager.

"Mike?"

Northern Mike looked up from the body at their feet.

"Boss?" he replied.

"Get this bleeding carpet cleaned up. Not a trace. Understood?"

Northern Mike nodded, but he looked hesitant.

John placed a reassuring hand on Mike's shoulder, just as his phone vibrated in his pocket. The number was blocked and the small screen read '*Unknown Caller*,' but he didn't need to be a rocket scientist to know who it was.

He hit the green button to answer the call and waited for the familiar gravelly voice.

"Checkmate," said Dixon.

CHAPTER FIFTEEN

"How did it go?" asked Melody. "Did you find it?"

"Yeah, I did," replied Harvey.

"So are you coming back to Reg's place? We're going out for dinner tonight. The wedding is in two days and they want to say thanks."

"Yeah, I'll be back," said Harvey. He switched the lights off, pulled the car to the side of the road and watched as the man in the hat disappeared through a doorway beside some shops.

"Okay, but don't be too long," said Melody. "This means a lot to them."

"I'll be back soon," said Harvey. "I'm just finishing something."

He disconnected the call, turned the car off and waited. As if on cue, a few light raindrops dotted the windscreen. The street lights ahead magnified and fragmented the light but Harvey's eyes remained fixed on the doors. A light flicked on in a first-floor window and a figure passed across the frame but too fast for Harvey to see who it was. A few minutes later, the light flicked off.

Ahead of where Harvey had parked, on the opposite side of

the road, a black BMW pulled over outside the doors Harvey was watching. The lights flicked off and the plume of smoke faded into the night. A van pulled into the street behind the car; for a brief moment, its headlights washed across it and silhouetted two men sitting in the front.

A flash of lightning lit the sky in Harvey's rear-view mirror. The light patter of rain on the car's bodywork grew into heavy drumming as the downpour began and the windscreen was obscured. Harvey turned on the ignition and cracked the car's electric window, but in the narrow field of view, all he saw was the door. It was closing. He flicked the windscreen wipers on to see the struggle of the two men forcing someone into the back of the BMW.

Harvey reached for the door handle, but it was too late. The BMW doors slammed, the engine fired up, and the headlights lit the street as the driver planted his foot to the floor and sped out of the parking spot. Harvey bent down out of sight, started the engine of Melody's little sports car, dipped the clutch, and found first gear. By the time the BMW had shot past, Harvey was accelerating out of his parking spot in the opposite direction. In his mirror, he saw the BMW turn left on the highway, so Harvey dropped into second, lifted the clutch and let the gearbox slow the car to make the turn. As soon as the car nosed out of the bend, Harvey slammed down the accelerator. It had been years since he'd been in the neighbourhood but he knew the streets well.

At the first crossroads, Harvey wrenched the wheel to the right. The highway was at the end of the street; he was only halfway down it when the BMW flashed past, faster than the other cars on the road. Harvey slid onto the highway, nosing between two cars and upsetting the driver behind. The BMW was four hundred yards in front. The highway was the main artery into the City of London and traffic was monitored.

Harvey settled in and focused on the rear lights of the BMW in front.

His phone vibrated in his pocket and Melody's number flashed up. He put the phone away, checked his mirrors and closed the distance between him and the BMW.

The lights of the Limehouse Link tunnel loomed ahead, bright like a portal in the night. The BMW entered it, followed thirty seconds later by Harvey in Melody's little Mazda. A van and a taxi travelled side by side at the same pace to avoid the speed cameras in the tunnel. But the BMW was moving fast, not slowing for the cameras. Harvey eased the Mazda behind the taxi in a signal that he wanted to pass. But the taxi driver entered a power game and held fast. Aware of the bright lights illuminating Melody's very identifiable car, Harvey hung back behind the van but watched the BMW through the long, sweeping bends until, at last, the end of the tunnel was in sight. The car broke free into the rain and the darkness.

By the time the taxi, the van and Harvey left the tunnel, the BMW was nowhere to be seen.

Rain pelted the car once more. Canary Wharf and the Isle of Dogs were on Harvey's right. Another road merged at the tunnel exit. All Harvey could see were dozens of tail lights of the cars ahead, magnified and distorted by the rain, and unidentifiable in the dark. The taxi eventually moved into the next lane and Harvey accelerated past him.

Half a mile in front, Harvey knew there was a junction, where the BMW would be lost for sure. Before that was a slip road off to the left; a few cars in the left-hand lane were taking it. Harvey studied the tail lights but recognised none as the BMW. He kept looking at the cars as he drove onto the slip road and rose up onto an overpass, but saw nothing.

He slowed for the junction, scouring the cars that peeled off and the others that waited for a gap. But again, he saw nothing.

He joined a group of cars three lanes wide and three cars back from the roundabout. He pulled to a stop. While everyone else was looking right for a gap, Harvey looked left, and came face to face with the driver of the BMW. He feigned disinterest, saw a space in the traffic, waited for the BMW to join the flow, and then slipped in behind it.

The BMW had slowed down, a move that Harvey presumed was to avoid being stopped by the police with a kidnapped man in the back. It turned onto East India Dock Road, matched the speed of the traffic and remained inconspicuous until it turned off Prince Regent Lane, where the driver found the maze of back streets and opened up the engine.

To follow them directly in Melody's little convertible would have been too obvious. Knowing the streets well, Harvey took the next left and caught up to them as the driver parked outside the Golden Ring Pub. Plaistow had been Harvey's stomping ground when he and Julios had worked for Harvey's foster father, John Cartwright. The only time Harvey had ever been in the Golden Ring was to find a man who owed John money.

They'd waited in the car park. It was rare that Harvey and Julios would talk while they stalked their prey. There was never much to be said, and Julios' ethos was to remain focused at all times. It was a testament to the length of his career. Until the end. And then it was Harvey who had been distracted.

Harvey drove past the pub, turned into a side street, killed the lights, and switched off the engine. He got out of the car, leaving the doors unlocked to avoid the flash of the indicators, and edged to the end of the road, out of sight. The muffle of men's voices followed. Then the dull thud of body blows and accompanying groans were the only sounds Harvey heard above the rain splashing in the puddles and hitting the roofs of parked cars. He watched from afar as one of the two men held the door of the pub open. The other marched the kidnapped guy inside at gunpoint.

To pull a gun in the open street, regardless of the time of night and torrential rain, was a brave move. Either things had changed since Harvey had worked the area or these men ran the neighbourhood. Harvey presumed the latter, which would mean there would be more men.

The phone in his pocket vibrated. It was Melody. It had to be. She was the only person who ever called him. He ignored the call, pulled his jacket around him, and marched across the street. He looked both ways, but the road was quiet and nobody had seen him.

He stepped into the Golden Ring.

"Sit down," said the man with the silver hair. He was dressed well in an expensive-looking shirt, smart trousers and shiny shoes. A nice watch peeked from his cuff and he sat relaxed in an armchair beside the fire as if he owned the place.

Tyler checked around the room. Although the bar next door sent a hum of activity through the adjoining door, the room Tyler had been brought into was empty, save for the two men who had picked him up, and the old man in the chair.

"I'd rather stand," said Tyler. "This won't take long, will it?"

"It'll take as long as I want it to take, and it'll be quicker if you do as you're told," said the man. "So sit down." He held out a hand, offering the chair opposite him. "Mick, get the boy a drink, will you? What do you want, son?"

"I don't drink," said Tyler, unable to meet the man's eyes.

"Another one that doesn't bleeding drink. What is with you people?"

Sensing the question was rhetorical, Tyler remained silent. He studied the intricate patterns of the old carpet at his feet.

"Let me introduce myself," said the old man. "You can call me John." He held out his hand once more, this time for Tyler to shake. Short, fat, ringed fingers gripped Tyler's hand with a positive strength. The shake was barely perceptible; John allowed the squeeze to do the talking.

"Look, John," said Tyler, "I haven't done nothing wrong. I don't know who you are, but honestly, I haven't done anything."

"I know, son. I know." John raised his hand. "Don't worry. You're not in any kind of trouble."

"So what am I doing here?" asked Tyler. "This bloke shoved a gun in my face." He jerked his thumb at Mick who placed a bottle of sparkling water on the table in front of him.

"No harm done, Tyler," said John. "I'm sure it was all meant in good spirit." He eyed the man he'd called Mick and nodded. It was a slight movement, enough to reassure his subordinate that he'd done the right thing.

"How's your mum, Tyler? I hear she's ill."

"What? How do you know about-"

"Look," said John, his face twisted as if he'd had enough of the back and forth, "let's clear up any ambiguity, shall we? Then perhaps we can move onto business."

"Business?" asked Tyler.

"I'm a very well-known man, and a very well-known man knows lots of people. It's my business to be in the know. So anything I know about you shouldn't come as a surprise. Now, I know that your old mum is sick, and I asked how she was."

"Today was a good day," Tyler replied.

"A good day? Well that's something," said John. "Tell me what a bad day looks like."

Tyler felt his throat close and his eyes bulge as the memories showed themselves to him alone.

"Delirious. Incontinent. Passing blood, vomiting blood, and pained to the point of pulling her own hair out of her head and clawing at her skin to get to the pain." He paused. "Shall I go on?"

John held his gaze, his expression serious. Regardless of the surroundings, he seemed somehow empathetic.

"That's a lot for a boy your age to deal with."

"I'm not a boy and I'm dealing with it the best I can."

"That's admirable," said John, with an accompanying smile. "I hear you're a boxer?"

Tyler nodded. "Yeah. I'm supposed to be there now. My trainer won't be happy. He's giving me extra time in the ring."

"Personal attention from Old Man McGee?" said John. "You are privileged."

"You know him?"

John laughed. "Yeah. Anyone who's anyone in this world knows the old man. Does he still have that big guy mopping up after him?"

"Lloyd? Yeah, he's still there. Look, is this going to take long? I don't want-"

"I know. You don't want the old man to think you've skipped a training session and wasted his time. That's okay. We can take care of the old man for you. I'll tell him you're with me."

"No," said Tyler, a little brash. "It should come from me. Are we done?"

"No, Tyler, we are not done. I'll get Mick here to drop you at the arches when we're finished. How does that sound?"

It was only then that Tyler turned to look at Mick and recognised him as the man from the gym the previous night. He turned again and eyed the man by the door. It was both of them.

"What do you want with me, John?"

"Simple," said John. He leaned forwards, resting his elbows on his knees, then collected his brandy from the small table between them. "I want to put you in the ring, son."

"I can't do it," replied Tyler. "The old man-"

"Yeah, yeah. The old man said you can't fight for anyone else or he'll stop training you. So what? From what I hear, you don't need him anymore anyway. Look at the bleeding size of you."

"I can't let him down."

John listened and nodded.

"So much honour. But so little brains," he said. Then he sat back with his glass of brandy and took a sip without removing his eyes from Tyler's. "What if I told you that the winnings would get your mum private medical attention? No more of this waiting around for some old fart on the National Health Service to procrastinate and worry about making a decision. You could afford to let the professionals look after her."

"I can't do it," said Tyler. "The old man-"

"Sod the old man, Tyler. Think about your poor old mum. Delirious, you said. In so much pain she's clawing at her own skin. You could stop that, Tyler. Look at me when I'm talking to you, son."

Tyler looked up from the floor. He felt his eyes redden.

"Don't be ashamed, Tyler. Be proud of who you are." John took a sip of his brandy. "She's dying, isn't she?"

A single tear rolled down Tyler's cheek. He bit his bottom lip.

"Let it go, Tyler," said John. "I'm giving you the chance to stop it, son. No-one knows how long she has left, do they?"

Tyler shook his head. At the same time, the door opened and a man entered. Tyler glanced up to see who it was, but tears fogged his vision. He let his head drop back down. His silent tears fell to the floor. John leaned forwards and spoke quietly.

"So here's your chance to make her last days as nice as possible."

CHAPTER SEVENTEEN

"Sorry, mate, this bar is shut. You'll have to go next door," said Jack, who was leaning on the bar with a pint.

The man let the door swing closed behind him, looked around the room, and let his gaze fall on Tyler, who was wiping his eyes.

"It's a bit noisy for me next door," replied the man. He took three strides towards the bar where he stood with his back to John and Tyler, and with Mick and Jack to his right.

"I said the bar is closed, sunshine," said Jack. "You'll need to go next door to get a drink."

"And I said it's a bit too noisy for me next door," replied the man.

John grinned at Jack's failed attempt to impress him. He glanced back at John, embarrassed by the lack of fear he'd instilled into the man.

"Listen, pal, you've got five seconds to get out or-"

"Or what?" said the man. He turned to face Jack, but his stance wasn't threatening. In fact, it was as casual as if he was waiting at a bar for a beer.

John sipped at his brandy and admired the man's control.

"That's five seconds. The way I see it, it's you who has options. You can either try to throw me out in the pouring rain." He held his arms up as if he was waiting for Jack to make a move, then dropped them to his sides and rolled his neck from side to side. "Or you can shut up and leave me to dry off."

The two men stared each other down. The anger was clear in Jack's eyes, but still, the stranger remained unmoved. Northern Mike appeared through the service door that linked to the two bars. He glanced at the stranger and at John.

"Another brandy, John?" he called out, ignoring the standoff between Jack and the man.

"Why not?" John replied. "And can you get our friend here a drink and a towel or something please, Mike?"

A towel landed on the bar beside the stranger, then Mike's face appeared beside him.

"What can I get you, mate?" he asked.

"Water's fine," came the reply.

A bottle of sparkling water was placed beside the towel. Mike brought the brandy to John's table.

"Mick, do me a favour. Take Jack for a walk in the rain. He looks like he could do with cooling off."

"I don't need a-" began Jack.

"Jack, go for a walk," said John. "Mick, go with him."

A look of contempt flashed across Mick's face. He pulled his coat on and threw Jack's to him, a little harder than necessary.

When the door swung closed and the sound of the rain was quietened, the stranger turned and leaned on the bar. He nodded once at Northern Mike, then cracked the lid off the water bottle. In the mirror behind the optics, John found the stranger staring at him.

"Can I go now?" asked Tyler.

John broke the stare and addressed Tyler.

"So you're going to do it?"

"Can you make it so that the old man doesn't find out about it?" replied Tyler. "He's been good to me, and, well-"

"Listen, son. You leave the old man to me. Meet me here tomorrow night. Six o'clock. Bring your gear. We'll get you in the ring and see what you're made of."

"And can I ask what I get?" said Tyler. "I mean, if I win. What's the pay-out?"

"What if I said fifty grand?" replied John, taking another sip of his third or fourth brandy.

The eyebrows on Tyler's face rose, showing bright red lines in the backs of his eyes.

"Is that enough?" asked John.

"I'm in," replied Tyler. He leaned across the table to shake John's hand. A smile of hope spread across his face. He sat back in his seat, cracked the water bottle with shaky hands and took a long mouthful. But then a thought hit him. His expression changed to curiosity. "Do I need to sign anything? Are there insurance papers I need to sign? I had to do that before, for my last fight."

"Your word is good enough for me," replied John. He sank his brandy and felt the satisfying burn as it made its way down his gullet. "People rarely let me down, Tyler."

"I need to think about it. What happens if I say no?" Tyler asked.

John set his glass on the table. He leaned in, beckoning Tyler to meet him halfway, and lowered his voice to a whisper.

"We just made a deal, Tyler. If you back out now, they'll be scraping bits of your poor old mum off the kitchen wall for a week. Do I make myself clear?"

The phone in Harvey's pocket vibrated. He couldn't ignore it any longer. With a nod of thanks to the man sitting by the fireplace, Harvey pulled the phone out and stepped outside into the rain. He checked both directions and crossed the street.

"Harvey, where are you?" asked Melody. "You said you'd be back."

"I'm coming back now," he replied. "I stopped to see someone."

"See who? You've been gone hours, Harvey."

"Well, I'm coming back now. Get yourself ready to go out. I'll be thirty minutes."

Harvey disconnected the call and turned into the side street where he'd parked Melody's car. Something wasn't right. The way the car was sitting was off; it was leaning to one side. He edged along the wall of the end-of-terrace house and saw the huge frame of the boy sitting in the passenger seat.

Harvey stepped into view and, although the street was dark and any moonlight was blocked by the heavy clouds, he saw the white face of the boy turn towards him through the rain-spattered glass.

The door opened and the car's suspension seemed to sigh with relief as he eased one long leg out of the small vehicle and pulled himself out into the rain. The boy towered over Harvey and was nearly twice as wide, but his hands fumbled with a nervous energy as if they sought something to do.

"I'm sorry," said the boy. "I saw you park here. That's how I knew it was your car."

"So you sat in it?" said Harvey.

"The way you spoke to them in there. You wasn't scared. They're dangerous. One of them had a gun."

Harvey studied the boy's proportions.

"Having a gun is one thing. Using it is another. And using it properly is another thing altogether."

The boy was silent.

"It's Tyler, isn't it?" asked Harvey. "I heard that bloke call you Tyler."

The boy nodded.

"You want my advice?" said Harvey.

Another silent and ashamed nod.

"Run away. Get away from them and don't look back," said Harvey. "You seem like a good kid. But if you carry on with those guys, it's the beginning of the end. Trust me."

Tyler's face seemed to drop as if every muscle in it had relented to the pressure of holding back the emotion.

"I'm in trouble," he said. His voice had raised an octave. "I don't know what I've got myself into."

Harvey watched the boy fight his emotions, but didn't try to stop him. Instead, he checked both ways in the dark street then sighed.

"Get in the car," said Harvey.

He walked around to the driver's side, opened the door and climbed in. The sheer width of Tyler's frame occupied most of the space inside and when Harvey pulled his door closed, the two men's shoulders had nowhere to go but rest against each other.

"How do you know them?" asked Harvey. He started the engine and set the fan to clear the windscreen, which was fogging up.

"I don't know them. They came out of nowhere. I left my flat to go to training and they jumped me. They hit me and put a gun in my face."

"And you didn't fight back?"

"I wanted to," said Tyler. He stared out of the windscreen, his eyes shining in the dark. "I should have, but..."

"But what?" asked Harvey. "If two guys jump me, I fight back. I'm guessing you're strong. You could have handled them."

"Not with the gun. Plus, I'm not allowed."

"You're not allowed to fight back when two men put a gun in your face?"

"I did it once before. I hurt someone pretty bad," said Tyler. "The police arrested me, but the guy came around in the end and they dropped the charges."

"Came around?" asked Harvey.

"He was in a coma."

"You put him in a coma?"

"I didn't mean to. I only hit him once or twice, not a lot."

"You can't remember?" asked Harvey. "Is it hazy?"

Tyler nodded. "I remember it, but the details are cloudy, like..." Tyler searched for the right words. "It's like I was drunk, but I wasn't. I don't drink."

"It's okay. I know what you mean. But you need to control that. You need to channel the anger and control it."

"That's what I did earlier. I held it back."

"You held it back and had a gun put in your face, then you were chucked into a car and driven off. That's not channelling the anger. That's called being kidnapped, Tyler. You need to take that energy, but instead of suppressing it, you need to drive it to where you want it to be. When you feel that anger coming on and all you want to do is hurt someone, you need to remember your training. You need to go back to basics and let that anger bubble away in the background. Don't push it away but don't let it overtake your training."

The two sat in silence for a moment. A car drove past and its headlights flashed across the dashboard.

"You sound like you have it too," said Tyler. "The temper."

"It's not a temper," replied Harvey. He questioned if he should continue; he'd already said too much. But the boy was genuine, and he had a familiarity that had caught Harvey's attention. "I don't know what it is, but you're right, it's inside me."

"How did you learn to control it?"

The question came out of nowhere. It shouldn't have. Harvey should have seen it coming. But it hit him hard.

He didn't reply.

"Did you end up in trouble like me? Is that it?" asked Tyler.

"Somebody showed me, Tyler. Somebody saw it in me and helped me."

Harvey's phone began to vibrate once more. He put his hand in his pocket.

"Can you help me?" asked Tyler. "I mean, do you think you could? I can fight, but I'm in trouble. If I lose my temper, it'll all be over."

"I'm not the man you need, Tyler. Trust me."

"I do," said Tyler. "I don't know why. I don't know you. But do you think you can show me how to channel it? Or at least get me started? I could pay. I have money, a little."

"I'm not the man you need, Tyler," said Harvey. "Nobody needs advice from me."

He put the car in gear and pulled his phone from his pocket.

"You can get out here, or I can drop you on the way. That's about all I can do for you," said Harvey. He hit the green button on his phone.

"One second, Melody." He looked across at Tyler. "What do you want to do?"

"It was you, wasn't it?" said Tyler. "Earlier?"

Harvey didn't reply.

"I saw you. I know it was you."

"Where?"

Tyler looked at his feet again and scratched at his hand.

"At my dad's grave."

CHAPTER NINETEEN

"So I was wondering if maybe we could talk, you know, about my Dad," said Tyler, as Harvey pulled the little Mazda up to the entrance of Tyler's building.

"There's not a lot I can tell you," replied Harvey.

"It doesn't have to be a lot. It doesn't have to be much at all. It's weird, but I feel this connection to him somehow through you."

Harvey didn't reply.

"Can I call you? Or you could call me? I don't know anything really. I only know what he looked like from photos and Mum doesn't say much about him. She shuts down if I mention his name."

There was a naivety in the boy's language that Julios wouldn't have tolerated, but also a softness in his eyes. There was no denying the boy was Julios' son. Harvey could see it in his size, and his features in profile with the large square jaw, piercing eyes and an over-sized nose.

"You can call me," said Harvey. "Do you have a pen?"

Tyler rummaged through his bag and wrote Harvey's number on the back of his hand.

"It really means a lot to me. Thank you for this."

"I'm in London for a few days. After that, I'll be gone and I doubt I'll be back."

"I'll call. I promise," said Tyler. "Can I ask one thing?"

Harvey's eyebrows raised in anticipation.

"Can I ask what your name is? You didn't say and maybe my mum knows of you."

"Your mum doesn't know me," replied Harvey. "What's her name?"

"Leah. Her name's Leah Thomson."

Harvey didn't reply.

"She knew all the faces around here. Anyone that was worth knowing, that is. She was married to some gangster bloke, but they were divorced before I was born. Mum said they got married too young. Mum started seeing my dad, on the quiet, you know? She wouldn't have people talking about her."

"And what happened to the gangster?" asked Harvey.

"He was killed eventually. I guess when you walk that line you have to expect it might happen one day, right? Good riddance, I say."

"And you never met your dad?"

"No, he stopped coming round but used to send mum money. It's weird. It was as if she didn't want him there, but she never speaks bad of him, not like the other fella, the gangster." Tyler paused. "Didn't he ever talk about me?"

"Your dad didn't say much at all, Tyler. He was a private man."

"I wish I knew him. From what Mum says, he was a great man. But he just couldn't commit to us. It's weird though, a couple of times while I was on my way to school or out with my mates, I'd imagine I saw him driving past or walking nearby. But whenever I looked again, he'd be gone. It's almost as if some part of me wanted him to be there."

"How long have you been going to the grave?"

"A few years now. Mum found out where it was and told me. I don't really know why I go. I guess it's just a connection. I talk to him about mum and about my training." A solitary, weak laugh broke Tyler's memories. "He's a good listener."

Harvey left Tyler with his thoughts for a few seconds and considered what to say. For the first time in a long while, there was so much Harvey wanted to say, but there was also so much he couldn't. A memory here and there might open the boy's wounds. But nothing might close him off, and he was the closest Harvey had to having his old friend back.

"I should go," said Tyler. He reached for the door handle and glanced through the windscreen at the torrential rain. He turned back to Harvey as he pulled on the door handle. "Thanks. I *will* call you, maybe tomorrow."

"Wait," said Harvey. He'd started. He couldn't stop now. "Close the door."

Tyler pulled the door shut and the interior light flicked off.

"Do you want to know about your dad?" asked Harvey. "I didn't know my dad either. I know what it's like, the wondering."

"Anything," replied Tyler, his eyes wide in the semi-light of the dark street.

"My dad was killed. My mum too. We were fostered by a man, not far from here. I don't remember it happening. I was just a baby. But my sister and I were taken in by this man and his wife. It was the same man your dad worked for. He was his security."

"Like a minder or a bodyguard?" asked Tyler.

"Exactly that," replied Harvey. "I ended up in some trouble. I was heading the wrong way, probably just like a million other boys out there right now. But my foster father asked Julios to take me under his wing, you know, show me a better path."

Tyler nodded. His eyes glistened at Harvey mentioning his dad as if the words had added a reality to the name, the photos and the grave marker.

"I was only young, about thirteen years old, I think. Maybe older. He started to train me, taught me to swim, made me run and do push-ups. All the things a kid hates, right?"

"Right," said Tyler with another single laugh enthused with an anxious energy.

"Then he started to teach me defence. I loved it. I ended up spending more time with your old man than my own foster father. We grew very close."

"So he taught you to fight?" asked Tyler.

"He taught me a lot of things, Tyler. Yeah, fighting was one aspect of it. But it was more than that. The fighting, the training and exercise, it all came second to a mindset, a way of thinking."

"What do you mean?"

Harvey turned in his seat and edged into the corner, allowing him to see Tyler without turning his head.

"Everything your dad ever did was part of a plan. If he put his keys on a table, he'd do it a certain way. If he opened a door, he did it a certain way."

"Why?" asked Tyler. "I mean, why open a door a certain way? How many ways are there?"

Harvey looked up at the street outside.

"Do you see that door there?" he asked.

"The green one?"

"How would you open it?"

"I'd pull the handle and walk inside."

"Who's on the other side?"

Tyler shrugged. "I don't know."

"Exactly."

"Was his job dangerous?" asked Tyler.

"Sometimes," replied Harvey, but redirecting the trail of

conversation. "Everything he did was meticulous. Parking a car, he'd drive up and down the street twice before even attempting to park. Your dad was a smart man, and that mindset was habitual. It drove his life and he passed that on to me. I think, more than anything, that's what I learned most from him. The mindset."

"But you didn't drive up and down before you parked," said Tyler.

"I'd like to think that part of my life is over. What I'm trying to say, Tyler, and believe me, this is the hardest thing I've ever had to say, but your dad meant the world to me. More than anyone I ever met. If you turn out to be half the man he was, you're onto a winner."

Tears had overflowed the wells in Tyler's eyes and a single drop rolled down each of his cheeks.

"I'll call you tomorrow, yeah?" said Tyler. He gave Harvey a thoughtful look and hid his face, embarrassed by his tears.

Harvey didn't reply.

Just as the car door was about to slam, Tyler ducked inside once more. Harvey had straightened and put the car into first gear.

"You didn't tell me your name," said Tyler.

Harvey stared back at him, considering the consequences and weighing up the odds. But his affection broke through the defences that the boy's father had taught him.

"Harvey," he said. "Harvey Stone."

It took just a few seconds for the downpour to soak Tyler through. He looked up at the windows of his flat. The lights were off. If his mum had been up, he'd see the flickering of the TV through the kitchen window. It was a trick he'd learned as a kid when he'd stayed out too late.

He pulled his hood up as Harvey drove away and checked to see if he looked in his mirror, but the rain, the dark and the tiny window made it impossible to see.

Tyler watched the little Mazda drive to the end of the street, where it turned right onto the highway towards Tower Bridge. Tyler turned and fumbled in his pocket for his keys, but as he did, a shadow stepped out of the neighbouring doorway, broad and as black as the night.

The movement caught Tyler off guard, and he stumbled backwards. The man moved towards him, his hands in his jacket pockets and a dark hood pulled over his head, which covered half of his face.

"You let him down, Tyler."

It was only when the man spoke that Tyler's fear sank

further into a sense of dread, a tightening at the bottom of his stomach.

"Lloyd, I can explain."

"So explain," replied Lloyd. "Do you know how many people get the chance you had? You missed training, Tyler. Would you rather be out with your mates than-"

"It's not what you think, Lloyd. Honest. I can explain."

"So tell me," said Lloyd.

Tyler took another glance up to the windows.

"Shall we talk inside?" asked Tyler.

Lloyd looked up too, and then shook his head.

"I don't need to intrude. I just came to warn you. You have everything going for you, son. You have the talent and you have the trainer that will take you to the top. What you don't have is the mindset."

"Mindset?" said Tyler.

"Did I say something?" asked Lloyd.

Tyler was looking past him to where Harvey had disappeared around the corner.

"No," said Tyler. "No, I understand."

"Do you? Do you understand that right now, the old man is talking about not even letting you back in his gym, let alone training you."

"I told you," said Tyler. "Something came up. Family stuff."

"You can't kid a kidder," said Lloyd. "If there's one thing a lifetime of being around juveniles has taught me, it's how to spot a lie."

"It was," said Tyler. "Honest."

"And the man in the car was family, was he?"

Tyler fought to keep eye contact with Lloyd.

"Yeah. Yeah, he was, in a way."

"Training tomorrow. I'll talk to the old man, but it's the last time. You let us down again and you lose it all. And don't think any other gym will train you once the old man drops you. If you mess this up, that's it. That's your career in the ring over."

"Thanks, Lloyd. I won't let you down. I promise."

"Don't come by tomorrow. Let me talk to him. Come on Saturday night. Double session. Be prepared to work hard."

"I will," said Tyler. "No, wait. Saturday. I can't."

Lloyd cocked his head and even in the darkness beneath his hood, Tyler could see his eyes narrow.

"And why can't you come in on Saturday? You either want my help or you don't."

"I, erm, I said I'd help a friend."

"A friend?"

"Yeah. He's only in town for a few days and I said I'd-"

"Saturday night, Tyler. The old man won't wait any longer. What's more important to you?"

"Training, of course it is."

"So be there. I'm sure your friend has other friends to call on."

Lloyd finished with a cold, hard stare, which Tyler knew was him searching for sincerity.

"I'll be there," said Tyler. "Double session."

Lloyd turned away and pulled the collar of his jacket close to his neck as he walked.

"Hey, Lloyd," called Tyler. He'd been standing in the rain for more than ten minutes but had only just begun to feel the cold as the damp seeped through to his skin.

Lloyd turned but only a shadow beneath his hood looked back.

"Thanks, yeah?" said Tyler. "Thanks for your help."

Lloyd nodded once and slipped around the corner.

The entrance to the flats was still broken, but the front door was locked. Tyler let himself in, avoiding the noisy parts of the floor, just as he had for the past ten years since he'd been coming home late.

He switched the kettle on and grabbed his favourite mug from the cupboard. It was white with the words 'Education is important but boxing is importanter' in bold black letters. His mum had seen it in a cheap store and bought it for him back when she was able to go to the shops alone. He spooned in two spoonfuls of cocoa. It was a luxury he allowed himself after training, and although he hadn't trained that night, he felt he needed something to help him sleep.

A whining in his ear, relentless and monotone, sang through his head and he felt the familiar restless toe-tapping that came when he was anxious. While the kettle boiled, he removed his wet clothes, stripping to his shorts in the kitchen, and hung them over the radiator beneath the window. It was as he did so that he saw them. Two men sitting in a car outside the flat. The glow of a cigarette occasionally lit the dashboard in a weak orange light.

Tyler flicked the light switch and stepped back to the window.

"Maybe Harvey could help," he whispered to himself.

He dug his mobile phone from his bag and hit the on button. The little screen glowed in a green light. He held it beneath the window so he could watch the two men. He used the light to see his hand, where he'd written Harvey's number. But instead of the neat little numbers, he found a blue ink smudge across his skin. Only two of the digits even resembled numbers.

Tyler sank to his haunches with his back against the fridge and let his head fall down. There was no way he could find him now.

A car door closed outside. Tyler peeked through the window, but all he saw was the empty car with no orange glow of a cigarette lighting the dashboard.

CHAPTER TWENTY-ONE

"Did he say he'd do it, John?" asked Mick, as he poured himself and John a drink from behind the bar.

John was still sitting in his chair with the fire burning low, a bed of hot embers pulsing with rage beside him. He waited for Mick to hand him a drink, took a sip, puckered his lips then set the glass down on the table.

"Of course he did," replied John. "You leave the boy to me. What I want you and Jack to do is give the opposition a disadvantage."

"You mean you want us to take his boy out?" asked Mick. "What was his name?"

"Mackie," said John. The name was at the forefront of his thoughts.

"That's it," said Mick. "Do you want us to take care of him?"

"No, no. Dixon already played that card. He'll be expecting a retaliation. No, that's not the way. You see, while you two were out for a stroll in the rain, I did a bit of thinking. Brandy's good for that, Mick, thinking. There's nothing quite like being warmed by an open fire and sipping at a nice brandy to keep the creative juices flowing."

"You've had some ideas then?" said Mick. He rubbed his hands together and turned one of the chairs opposite John to face the fire, then laid his jacket across the back to dry it out.

"Tyler Thomson," said John. "That's our boy. I haven't seen anyone that big for a long time, and if he can fight like I've been told he can fight, then we're rock solid, Mick. Rock solid."

"I hear good things, John. The old man wouldn't be wasting his time training a nobody."

"No, Mick. No, he wouldn't. But, you see, the old man can't give the boy the training he needs. What that boy needs, the thing that will take him to the top, is up here in the grey matter, Mick." John tapped at his temple with his index finger. "He doesn't have the killer instinct. Not yet anyway. But if he gets through this fight, he'll be a changed man."

"If he gets through this fight, he'll be a killer, John. A thing like that can really affect somebody, mentally, I mean."

"You mean *when* he comes through this fight, and he will. Nothing hardens someone up better than a few sleepless nights of restless remorse. If he comes out the other side unscathed, he'll be unstoppable, and he'll be someone we'll want on our side. He'll be going places and he'll have yours truly to thank for his success."

"So you haven't told him it's a fight to the death?" asked Mick. "He thinks it's just a normal boxing match?"

"Of course I haven't," said John. "He doesn't even know it's bare-knuckle, but he won't back out now. Besides, the bloke was in bits already. I don't know which one of you hit him or how hard you did it, but you scared the hell out of the kid."

"It was Jack. He always gets carried away," said Mick.

"Well, young Jack wants to control it. He's not as tough as he thinks he is. Did you see that muppet walk in here earlier? All the poor bloke wanted was to get out of the rain and Jack starts mouthing off and giving him stick trying to impress me.

Giving someone a hard time isn't going to impress me, especially when that someone happens to shut him down. Now, if Jack decided to stick one on him, that would impress me. Anyway, pissing people off is one sure-fire way to bring attention to the place. He's got to learn how to treat people. Mark my words, Mick, *when* young Tyler gets through this *and* handles the ensuing nightmares, he's going to be a monster, and that monster will remember the beating that Jack gave him way back when. I'd like to be there for that one."

"Do you want me to have a word with him?" asked Mick. "You know, calm him down a bit?"

John reached for his drink, shifted in his seat, and shook his head.

"No, Mick. In matters such as these, I prefer to let nature take its course."

"So how are we going to get at Dixon's boy?"

"Ah, we digressed," said John. He felt a smile warm the muscles on his face. "Like I said, Mick, it's all in the mind. Find out who he is. Where he's from. He must have family. He must have a weak point. Find it and bring it to me. We've got two days until the fight so I want something to work with by tomorrow night at the latest. We're going to break that boy from the inside out and there won't be a thing Dixon can do to stop us until it's too late."

"What about the old man?" asked Mick.

John's left eye twitched at the question. It was an annoyance, a potential thorn in his side.

"Take care of it, Mick."

CHAPTER TWENTY-TWO

"Oh my god, Harvey, where have you been?" said Melody.

She looked up at him, concerned and with a glass of wine in her hand, then quietened when she saw the look on his face.

The waiter pulled his chair for him, but Harvey issued him a look that told the man he didn't require assistance to sit down. He seated himself and collected a menu from the centre of the table. Melody took it from him with her spare hand.

"What happened?" she whispered.

Harvey didn't reply.

"Can I get you a drink, sir?" asked the waiter.

"Water's fine," replied Harvey, and he glanced around the room, where tables of twos and fours hosted couples and four-somes. The new couples laughed and were lost in their own little worlds. The seasoned couples sat in near silence. The four-somes each battled with two streams of conversation, fighting to be heard above the other.

There were no lone diners and no groups of men that rang alarm bells, but still, Harvey positioned his chair with its back to the wall to maintain a full view of the room. It was an old habit he'd never be able to break.

"We didn't think you'd come," said Jess. "But Melody said you wouldn't miss it."

The waiter delivered his water to the table, then cracked the lid and offered Harvey a slice of lemon. He refused the lemon and poured his own water.

"Don't you ever drink?" Jess asked.

"I never have done. I got this far without it. It would be a shame to start now."

"Harvey has never had alcohol and never worn anything apart from a white t-shirt," said Reg, offering Harvey a smile to let him know he was only joking.

Melody sidled up beside Harvey and worked herself under his arm.

"But he sure knows how to wear those white t-shirts, Reg," she said, and winked at Jess, running a playful hand down Harvey's chest.

"Well, I hope you brought a suit or something for the wedding," said Reg.

Harvey looked at Melody for a response.

"He's got a suit. He scrubs up well," said Melody.

"So, Harvey, how did it go? Did you find your friend?"

"My friend?" said Harvey, a little too brash.

"She means Julios," said Melody.

"Yeah, I found Julios. It was a little anticlimactic, but at least I know where he is. Thanks for arranging that. I hope you didn't have to break any rules," he said with a smile.

"It was nothing," replied Jess.

"So are you guys all set for the big day?" asked Harvey. "I feel I missed all the conversation."

"That's okay," said Reg. "We know how much he meant to you, Harvey."

Harvey offered Reg a curt nod.

"And yeah, we're all set," Reg continued. "In two days' time, we'll be Mr and Mrs Tenant."

"What about the honeymoon?" asked Harvey. "Have you made big plans?"

Reg and Jess looked at each other and the table fell silent.

"Well, we kind of spent everything we had on the flat, the wedding and the van."

"I've offered them our house for a few weeks," said Melody. "We'll stay here and they can enjoy the beach and the fields."

It wasn't often Melody drew a line in the sand with Harvey, but he knew her tone when she had.

"Okay," he said, realising that their little pocket of paradise in southern France would be more memorable than a wet weekend in Clapham. "You'll love it. The mornings are crisp and the sea's cold, but I've never experienced peace like it."

"We can't wait. It feels like I haven't had a holiday for years sometimes," said Jess. "It can't be healthy, going to work in the dark and coming home in the dark, only to wake up a few hours later to do it all over. A few weeks by the sea is exactly what we need."

"Excuse me," said Harvey. "I'll just find the washroom."

The conversation faded as he made his way between the tables, past the reception and into the toilets, where he splashed cool water onto his face. He leaned on the basin and stared at his reflection, pondering the small talk. He loved Reg and Jess but somehow never managed to fit into any of their conversations. He thought of the two men on the table of four, probably discussing business or sport, while their wives chatted about plans for children. He let out a long exhale then dried his hands and face using a rolled-up towel from a neat pile on the marble surface.

From the washroom door, he looked out across the restaurant. In the far corner, Jess, Reg and Melody were all discussing wedding plans, a subject on which he could offer no real input. To Harvey's right was the reception, a small counter with a cash register up top and small TV below showing a London news program. A reporter was standing beneath an umbrella in the rain as firefighters behind her rallied to put out a huge fire. The scene was lit by the flashing blue lights of emergency vehicles while the fire cast an orange haze over the surrounding cars and buildings.

The receptionist saw Harvey staring at the TV, and with an apologetic smile, she moved to switch it off.

"Wait," said Harvey. "Where is this?"

"Poplar," said the girl. "It's been burning for a while. I think it's the arches."

"Can you turn the volume up?" asked Harvey as ambulances arrived on the scene.

"Sorry, sir, I'm not really allowed to have it on."

He glanced back at the table where Melody, Reg and Jess were still absorbed in conversation.

"Can you do me a favour?" he asked, pulling his phone from his pocket. "Do you have a pen and paper?"

On the paper the receptionist slid across the counter, Harvey wrote the words 'I'm sorry.' He placed his phone in the centre of the paper and folded it into a parcel, then slid it towards the girl.

"Can you wait five minutes, and then deliver this to the table in the corner?"

CHAPTER TWENTY-THREE

"Mum, you need to get up," said Tyler, nudging his sleeping mother's shoulder. "Come on. Wake up, Mum."

Tyler flicked the lights on as she stirred and pulled the covers over her face.

"Come on, Mum. Wake up," he said with a little more urgency.

"What time is it?" she mumbled, just as there was a gentle knock on the front door.

"Mum, I'll explain later. But you need to wake up." He pulled the covers from her face then began to pull clothes from the cupboard and stuff them into a bag. Shielding her eyes from the light, his mum sat up and swung her legs out of the bed.

"What's going on?" she asked.

"Put your slippers on, Mum. There's no time to explain."

Another knock, louder than the first.

"Who's that at the door?" his mum asked.

"Mum, please," said Tyler. He could feel the frustration sending his heart rate skyward.

"Okay, okay. No need to rush me," she said, as she pushed

herself to a standing position. Tyler helped to steady her, a little harder than usual.

"Easy, Tyler. I'm not as young as I used to be," she said. "Now, where are my slippers?"

Three hard knocks on the front door.

"Who is that at this time of night?"

Tyler finished stuffing his mother's medication into the bag, then dropped it on the bed and took hold of her shoulders.

"Mum, I need you to listen to me. There's some bad men out there that want to hurt us."

"But why?"

"There's no time to explain, Mum. I need you to follow me. We're going out onto the fire escape and I'll find us somewhere safe," said Tyler, although he couldn't think where. His mind raced with the words of John Cooper. "Your slippers are there by your feet. I have your pills and some clothes. Let's get out of here and we can talk about it when we're safe. Okay?"

"Oh," she said. It was the start of a panic attack. Tyler had witnessed many of her panic attacks begin with that word.

"No time to worry, Mum," he reassured her. "Let's go. It'll be like an adventure, okay?"

Tyler took his mother's hand and led her from the bedroom just as the front door began to pound.

"Quick, Mum, in here," said Tyler, leading his mum into the rear bedroom, which was too small for anything other than storing boxes, but the window opened onto the iron fire escape, which led to the ground floor alleyway that ran behind the buildings.

"Out there?" she said. "I can't go out there like this."

"Mum, please," said Tyler. "Please just do as I ask."

He forced the window open, which required a particular knack he'd learned as a child when he'd sneak out late at night to meet his friends.

The pounding on the door stopped, allowing for a moment of peace.

"Come on, Mum," he whispered, and held his hand out to help her through the gap.

She sat on the window ledge and swung her legs over until the brisk, cold wind lifted the edge of her dressing gown.

"Oh, Tyler, it's freezing," she said.

"I know, Mum. But not for long, I promise," he said, as the front door boomed with the shoulder of a man trying to get inside.

Tyler climbed through after his mum and leaned inside to grab the bag, just as he heard the front door explode open and a man stumble inside, followed immediately by two rough angry voices.

"Go down," whispered Tyler to his mum, as he pulled on the window to close it behind them. The men wouldn't know how to open it, which would give Tyler a head start.

Heavy footsteps on the lounge floor approached the tiny room. Just as the shape of the first man became silhouetted in the doorway, the window gave and slid shut with a click.

With the hard rain hitting his face, Tyler stepped back as the man pressed against the window, struggling to see through the frosted, reinforced glass. The face appeared to smile as Tyler moved to the top of the stairs. He glanced down at his mum who was carefully placing her slippered feet on the slippery iron stairs and clinging to the wet, slick handrail. Tyler looked back. The face moved away from the glass, but Tyler's hope lasted a fraction of a second before a piece of furniture was hurled at the window. The reinforced mesh held the glass together, but it fractured; it wouldn't take long to break through.

Tyler edged down the stairs.

"That's it, Mum," he said. "You're doing great. Are you okay?"

His mother didn't answer.

Another crash of the furniture smashing through the window. This time, tiny pieces of glass rained down onto the iron platform and to the ground below. A hole had been made in the mesh, and the man began to hammer with something, trying to smash through to outside.

"Keep going, Mum," said Tyler, keeping his eyes on the window above.

A man's head poked through the hole, searching around in the darkness until he caught the movement of Tyler on the stairs. With reluctance, the man pulled his head back inside. The crunch of stones and glass beneath his feet told Tyler he'd reached the ground, but he dared not take his eyes off the window above.

"Are you okay, Mum?' he asked.

But she didn't reply.

"Mum?"

Tyler turned to find a handgun pointing in his face. The one John had called Jack was staring back at Tyler with his hand over his mum's mouth.

"Going somewhere?" he asked.

CHAPTER TWENTY-FOUR

"So you thought you'd do a runner, did you, Tyler?" said John. "After our agreement, that's most unprofessional."

"No, it wasn't like that," replied Tyler. His voice was muffled by the thick hood that had been pulled over his head.

"Oh? Jack tells me you were climbing down the fire escape, Tyler, in the rain with who he can only imagine is your mother. Jack, remove her hood, mate, and get her wrapped up in a blanket or something. We don't want her bleeding dying on us yet."

Jack carefully pulled the hood off the lady's head to reveal a pair of wide scared eyes behind a thin facade of steely resentment.

"Can you get her a chair or something?" asked Tyler. "She's sick. She's supposed to be in bed, resting."

John took three paces forward until he was just inches from Tyler. He had to reach up to grab the hood, but he caught it and tugged until it fell from Tyler's face.

"That's better. I like to look a man in the eye when he's upset me," said John, aware that Tyler was a full twelve inches taller than himself. "What's wrong with your dear old mum then? She looks fine to me. A bit cold maybe."

"She's sick. It's cancer," said Tyler. "Please. I said I'd do what you asked. Get her a chair before she falls."

John studied the frail lady who seemed half the size of her son but could easily have once been a strong woman. He nodded to Jack who slid a chair behind her legs.

"Take a seat, Mrs Thomson," said John, and offered his hand to help her lower herself into the chair. "Find a blanket, Jack."

"Thank you," said Tyler. "I appreciate it."

"It's nothing. Where were you going?" asked John.

"Your men came for us. I didn't know what else to do."

"What are you talking about?"

"When we spoke, in the pub, you said you'd..." Tyler swallowed to control his voice. "You said you'd hurt my mum if I didn't do what you said."

"Right. So?"

"So when your men came, I thought you'd come for us. I didn't see any other way."

"You didn't see any other way," repeated John. He pronounced the words with slow and clear pronunciation. "These men, did they tell you they worked for me, Tyler?"

"Well, no. But we didn't hang around to talk to them. I woke my mum up and got us out of there."

"And where exactly was you planning to go?"

Tyler hesitated.

"Tyler?" John urged. "Is there something you're not telling me?"

"No. I didn't have a plan. I just knew I had to get out. They were kicking the door in. What was I supposed to do?"

John began to pace. He stuffed his hands into his coat

pockets and took five steps to his right, letting the wooden heel of his Italian shoes click on the concrete floor. The noise reverberated in the large space and the tiled walls toyed with the sound until it faded away to nothing.

"Did you manage to get a good look at these men?" asked John.

"Not really," said Tyler. "Well, one of them, but I only saw his face in the dark, like a silhouette."

"As it turns out," said John, "you did the right thing. You should give yourself a pat on the back, Tyler."

"I did? So why are we here? And where are we?"

"Look around you, Tyler."

The boy turned to let his eyes wash across the tiled walls and cubicles where animals had once queued for the slaughter. He stopped when he saw the punch bag and weight bench. A rack of dumbbells lay against the tiled wall and a mat covered an area ten metres by ten metres.

"It's not much right now, Tyler. But one day, Cooper's Gym will be big, you mark my words."

"What's with the tiled walls and the smell?"

"That, Tyler, is the smell of fear. Fear and death," said John. He watched as Tyler's face sank even further. "It was a slaughterhouse. I bought it a few years ago. It comes in handy for times like this, you know? Sometimes a man in my position needs to be able to hose the blood off the floor."

Tyler gave him a sideways glance.

"They were going to tear it down and build some new swanky apartments, but the locals were against it. They said the building is a part of Plaistow history. So I bought it and I gained a few loyal fans in doing so. It's always good to have the public on your side when you're in the spotlight, Tyler. That's a lesson you should learn if you're going to be on stage."

"On stage?"

"In the ring, Tyler. If the crowds are with you, cheering your name, you'll feel on top of the world. If they're not, you're just queuing for the slaughter."

"So who were those men, if they don't work for you?" asked Tyler.

John took the five steps back to stand in front of the huge but naive boy.

"Those men, Tyler, were the opposition. I don't know how they found out about you, but they obviously did, and tried to put you out of the game. It won't happen again."

"They were going to kill us?" asked Tyler.

"I don't know," replied John. "I doubt they'd kill you. But they'd hurt you enough so you couldn't fight."

Tyler looked down at his mum who had fallen asleep in the chair.

"She looks comfy," said John.

"It's the meds," replied Tyler. "Look, John, I said I'd fight for you. And I will. But she's really sick. Can we get her somewhere? She needs rest."

"And what about you?

"What about me?" asked Tyler.

"Do you need rest?"

"No," replied the boy. "I need to train. I can feel the energy inside me. I won't sleep until I've worked out."

"Jack?" called John.

"Yes, boss."

"Get Mrs Thomson to the flat above the pub. She can have the spare room." He turned to Tyler. "Is that alright for you?"

"She needs care," said Tyler.

"I'll make sure she's looked after."

"And her medication."

"Painkillers?" said John. "I presume they're in the bag."

Tyler nodded.

The double doors at the end of the room swung open with a crash and Mick walked in. He saw John talking quietly to Tyler and kept his distance. He'd been trained well. John turned his attention back to Tyler.

"Tyler, you have to understand one thing. I'm a businessman. I'm hard but fair. And you are a fighter who now works for me. It might seem like a rough deal, son, but if you win this fight for us, you'll be welcomed into this family and your poor old mum will want for nothing. You got that?"

Tyler nodded once more.

"Good. From now on, you train here. You eat here and you sleep here. You need to be on top form, son."

"What about my job?" said Tyler. "I'll be letting my boss down."

"You leave your boss to me. Give Mick his number and he'll take care of everything for you."

"He'll fire me. I was going onto the tools."

"Listen, Tyler. When you win this fight, you'll have more money than you know what to do with. Forget about your job. I'll have Mick take care of it for you. We'll tell your boss you're sick or something, you won't be coming back, and you're really sorry. We'll be convincing. That's something that Mick happens to be particularly good at."

"What about the old man? I'm supposed to train. I can't let him down."

"You leave the old man to me, Tyler. Stop worrying and focus on the fight. I've got a lot riding on you. I can't risk having you leave my sight."

"But who will train me? I need a trainer."

Tyler eyed John up and down and spent a little longer on the paunch John had been developing.

"My trainer. He's the best. He'll be here later. You do everything he says when he says it and you won't have any trouble. You deviate from his plan and you'll find yourself in hot water. Is that clear?"

"It's clear," replied Tyler, but his enthusiasm had plummeted.

"Don't worry about the old man and don't worry about the job. I told you. Leave them to me. I'll have someone swing by your flat and get you a bag of clothes."

"And my mum?" asked Tyler.

"Well, as nice as this place is, Tyler, it's really not accommodating enough for the likes of your lovely old lady. She'll be staying at my pub in the flat upstairs. It's lovely. I'll see to it that the girls behind the bar pop up and see her to make sure she's okay. Poor old girl could probably do with a drink, couldn't she?"

Tyler managed a weak smile at John's attempt to finish on a high, positive note.

"Go say goodbye to her," said John. "If you play your cards right, Tyler, the next time you see her, you'll have cash in your pocket and a smile on your face."

A curt nod at Mick summoned John's number two while Tyler settled next to his mum and reassured her that everything would be okay.

"How did you get on with Dixon's boy?" asked John.

"He's a rock, John. No family. No weaknesses."

"He must have something. Keep looking," said John. "What about the old man?"

"I sent Nobby and Jack round to sort him out."

"Good. The last thing we need is that nosy old bastard sticking his two pennies worth in. He's well connected and could be a lot of trouble for us."

"Oh, he won't be any trouble, John."

"You sound sure of yourself, Mick."

"I just drove past his gym on the way back from south of the water. They torched the place with him inside. He won't be sticking his two pennies in anywhere ever again, John."

CHAPTER TWENTY-FIVE

Although the flames had been extinguished, huge, thick plumes of black smoke billowed from the charred remains of the gym and the tyre shop that occupied the arch beside it.

Harvey stood in the shadows across the road and watched as the firemen began to roll the hoses into neat stackable rolls, and the last of the ambulances waited with open doors. A window of light in the darkness. Its counterpart had sped off twenty minutes previously just as Harvey had arrived on the scene.

A few junior police had cordoned off the road and senior officers spoke with senior firemen, presumably discussing probable cause and managing the scene of the crime. If it was indeed a crime. Harvey had no doubt the fire was the result of arson.

As the final gurney rolled unhurried towards the waiting ambulance, Harvey felt a stab of guilt and loss. The sheet that covered the huge corpse differentiated its load as a body and not a survivor with an oxygen mask over their face. The sheet, much the same as the one that had covered Harvey's sister all those years before, was not blood soaked like they were in the movies. In Harvey's experience, they rarely were. A blood-soaked sheet would indicate a pumping heart. But there was no way anybody could have survived the hellish blaze that Harvey had witnessed. The size of the body beneath the sheet was unmistakable.

Harvey watched as the two paramedics struggled to load the heavy gurney into the ambulance then secured it in place. The driver called through on his radio to the hospital.

"Male. One hundred and thirty-five kilos. Dead on arrival."

A crackle of radio returned as the doors slammed. Harvey edged back into the shadows, stumbled against the wall and took three deep breaths.

For the second time in Harvey's life, he'd failed a Saville.

Another car door slammed close by and men's voices grew louder, rousing Harvey from his thoughts. He stepped back further into the shadows, but his boot nudged a discarded glass bottle, sending it rolling. The chink of glass against concrete was loud in the quiet alley.

The voices stopped as if the bottle had caught their attention. Harvey checked his exit, glanced back at the ambulance one last time, turned, and ran through the series of alleys to where he'd parked Melody's car.

The doorway of a corner shop provided a place to hide and check to see if he'd been followed. He waited a full minute then walked calmly to the car.

The rain had cleansed the street but the nearby fire had tainted the air as far as three streets away. Harvey took the back streets through Poplar, passing old pubs and gambling houses his foster father used to own. But none of them brought back fond memories. They had been violent times when Harvey was only ever called out to take care of someone, leave no trace, and then crawl back to his little house. Each time, it was as if he paused his own existence while people searched for the missing man, retaliated, and then carried on with life.

Tyler's flat looked very different in the half-light of dawn. A corner shop was opening up a few doors down, its owner heaving in the bundles of newspapers. The highway at the end of the road was growing busier and soon London would be a hive of activity. Harvey turned and gave Tyler's flat another pass, checking the parked cars as Julios would have him do. The sentiment seemed like the right thing to do and Harvey couldn't shake his mentor's words from his mind.

He parked five cars down from the entrance to Tyler's flat and sat with his hands on the wheel, questioning what he was doing. He was just some kid who said he was Julios' son. But with no real proof. If he'd meant that much, surely Julios would have said something.

But he wouldn't have.

The line in the sand was never crossed. It was part of who Julios had been. And Julios was gone. So the only person left to look out for his son was Harvey. He couldn't walk away. He had to know if it was true, if it really was him in the fire.

He found the ground floor entrance to the flat. The door was broken as if it had been forced. Harvey slipped inside and took the single set of stairs to the first floor where he saw two doors.

The first one, on the right-hand side, was adorned with religious beads and had the spicy smell of curry emanating from inside. The second door had been smashed off its hinges and was laying on the floor inside the flat. On the wall in the hallway inside, three photo frames took pride of place, as if they were memories that welcomed Tyler home each time he walked through the door.

The first was of Tyler and who Harvey assumed to be his mum. The second was an image of a much younger Tyler leaning on the ropes of a boxing ring. The third caught Harvey off-guard. Standing with a baby in his arms, and wearing his trademark three-quarter length leather jacket, was Julios.

A man's voice came from inside the flat, dull and monotone. Harvey unsheathed his knife from his back pocket and traced the voice to a small room at the back of the flat. A cold breeze flowed through as if a window was open. Apart from the broken door, there were no signs of struggle or robbery.

A large crash sounded from the same bedroom as the voice, loud but muffled. Harvey crept across the threadbare carpet and peered inside to find a man in a dark green bomber jacket smashing a small chest of drawers into the frosted, reinforced window. With the knife held by his side, Harvey watched as the man leaned through the hole he'd made and called down to someone.

Harvey stepped into the room.

But as he did, a blow from behind slammed into his lower back, sending a wave of dull, agonising pain through his body. With no time to turn and defend himself against a follow-up attack, he dropped to the floor and kicked out at his attacker's legs. It was a move Julios had taught him. The natural reaction for someone being attacked from behind is to turn and face the attack. But to drop to the ground out of harm's way and smash the man's knee was nearly always unexpected and extremely effective. His attacker fell to the floor behind Harvey, who rolled, swiped the blade cross the inside of the man's thigh, and then stood with his heavy boot held hard down on the man's throat as he began to bleed to death.

The first man pulled back into the room and reached inside his jacket for a gun. But Harvey was faster. With his boot firmly in place and resisting the struggles of the dying man, Harvey put his blade against the first man's neck.

"Don't move," said Harvey.

The man froze. "Who are you?" he said, clearly angered but controlling his voice.

"Listen carefully," said Harvey. He increased the pressure

of his boot on the dying man's throat, which raised his heart rate. The pool of blood between his legs grew wider, spilling out in heavy spurts from his femoral artery. They could hear the gargled chokes of the dying man taking his last breaths. "Do you hear that?"

"I hear it," replied the man with the knife to his throat. He glanced down as his friend's body twitched for the final time and was still.

"What are you doing here?" asked Harvey.

"Looking for someone."

"Who?"

"A friend," the man replied.

Keeping his eyes on the man, Harvey gestured with a nod of his head at a framed photo on the floor, which must have been on top of the furniture he'd used to smash the window.

"Him?"

The man glanced down at the photo and nodded, being careful not to move his neck.

"Yeah, him," he replied.

"I just watched his body being dragged out of a fire," said Harvey. "And now I find you in his flat. Tell me why I shouldn't cut your throat right here, right now."

The man's eyes watered. He kept his cool, but Harvey saw the fear building inside.

"Who are you working for?"

"Why should I tell you that?" the man answered.

"Because I just killed your friend here in less than two seconds and I'd like to see if I can kill you faster."

"Dixon," replied the man with no hesitation. "Del Dixon."

"Take me to him."

CHAPTER TWENTY-SIX

Left to his own devices, Tyler sat on the end of the bench press that John had provided. He let his head drop into his hands and fought back the hot tears that reddened his eyes. Ahead of him, thirty metres away at the far side of the room, the two double doors invited him to leave. But his fight had gone. While John Cooper had his mum holed up, he needed to do everything he could to get her back safe.

His fat fingers covered his face, but he opened his eyes and stared at the doors, then exhaled, long and slow.

"You can make a try for them if you want," said a voice.

Tyler looked up. His eyes were foggy but allowed him to focus on a man of average build standing a few feet away.

"The doors," he said. "You can make a run for it if you want."

"What's the point?" replied Tyler, and he let his head fall back into his hands.

"So stop thinking about it."

"How would you know what I'm thinking about?"

"Intuition," the man replied in a whisper.

"Where did you even come from?" asked Tyler. "I didn't hear-"

"How could you have heard me?" the man replied. "You were too busy listening to the demons in your head argue over running for the doors or killing yourself."

"I wasn't thinking about that," said Tyler.

"You will be when I'm finished with you."

Before Tyler could respond, a hammer-like punch caught him on the side of his jaw, knocking him from the bench to the mat, where he rolled to his knees and held his face, working his jaw to test for damage.

"What the-"

A kick to his gut doubled him over and he rolled to his side sucking in air.

"Get up," said the man. The order wasn't barked or shouted. There was no emotion whatsoever in the words.

"Who are you?" asked Tyler, as he scrambled across the floor away from the man.

"You haven't earned my name yet," the man replied. "Come on. Fight me."

Pulling himself to his feet, Tyler straightened. But he wasn't ready for the three-punch combo to his kidneys. A crippling backache set in with immediate effect. Tyler tried to walk it off with his hands on his kidneys and his spine arched back, but another blow came from nowhere. The man's fist connected with the side of Tyler's head, rocking his vision into a dizzying swirl of white tiles and early morning sunlight beaming through the frosted windows high on the walls.

He dropped to his knees then fell to his side and assumed the foetal position, waiting for the world around him to stop spinning.

Not a sound was made by the man's feet, but Tyler heard him from the far side of the room, talking on his phone.

"You've got yourself a dead boy, John."

Tyler closed his eyes. A wave of nausea flowed through him and hung at the back of his throat, threatening to advance if he moved even a finger.

"No. There's no fight in him. He might be big, but he's soft," the man continued to say.

But Tyler pushed his voice away and tiny roots pushed through the shells of the seeds of suicide the man had planted. It was the only way out. They wouldn't hurt his mum if he was dead. She'd be taken into care.

"He wants to talk to you," said the man.

Tyler opened his eyes to find the man standing beside where he was laying, holding out a mobile phone. He hadn't made a sound. The man hit loudspeaker and held the phone at arm's length.

"Tyler?" It was John's voice. "Answer me, son. You're testing my patience."

"I'm here," said Tyler. He heard how weak his own voice sounded.

"You need to fight, son. If you can't fight, you're no good to me. And you know what happens if you're no good to me?"

Tyler let the words play over in his mind, but couldn't respond without releasing the damn that held back his tears.

"You disappear, Tyler," John continued. "You just vanish like you never existed. And your mum? Well, I haven't made up my mind yet. But you can guarantee the last few days of her life will be spent laying on her back earning all the money I've wasted on her sorry, waste-of-space son."

The heat behind Tyler's eyes drained to his face, sending a tingle of rage across Tyler's skin. He felt his cheeks tighten. His eyes pulsed once as his heart fed a shot of adrenalin into his bloodstream.

"Don't you dare lay a finger on her."

"You don't call the shots, Tyler."

He got to his knees.

"Here we go," said the man who held the phone.

"You know what I'm going to do, Tyler? Just to make sure you know I'm a man of my word. I've took your mum's medication and hid it. How long before she starts to really hurt?"

"That wasn't the deal," said Tyler.

"So fight," replied John. "There's a man standing in front of you. He's half your size, a third of your weight, and he's ready to slap you around the room. He's one of the toughest men I know. He's going to put the phone on the bench. If you can put him down long enough to hit redial, I'll give your poor old lady a dose of painkillers. If not, she suffers until you fight like a man and beat him. Each time you beat him and call me, your mum gets a painkiller. The next call I receive will either be from you asking politely for me to ease your mum's pain, or it will be from my friend telling me you haven't grown a pair of balls big enough for your mum to deserve a painkiller, and that she deserves to suffer."

The call disconnected.

Tyler studied the man who turned his back and walked to the bench to place the phone down in clear sight. With casual indifference, the man stood opposite Tyler. He bounced a few times on the balls of his feet and threw a rapid combination of punches into the air before eying Tyler.

"I imagine, right now, your poor old mum is locked in a padded room with a bucket to piss in and only the memories of her dead son to keep her company," he said.

The thought of his mum lying in a strange room, sweating and clawing at her skin, washed over Tyler's mind.

'Control it,' Harvey's words whispered.

But Tyler's mind focused on his mother's anguished face, wrinkled with agony and suffering.

"How's she going to feel when she learns her own son wasn't man enough to come to her rescue?" said the man. His taunts faded to a monotonous, heartless whisper.

Through eyes blurred by tears, Tyler focused on the callous and cruel grin that beamed from the man's face, bearing yellowed teeth, broken and stained. Tyler felt rather than heard the rasp of the growl that emerged from his throat, its rhythm in perfect time with the blood that pulsed behind his eyes.

'*Use it*,' said Harvey.

And the man came for him.

"What do you mean you bloody killed him?" said John, sitting forwards in his chair and gripping the edge of his desk. "I didn't tell you to kill the bloke, did I? No, I did not. Oh, Jesus. We're going to have the whole bleeding who's who of East bleeding London on my bleeding doorstep, and let me tell you something, Mick, it will not be me that takes the rap for it. I've got a lot riding on this fight tomorrow night and what I don't need right now is enemies. Opponents, yes. Dixon is an opponent. But when you kill someone like Old Man McGee, you might as well go round to the neighbourhood villain's house, wake them up, spit in their tea, and jump into bed with their wife, Jack. Do you understand the gravity of the situation?"

With both hands flat on his desk, John splayed his fingers and could feel the sweat from the antique desk's fine leather inlay warming his hands.

"Mick said to go and sort him out," said Jack, and glanced across to Nobby for support.

"That's right, John," said Nobby. "He didn't tell us not to kill him."

It was too much for John.

"Jack, pour me a drink, will you?" said John. He pinched the bridge of his nose to try and stem the headache that was forming. "Tomorrow night, I have got every villain worth his salt in London coming to watch my number one fighter take on Mackie in a fight to the death. It just so happens that my boy was being trained by the old man himself and now he suddenly trains with me the day after the old man gets bleeding offed. These villains, Nobby, are not like you, mate. Oh, no. They're intelligent men. That's why they're good at what they do, and that's how they manage to stay out of prison."

He took a sip of the brandy Jack had placed on the desk and pulled a tissue from a nearby box to wipe the ring mark from the leather.

"Another trait of these men, Nobby, is that they are extremely dangerous and not men that I want as enemies. Especially when I've invited them into my bleeding pub to watch the fight."

"Can't we just deny it?" asked Jack.

"Deny it, Jack?" A pulse of tension washed across John's temple. "And how the hell am I supposed to do that when I've got the old man's best fighter working for me? I'll be bleeding slaughtered."

He stopped, put his glass down on the wooden coaster beside his desk phone, and tried to make sense of the ideas that ran amok in his mind.

"Is that what this is about?" he asked. "Are you two trying to have me taken out? Is this some ploy to land me in hot water because I can assure you if it is-"

"No, John. I swear," said Nobby.

"I didn't ask you to talk. Shut up," said John. Then he calmed. "Let me finish. It makes perfect sense. You get the entire community of villains to outcast me and you both get to go and work for who you want. Who is it? Who's contacted you?"

"No-one, John," said Jack. "Honest. We haven't been anything but loyal. I've been with you from the start."

"I know you've been with me a long time, Jack. That's how I know your two weaknesses. The slightest sniff of a pair of panties or the alluring waft of banknotes and you're away with the fairies."

"We're not trying to set you up," said Nobby. His voice had calmed and he spoke with reason and without fear. "Mick told us to go and make sure the old man doesn't stick his nose into the fight, being that he was training the boy. So we went down there, to his gym-"

"Okay," said John. He sat back in his chair with his glass, admiring the way Nobby was handling the situation and wasn't falling to bits like Jack. "And did you talk to the old man?"

"No, he was out the back."

"So who did you speak to?"

"Some big fella. Black as they come, he was, and with a voice like a trombone."

"Lloyd?" asked John.

"That's it. Do you know him?"

"Everyone knows Lloyd, Nobby. He's the old man's able-bodied partner, and he's just as well connected as the old man. He comes from a family of drugged-up yardies in Bow. He's the only one in the family that doesn't crush scrap cars for a living, and he was one of the old man's first success stories until the booze and the pills got him."

"He's an alcoholic?"

"Que sera sera, Nobby," said John, and took a sip of his brandy.

"Right," said Nobby. "Anyway, he told us where to go, you

know? Didn't want us around and made it very clear we weren't welcome there."

"And then what?"

"Well, what would you do if someone insulted you, John? What did you expect us to do?"

"You torched the place?"

"Just the front door, but I guess the rest of the place just took off."

"And what did you do?"

"Nothing we could do, John. It was out of control in seconds."

"You ran?"

Nobby answered the question with raised eyebrows and tight lips, and he held John's stare, aware of the immorality.

"Well, at least you're honest, Nobby. Bleeding stupid, but honest."

"So what do we do?" asked Jack. His voice was still trembling and stained with panic.

"What you two pair of clowns have done is start a war, Jack. There's going to be fifty of London's most fearsome gangsters in this pub tomorrow night and each and every one of them was friends with the old man, and that's not to mention the family of angry yardies that will be kicking doors in looking for an answer to who killed their brother. And right now, all roads lead to the Golden Ring. So in answer to your question, Jack, we prepare for the worst, and you better get your backside out on the street and make it right."

"How are we-"

"Just listen, Jack," said John. He sank the remainder of his brandy and slammed the tumbler back down on the wooden coaster. "I want you to do exactly what I say. If you cock this up, everything I've worked for is going to come crashing down, and it'll bury us alive."

CHAPTER TWENTY-EIGHT

In an old power station in the heart of South London in the shadow of towering, concrete blocks of flats, and surrounded by pockets of small, green parks and old office buildings, a make-shift boxing ring had been put together.

Years of damp had tainted the stale air. It was flavoured by a history of under-paid union worker's sweat, thick grease and heavy, iron machinery that had long since been sold for its scrap value, or reconditioned and sold to the highest bidding emerging market.

The rhythmic grunts of the two men in the ring echoed off the bare, Victorian, brick walls, accompanied only by the dull thuds of gloves on pads and the gruff, angry voice of a man in a sheepskin jacket and thick tortoise-shell glasses who leaned over the ropes, shouting at the larger of the two boxers. The bigger man sent a perfect hook through a poor defence, stunning the smaller boy, who rocked forwards then back.

"Don't just bleeding stand there, Mackie, you big girl," he shouted. "When you hit someone that hard, you follow up with more. Put him on his arse and don't let him up."

The man Harvey had found at Tyler's flat entered through

the small side door and put his hand on Harvey's arm. It was a move Harvey presumed was designed to inform his boss that Harvey had been forced to accompany him, as opposed to the truth of the matter, that Harvey forced the man to lead him there and into the jaws of death.

The hand was removed moments after Harvey had delivered a silent glare, and the two men walked towards the ring. They stopped behind Del Dixon with room enough to watch the sparring.

"That's it, Mackie. Get in there," the older man shouted, his enthusiasm fully supported by the ropes. A cigar was lodged between two of his fingers while the others gripped the rope. Both hands were adorned with an array of sovereigns, signets, five-row keeper rings and a heavy gold watch that rested on his angled wrist. "Now take him down and keep him down."

Spittle shot from the man's mouth and his cigar waved in the air as the larger of the two fighters took the advantage on his opponent who stood swaying in the centre of the ring. He delivered a wild but powerful hook that lifted the boy's feet from the ring floor, causing him to land in an unceremonious heap with blood leaking from his mouth.

But the fight wasn't over. Harvey expected Dixon to give his fighter a pat on the back and turn to see Harvey. But instead, Dixon leaned further into the ring.

"Now, Mackie, don't let him wake up, son."

The fighter was standing over his opponent, a tentative look of fear etched onto his young face as he locked eyes with Dixon, who leaned further into the ring.

"Finish him, you big dumb bastard," he screamed. "If you don't finish that boy, I'll wake him up myself and let him give you what for."

The veins on Dixon's temple were visible even from the distance of a few metres away, where Harvey stood.

The boy looked down at his opponent, whose eyes flickered once and whose arms began to move.

"Now, Mackie," screamed Dixon.

Mackie dropped to his knees beside the younger boy and placed his hand on his opponent's head as if to offer a silent apology.

"Mackie," screamed Dixon again, his voice rising several octaves.

It took Mackie three hard punches to the boy's head before the crack of bone could be heard.

"That's it," said Dixon, his voice quieter. "You've done the worst of it. Send him on his way."

Mackie hovered above the dying boy as a pool of blood began to form by his knees. Then he brought his arm up for one final blow, raising it high above his head, clenching his gloveless fist and, with his eyes focused on the side of the boy's head, he delivered the fatal blow.

The crack of bones and grunt of Mackie's exertion echoed in the vast room, but the sound faded as fast as the boy's life. Mackie wiped the blood spatter from his face with his forearm and fell across the body at his knees. The man beside Harvey turned away and exhaled, long and slow.

Dixon nodded his approval, then straightened.

"Good lad," he said, and took a long pull on his cigar. The ember crackled amid the smoke that swallowed Dixon's wrinkled face. "It gets easier, Mackie. The more you do it, the easier it gets. Now get yourself washed up and go for a run. One more tonight then tomorrow is the big day."

Dixon stepped down to the concrete floor using the three ropes for handholds and with his teeth clenching the cigar butt between his thin lips. Then he wiped his hands on a towel that was draped over the lowest rope and tossed it into the ring, catching sight of Harvey and the man beside him as he did.

Dixon's head cocked inquisitively, and with a subconscious habit, he pushed his thick glasses onto his nose before retrieving his cigar. The soles of his brogues clicked on the concrete floor as he took five steps towards Harvey. His right hand found the fat sovereign on his left and turned it a full circle before positioning the coin flat on his fist as if he was readying for a punch using his rings for maximum results with minimum damage to his hands.

Then, as if asking a question, he searched from his man to Harvey and back again, finally resting on Harvey with magnified cold eyes, tinted brown by the lenses of his thick-framed glasses. He took a final, long pull on his cigar, tilted his head back and blew the smoke above him, where it was lost to the dank, stale air.

Finally, he tossed the remains of his cigar to the floor, crushed the ember with the heel of his shoe, and placed his hands inside the deep pockets of his sheepskin jacket.

"Who the bleeding hell are you?"

CHAPTER TWENTY-NINE

The first punch connected with Tyler's nose, smarting his eyes. The second found his kidney, followed by a third that broke through Tyler's guard and glanced off his brow. In an instant, the warm sting of blood found the corner of his eye. Tyler jumped back, maintaining his guard, and worked the mix of tears and blood from his sight with rapid blinks of his eye.

"Can you see her, Tyler?" said the man. "Can you see her doubled over in pain, clawing at the door for someone to help?"

Tyler launched an attack. A quick succession of body blows were all blocked, and a final hook to the man's head fell short by a whisker as he dodged back.

"But there's no-one to help her, Tyler," he continued.

Then the man dodged and weaved a series of head blows. The final jab connected square on and sent him reeling back. But he recovered and came at Tyler with a relentless succession of kicks and punches that forced Tyler back against the tiled cubicle where, long ago, livestock would have been dragged and bolted and strung up to drain.

No matter where Tyler guarded, the blows landed elsewhere. Rock hard fists, delivered with precision and power, slammed into Tyler's body with tiresome energy, until the man was so absorbed in his rhythm and breathing that he got close enough for Tyler to open his arms wide and smash his massive forehead into the man's face.

He stumbled back, but the reprisal was brief. Within two seconds, he was ready to fight again, his mouth running with blood.

"Is that it, Tyler? Your poor old mum is banging on the door, begging for help, and all you can do is stand in the corner and take a beating."

Tyler shoved off the wall.

"They'll need to tie her down. You know that?"

With his shoulder set, Tyler charged at the man, but he side-stepped and delivered a kick to the back of Tyler's head.

"They'll be so bored of listening to her sobs and screams, she'll be gagged and tied to the bed."

Tyler charged again, but this time, the man didn't side-step. He stood his ground, coiled and greeted the charge with a powerful uppercut that rocked Tyler's brain. Tyler stumbled then dropped to a knee to steady himself.

'*Control it*,' Harvey's calm voice came to him.

He ducked a sidekick. The man's leg passed over his head and Tyler reached up, catching it in the crook of his left arm. Instinct took over and he stood, kicking out at the man's legs and sweeping him off his remaining foot.

The man went down but Tyler still had his leg. He began to twist, fending off futile kicks until the man rolled with the twist and lay on his front. Tyler placed a huge foot on the back of his neck and bent his leg up towards his head until the man's body arched to its maximum stretch.

Three slaps of the man's hand on the floor and Tyler released him. He turned and walked towards the bench where the phone lay waiting. His mum would be suffering just a call away.

"Where do you think you're going, big fella?"

Tyler stopped and turned, and a hard jab found its mark on his face.

"You haven't earned that yet."

"I got you down," said Tyler, blinking away the throb of the punch.

"And I got back up again," the man replied. "If you want to survive this fight, you'll need to do better than that."

The man's smaller size seemed to have no bearing on his confidence. He began to dance around, hopping from foot to foot.

Tyler raised his guard.

"Jerry," said the man, and offered Tyler a smile.

"Jerry?" replied Tyler. He planted his feet and met the man's eyes while his brain focused on his arms and legs.

"My name," the man replied. "That's all you earned. I was told you can fight, but all I've seen so far is a big, muscle-head cry-baby who misses his mum. This time, we fight for real. No tapping out. No going easy. I want you to hurt me. I want you to pick up that phone with pride and tell John Cooper to feed your mum those painkillers. So hit me."

Tyler didn't move.

"I said hit me, you big dumb idiot."

'*Use it.*'

"Fight me," said Jerry. His smug face dropped as frustration set in. "Hit me. Or I'll call John myself and tell him to strip your mum naked and send the boys into her room."

'*Control it.*'

"Are you retarded? Hit me."

'*Use it.*'

The first jab was easily dodged with a duck of Tyler's head

and he responded with a hook that found Jerry's jaw. But the punch hadn't perturbed Tyler's aggressor. He retaliated with a hook that Tyler ducked back to avoid, then delivered his own that found its mark.

Seeming to take delight in the volley of punches, Jerry launched into a frenzy of failed attacks with Tyler managing to duck or block each one with a new-found calm composure. The few hits that he did take didn't hurt but only seemed to strengthen his resolve. Even when Jerry slipped a few wild kicks at Tyler, he absorbed them and replied with his own, which were more powerful.

The volley grew in intensity when Jerry's punch cracked Tyler's jaw. Moments later, Tyler smashed Jerry's nose and the two men entered into a rhythm of punches and kicks, neither blocking nor dodging but matching each other one for one.

The only difference between the two men was that with each blow Tyler landed, the control over Jerry's rage weakened and each punch he replied with grew in anger. But Tyler had found a state of emotionless calm. He could read Jerry's next move by watching the way his body leaned or catching the flick of his eye to its target. Jerry's rage grew to a point where he dropped his guard to coil for a punch. Tyler's hand shot out, grabbing his throat and squeezing hard.

Jerry fought back. The volley was over and he pounded Tyler with both arms, each punch easily absorbed with the resilience of a rock. Tyler tensed, gripped harder than before and lifted Jerry from his feet. The punches turned to kicks as Jerry tried to pry Tyler's hands from his throat, lashing out at whatever target his feet could find.

But it was too late. Tyler's left hand found the waistband of Jerry's loose sweatpants. He took a long deep breath, then raised the smaller man above his head, kicking and flailing.

A stream of abuse aimed at Tyler's mother began to run free

from Jerry's spiteful mouth, but the sound was a distant noise, irrelevant and unfathomable.

'*Use it.*'

Tyler arched his back, sending all the energy he could muster into his huge, broad shoulders, then with the power coursing through his body, he slammed Jerry down onto the hard, concrete floor.

CHAPTER THIRTY

"Take her pain away," said the voice on the other end of the phone.

John recognised the number, but the confidence in the voice was new.

"I knew you had it in you, Tyler."

"I want to talk to her."

"All in good time," said John.

"I want her taken care of."

"You're in no position to make demands, Tyler. I told you to trust me. Do you?"

"You have to earn trust," replied Tyler.

"How ready are you?" asked John, leading the conversation towards the big fight.

"My mother, look after her or I won't be fighting."

The call disconnected. The doors of the pub opened up onto a cold and miserable morning. A car drove past with a swish as its tyres cut through the surface of water and the car's rear lights reflected, fragmented and multiplied in the road.

John stepped across the street, mindful of ruining his shoes in the deep water, then turned and looked back at the Golden

Ring. The building was symmetrical with two windows, a door, and a patch of mismatched brickwork that betrayed the old off-license window, where the landlord would have served thirsty customers during the forced out-of-hours periods. The window had been bricked up long before John had taken on the pub.

The lights on the top floor of the house were all off, except for John's office at the front and the small spare bedroom at the back where the boy's mum was likely lying in a pool of her own pain-filled tears. He'd ask one the staff to take her a painkiller when they arrived.

The car park to the right-hand side of the old building was empty. John's Range Rover was parked around the back behind locked gates. He pictured how it might look that evening. Instead of the usual vans, hatchbacks and boring, cheap family wagons, the car park would be filled with the finest selection of cars that ever graced its tarmac. Tonight would be the night to forge alliances. Nothing formal, but a display of wealth and power would go a long way with the men that he'd invited. When the time was right, he'd have men to call upon. Behind the scenes and buried in the facades of conversation, the evening would host a plethora of back scratching. The time to stand out was now. The time to be recognised was now. The time to sow the seeds that would see John rise up was now.

The night needed to go without a hitch.

The headlights of an approaching car turned into the road a few hundred yards away. In the dawn light, John couldn't make out the model so he stepped back out of sight until it reached him, slowed then pulled into the car park. Mick climbed out carrying two coffees in takeaway cups. He shut the door with his foot and hit the fob to lock the car. The indicators flashed once and the interior light faded to nothing. Mick was John's best man. He was reliable, loyal, and as tough as they come. Plus, he had brains, a trait that rarely went hand in hand with brawn.

Keeping to the shadows, John watched as Mick approached the pub with furtive glances at his surroundings. He saw John, checked the street both ways, and crossed over to join him, handing him a coffee. Mick let a few seconds pass before speaking, apparently gauging John's mood at Nobby and Jack's cock-up.

"Big night tonight, John," he said.

"It'll be big alright, Mick."

"I heard about Nobby and Jack," said Mick. "I didn't give the order, but I take responsibility. I obviously wasn't clear enough."

John glanced to his side. Mick was looking at the pub, his face strong. His eyes showed no sign of fear.

"Jack's a liability, Mick," replied John. "Even if we get through this tonight, he'll still be a problem."

Knowing that Mick would understand the underlying tones and find a way of getting rid of Jack, John turned back to look at his pub, leaving Mick to ponder on a solution. He was good at solutions.

"Do you think the other firms will go for it?" asked Mick. "I mean, word from you would be one thing, but spreading a rumour that Dixon killed the old man, well, who would believe them?"

John smiled.

"That's the game, Mick. All this might even work in our favour and nothing pleases me more than profiting from disaster."

John took a sip of his coffee. The steam fogged his glasses. He licked his lips, cleared his throat, and let his lenses clear.

"If I were to contact the other firms," began John, "and tell them it was Dixon that had the old man taken out in an effort to upset my fighter enough to lose the fight, I would have to go to the top dogs. The big boys, Mick. And I would have to stand there and tell them a bare-faced lie. Should, in the yet unforeseen turn of events, it be discovered that it was indeed my boys that took him out, then that lie, alongside the murder of one of London's most-loved men would see me buried alive. Probably in the same hole as you, Nobby and Jack."

Mick nodded.

"However," said John, "if Jack and Nobby were to shoot their mouths off in a bar, and just happened to be overheard by some keen and green upstart that worked for one of the other firms, then if and when the time came for me to defend my position, I would have told no lies."

"You'd still be killed, John. We all would."

"With honour, Mick. With honour," replied John. "And with any luck, I'd be buried in a different hole to the fool."

Mick gave a small laugh and a short exhale through his nose, then took a long sip of his coffee.

"How do you think it'll play out?" asked Mick.

"They'll wait. The firms will want to see the fight. Everyone's talking about it, you know?"

"Yeah, I hear."

"They'll all have wagers. The Robinsons will have wagers with the McIntyres. The MacIntyres will have wagers with the West London firms. And the paddies will be balls deep with the lot of them. Nothing will happen until one of our boys is lying in a pool of his own blood. Pockets will be fuller, smiles will be wider and the bubbly will be flowing. That's when it'll happen, Mick."

Mick nodded his head in agreement. "We need to be ready."

It was John's turn to issue a half-hearted laugh. "Listen, Mick. If there's one thing I've learned in this game, it's that the man with the biggest pair of balls doesn't always win. Nor is it the man with the biggest brain on his shoulders. You need to have both. You need balls of steel and you need to be smarter than anyone else. You don't need to be a rocket scientist, just smarter than the men you're up against. Did you ever hear about the guys in Africa? One of them asks the other what he'd do if a lion came, and he said, run."

"You can't outrun a lion," said Mick.

"That's what the other guy said. And the first guy replied, I know, I'd just have to outrun you. That's the point, Mick, you don't need to be faster than the lion. You just need to be faster than the blokes you're with."

John took a sip of his coffee, pleased with his analogy, and let his glasses de-mist.

"So do you reckon the other firms will go for it then, John?" asked Mick. "Like I said, we need to be ready if they don't."

John smiled. It was a question he'd thought about all night, lying awake in bed listening to the crying of the boy's mum a few rooms away.

"If it happens, Mick, there'll be absolutely nothing we can do about it. It's too late to cancel now, and besides, it would make us look guilty. We'd need more than a hundred men, which we don't have. We'd need firepower, which we don't have enough of. And we'd need friends to get us out, which at this point, we wouldn't have at all. If they don't fall for it, and all fingers point at us, the best thing we can do is take it like men. I'm not going down like a coward, Mick. If it comes to it, I'll stand there and tell them all it was us, and tell them to do their worst. In years to come, they'll be talking about me with a degree of respect. If we run, we'll just be another firm that came and didn't have the balls to see it through."

CHAPTER THIRTY-ONE

"The way I see it, we both have a common enemy," said Harvey.

He walked beside Del Dixon along London's River Thames. Although Harvey had grown up in East London, the south side offered a far better view of the city that even he couldn't deny.

"So you want my help to get at John Cooper?" said Dixon. "You killed one of my men and walked into my manor, bold as brass, and you've got the audacity to ask for my help."

"It's *you* that needs *my* help," said Harvey. "And I killed a man who attacked me. It was him or me, and I'm not in the habit of asking who someone is before they slot me."

"Well, perhaps you bleeding well should next time," replied Dixon. "You don't know who you might upset."

Harvey didn't reply.

"What's he done to you anyway?" asked Dixon. "Why do you want to get at John Cooper?"

"Does it matter?" said Harvey. He stopped to lean on the iron handrail that ran alongside the pathway. The river flowed past, fast with the morning tide.

Dixon joined him and leaned on the railings. The body

language wasn't threatening, but Harvey could see the older man trying to maintain the upper hand.

"As it happens, yes, it does matter," said Dixon. "When a man I never clapped eyes on before kills one of my best men, then forces the other one at knife point to bring him to me, it raises eyebrows. In particular, my eyebrows. Can you see them? My eyebrows. They're raised, are they not?"

Harvey gave him a brief glance, then turned back to the river.

"I'd say so," he said.

"Right. So when my eyebrows are raised," continued Dixon, "it is not a good sign for the man that raised them."

"So take care of me," said Harvey. "We're standing by the river. All it would take would be for you to shoot me and throw my body over the side. Why don't you?"

"Are you bleeding mental?" said Dixon. "You're either extremely stupid or extremely brave. Which is it?"

"Why don't you shoot me and throw me in the river?" said Harvey. "You'll soon know."

Dixon shook his head in disbelief.

"So?" said Dixon.

"So what?"

"So it does matter. It matters why you want to get at John Cooper. Of course it matters. Everything matters. For all I know, he sent you here."

"He killed a friend of mine," said Harvey.

"And who was your friend?"

"*That* doesn't matter," replied Harvey. "What matters is the fire he started last night."

"Fire? What fire?"

Harvey checked Dixon's expression with a sideways flick of his eyes. He genuinely wasn't aware of any fire.

"Well, if you don't know by now, I'm pretty sure you're about to find out," said Harvey.

"Don't play games with me, sunshine. You've pushed your luck too far already. What fire?"

"Do you know the gym in the arches in Poplar?"

"In Poplar?" said Dixon. "You mean Old Man McGee's place?"

Harvey didn't reply.

"He torched it? John Cooper? Are you sure?"

"It was either him or you, and your men were busy elsewhere."

"Why would he do that?" asked Dixon. "Why would he torch the old man's place?

"To get at my friend," said Harvey. "But if I were you, I wouldn't be concerned with why he did it. I'd be concerned with the ramifications."

"Explain," said Dixon. He pushed off the rail, planted his hands into his sheepskin jacket and pulled out a fresh cigar.

"Don't do that near me," said Harvey. "It stinks."

Dixon cut the end of his cigar, flicked open his Zippo lighter, and lit it.

"Like I said," said Dixon. "Explain."

"When I walked into your makeshift gym this morning, you were watching your fighter beat another boy to death."

"So?"

"So I happen to know that John Cooper is also preparing for a fight. It's not difficult to see that your boy is up against his boy, and judging by the mess your boy Mackie made, it's a fight to the death."

"So you're observant. Tell me about the ramifications."

"I haven't seen a prize fight like that for a long time. They stopped years ago," said Harvey.

"We reintroduced them," said Dixon. His smile spoke volumes about how much money the man had made.

"Bigger stakes," said Harvey. "Bigger stakes means bigger risks. I'm guessing that this isn't the first fight."

"There's been a few," replied Dixon.

"And if it's anything like how it used to be, John Cooper has been trying to get to your boy, and you've been trying to get John Cooper's boy. Hence why I found your men in his flat last night."

"Just get to the point," said Dixon, urging Harvey forward with his thoughts. Revealing the thought process piece by piece was Harvey's intentional way of seeing who Del Dixon really was. And with each word Harvey spoke, the man beside him grew tense and agitated.

"What would you do if your boy Mackie said he was out? If he said he wasn't going to fight for you?"

Dixon shrugged.

"You wouldn't just send him back to his old life to carry on as normal, would you?" said Harvey.

"Probably not, no," said Dixon.

"So what do you think Cooper would do if his boy told him he wasn't going to fight for him anymore?"

"The same as me, I guess."

"And what do you think John Cooper would do if, whilst he was taking care of the boy, he accidentally took care of Old Man McGee, who incidentally trains some of the best prize fighters in London, and who incidentally works for some of the biggest faces in the city?"

"How do you know about the old man? Who are you?"

"Who I am doesn't matter. But I've been around a long while, and the old man was the best trainer around even when I was a boy."

The slow realisation of Harvey's words took its place on

Dixon's face. His cigar hand fell to his side and his eyes grew huge behind his thick glasses. He regained his composure and leaned on the rail beside Harvey again, but on the other side, so his cigar smoke was carried away by the wind.

"You think Cooper is trying to point the finger at me?"

"Like I said," said Harvey. "It's you that needs my help."

"And how, pray tell, do you plan on doing that? If what you just said is true, my photo will be pinned to every dartboard in every pub in London."

"How long have you got until the fight?" asked Harvey.

Dixon checked the heavy and expensive watch beneath the fur of his sheepskin cuff.

"Sixteen hours," he replied.

"Well," said Harvey, pushing off the rail and beginning the slow walk back the way they came, "I can't help you fight every face in town, but give me the day with Mackie, and I can make sure you beat John Cooper."

"What's in it for you?" asked Dixon. "What's your prize in this master-plan of yours?"

Harvey felt the familiar pang of retribution in his chest. He smiled and let it warm his veins.

"John Cooper," said Harvey. "John Cooper is my prize."

CHAPTER THIRTY-TWO

Breakfast consisted of eggs and bacon served up on a paper plate with a plastic knife and fork. It was wasn't the athlete's diet that Tyler had been hoping for, but having spent so much energy putting Jerry down, he devoured the food.

"Is he ready?" asked John, as if Tyler wasn't there.

Jerry nodded.

"He got through me twice," he replied.

"Good," said John. "So he's ready for the last part of his training then, is he?"

"The last part?" asked Tyler. He had envisaged a rest day before the fight. The other trainers all gave him rest days. But John ignored the question.

"He's ready," said Jerry. His eyes met Tyler's as he looked up from his plate of greasy bacon, but then looked away as if he was ashamed of admitting his defeat to John.

"What's the next part of the training?" asked Tyler. "I put Jerry down, twice now. I should be resting."

John span to face him.

"You should be doing what the bleeding hell I tell you to do. When I say eat, you eat. When I say stand, you stand. And when I tell you to fight, you damn well fight. Do you understand me, son?"

The words hit Tyler hard. Putting Jerry down hadn't bought him any favours. There was no new display of respect. He pushed off the bench, stood and dropped the empty paper plate to the floor. John's face twisted. One of his eyes squinted and one side of his teeth showed. They were straight and clean, but yellowed with age.

"I didn't tell you to stand," said John.

Tyler didn't reply.

John poked his index finger into Tyler's chest.

"Did you hear me, boy? I didn't tell you to stand."

Being a full twelve inches above John, and well over twice as broad, Tyler felt the urge to flatten him.

'*Control it.*'

He stepped back half a pace, away from the offending finger, but didn't sit back down.

"What's the next part of the training?" he asked.

"Jerry," said John, "I think you've done it, my old mate. I think you've turned this soft piece of mushy turd into a man. Did you see that? Did you see the way he tried to defy me?" Closing the gap between himself and Tyler, John looked directly up at the huge boy. "I like the new Tyler. He's got balls," he said. Then his hand shot out and grabbed Tyler's crutch, squeezing hard, doubling Tyler over and sucking the breath from him.

"Now you listen to me, sunshine. Until the fight is over, you're mine. Do you understand me?" He increased the pressure.

Tyler nodded, but John's hand tightened even more.

"I said, do you understand me, Tyler?"

"Yes. Yes. I understand," said Tyler, and let out a long breath as he fought to control the pain. As he did, the pain seemed to ease. His anger hovered at the forefront of his mind, but clarity began to emerge through the fog. He saw images of what John's face would look like when he squeezed the life from him. He would wait for the right time.

'*Channel your emotions.*'

John released his grip on Tyler's groin.

"Good," he said. "Now sit down. I haven't finished with you yet."

Tyler dropped to the bench. It was the right thing to do. The time to destroy John Cooper wasn't yet, not until his mother was safe. Until then, he'd play the game. He'd fight, and if it took every last piece of him to win, he'd make sure he did.

"The last part of the training," began John, as he put his hands into his jacket pockets and paced back and forth, "will be a test of your resolve. It'll make or break you. But remember, if you break, your poor old mum breaks too."

The mention of his mum sent a pulse of rage through Tyler. The pulsing behind his eyes was a familiar sensation now, as was the warm release of adrenaline into his blood, which heightened the feeling in his fingers. He watched as John pulled his phone from his pocket, hit the redial button, and put the phone to his ear.

"Mick? Bring the boy. It's time to see if our Tyler has what it takes."

CHAPTER THIRTY-THREE

The sound of car doors slamming outside initiated a wave of activity. Jerry had been tending to Tyler's wounds. He washed the blood from his torn eyebrow, applied heat packs to his bruised ribs and cleaned the blood from Tyler's nose, making him ready for another fight.

John sat and watched. Jerry was a good ally to have. The man was as tough as they come and had been around fighters all his life. He'd originally been a pikey that had taken the East London prize fighting scene by storm. John had recognised his talent, but the man couldn't be trusted. He could be called upon to help with training, but he'd run off with whatever you left laying around unless the job was worth more than whatever he could take. Once a pikey, always a pikey.

The doors opened and Jack fell through, stumbling to the floor. He pushed himself up onto his elbow and looked around the place with wonder as Mick closed the doors behind him. Mick then bent down and grabbed hold of Jack's jacket collar. The room sang with the echoes of shouts, Jack's voice rising an octave at a time, until Mick hoisted him up and onto the canvas floor of the makeshift ring. Jack rolled beneath the lowest rope, not with the keen desire to fight, as some men would, but just to get away from Mick, who had left his mark on Jack's face while persuading him to climb into the boot of his BMW.

"What's all this then?" said Jack.

He looked for a way out of the ring, but each side was covered by Mick, Jerry and John. The fourth side wasn't covered, but even if he managed to climb out of the ring, he'd have to get past all three of them to reach the doors.

"There's no use in running, Jack," said John.

"But what have I done?" Jack replied. He was gripped by fear, exactly where John wanted him. "I did what you said, and they fell for it. Honest. Everyone's talking about how Dixon's boys torched the gym. We're in the clear."

"Maybe so, Jack," said John. "But what's next? Where do you go from here?"

"I don't understand, John. You said it was all okay. I did what you asked."

John waited a few seconds, enjoying the panicked reactions of Jack as he sought to distance himself from Mick and Jerry, who had closed in and stood by the ropes watching him with as much satisfaction as John. Mick's gratification stemmed from his loyalty to John and nothing more. Jerry's grin, which seemed to broaden with every passing moment, stemmed from his lust for violence and his passion for watching people suffer.

John glanced behind him to where Tyler sat on the bench with a towel around his shoulders staring up at Jack. John could almost see the cogs falling into place.

"Even if tonight goes without a hitch, Jack, even when it's all over and Dixon is broken and destitute, I'm still left with you, aren't I?"

"I've always been loyal, John."

"You've always been a liability, Jack, is what you've always been. What am I supposed to do? Set you free? What would you do? You're like a dog, Jack. One that's bitten too many people and is too long in the tooth to set free. You wouldn't survive, mate. You couldn't get a job. Who'd have you?"

"John, don't do this."

"It's too late, Jack. I thought long and hard about this. About what to do with you."

"John, I'd do anything. You know I would."

John continued, ignoring Jack's pleas, much to Jerry's visible delight.

"I know you're loyal, Jack. I know you wouldn't go running to some other firm, even if you could find one that would take you on."

"No, John, I wouldn't do that. That would be betraying you."

"So, Jack, I wondered, how can Jack show me one last time just how loyal he really is? What can he do to demonstrate how sorry he is for the monumental cock-up that could destroy me and everything I've worked for?"

"Just tell me, John."

"And that's when it hit me," said John. "It was a revelation. This moment of clarity. The answer to the problem of what to do with a man whose stupidity has defied all odds, but whose loyalty has beholden him to me."

John kept his eyes on Jack but called out behind him.

"Tyler," he said, "this is the last part of your training, son. Get in the ring."

"You want me to fight him?" said Tyler. He was standing beside the ring, confused at what was being asked of him.

John pulled his phone from his pocket again and held it in front of him as if he were revealing a jack of hearts from a deck and asking him to memorize the card.

"At the end of this phone, Tyler, is your poor old mum. Right now, she's locked inside a room. The painkillers will be wearing off and her bucket will be full of a foulness that I just can't even begin to imagine."

"You told me you'd take care of her."

"I told you I'd give her a painkiller if you got Jerry down. And you did. Now I'm telling you I'll give her more if you finish off our loyal friend."

"What do you mean finish?" asked Jack. But John ignored him.

"Get in the ring, Tyler," said John.

"I can't do that," said Tyler. "That's-"

"Then your poor old mum suffers. I'll be sure to call the girls and have them pass the message on, shall I?" said John. "I'll make sure your mum knows that while she fights the pain that courses through her fragile little body, her son here, who has the chance to put a stop to it all, refuses to. Because it's what?"

"It's immoral," said Tyler.

"Did you hear that, Mick?" said John. "Immoral. Shall I tell you what Jack here did to deserve it?"

"John, I fixed all that," said Jack from inside the ring.

"Shut it, Jack," said John. He returned his attention to Tyler. "How close was you to the old man?"

"Old Man McGee?" asked Tyler. "Not close, but I respect him. What do you mean, was? What's happened?"

John let a smile creep onto his otherwise emotionless face.

"It's quite a story," said John. "And, if you can see past the emotion, it's actually pretty funny. See, Mick told Jack here to make sure the old man didn't get involved in tonight's fight. We didn't want to mess up your training, and after all, at that point, you were doing us a favour."

"Right..." It was clear that Tyler knew where the story was going but let John carry on.

"But instead of having a word in his earhole, polite like, he managed to upset the big fella, the old man's sidekick and able-bodied bodyguard."

"Lloyd?" asked Tyler.

"That's right. You're catching on," said John. "Well, Jack being Jack, the hard man he is, didn't let nature run its course. He didn't let sleeping dogs lie. No, Tyler. He offed them. Both of them."

Tyler looked up at Jack, who saw the rage in Tyler's eyes.

"He didn't just kill them, Tyler. He burned them alive," said John. "I don't think the old boy deserved that at all. He was, after all, a pillar of our society. But Jack thought he knew better."

"I didn't mean to-"

"So you see, Tyler," said John, overpowering Jack's whining pleas, "*Jack* needs a way of making amends. *You* need the training." He stopped and closed the distance between himself and the boy, placing his hand on Tyler's massive shoulder. "And your poor old mum needs her medication."

"What makes you think you can teach me anything Del's trainer hasn't been able to?" asked Mackie. He bounced from foot to foot and shook his limbs, then threw a combination into the air as Harvey eased himself through the ropes. "Nobody even knows you."

"And that's the way it's going to stay," replied Harvey.

He slid his padded leather motorbike jacket from his shoulders and hung it over one of the corners. Mackie eyed his physique and seemed to grow in confidence. While Mackie bounced around, Harvey took three paces forward and stood in front of him, two arms' length away with his hands on his hips.

"Come at me," said Harvey.

As expected, Mackie led with his weak hand into a straight jab, followed by a hook with his right. Harvey ducked out of the jab and before the boy had regained his guard, Harvey's hand had shot up and grabbed his throat.

Mackie's eyes widened with fright. He tried to prise open Harvey's hands but Harvey was too strong. He threw three wild punches to Harvey's gut, all weak and using more oxygen than he had left in his lungs, leaving him in a panicked state. Harvey shoved Mackie backwards and he stumbled, falling to the canvas.

"What are you doing, you lunatic? You could have killed me," said Mackie, his voice high and his confidence levelled.

"My point exactly," replied Harvey.

"I hope you know what you're doing, Harvey," said Dixon from his place beside the ropes.

Harvey didn't reply.

"Well, don't just sit there, Mackie. Get up and hit him," said Dixon in a cloud of cigar smoke.

Mackie scrambled to his feet. He shook off the defeat with a dance of his feet and show of speed with the same combination he'd used a few minutes before.

"Stop dancing and come at me again," said Harvey.

"What do you mean, stop dancing?" said Mackie. "I'm keeping agile."

Mackie stepped forwards and offered the exact same combination of punches he'd just thrown. Harvey ducked down, slammed his fist into the boy's gut, then stood through his defence and took hold of his neck again. But this time, he used his momentum and lifted Mackie while kicking his legs away, then slammed him down onto the canvas and held him by his throat.

Mackie rolled away the second Harvey released him, then stood and let the flush of embarrassment drain from his face before beginning his bouncing again.

"Stop dancing and come at me," said Harvey, with his hands on his hips.

Mackie came to a stop. He strode up to Harvey, weaved in and out, from left to right, then issued a new series of punches, two body blows and the last aimed at Harvey's face. With relative ease, Harvey took hold of Mackie's arm and used the boy's momentum to force him into the rope, and once more, pinned him down with the heavy rope against his windpipe. It was only when he began to cough and splutter that Harvey let him go and moved to the far side of the ring to give him space to recover.

"You're not even fighting me," said Mackie. "What are you doing?"

Harvey collected his jacket from the corner and pulled it on.

"Where do you think you're going?" said Dixon.

"Does the boy want a lesson or not?" said Harvey. "Does he want to survive tonight? Because if he does, he needs to pay attention to what I'm doing."

"And what is it you're doing?" said Mackie. "And of course I want to survive."

"Listen, Mackie, you're a great boxer, or you will be one day."

"But?" said Dixon. "The boy has won every fight he's had."

"Boxing?" asked Harvey.

"Of course boxing," said Mackie. "Del, is this guy for real?"

Harvey listened to the boy's last words, then stepped over to him and watched as he scurried away until he was cornered.

"You're a good boxer," said Harvey. "You're quick, you're accurate and you follow through. Don't let them recover, whatever happens. No matter how good the punch was, don't admire it. Destroy the opposition."

"Cheers," said Mackie, unsure if Harvey's praise was genuine.

"But it's not enough," said Harvey.

"What's not enough?" said Dixon. He followed Harvey around the edge of the ring and stared up from the concrete floor below.

"The fight is not an ordinary boxing match. It's not even an ordinary bare-knuckle fight. It's a fight to the death."

"Right?" said Dixon.

"So what are you saying?" asked Mackie.

Harvey removed his jacket once more and hung it on the ropes. He rolled his neck from side to side, took a deep breath, and then coaxed Mackie to his feet.

"No dancing," he said.

"Right," said Mackie, and he stood on the balls of his feet with his guard up.

"Good," said Harvey. "Now forget everything you know about boxing."

"Eh?" both Dixon and Mackie said together.

"Put your guard down."

Mackie lowered his guard with a nervous look at Dixon, who was lighting a new cigar and looking on with growing interest.

"I don't know who you're going to be up against tonight. If Del's right, John Cooper will have found a replacement. He'll be a boxer. He might be good. He might not. But that's not a chance you can afford, is it? So let's assume he's very good."

"I guess so," said Mackie. He began to rub his arms as the chill of the huge power station found his white, sweaty skin.

"But you'll have the advantage, won't you?" said Harvey.

"Will I?" said Mackie, with another glance at Dixon.

"Whoever it is that stands in front of you tonight, Mackie, will try to out-box you. He'll fight dirty if he has to. There's no rules in these matches. Am I right, Del?"

Dixon nodded.

"But you're not going to box him. You're going to watch his every move, dodge, duck, weave, whatever it is you need to do to work out how he fights."

"And then what?" said Mackie.

"When I'm done with you, Mackie, you'll no longer be a boxer. Being a boxer isn't good enough for what you need to do. In fact, I don't know how you've survived this long. I can only assume you've been up against like-minded mediocre boxers. But, like I said, being a boxer isn't good enough."

"So what do I need to be?" asked Mackie with apprehension in his voice.

Harvey closed the gap between the two men, stared the boy in the eye, and then shot his hand up once more to his throat.

"What you need to be, Mackie, is a killer."

CHAPTER THIRTY-FIVE

The car ride from the old slaughterhouse to the Golden Ring was short, but Tyler felt every bump in the road and swayed giddily with every turn they took. Nausea hung at the back of his throat with a wave of hot acid behind it. A layer of cold sweat formed on his brow in contrast to the hot, damp patches beneath his arms and the burning heat in the centre of his chest.

He stared at his open hands on his lap as if they weren't his own anymore. They were now like two good friends that had betrayed him. In the background, John Cooper spoke, slow and rough. Blurred slices of Jerry's rapid Irish filled the gaps.

Before his previous fights, his trainers had kept him focused, relaxed him with massages, and drowned him in sickening positive energy. John and Jerry's conversation was clouded in a deafening hum, and all Tyler could hear was Harvey's voice.

'*Control it.*'

He'd spoken the words matter-of-factly. It wasn't some hippy state of play on the mind. It was real.

'*Use it.*'

Although his sweaty hands were empty, they pulsed with electric tension. The fingertips twitched as unspent adrenaline sought a place to break free. The crunching of gristle and breaking bones from Jack's neck played on repeat. It was a feeling Tyler would never forget. How the man's head had reached its limit. How the muscles had stretched in Tyler's hands until the only resistance had been the spinal column, which snapped after the third brutal wrench.

Even Tyler's legs, which had wrapped around Jack's torso, still felt the twitching of his body. Even when the struggle had stopped and Jack's head had fallen forwards, twisted unnaturally, and his hands had ceased scrambling and fallen to the canvas, the body still twitched. Much like the adrenaline in Tyler's hands, the electricity within Jack's broken body sought an exit.

The stench of urine had come last. Tyler had heard about the muscles of a dead body relaxing. He'd seen it in documentaries and movies where a hard-nosed detective covers his face and offers a reticent quip. But all Tyler had felt as Jack's racing heart had reached the peak of its climbing crescendo and stopped as suddenly as if a switch had been flicked was pity.

He'd wanted to hug the man. He'd wanted to say he was sorry and take it all back. But John Cooper stared up at him through the ropes with glory in his eyes and had spoken those words.

"That's it, Tyler," said John. He slammed his hands onto the canvas in elation and laughed like a madman. "You're a killer. Did you hear me? You're a bleeding killer, Tyler."

"Tyler? Tyler. Did you hear me?"

The words were loud. Memories of how he'd cradled Jack's body were sucked into nothingness and John's sour breath roused Tyler from his daze as he leaned across the seat.

"Get out of the bleeding car, son. We're here."

Tyler peered through the car's side window as the front

doors opened and filled the rear with a blast of cold air that found Tyler's damp sweat patches.

"The Golden Ring?" he asked.

"Where else?" said John, as Jerry pulled the rear door open for Tyler to get out. "As soon as we get inside, get yourself downstairs and into the changing room. Don't talk to anyone. They'll mess with your head, especially if they're betting against you. Jerry, see to it he gets there. Mick, upstairs in my office."

"Right you are, John," said Jerry, and led the way into the pub with Tyler behind and John bringing up the rear. But just as his hand reached for the handle, Tyler spoke out.

"Wait," he said.

Jerry stopped.

"Tyler, this is no time to cock about, son. Remember what I told you would happen if you pulled out of the fight?"

"I'm not pulling out," replied Tyler. "But I want to see her. I want to see my mum before the fight. Just in case-"

"Just in case what?" spat John. "In case you don't make it? Don't be soft, Tyler."

John spoke the words with a warning tone and allowed a shadow of a doubt to wash across his face.

"I'll fight," said Tyler. He backed away from them both, and filled his chest with a deep long breath. "But only if I see my mum first. I need to see her. I need to say goodbye."

CHAPTER THIRTY-SIX

"Close the door, Mick," said John, as he dropped into his leather office chair and pulled himself close to the desk. "I've done a bit of thinking."

"Do you want a drink, John?" asked Mick, standing beside the crystal decanter, poised and ready to pour.

"No, Mick. Not tonight, mate. And you shouldn't either. We need to be on top form tonight. If it all kicks off downstairs, I don't want anyone's judgement clouded by booze, which leads me nicely into my idea."

"Are you getting everyone drunk, John?" said Nobby. "So they can't fight?"

"No, Nobby, but you're close. Keep your eyes and ears to the ground. If it sounds like all fingers point at us, I need to know. As soon as the fight is over, I'll send the girls around with trays of champagne. Whatever you do, don't bleeding drink it."

"You're not planning-" said Mick.

"Yes, I am, Mick. Remember, these men will be out for blood, potentially my blood, your blood and anyone's blood they can get their hands on. If it all goes south, it won't be until after the money has changed hands. By that time, the basement will be full of London's most dangerous criminals, all having a nap, leaving us enough time to make a getaway."

"You're going to run?" asked Mick. "After everything we've built here?"

"Everything we've built here won't be worth a lot if those slimy bastards downstairs have us in their cross-hairs, Mick. You'll be a wanted man. So will you, Nobby. You won't be able to walk to the shop to buy a paper and a pint of milk without looking over your shoulder. And it'll happen one day, when you least expect it. When we think we got away with it, we'll be taken down, cut into pieces, and slung in the river. When you was a kid, did either of you ever have races with your friends where you both throw a stick in the river and see which one reaches the bridge first?"

"Yeah," said Mick, nodding.

"Well, they'll be doing that with your legs and the legs of your wife. Do you get the picture?" said John.

Both Mick and Nobby nodded.

"Right. Good," said John, regaining his stride and opening his desk drawer. "I've made the arrangements. There's two tickets each for the Eurostar first thing in the morning."

"Are you sure about this, John?" asked Mick. "This is serious stuff. We can't go drugging the entire criminal community."

"So what's your plan then, brains?" said John. "You've had just as much time to think about all of this as I have. What plan did you come up with?"

"Well-"

"Well nothing," said John. "Believe me, I'd hate to leave this place behind and everything we've worked for, but if push comes to shove, we can start again. Maybe somewhere sunny?"

Nobby glanced up at Mick who turned away.

"Are you both clear on the plan?" asked John. "Keep your

ears to the ground. I want to know if we're under suspicion. If we are, I'll signal the girls to do their thing, and we'll make our exit before the ceremonial exchange of money and while everyone is filling their gullets with champagne."

"What about the boy?" asked Mick.

"The boy? He'll be okay. A lesson learned and all that, Mick. Where is he anyway?"

"He's with his mum," said Nobby.

"Well get him out," said John. "He's been in there long enough. I want a word with him before the fight."

CHAPTER THIRTY-SEVEN

The car park of the Golden Ring was brimming with expensive luxury cars when Dixon's driver entered with the Mercedes. He was a quiet man who reminded Harvey of the man that used to drive his foster father around. Quiet, observant and in control. Harvey didn't ask his name. He just sat in the passenger seat preparing himself while Dixon reeled off endless spurts of spiteful monologue, mostly about the look on John Cooper's face when Mackie won, and how good it would feel to take the money off him.

"The first thing I'll do when Cooper hands me the keys to the ring is buy everyone a drink," said Dixon. "He's only had a few days to find a replacement. Mackie has been with me for over a year. Never lost a fight, have you, son?"

Harvey heard the slap of Dixon's hand on Mackie's leg, but Mackie was quiet. The words of wisdom Harvey had passed on were most likely running through his mind. The confident look on the boy's face had dropped to an expression of fear and self-loathing.

The driver turned and parked in a prime spot close to the building and facing the exit. The engine died. But before any doors opened, they waited for the van to park behind them. It was full of Dixon's men, all armed to the teeth and prepped for action.

"Right, boys," said Dixon. "Remember, nothing is going to happen until after the fight. So I've got until then to make some friends. Harvey, you concentrate on Mackie. Keep his chin up and keep him focused. If you hear anything, warn me. When the fight is over, and John Cooper has given me a bag full of money and the keys to his pub, that's when one of us will be slotted. Until then, it's a normal night at a prize fight, and we've got the winning boy. Is that clear?"

"Crystal," said the driver.

Harvey didn't reply. He pushed open his door, straightened his jacket and searched the parked cars for signs of life. Through the windscreen of a van parked fifty metres away, a few orange glows of cigarettes could be seen. But it wasn't a sign of someone about to jump them. With some of the most powerful men in London attending the fight, Harvey imagined there would be several armies nearby waiting for it all to kick off.

Dixon opened his door and climbed out, giving Harvey a distasteful look, as if he should have opened the door for him, as if he was some sort of king.

"Keep your men in the van," said Harvey, "and stay behind me."

"What, are you my minder now?" asked Dixon. "You just look after Mackie. I'll take care of myself. I didn't get this far having my hand held."

Harvey didn't reply. He led the way into the rear doors of the pub, which took him into the public bar. A band was warming up and a few of the locals glanced his way. But they turned away when Dixon followed him in. He walked straight through the bar hatch, and through another door that led down to the cellar.

The busy hum of multiple hushed conversations filled the space, which Harvey guessed to span further than the floor plan of the pub itself, with eight large columns that supported the building and framed a boxing ring in the centre of the room. The smell of old beer and cigar smoke tainted the air, and fluorescent lights created areas of intense brightness ringed by shadows. Harvey took a guess at the crowd being one hundred strong. Instead of the ring being surrounded by lines of chairs for the audience, a series of high tables had been provided, allowing five to six men at each table to enjoy an unobstructed view of the fight, and a place in the shadows to stand.

On each of the four sides of the ring, two tables were fortuned prime position. The tables were all taken except one, which Dixon claimed. He set his cigar down in the ashtray, slid his coat from his shoulders, allowing a girl in hot pants and a tiny top to take it from him, and then took a glass of champagne from the tray her colleague offered.

The girl turned to Harvey, smiled at him, and moved close enough for him to smell her thick perfume and say no to the drinks she offered.

Dixon leaned forwards to speak in Harvey's ear.

"Cooper isn't here yet. He'll make a grand entrance. Why don't you take Mackie out back and get him ready? I don't want him getting nervous," said Dixon. "The fight won't start for an hour, but warm him up, keep him hydrated and five minutes before you come back out, give him this."

Dixon slipped a little polythene bag of white powder into Harvey's inside pocket and tapped it twice. Then he turned to talk to the table behind them. Four unsmiling men with shaved heads, long Kashmir jackets and open collars stood with their hands in their pockets, eying Harvey with narrowed, suspicious eyes.

"Boys," said Dixon, in mock surprise as he turned away.

Then he glanced back at Harvey. "I don't have to repeat myself, do I?"

Harvey gestured for Mackie to follow him through a set of doors. The hum of the room faded to a dull murmur, and flickering light lit a small corridor with one room on each side. Two dressing rooms.

A letter-sized piece of paper with the name Dixon in bold, black letters was pinned to one of the doors. Harvey walked inside. The room was small but clean with a slatted wooden bench, a single locker and walls that were thick with years of grey paint. A small shower cubicle and a toilet were at the end of the room with a tiled floor that reached out to the corridor.

Harvey dropped the cocaine into the toilet, flushed it and eyed Mackie, who looked nervous but was getting through it.

"Do you need help?" asked Harvey.

Mackie shook his head. "No."

"Good. I'll be back in a while," said Harvey. "Warm up while I'm gone."

"What do you mean warm up?" said Mackie, looking around the dingy changing room.

"I don't know. Do a dance or something," said Harvey.

He left Mackie to his own devices and stepped back into the corridor with the flickering light. Through a small window in the doors, Harvey could see the four men all listening to one of Dixon's anecdotes with a less-than-impressed look mirrored across all four of their faces.

Harvey pushed through the doors and headed straight to the stairs. At the top was the entrance to the bar where another staircase led up to the first floor. With a quick look both ways, he took the next staircase and reached a landing with four doors leading off it. The door to the front of the building was closed. From inside, Harvey recognised the deep, authoritative voice of

John Cooper. There was the occasional pause as somebody else spoke, but it was too quiet for Harvey to hear.

Keeping close to the walls, Harvey edged away from Cooper's office and along the hallway. The next door was ajar with an oak floor, large leather couch and a big flat-screen TV on show through the small gap. Harvey moved past, but as he did, two men climbed the staircase behind him. Their voices grew louder in the stairwell and their heavy boots thundered on the old, wooden stairs.

Harvey froze then slipped into the room.

He watched as the three men appeared. One of them had been in the pub the night Harvey had met Tyler. The others were unknown but one had a thick Irish accent, was smaller and had the rough edges of a pikey. The old upstairs hallway echoed with their voices but another noise cut through the dull monotones of the men.

The stifled mumble of tears was coming from the door at the end of the hallway.

CHAPTER THIRTY-EIGHT

Something clawed at Tyler's insides as he pulled the door closed. He held his mum's sorrowful gaze until the last moment, and then let his fingers slip from the door handle. Closing off the sound of her tears inside, he placed the flat of his hand against the wood, as if somehow she would know, and would realise how sorry he was that all of this happened.

He felt, rather than heard, John Cooper behind him at the doorway to his office, so choosing to leave his mum on his own terms, Tyler let his hand fall away, then turned and joined John.

In the office, he chose a seat to the side of the desk, a wide armchair with artificial leather upholstery. It was a cheap choice in comparison to the luxurious recliner John had selected for his own comfort. It was symbolic, thought Tyler, of the man's greed and selfish style.

A true narcissist.

But as with many narcissists, John opened with artificial understanding and comfort, much like the chair Tyler had chosen to sit on.

"I need you to focus now, Tyler," said John. "Now is not the time to fill your head with thoughts of your mother."

Tyler nodded. He couldn't meet the man eye to eye. Instead, he stared at the intricate patterns in the oak floor.

"In less than thirty minutes, you'll be toe to toe with Dixon's boy." John paused while Tyler began to think about the fight. "Are you ready?"

Again, Tyler nodded.

"Usually when you fight, you have a goal in mind. A belt or a trophy. Right?" asked John.

"Trophies," replied Tyler, still staring at the floor with his elbows resting on his knees.

"Look at me, son. I'm not talking to the top of your head," said John. The warm, faux comfort was lost and the words came out sharp and cold.

Tyler looked up at him.

"Do you want some advice, son?" said John, retaining his harsh tones. "Forget about your mum. For the next hour or so, at least. Just forget about her. She's not going anywhere. We've given her painkillers. She's in good hands, Tyler. Focus on the fight. Focus on getting Dixon's boy down."

"Have you seen him?" asked Tyler, his voice still thick with emotion.

"Mackie?" asked John. "Of course I have."

"Did he beat your last fighter?"

With a slow nod of his head, John confirmed.

"He died then?" asked Tyler. "Your fighter? He died."

"Yes, Tyler. He died. It was…" He sought the words, but Tyler knew whatever word he chose would sound callous from the man's bitter mouth. "Unfortunate."

"How long did he last?"

"How many rounds? Or how many fights?"

"Both."

"One and one," said John. "I was told he was a dead cert."

"What was his name?"

"Oh, Tyler. What does it matter?"

"What was his name, John?" Tyler's voice rose and shut down John's attempt to make the dead boy insignificant.

"Fraser," said John. "His name was Fraser. That's all we knew. He was a street kid. Nothing to lose. You know the sort?"

"And how much do you stand to win if I beat Dixon's boy?"

"That's not something you need to trouble yourself with, is it, Tyler?" said John. "In fact, that's getting awfully close to the line that you, sunshine, do not cross."

"What about me?" asked Tyler. "You said we wouldn't have to worry about money. You told me I'd be able to afford proper care for my mum. How much will we get? My mum and me?"

"If I was you, Tyler, I'd be more concerned with what happens to her if you lose."

"That's not going to happen, John," said Tyler, standing and shunting the chair back. "When I go into that ring tonight, I'm not going in there for you. I'm going in there for Fraser. I'm going in there for myself. And I'm going in there for my mum. I'll be taking my winnings and you won't see me again."

"You're not in the best place to make demands."

Quick as a flash, Tyler reached across the desk, grabbed John by his collar and hauled him out of his chair, dragging him across the leather insert and knocking the phone and pens to the floor. He slammed John into the wall with one hand on his throat and the other poised to deliver a deadly punch.

"Now you listen to me, John Cooper," said Tyler. "I got myself into this. I'll get myself out of it. A deal is a deal."

"You just overstepped the mark, Tyler," said John, trying to regain the upper hand.

"Look around you, John. Your bodyguards aren't here and don't even think about reaching for your pocket."

For just a fraction of a moment, John's eyes betrayed his fear, then returned to their cool, controlling glare.

"One hundred thousand pounds," said John. "I'll give you one hundred thousand pounds to go down there and kill Mackie with your bare hands."

Tyler let the number hang in the air for a moment then lowered his voice.

"Two," he said. "I want two hundred thousand pounds. One for me, and one for my mum."

"Oh, come on-" John began, but Tyler strengthened his grip.

"Two hundred thousand pounds, and if you try anything, I'll tear you apart limb from limb."

"Okay, okay," said John. "Two hundred grand. I can do that."

The two locked eyes for a moment then Tyler relaxed his hand.

"So now we've come to an agreement, Tyler-"

"And what about my mum?" said Tyler. "If I lose, she needs care."

But John Cooper emitted a cruel and hate-filled laugh.

"After that little demonstration of your emotional instability, Tyler?"

He straightened his jacket and smoothed out the non-existent creases with the palms of his hands. He snatched a handgun from inside his jacket and pointed it at Tyler. He stepped closer, then placed the gun beneath Tyler's chin, pushing up and back until Tyler's head hit the wall behind him.

"I'll tell you what I'll do. If you win, you'll get your two hundred grand. But how about this for motivation? If you lose, I'll take this gun, and I'll stick it in your dear old mum's mouth. But before I pull the trigger, I'll tell her how much of a coward her son was. And I'll tell her exactly how Mackie crushed your skull. I'll be sure to include the gory details, Tyler. And only then, once I've seen her fall apart at the seams at the loss of her beloved son, will I pull the trigger and end her misery and pain.

So stop cocking about, get downstairs, get in that ring, and win that bleeding fight."

CHAPTER THIRTY-NINE

"I'm not going to hurt you," said Harvey with his finger to his lips.

He checked to make sure the landing was clear and John Copper's goons weren't loitering then pushed the door, not closing it fully, as the handle had been removed from the inside. The woman was silent, but her eyes were wide and fearful, watching Harvey's every move. A foul stench came from the corner of the room where a bucket had been placed. The curtains were closed but were thin, allowing a fog of streetlight to pass through, ghostlike, and touch the edges of the items in the room like a mother might smooth a child's hair.

"Are you Mrs Thomson?" he asked, his voice reduced to a whisper.

Mrs Thomson's eyes shone in the poor light like glistening diamonds on the carcass of the dead. She waved him over with two feeble flicks of her wrist, then patted the mattress for him to sit beside her. The fear had gone from her eyes, replaced by an inquisitive, curious stare.

Harvey took a step forwards, checking through the tiny gap in the door again.

"Sit with me," she said, her hoarse voice no louder than a whisper. "Where I can see you."

There was a confidence in the woman's voice; she was unafraid. He sat on the side of the bed with his back to the window. Her hand reached up from where she lay, felt his face and turned it to the light, left then right.

Harvey remained silent.

It was coming.

She licked her lips in a futile attempt to ease her speech. There was no water for her and Harvey could have crept out to find some, but something held him still.

"I know you," she said.

Three words.

"Like the angels above know the devil below, I know you."

She let her hand fall and lay it across her stomach. She turned away and stared back at the ceiling.

Harvey didn't reply.

"You're the foster boy who lost his sister. He spoke of you. It was like you were his boy. So proud, he was." It was clear she was recalling memories from a time long ago. Even in the dim light, with her prominent features, Harvey could see she would have been a beautiful woman in her day. "I know what he used to do, the type of man he was." She paused as if wondering if she should carry on, then sighed and gave in. "I know what you do. I know what he trained you to do."

"I'm not here to hurt you," said Harvey.

"Well, you should be," she replied. Her whisper was cold and sharp. "Take me away from all this. Put an end to it all."

Harvey didn't reply.

"He could have. He would have too if he saw me like this."

"You're wrong," said Harvey. "He was a good man. He'd never-"

"You didn't know him like I did," she said. "My Julios."

Hearing somebody speak with so much affection for Julios warmed Harvey. He'd never heard it before and he wanted her to carry on. But it wasn't the time.

"Mrs Thomson, I need to tell you something," said Harvey.

"Don't waste your breath. I'm dying," she replied. "If you're not here to help me, then go. You may as well leave."

Her hand slid across the old mattress and found Harvey's. Though her hands shook and her body clenched from visible stabs of pain, the strength of her grip surprised Harvey. Wide, moist eyes followed his as her cold, trembling hand led his to her chest.

"Do you feel that, Harvey Stone?" she asked.

It was the first time she'd spoken his name. A confirmation of the things she knew.

Harvey shook his head.

"No," he whispered. "I feel nothing."

"That's because there's nothing to feel," she replied.

"I was there, you know?" said Harvey. He didn't know why; it just came out.

"I thought you might have been."

A burning behind Harvey's eyes and a swell in his chest took the words by the hand and together they ventured into the light.

"It was my fault. I saw it all," said Harvey. "But I couldn't stop it."

Mrs Thomson peered up at Harvey, but let him speak. There was no malice or anger in her eyes, just understanding.

"There's nothing I wouldn't do to bring him back," he finished.

She squeezed Harvey's hand.

"Take me to him, Harvey," she said. He felt her pull his hand upward, to which he offered no resistance. Even when she opened his fingers to encircle her throat, he dared not pull away.

And when she closed his hand around her tiny, feeble neck, she smiled.

"I'm glad it was you," she whispered. "He would've wanted this."

She increased the pressure on his fingers, a signal that she was ready. Although her eyes glowed in the pale orange light, the tears that moistened them did not roll onto her face.

"Do it, Harvey," she whispered. "Take me to him. There's nothing for me here now."

Countless times, Harvey had squeezed the life from men. But never a woman. Never someone who had been so close, yet so far away. There were ways of easing the passing without the need for brutality. His fingers sought her windpipe through the loose flesh on her neck until the muscles around it fought to protect the airway.

He began to squeeze.

"Look after him, Harvey," she rasped, squeezing her eyes closed, and embracing the oncoming journey with what appeared to be delight. "Take care of my boy."

Harvey released her, drawing his hand away.

In a panic, she reached for his hand, easing it back to her throat.

"Don't stop," she whispered.

"I'm sorry," said Harvey, searching for the words that would make it right, but knowing deep inside that nothing could ever repair the damage he'd done. Despite only knowing the woman for a few minutes, for the second time in his life, he'd failed to save the ones she loved. "I couldn't stop it. He's gone."

Thoughts of her own death sank from the frail lady's face and motherly love coaxed energy from some hidden part of her.

"Where?" she said. Her wild eyes began to stream. "When?"

"Two nights ago," replied Harvey. He couldn't meet her eyes. "There was a fire."

"That can't be," she said. "You're lying."

"I wish I was. I let him down. I let you down. And I let Julios down again."

"No, it can't be," she said. "He was just here."

CHAPTER FORTY

"Ladies and gentlemen," began the master of ceremonies, as Harvey stepped into the basement and headed towards the changing rooms. "Welcome to the Golden Ring, the home of the back street, bare-knuckle boxing tournaments for as long as I can remember. And tonight, have we got a treat for you. But before we introduce our two very brave boys, I'd like to say a few words."

The voice of the MC faded away to the hum of the air-conditioning as Harvey stepped into the narrow hallway with a flickering light. To his right, Harvey now realised, Tyler would be preparing himself, psyching himself up for the fight.

He stopped at the doorway. Behind him were all of London's hardest men in one room. Every single one of them would have a wager on and every single one of them was there to see a fight to the death.

Harvey stepped back. He glanced through the small window in the door. Escaping unseen would be impossible. There were van loads of armed men in the car park. Even if he did take Tyler and run for it, they wouldn't get far. Whatever happened, nothing could wipe the shame Harvey felt. Guilt and sorrow hung like weights from some place inside of him, some place he'd never been able to reach. Like an itch, it tormented him and meeting Tyler had awoken it.

Whatever happened, the boy needed to survive. It was the last thing he could do for Julios.

"And without further ado," said the MC, "let's meet our first fighter. Ladies and Gentlemen, let me introduce you to Tyler Tornado Thomson."

Before Tyler emerged from his changing room and while the criminal audience erupted in eager applause behind him, Harvey lifted a fire extinguisher from its hook on the wall and stepped into Mackie's room.

The boy was sitting on the slatted wooden bench, his head resting in his hands. He looked up just as Harvey slammed the fire extinguisher into his face. The force of the blow sent the boy reeling backwards over the bench. But he stood and launched the bench at Harvey, following it up by running at him and slamming his shoulder into Harvey's gut, forcing him against the hard, painted brick wall.

Pinned to the wall, Harvey used his elbows to knock the boy backward, but in the limited time he'd had with him earlier that day, Mackie had listened to everything he'd said. With an animal-like strength, he tossed Harvey across the room into the wash basin. It ripped from the wall and tore the water pipe.

Freezing water gushed into the air and rained down on them both. But the reprise gave Harvey enough time to pull off his wet jacket. He rolled his neck from side to side and coaxed Mackie toward him.

The boy had listened to what Harvey had told him. He stood there waiting for Harvey to attack with water dripping from his brow.

"I thought you were on my side?" said Mackie.

"You can't fight him," said Harvey. "I can't let you go out

there. I don't want to hurt you any more than I have to, but one way or another, you aren't fighting tonight."

"Why not?" replied Mackie. "That's why I'm here. I'm going to tear his head off." His teeth were bared and his wide eyes showed black holes for pupils.

"I can't let you do that," said Harvey with a sigh. He rolled his neck, felt the familiar bite of his inner beast, and then stepped forward.

There was no combination of rehearsed punches offered to Harvey, and Mackie didn't bounce from one foot to the other. He stood ready, watching Harvey's every move. In just a few short hours, Harvey had taught the boy how to kill, not fight. The difference was what had separated Harvey from nearly every man he'd been up against in his life. Fighting is one thing; you train to hurt people. Killing is another; usually, the first move is the last if done right.

Mackie had shown promise. His strength and speed combined with Harvey's knowledge had formed a lethal young boy.

"It needs to be me," said Harvey, and he launched an attack while the boy contemplated the words. Harvey gave an open-handed stab at his windpipe. But Mackie was quick. His reactions were lightning fast and he knocked Harvey's hand away with ease, sidestepped, and delivered a sharp blow to Harvey's kidney.

Deep breaths eased the shock and Harvey stepped away.

"I thought I told you to follow up, not to wait?" said Harvey.

"I thought I'd give you a chance," replied Mackie.

Harvey straightened, dropped his arms to his sides and picked up his jacket.

"Where are you going?" asked Mackie, stepping over to block Harvey's exit.

Harvey swung his jacket round in a wide arc. He caught the

sleeve as the confused-looking Mackie turned to see what was happening.

But it was too late for him.

Harvey pulled the thick leather tight against Mackie's neck, twisting it to tighten the grip and close off the boy's airway. A sharp kick to the back of his legs dropped Mackie to his knees and both hands gripped the jacket, trying in vain to pull it from his throat.

Harvey slammed his knee into the back of his lungs, forcing the last remaining breath from Mackie's body. Then, keeping his knee in place, he forced Mackie's head back with the taught leather jacket fastened around his neck.

"That's the last lesson you'll ever learn, Mackie," said Harvey, as he strengthened his grip. "Never give anyone a chance."

He squeezed harder and watched as the boy's face morphed through shades of red, from pink flesh tones to the deep, cherry colour of blood. Tiny spatters of saliva flew from Mackie's lips with the last breaths his body would take. The battle-hardened boy whimpered as he succumbed to death.

It was a sound Harvey had heard too often. The brave face of masculinity was typically a facade, underneath which, in most men, a child lives and breathes, and when the cold hand of death approaches, the child cries out.

It wasn't until Mackie's lifeless hands released their grip on Harvey's jacket and his body slumped to the cold, concrete floor that Harvey released the pressure. Water continued to rain down on Harvey, breaking the silence as the amplified and muffled voice of the MC came through the thick walls.

"And now, on behalf of the one and only, Mr Dixon, our guest fighter tonight and current champion, let's hear it for Mackie." The audience applauded once more as Mackie lay motionless at Harvey's feet in a pool of cold and bloodied water.

Harvey hung his jacket on a hook fixed to the wall. He pulled off his soaking white t-shirt and hung it beside the jacket, then took three deep, long breaths before stepping out beneath the flickering light and through the double doors to where a sea of confused faces greeted him with wide eyes.

But above the heads of the confused, criminal faces, standing alone in the centre of the ring, one face stared at Harvey.

Harvey met Tyler's gaze. They locked onto each other as the murmurs around them rose to a deafening hum of curses and taunts. But nothing could break Harvey's focus. No crude curse or threatening taunt found its way to Harvey's mind.

It was payback time for Julios and his son was ready to receive the payment.

CHAPTER FORTY-ONE

A murmur among the men below and all around Tyler grew into a hum of confused questions as each of the guests looked from Harvey to Del Dixon and back to Tyler, whose heart sank in the pit of his stomach. He backed into his corner to watch Harvey Stone pull himself to the edge of the ring and step through the ropes.

With outrage written all over his face, Del Dixon shook his head at Harvey, who ignored the gesture and began to roll his neck from side to side. He didn't offer a menacing look or a threatening stare. Instead, Harvey simply nodded once at Tyler and prepared for the fight.

The hum of the crowd had worked itself to an excited buzz. New bets were being placed, cigars were lit and trays of champagne seemed to float across the tops of the grey, bald and shaved heads as if they were at the whim of a river that ran around the ring.

The ref took to the centre of the ring, held his hands in the air to silence the buzzing crowds, and cleared his throat.

He waved for both Harvey and Tyler to join him.

The fascinated crowd listened on with awe.

The ref looked between Harvey and Tyler as if he were delivering bad news.

"Tonight, one of you will die," said the ref. His choice of words was designed more for the crowd's amusement than as a warning to the fighters. "There's no gloves and no rules except one. The last man standing wins."

The crowd erupted into a frenzy of cheers and taunts aimed mainly at Harvey, the smaller of the two men.

"Lights please," called the ref.

The lights dimmed all around, leaving the ring lit by two huge spotlights in the ceiling. The hum of the audience fell to a whisper and the ref ordered them both back to their corners.

Finding John at the most prominent table, Tyler searched for answers, but received only an unsmiling nod of the head. John ran his finger across his throat then pointed to the ceiling.

"Are you ready?" asked the ref, as if Tyler's distraction was holding up the fight.

He nodded.

The ref caught his eye one last time then glanced at Harvey. He brought his arm up then swung it down, issuing the command to fight. Then he stepped out of the way and climbed through the ropes. As the ref in a fight with no rules, his job was over.

Harvey stepped forwards and gestured for Tyler to come at him. But Tyler froze. It was his father's only friend. He couldn't fight him.

The murmur of the crowd grew in volume like a slowly approaching wave. But when Harvey landed the first punch, a jab to Tyler's gut, the wave crashed and the crowd erupted.

In their eyes, the fight had begun. But in Tyler's, he saw only one way out.

"Fight me," said Harvey over his guard as he ducked and

weaved and planted a series of jabs into Tyler's ribs. "Don't just stand there. Fight me."

Harvey landed one more across Tyler's jaw. It was a sweet punch that rocked Tyler from his daze. Something stirred inside him. A growl of distaste and the warmth of emotions.

"That's it," said Harvey as Tyler pushed himself out of the corner. "Control it."

As if to make sure the beast was indeed waking, Harvey jabbed twice then landed a hook that grazed Tyler's ear and enabled Tyler to grab hold of Harvey and bring him close.

"What's going on?" he asked, "I thought-"

But Harvey delivered an uppercut to Tyler's gut in the same spot as before. The punch caught Tyler off-guard and left him winded, so he moved away, and began to bounce from foot to foot.

"Get on with it," shouted a bald man from the crowd. His thick London accent made the sentence sound as if it were all one word.

Raising his guard, Tyler moved in with a combination of his own. The final of the four punches caught Harvey square in the face and sent him back to the corner, where Tyler followed him and rained in blow after blow to Harvey's stomach. Feigning fatigue, he leaned in close to Harvey.

"Fight me, Tyler," said Harvey, and he shoved him away.

Before Tyler could recover, Harvey was back on him. A beer bottle skidded across the canvas as Harvey rained punches in from every angle, the last of which caught Tyler's nose, causing the growl in the pit of his stomach to claw up to his chest.

"For your dad," said Harvey, as he came in for another attack.

But the beast saw it coming. Tyler dodged to one side and

coiled like a spring then landed a blow to Harvey's face with the full weight of his body behind it, which sent Harvey to the floor.

"That's more like it," shouted one man who hung onto the ropes like he was a caged animal. "Get in there, son."

But Tyler watched with his arms by his sides as Harvey stood and came back at him with a series of punches.

"Hit me," shouted Harvey, and punched Tyler. "I said fucking hit me." He punched Tyler again then waited for a reaction.

But none came.

"Come on, Tyler," said Harvey, as he punched Tyler square in the gut. "Hit me."

'Control it.'

"Hit me," shouted Harvey.

'Use it.'

With his face up close to Tyler's, Harvey leaned into him, resting his fatigued arms on the boy's shoulders.

"Kill me," he whispered, then moved away to catch Tyler's eye. He nodded. "Kill me for your dad. It's all I have to give."

Tyler stared down at the man he'd met only a few days earlier but what seemed like a lifetime ago. The last connection to his father was standing in front of him, coiling for a punch and then releasing.

The blow rocked Tyler back to his heels.

"Hit him, Tyler," screamed John from the side of the ring. "Don't just bleeding stand there."

But Tyler couldn't move.

"I said kill me, Tyler," Harvey screamed in his face, and shoved him backwards. "Kill me, Tyler." Harvey stood in front of him, opening up his guard, and planted his feet flat on the canvas floor. "Come on. Hit me. Just do it. Kill me, Tyler. Please."

"Tyler, you've got three seconds before I go upstairs and

open your mum up, sunshine. I'll cut her bleeding heart out and bring it down here for you to see," said John.

The beast climbed into Tyler's mind.

"Kill me," said Harvey, his anguished face pleading with Tyler as he shoved him across the ring.

"Three," called John. "I'll cut her from top to bottom, sunshine."

The beast took a deep breath.

"Come on. For your dad, Tyler. I'm open," said Harvey.

"Two. Tyler, this is your last chance," said John, and from the corner of his eye, Tyler caught the glint of a blade being pulled from John's jacket.

The beast rolled its neck from side to side. Tyler's huge frame coiled like a snake with his massive fist clenched tight.

Harvey dropped to his knees and held his arms out wide, inviting Tyler to attack him.

"Just do it. Just finish me, Tyler," screamed Harvey.

"One."

The sound of the automatic gunfire that shredded the ceiling and rained broken glass down on the crowd cut through the tension like a hot knife through butter. The excited audience of hardened men and trophy wives dropped to the floor with a crash of broken champagne flutes and sought refuge behind anything solid. Tables were dragged to the floor and the sea of heads that had gazed up at Harvey became a tangled mass of arms and legs, as men covered their wives from danger.

The gunfire stopped.

Harvey, who was kneeling in the centre of the ring with Tyler lying flat on the floor beside him, looked out at the door to the staircase. Five men, black as the night, took confident steps across broken glass into the room. They strode in formation with the largest and ugliest at the front and his men behind him in a V-shape.

He let loose another short burst of gunfire and the last of the lights blew out.

Harvey didn't move an inch.

One of the men with a shaved head who had spoken to Dixon earlier raised a handgun above the toppled table he was hiding behind. He fired off three rounds, all of which found the rear wall.

One of the intruders stepped out of formation, strode across the floor and opened up on the mass of people hiding behind the tables. The gunfire fell silent again, leaving the grunts of dying men and the whimpers of injured and dying women to fill the space.

"Any more brave men in here?" said the lead man.

The room fell silent.

"I didn't think so," he said. His voice was deep like a bass, and his accent was London through and through. "How about you?" He kicked out at a fat, bald man who lay across his wife on the floor in a protective pose, which gave way as he scrambled away from her and the man's boots. "No brave men in here then?" said the man, as he raised the automatic weapon and tucked his elbow into his side to take the weight.

"How about you, fella?" he said, as his eyes landed on Harvey. "Feeling brave tonight?"

"You've got no idea, mate," replied Harvey.

"Is that supposed to be funny?" said the man, as his four men joined him by the side of the ring. "What are you, some kind of tough guy?"

Harvey didn't reply.

The man looked down at Tyler on the canvas and then back at Harvey.

"Who's winning?" he asked.

"You're the one with the gun," said Harvey. "I'd say you're winning for the time being."

The intruder gazed up at Harvey and cocked his head with what appeared to be fascination.

"I'm looking for Del Dixon," he said at last. "Where can I find him?"

Harvey didn't reply.

"For a man with a smart mouth, you don't say much, do you?"

"Do I look like an information kiosk? Why don't you ask a few of the guests? I'm sure they'd be only too happy to oblige," replied Harvey.

Beyond the shoulders of the men, a single figure crawled towards the doorway.

The man talking to Harvey snapped around to his friends. His long thick dreadlocks trailed the movement of his head and swung around to his front.

"Find him," he ordered. "If anyone lies, shoot them."

The comment raised a few gasps and murmurs from the crowd on the floor all around the ring.

"Silence," the man shouted, and let a three-round burst pepper the ceiling. "Del Dixon, where are you?"

"He's by the-" called a woman, who was quickly silenced by her husband.

The man focused on the voice in the dark and trod across the broken glass to where he found her, wrestling her husband's hand from her mouth. "If they want Del, they can have him," she snapped at her husband. "Then they can get out of here and leave us alone."

The hot muzzle of the automatic grazed her rosy cheek. She winced and pulled away.

"Where?" said the man.

"By the door," the woman replied with regret in her voice. Harvey caught the shine of her husband's bald head as he shook it from side to side in dismay.

Beside the door, two of the intruders hauled Del Dixon to his feet and dragged him by his armpits through the tangle of limbs. They heaved him onto the canvas where he rolled to the centre away from their hands and stood beside Harvey, eying the men with caution as each one of them moved to guard one side of the ring.

There was no escape.

"If anyone tries to run anyway," the lead man announced, "there's an automatic rifle waiting to say hello at the top of those stairs. For the time being, this fight is over. All bets are off."

He climbed up onto the canvas and ducked beneath the rope, then circled Del Dixon as a lion might orbit its prey.

"You all might be wondering what my brothers and I are doing here. What is it we want? So I'll tell you."

He towered over Del Dixon, placed one big hand on the smaller man's shoulder, and looked out at the crowd.

"Up until two days ago, my brothers and I had one more brother, our youngest sibling. He chose not to work in the family business and we didn't see him often. But we loved him nonetheless." He nodded at one of his brothers who slid a small fuel can beneath the rope onto the canvas. "Two days ago, Del Dixon killed him in an attempt to win this fight."

Murmurs and whispers started to grow as the crowd began to see the outcome.

"Silence," the lead man said. "The next person to speak or move will be shot."

The room once more fell silent and the lead man turned to Harvey.

"You, grab that can."

Harvey got to his feet and collected the fuel can.

The lead man nodded at Del Dixon. There was no instruction necessary. Del Dixon's angry face turned to horror as the smell of the fuel hit him and reality set in. Harvey soaked Dixon's clothes and hair, and paid special attention to Dixon's feet, making sure his leather shoes were saturated. It was a trick he'd learned from Julios to ensure the victim couldn't run away.

"No," said Dixon. "Stop. It wasn't me."

"You look like you've done this before," said the lead man,

ignoring Dixon. He held out a lighter in his steady hand and gazed at Harvey with wonder.

Harvey didn't reply. But for a second, the light from the stairwell caught movement. It was John Cooper.

Taking the lighter and crouching at Dixon's feet, Harvey looked up to enjoy the final expression of terror on Dixon's face.

"It wasn't me," said Dixon. "Don't do this. It wasn't me or my men."

"Any last requests?" said the man. "Is there anything you want the world to know?"

Dixon was breathing hard, the fumes accelerating his hyperventilation. He stared up at the intruder who loomed over him.

"I'm going to come back and bleeding haunt you."

"Not if my brother haunts you first," said the man, and nodded at Harvey.

Harvey sparked the lighter.

CHAPTER FORTY-THREE

The rush of flames igniting Dixon's agonised body sent the man into a blind frenzy. He bounced from the ropes as he tried to escape the ring and fell backwards, writhing and screaming.

But the scene was too much for the hardened crowd. As if it were coordinated, men emerged from the tables they hid behind, wielding handguns, and all hell broke loose. Harvey dove to the floor, covering Tyler as the lead man's body was peppered with shots from all angles until his knees buckled and he fell forwards onto Dixon.

Harvey rolled, pulling Tyler with him until they dropped from the ring and landed beside the still-twitching body of one of the brothers.

Automatic gunfire from the far side of the ring, along with many single handgun shots, sang out in the darkness. Only the burst of muzzle flash and the flames of Dixon's charred and squirming body lit the scene.

Flashes of muzzle fire near the stairwell blocked the exit. With one hand holding Tyler down, Harvey reached into the ring, grabbed the fuel can and began tearing a strip of clothing from the body of the dead yardie brother.

In near darkness, he knotted the strip of material, soaked it in fuel, and then stuffed it into the fuel can, wedging the knot tight into the hole.

"Get ready, Tyler," he said, as he lit the end of the rag, reached back and launched the can at the wall beside the stairwell. Flames burst from the wall as the plastic can split and burning fuel sprayed out in all directions.

"Now. Go."

He pulled Tyler to his feet and, for a brief moment, the gunfire stopped until they were halfway across the room. Then the automatic weapons opened up again. The wooden beams that supported the floor above took the flame, and like dry grass in a breeze, the fire rushed across the ceiling, burning blues and yellows.

Then the screams started.

Women made a beeline for the door as Harvey and Tyler reached the stairwell, but the intruders gunned down the criminal wives where they stood. With one foot on the first step, Harvey looked back to see two men with shaved heads attacking the last remaining brother. Both of them were cut down, and they skidded face first on the broken glass across the floor.

The flames now encircled the room. The dry, wooden, panelled walls crackled and popped as the heat intensified and the flames found fresh fuel. More than a dozen people remained alive, hiding behind furniture but too scared to run for the door.

The remaining brother looked up at Harvey. He cocked his head at Harvey's lack of fear, then nodded. A sign he was free to run. The man would die with his brothers.

Harvey shoved Tyler forwards and the two men ran up the stairs and found relative cool air on their scorched faces. The public bar was empty and the pair stopped at the top of the stairs, hearing the screaming of burning men and women below.

"I need to get my mum out," said Tyler, forcing the sounds of the dying from his mind.

Harvey nodded and glanced up the stairs.

"I'll wait for you out the back," he said. "I'll find us some wheels."

Tyler held his gaze, finding it difficult to break away, until Harvey turned to leave.

"Don't leave without us," said Tyler.

Stopping in the doorway, Harvey looked back and met his eyes.

"I won't," he said.

Tyler took the stairs two at a time. The door to his mum's room was locked, so he stepped back, his adrenaline still pumping, and slammed the heel of his foot into the wood. The door crashed open with the sound of splintering wood and Tyler crouched down beside his mum.

"Mum, it's me," he said. "We've got to go."

He nudged her shoulder to wake her.

"Mum, come on, it's me. You need to get up," he said, and nudged her harder. Her body rocked but still, she didn't move.

Using both hands, he gripped her shoulders and shook her.

"Mum, the place is on fire," he said, as the tears began to well up and his throat swelled. "Mum. Please."

He gripped her lifeless hand, resisting the urge to scream. Instead, he let his head fall onto her stomach.

"Please," he whispered, and brought her hand to his mouth to kiss the cold skin.

"Very touching," said a voice from behind him. The accent was familiar, but far removed from Tyler's mind. "I think you'll find you're a touch too late."

The beast growled inside Tyler's chest, long and guttural.

"John said you wanted to be with her. At least now I won't have to drag your fat carcass up the stairs."

A flash of light pulsed behind Tyler's eyes. He lifted his head and took a final look at his mother, wiping her loose hair from her brow and smoothing it behind her ears how she liked it.

"Up," said Jerry. "I haven't got all day. Some of us have trains to catch."

A twitch of nerves in Tyler's neck faded when he rolled his head from side to side, stretching the muscles.

He lay his mother's hands on her lap then bent forward to kiss her forehead.

The noise of a shotgun being armed cracked in the tiny room.

"Goodbye, mum," he said. But he found no more words to accompany them.

The twin barrels of the shotgun touched the back of his head, hard and steely cold, like the fingers of death himself.

With slow and deliberate movements, Tyler raised his arms and stood, then turned to find Jerry staring back at him with the cold, hard stare of a man who'd won.

The beast smiled.

The rear doors of the Golden Lion smashed open with the hard kick of Harvey's boot. The bite of the freezing wind found his naked torso, but the adrenaline that flowed through him blazed like the fires of hell. He was greeted by five men who all stepped from the side door of a van with shaved heads, tattoos and bomber jackets. Each of them brandished a selection of bats and knives.

"You've got to be kidding me," said Harvey.

"Nobody gets out alive," said the frontman.

A burst of automatic gunfire could be heard from the basement below then two single shots of a handgun silenced it. A lick of flames showed itself in the stairwell then retreated, leaving behind a mask of flickering oranges and yellows as the fire crept up the stairs in its unquenchable hunger for fresh fuel.

"I don't think there's much chance of that happening," replied Harvey.

But he was cut short as one of the men came at him with a wild swing of his bat. Harvey ducked as the bat missed his face by a few inches then reached up, grabbed the man's arm and twisted it until the wooden weapon fell from his grip and into Harvey's hand.

Keeping the grip on the man's arm, Harvey swung the bat in his left hand, familiarising himself with its weight. Then he gave the arm a final twist and pushed up until the crack of shattering bones induced agonised screams from the man. Harvey let him drop to his knees, then passed the bat to his right hand, swung it and delivered a blow to the man's head that spattered blood across his awestruck friends.

"Now we're equal," said Harvey, kicking the man's body to the ground. He rolled his head from side to side, felt the two satisfying clicks, and waited for the men to come at him, as they always did.

And they did.

Another man ran at him, carving a knife from side to side in long, sweeping arcs designed to break Harvey's guard. Taking one step back, Harvey shunted the blunt end of the bat into the man's face, stunning him long enough for Harvey to turn the blade in the man's hand and force it into his throat. Another forceful kick with the heel of his boot sent the second man onto the first. But there was no reprise.

All three remaining men came at Harvey, two with bats, one with a knife.

They closed in on three sides, attacking all at once. The first swing of a bat sent Harvey ducking low where he destroyed the kneecaps of the man to his right. But the knife lunged at him while he was low in a straight stab aimed for his gut. Harvey dropped onto his back, swung up with the bat and felt the man's wrist shatter under the blow. The last man with the bat took aim at Harvey's legs. There was no time to move or attack and the blow found his thigh with a hard, dull stab of pain.

The man with the broken wrist began to kick as Harvey rolled to his side, and once more, the bat found Harvey's back. A boot connected with Harvey's face, shattering his nose. The man with the broken wrist leaned over Harvey and peered into his eyes, looking for some kind of understanding.

"I told you, nobody gets out alive," he said, then spat in Harvey's face and waved the man with the bat closer. "Finish him off, Ted."

Ted stepped closer. He positioned himself beside Harvey's head then raised the bat high, coiled to deliver the hardest blow he could. Harvey braced for the hit. There was no room to move and not enough time to think. But as the man's back reached its zenith and his face contorted to summon all his strength, the sound of shattering glass from above tore his eyes from Harvey's head and the lifeless body of a man took him to the ground.

With barely a pause to think, Harvey swung at the last man's legs, rolled, then stood over him. He lifted his chin with the end of his bat then raised it for the final blow.

A screech of brakes and the crunch of tyres on gravel a few metres away stopped him. The side door slid open. Its metallic click was loud in the now-silent night, filled only with the distant sirens of the fire brigade and police. A familiar voice called out. The voice of reason.

"Harvey," cried Melody, "get in the van."

He stopped and met Melody's eyes. She was half in and half out of the van, reaching for him with a pleading gaze.

"You don't need to do this," she said. Her eyes darted to the building behind him. Tiny orange sparks found the cool night air and wafted past Harvey's face. Then, like a pack of hungry wolves, the flames reached out of the doors, searching for food to devour. "Come on."

Harvey stared back at the man on the ground, who waited for him to make his decision with wide, hopeful eyes.

With a glance back into the fire and then to Melody, Harvey tossed the bat across the car park. There was something missing.

A feeling. He no longer felt the warm, guttural growl of his inner beast. The desire to punish the man was further from his mind. He saw with clarity a human being lying on the ground beneath him, beaten and broken.

Harvey stepped away. He could hear Melody and Reg calling to him from Reg's van. But their voices were no match for his thoughts as they sought to ease the beast inside him. He clung to the side of the van, felt Melody's hands clawing for him to climb inside, and heard the growing wails of the approaching emergency services.

He tore himself away from Melody, but locked eyes with her in the firelight.

"Tyler," said Harvey. "I can't leave him." He felt her grip loosen as he stepped back towards the fire. He turned and was about to launch himself through the flaming doorway when, from inside, he heard the snapping of wood and breaking of glass.

A figure appeared, lit briefly by the angry flickering of flames and framed in the centre of the burning doorway. A heavy foot smashed the burning doors from their hinges, and they fell to the ground beside the group of men who had attacked Harvey and now writhed on the cold, hard ground.

From the flames, with the body of a woman lying limp in his strong arms, stepped Tyler. He emerged from the fire like the devil himself, his face a picture of hate, love and loss. It was a face Harvey had worn for many years.

CHAPTER FORTY-FIVE

"Lay her down here," said the woman in the back, taking control. She moved aside and let Tyler lay his mother on the carpeted floor of the Volkswagen van.

"We need to go," said the man at the wheel. Beside him sat another woman. She had a laptop on her legs and the screen showed a live satellite view of the area with icons closing in on one place.

The Golden Ring.

"In the van," said Harvey, and shoved him inside. "Go, go, go, Reg." Harvey stepped in and slid the door closed. He knelt beside Tyler's mum, refusing to meet Tyler's stare.

The van roared into life. It slid sideways out of the pub car park onto the wet tarmac, and Reg fought to hold on. Tyler found a handhold but couldn't tear his eyes from his mum's dead body as it rolled from side to side with the movement of the van.

"Get us somewhere safe, Reg," said Harvey, as the woman tried to find a pulse on Tyler's mum. She looked up at Harvey, and offered him a faint shake of her head as if shielding the news from Tyler.

"It's okay," said Tyler. "I know. She's been dead for a while."

"I'm sorry," she said, as she pulled a blanket from the small couch beside her. "You did a brave thing to get her out of there."

"No," said Tyler. "Don't cover her. Please. I want to see her. For a while, at least."

"How did you even find me, Melody?" asked Harvey. "I left my phone at the restaurant so you couldn't find me."

The woman in the front passenger seat turned to face the rear and found Harvey staring back at her.

"Easy," she said. "We just followed the trail of death and destruction. The police found a body in an old disused power station in South London. I found the satellite feed and video footage and saw you leaving with two men. I took the license plate of the car you got into and tracked its inbuilt GPS to the Golden Ring."

Harvey stared back at her in disbelief.

"You know you two really are made for each other?" he said. "Jess, how about you use those skills and get us somewhere far, far away."

They sped from Plaistow and slowed when they reached the relative safety of Silvertown's backstreets. The engine quietened and the sirens faded away, leaving only Tyler's occasional heavy exhales as he sought to make sense of the situation.

Suddenly, the car behind flicked on its full beam headlights, filling the interior of the small van with harsh light.

"Who's that?" asked Reg, squinting as the car grew closer and nudged into the back of the van. Reg barely maintained control and took the side mirrors off a row of parked cars in a spray of orange sparks.

"Open the rear door," said Harvey, searching for a weapon of some kind as the car once more smashed into the back of the van.

But as much as Tyler tried, the door wouldn't budge. The hits from the car had wedged it closed.

"Left turn coming up," said Reg. "Hold on."

A squeal of tyres, piercing and shrill, filled the van as it lurched to one side at the limits of its stability. Harvey wrenched open the side door as the car came in for one last hit, a hit that would topple the van. But Harvey launched himself onto the front of the car, as the van careened around the corner, taking out two more parked cars and barely making the turn.

The van rolled to a stop as everyone inside looked back in horror. The speeding car had made no attempt to turn or stop. It smashed through the two parked cars, tore down an iron safety barrier onto wasteland and launched off a pile of rubble. Its engine roared and the wheels span uselessly before the front of the car plunged into the inky-black water of the River Thames.

Only the idling rumble of the van's engine could be heard as everyone took in the sight and feared the worst.

Tyler was up and out of the van before anybody spoke. Inside him, as he ran, a warm, familiar feeling clawed its way from the very pit of his stomach, through his chest and found solace in Tyler's mind.

The car was gone, completely submerged. Only the headlights shone with fading enthusiasm, which then disappeared as the car sank to the river's depths.

Tyler pulled off his top mid-run. He threw it to the side and began to kick off his trainers when Melody tackled him to the ground.

"No," she said. "Don't be stupid."

But he rolled her away and sprang to his feet, just before Reg and Jess took him down in a joint effort. He struggled, but Melody joined them, and together, they pinned him down.

Inside, the beast roared. It kicked out at Reg, sending him flying backwards. Melody dove on top of Tyler's free leg as the beast threw Jess away like a rag doll. But as he reached for Melody, she twisted his leg. A pulse of anger flashed through his eyes and he kicked out violently.

Melody was ready for it. She moved to one side, collected both legs and bound them together with her belt. Tyler lay face down, his legs forced up and back by Melody's surprising strength. His face was forced into the mud and gravel.

"Let him go," she said, her face beside his. His arms tensed with the raging beast inside him, seeking a way out. But it was futile. "Let him go."

A coolness washed over his face, leaving only burning tears behind his eyes as the beast sank back to the depths. His muscles relaxed and grief overcame him. With the anger gone, Melody released her belt and dropped down beside him. He rolled to one side to look at her. Reg and the other girl stood on the river bank calling out Harvey's name. But Melody seemed content to sit with her legs tucked up to her chest with her arms wrapped around them.

"Let him go," she whispered once more, as if the words she had spoken had been shared for them both.

CHAPTER FORTY-SIX

A dark sky loomed ahead and in front, lit only by the ambience of a hundred million lights scattered across the City of London and beyond. At the peripherals of his vision, the world passed like looped scenery and faded away before any focus of vision determined its nature, purpose or identity.

Travelling at the whim and mercy of the moonlit tides, with only the breath in his body to keep him afloat, he lay calm and still and contemplated life itself in waves of guilt, loss and shame. Each memory held the touch of an angel. Each was a step closer to heaven and the closing of heavy, dark doors.

A searing pain jabbed at his leg, but there was no need to reach down. He'd felt the sharp shard of bone split his skin the moment the car had hit the water. The current was strong and, for a brief moment, he considered using his arms to take him to the shore. But a warm feeling of closure accompanied the idea of floating out to sea. To be swallowed whole by nature's most fearsome weapon. To die silently beneath a sky of stars.

The river widened as it neared the estuary and its shallow waves rushed up onto the nearby mud flats then broke with a rhythmic percussion. Two strong hands hauled him from the water and onto the deep muddy banks where they dropped him beside a rotted, wooden post that maybe, one day, in a time long forgotten, formed part of a jetty. Now it sat alone, exposed by the moon and its tides, waiting for the river to return to full height.

He closed his eyes, and as the cold wind rushed across the River Thames, sending his body into uncontrollable spasms of shivers, he was lulled to somewhere warm. It was a memory of fire and death, where distant screams hung like haunted voices, and chaos ensued at the centre of a rioting mass of charred and burnt human forms.

But it was warm.

He woke to the kiss of lapping water by his side while behind him, two heavy boots slipped and stomped in the thick, dark mud. Any inquisitive thoughts as to who, why or how succumbed to his desire to let the river wash him away along with the guilt, loss and shame that still stained his thoughts. The devil's hand still warmed his shoulder while the rest of him succumbed to shivers.

"You don't need to do this," he said, as a leather belt was passed around his neck and fastened with two sharp jerks to bring it tight. "You should have left me in the river. I'm ready for it."

The shivers set in as fits of body-shaking convulsions forced his body to stay alive, while his mind was far out to sea.

"I considered it," came the reply.

"So why didn't you?"

There was a silence as an answer was sought.

"I considered taking the journey with you."

"So why didn't you?" he replied. "What better way to go than on your own terms with darkness above and darkness below, and nothing but the whispering wind to hear your confessions?"

The boots slopped in the mud and stopped beside him. A dark shape loomed above, blacker than the night's polluted sky.

"I wanted to see you die," came the reply.

He laughed, a single laugh that sounded more like a breath.

"I can't remember the last time I laughed," he said, and rested his head on the rotted, wooden post behind him. "It's funny. It's only when the end is near that you realise these things."

There was no reply, just the shape above him and beside him, unmoving.

"How about you?" he said. "Who gets to watch you die? Surely there's someone who deserves to see that show?"

"I could fill a room with people who deserve to watch me die, John," said the man.

"So why don't you join me?" he said, and reached for a rock beside his leg at the limit of his constraint. It sucked at the mud as he dragged it close, and jarred when it found exposed bone. He breathed once, long and deep, then rolled it onto his lap. "Pull up a rock. The tide's coming in."

But the dark shape beside him had vanished, and the cool bite of the water washed over his legs, broke, and then ran back to the river. With each wash of the water across his body, a renewed energy shook him with vigour as still, his body fought to stay alive while his mind welcomed the rising tide.

He called out to the night but only the wind replied, seeking his confession with its whispering promise of death. With each whisper, the water rose higher, until it licked at the skin on his face, then receded to allow one more memory, one more confession and one more burst of lonely tears to leave him.

At last, there were no more memories, no more stories of horror to confess, and his last remaining tear was washed away with the tide that swallowed him.

CHAPTER FORTY-SEVEN

The avenue of trees shielded the small congregation of mourners who stood beside the open grave among the fortunate dead, whose lives were celebrated and marked with statues of angels. The mood was sombre but few tears fell. Each member of the congregation waited patiently to shake Tyler's hand or offer the estranged boy a hug before walking away and disappearing into the maze of graves. The minister was the last to leave. He placed his hand on Tyler's shoulder and spoke a few unheard words. Tyler gazed past him into the hole in the ground, searching for some kind of answer, or a clue to where his life should lead.

The fact was cold but true; he was free now to go wherever his heart would take him. He was no longer bound by the restraints of his dying mother. He was no longer the lifeline that brought her food and water, and worked to keep her warm and safe. He was no longer the lifter of spirits in those hideous dark days. The days when death had stepped closer and teased her until she tore at her skin with savage nails, frustrated, agonised, and tortured to the point of despair.

But that wasn't how she should be remembered.

She deserved more. She was more than a dying woman who had demanded for her son to grow into a man, denying Tyler the final part of his childhood. She had been beautiful. The photos in their flat were proof that she was once full of vibrant life, strong and resilient. That was how she should be remembered.

The minister, with his hands folded respectfully, stepped away with silence and grace, leaving Tyler to share a few silent moments with his mum. Remembering the good times, the laughs and her beauty, he stepped forward and fell to his knees. He closed his eyes, searching for a connection. A sign. Anything.

He raised his face to the grey sky above, but no sunbeams broke through the clouds to warm his skin. Just the rustle of leaves and the distant hum of the city behind the walls of the cemetery.

He spoke his last goodbye then rose, turned and walked away. His lower lip was hidden beneath his front teeth and his eyes were narrow and dark. He was channelling the emotion, sending it to the pit of his stomach where the beast slept. One day, when the time was right and the beast opened its eyes, he would feed off that emotion. It would grow in size and strength, tamed, but deadly if not controlled.

Familiar with the maze of the surrounding graves, Tyler took a slow walk past Mary, the angels and Jesus, who regarded him, unafraid, like an old friend. An old Celtic cross dating back to the eighteenth century, with two hundred years of moss and mould embedded into its hard surface, marked the turn. Soon enough, Tyler stood in front of his father's bland grave marker. Only the other names of the shunned were witnesses to his grief.

Once more, Tyler dropped to a crouch, then fell forward to one knee. His hand reached out to stop his fall and found the soft dirt that he'd so often cleared of weeds. His head fell forward too as if the muscles had succumbed to its weight. Then the tears came. They rolled across his tired skin, finding the lines on his face formed by sleepless nights, and channelled into a single drip, which fell onto the factory-stamped letters that formed his father's name.

Julios Saville.

He sat for a long time in that position, hunched above a hidden memory of his father, and fighting for an image of them both together. He longed for a memory of his family, one of laughter and love. The image remained hidden if indeed it had ever existed. Only a reel of old photos played on repeat in his mind.

Never before had Harvey felt such a connection to someone. Never before had he wanted so much to reach out and help somebody grieve as he had grieved and to share the burden of loss.

A hand gripped his suit jacket. Another found the thin material of his new shirt and traced the outline of his chest with soft fingers. Her head fell against his back, letting him know she was there if he needed her.

Something stirred inside his chest. It wasn't the familiar, cold, sharp claws of the beast, but a warm, silky energy that found his veins and a single tear formed in the corner of his eye. His arm reached out, sliding around her waist and across the smooth material of her dress.

"It's time," said Melody with a gentle squeeze.

Harvey didn't reply.

The End

STONE ARMY

CHAPTER ONE

Headlights shone like two dying suns at the far reach of Gabriella's vision, growing closer, burning brighter, and blinding her watering eyes. It was as if a searing needle had penetrated her visual organs and found the sensitive nerves cowering behind. Beneath her feet, the ground rumbled, silent but growing in intensity like the rising chaos of a stampede.

She turned to face the sound of breaking branches, barking dogs and men's voices, which had raised to a fever pitch. In the darkness of the forest, Gabriella saw torch beams cutting the night, leaving no escape except onwards across the railway tracks and into the unknown.

A distant scream pierced the blackness somewhere far away. The barking of dogs changed from the howl of an excited hunting pack to snappy snarls as they cornered their prey and pinned it to the ground.

"Donna," whispered Gabriella.

A faint cloud formed when she spoke as the night air met her warm breath.

Another scream sounded followed by frantic struggles as,

somewhere in the darkness, her friend fought off the dogs. A dark image formed in Gabriella's mind of the German Shepherds she had seen prowling the fence line of the laboratory. She saw an image of the pack, excited by the hunt as they tore at Donna's clothes, their teeth clamping down on her hands and arms, pulling her to the ground, their ferocity far outweighing that of the men who followed her with torchlights.

In front of Gabriella, two sets of railway tracks ran left to right from the coast to the mainland. Beyond the tracks, the ground fell away to fields and a forest columned by the night; dark outlines against a dark sky. Somehow, after her ordeal, the black unknown beyond seemed calm and safe in comparison to what lay behind. But something made her stand still. To cross the train lines and escape into the darkness would mean failure. But returning to the hunting dogs and torchlight men would mean certain death.

Some voices called out to others that they'd found one. Gabriella hesitated, undecided. A single gunshot into the air, followed by the lighting of a flare, marked the spot. The searching torches turned and headed that way, bouncing through the dark forest. The flash of the muzzle and burning flare found its way to Gabriella's watering eyes, registering enough danger to trigger the carnal instincts to run and find help. But a stronger fear of failure glued her to the spot.

"We got one," called a voice. "Find the other one. She went that way. She can't be far."

That voice. The voice that taunted Gabriella's drug-fuelled dreams and darkened her miserable days.

A torchlight span in a wide arc close by. It shone through the trees, tracing Gabriella's path through the long grass and up onto the embankment where she stood, frozen to the spot. The vibration beneath her feet was accompanied by the grumble of an approaching train.

The heavy pounding in Gabriella's chest amplified the sound of her breathing. She could feel the drug working. Whatever it was, it fuelled the familiar rush of blood to her head, the invincible surge of energy that coursed through her body, and the trembling of what felt like every muscle in her body, holding her taut like a runner on the starting blocks.

A man broke through the trees. His beam of light cut the darkness like a long, straight snake. The dark form was unmistakable. Broad square shoulders. His head cocked to one side. The swagger of a man who feared nothing.

That man.

He was different to the others. He was cruel, with a voice that violated Gabriella and the girls, and with eyes that did more than undress her; they seemed to tear at her clothes just like the dogs tearing at Donna.

His torchlight found Gabriella. It blinded her and fixed her to the spot. There was no need for words; she could sense his leering grin behind the light.

In the distance, the dogs silenced, and a group of torchlights flashed in all directions as they began their hunt for Gabriella. The dark man in front of her glanced back as if he was considering calling out. But he changed his mind and returned his attention to his quarry.

His prize.

Gabriella took one step back. Her bare foot found the track, cold and hard, but buzzing with energy like the muscles in her body that tensed and relaxed with adrenaline.

Gabriella held his stare. The man responded with a look, daring her with silent taunts to run and inviting her to him with unheard charm. He gave a flick of his eyes to the distant oncoming train. She saw his delight in the sight of her last remaining seconds on earth, half-naked, scared and broken.

"It seems to me that you have three choices," he said.

An agonised scream came from the woods behind him. But it wasn't a scream as Gabriella understood the word. It was more of the final, anguished wail of a tortured, dying girl, and a submission to death.

"Three choices?" said Gabriella.

She shunned the sound of her friend's death from her mind, seeking solace in the growing rumble beneath her foot.

"First choice," said the man, "you can run. You can cross those tracks and run like you've got the devil on your heels and he's mad as hell at you. But you won't get far. I know those fields like I know the skin on my hand. I'll find you before you even break for breath."

The concentrated torchlights in the forest dispersed as each of the men spread out to find Gabriella. A slice of light lit the side of the man's face, revealing a knowing smile that he had her all to himself.

Dogs barked in the trees to her left, where Gabriella had stripped and run through the freezing stream. The men called out, whooping with delight and joking that the last girl was already naked. Removing her clothes was intended to buy Gabriella time and throw the dogs off her scent. But the screams of Donna had stalled her escape.

"Second choice," said the man, "you can come down off the embankment. I'll give you my coat and I'll take you back. No-one will hurt you. I can assure you."

"Just like nobody hurt Donna?" said Gabriella.

But the man responded with a shrug.

Rounding the long bend, the headlights of the oncoming train swept across the trees, then lit one side of Gabriella's body. The rumbling beneath her foot intensified, vibrating through her body, and the sound of the horn broke the night as if marking her two choices. Run or return.

"And what's option three?" she asked between horns, shouting above the noise of the approaching train.

The torchlight flicked off.

In the darkness, only shadows and dark shapes moved. The headlights of the train passed by the tree line, lighting only the grass, the tracks and Gabriella herself, growing wider as the train thundered closer.

Another horn as the driver urged her to move.

The ground shook with a pulse matching Gabriella's heartbeat.

But she stayed.

A backward step would commit to the run, triggering the man and the dogs into action. A forward step would admit defeat. He'd take her into his lying, devilish arms and use her for the evil he'd been dreaming of since that first day. Then he'd kill her.

But staying on the tracks offered her only real chance of escape, to a place where even he couldn't reach her.

But death would mean failure.

Another horn, louder and longer.

The squeal of brakes as two hundred tons of steel anchored, spraying great washes of sparks into the forest.

"Option three," he said, appearing beside her from nowhere.

He smiled the smile she'd seen a thousand times in her dreams, in her waking tortured days, and now, as death held her in its bony grip. The surprise caught her off guard. She stepped back, and stood centrally between the tracks, where he seemed to dare not follow.

With half his face lit by the approaching train, he leaned across to her with an outstretched hand. "Don't be stupid, Gabriella. Come with me."

But Gabriella smiled and closed her eyes, letting peace find her, bringing with it the calm that allowed her to focus on cherished memories. She searched through her life in just a few seconds. An image of her father smiling in his garden as he stopped turning the earth and leaned on his garden fork to admire her, fanning himself with his wide-brimmed hat. Her brother shooting her a wink as he led Gabriella from their home on one of their many adventures. She would sleep in the car. Francis would drive then wake her up when they had reached the destination. Each time it was a different location, carefully planned and designed to enthral young Gabriella. Sometimes it was the beach. Sometimes Francis would park at the top of a hill to look down at the rolling forests below. They would sit and drink coffee from a flask and perhaps eat a croissant.

On one occasion, Francis had taken her to Paris to see the Christmas lights, but the memory was snatched away before she could relive the moment.

"Gabriella," called the man.

Her name came to her as he haunted her last treasured moments on earth. The images of her loved ones faded away, but without regret.

The train horn sounded once more, loud and urgent.

The beat of the tracks moved the ground on which she stood.

And the drug that coursed through her body woke every living cell, firing energy into every single muscle.

"*Gabriella*," said the man, his hand clutching for her arm.

Another loud horn. The headlights, as bright as the sun, held the two of them in limbo. The ground, the trees, the whole world, was white.

His outstretched arm.

Those evil eyes.

Men burst from the forest behind him and stopped as the

train bore down on her like a raging beast. She had just one second of life remaining. One second to deny evil its glory. One second to cherish living.

"I die for France," she said.

Then ran.

CHAPTER TWO

Thin, wispy branches of willow tore at Harvey's face as he broke new trails on the river bank in the South of France. But even the stinging slices to his face weren't enough to deter him or provoke a stumble. The rhythmic beat of his heart in time with his pace was enough to force him on, pumping harder, striding longer. The faster he ran, the harder his heart thumped.

A fallen tree blocked the path but he hurdled it with ease then ran down to a stream. His foot found the cold water; it splashed up his leg, fresh and cool. Beyond the stream was a long uphill stretch, littered with saplings and thorny bushes. Finding his way through without breaking stride was tough, and his legs took the brunt of the attack. Sharp pointed thorns dug into his skin and carved deep cuts across his legs. But with his arms pumping, and his mind fixed on reaching the top, he forced himself forwards, pushing the pain aside and focusing on one step after the other.

At the top of the hill, a narrow path led through the trees. It was a regular route for dog walkers who had trodden the path to a flatbed of dry mud. Even the trees had allowed a route through them. With every ounce of energy left in his legs, Harvey ploughed on. His downhill strides increased in length as gravity took hold. Then he broke through the tree line at the foot of the hill and entered a wide open field dominated by long grass and wildflowers.

The gate at the end of the field was just a dot. It was a goal to reach like so many other gates in Harvey's life. A place or a time where he passed from one field to the next. One battle to another. One life to more life.

The dog walkers' pathway circumvented the wild grass at the edge of the field, beside raspberry and blackberry bushes and dotted with rabbit holes. But Harvey stormed ahead, as he'd always done, forging his own way through the field, through the battles, and through life.

A glimpse of sun marked the end of the morning twilight. It was Harvey's favourite time, when enough light spilled across the earth to see the day after the night. But few did see it every morning.

For the last three hundred metres, Harvey gave everything he had. He searched deep for some pocket of power that his body had stored, some piece of mental strength that he needed now, to push harder than before.

Harvey slammed into the gate at full speed, using the flex of the wood to absorb his momentum. Then, with his hands raised behind his head, he stretched while gaining control of his pulse. A single bead of sweat ran down his face, hung from his chin, and then fell away as he lowered himself to his knees. The thunder of his heart in his ears eased to reveal a new sound, foreign to the early morning. The nearby thump of twin rotor blades grew closer as his body quietened. In the sky to his right, above the raised railway embankment, a helicopter hovered against the dawning sky with a bright spotlight washing from side to side and heading his way.

Dogs barked and deep voices called out, anxious and angry, like the voices of military men.

The five-hundred-yard walk back to his small house was Harvey's warm down. In his younger years, he would have run the entire way. But with each passing year, the warm down seemed to be getting longer. Harvey didn't mind. The time gave him thinking space. But the circling chopper was growing closer with each step. Whatever the police were looking for, Harvey wanted nothing to do with it. There were only three hundred yards to the main road, where Harvey could cross the small country lane and head into the fields to his small farmhouse by the beach, where a log fire would warm him and the views of the Mediterranean would occupy his mind.

He ducked beneath a copse of trees as the helicopter made a pass. The noise was deafening in the early morning silence. But it faded as the helicopter circled back towards the railway, giving Harvey a window to escape to the forest and into the fields behind his house, leaving whatever was happening behind him.

The roof of his house was visible through the trees and beyond the road. A thin wisp of smoke from the chimney, barely visible in the half-light, let Harvey know that the logs in his fireplace would need replacing.

Approaching the road, with just a wide ditch to hurdle, Harvey sprinted to make the jump, launching from his right foot and stretching out with his left leg.

But something stopped him mid-jump.

Two hands reached up and caught his foot then dragged him to the ground, where he slammed gut-first into the far side of the ditch. He rolled in time to see a girl throw herself at him. Her contorted face was a mix of anger and terror, and her muddied fingers were outstretched, ready to rip at his throat.

Harvey rolled to one side, avoiding the wild girl's hands,

then doubled back to pin her down. She landed with his leg across her back and his hand on her neck, forcing her face into the mud.

"Let me go," she begged, her voice muffled by the long grass. "Please. Let me go."

"Who are you?" said Harvey.

But the girl hesitated.

Harvey pushed harder.

In the distance, the thumps of the helicopter's rotors grew louder.

"Are they looking for you?" said Harvey.

Again, the girl failed to respond.

But as the helicopter grew closer, with surprising strength and agility, and in one smooth move, the girl twisted from Harvey's grip until they were face to face. She then slipped beneath him, like a slippery eel, and dropped back into the ditch.

Harvey spun around to find her pulling the long grass over herself and sitting with her back against the wall of the ditch. The helicopter slowed then dropped to a hover, sending loose grass and debris scattering across the field.

Harvey climbed to his feet as the chopper came down, then brushed the mud from his legs, catching the girl's wide, fearful eyes as he did.

A silent plea for Harvey's silence.

The helicopter doors opened on both sides.

Harvey glanced at the girl.

"Please help me," she mouthed.

CHAPTER THREE

"Find her," screamed Cassius Kane, before sweeping the contents of his walnut-wood desk onto the floor.

"We're trying, sir," said Jones.

"Someone is going to pay for this," said Kane. He kicked his desk telephone across the room and stepped out from the mess. Then he turned and raised a single index finger at Jones. "I've got one dead girl who looks as if she's been eaten by dogs and one missing girl who knows enough to have us put away for life. Everything the law would need to lock us up for good is in that girl's head and running through her veins."

"I'm aware-"

"Don't stand there and tell me what you're aware of. What are you doing here anyway? The last time I looked, she was out there somewhere, not in here."

"We're searching the area," said Jones. "It's like she vanished into thin air."

"If you don't find her, Jones, it's game over for all of us. You, me, and every single one of your men."

"We'll find her, sir."

"This isn't the military now, Jones. We don't have the

luxury of the government on our side. We crossed that line a long time ago. All she has to do is point us out."

"I'm aware of who we are, sir, and what we've done. And so are the men."

"Exactly how far are you willing to go?" said Kane. "And your men? How many of them would die for the cause?"

"Every single one of them. I can vouch for them."

"We're riding a thin line. If we succeed, we'll have a future. But if we fail, it's game over for all of us. We're talking life in prison here, Jones. No parole. No visitors. We'd all vanish like farts in the wind. We wouldn't even get an extra pillow if we asked for it. Do you understand the gravity of the situation?"

"I understand, sir. I remember the deal," replied Jones. The vein on his temple stood proud and blue as he cocked his head to one side. "You fund the project. We keep it secure."

"And have I funded the project, Jones?"

"Yes, sir."

"And have you kept it secure?"

Jones sucked at his top lip, which accentuated his lean features.

"No," said Kane. "No, you haven't."

"It would help if we had a few more details, sir," said Jones, meeting Kane's stare.

"Details?"

"What are we up against here?" said Jones. "We found two of our men with their throats torn out this morning."

Kane's eye twitched at the news.

"And it wasn't dogs, sir," said Jones.

"It's just a girl, Jones," said Kane, planting his hands behind his back and pacing the length of the room.

"Sir, we need to know the truth. We know it's some kind of drug. If it was *just* a girl, two of my men would still be alive."

"Do you have any idea at all where she went?" asked Kane,

ignoring Jones' whining and performing a relaxed turn to set his pacing off in the other direction.

"All we have is a pile of her clothes. The smart little bitch tore them off to throw the dogs off her scent," said Jones.

Kane stepped across to the window. His silver hair appeared almost blonde in the reflection, but the lines beneath his eyes were clear as the daylight now hovering over the horizon, where in the distance, the town of Saint-Pierre sat peacefully beside the calm waters of the Mediterranean.

"I want her alive, Jones," said Kane. He felt his eye twitch once more. "I've worked too hard to clear our names. I won't let this little French tart ruin it for us."

"It's freezing out there. No-one could survive the night without clothes. If we do find her, there's a good chance she'll be dead already."

"You don't know who we're dealing with here," said Kane.

"It's just a girl, you said."

"It's a girl alright. It was you who kidnapped her. I just enhanced her," said Kane. He smiled at Jones in the window. "Doctor Farrow has been pumping her full of chemicals for a month. She's high as a kite, charged like a battery and, by all accounts, doesn't die easily."

"Pumped her full of what?" said Jones. "What is she capable of? She tore the throats out of our team, sir, two fully grown men twice her weight and size."

"She's just getting started," said Kane. "But she'll hit withdrawal soon and come begging for more."

"Just getting started, sir? We only have fifteen men. We're down to thirteen and the prime minister arrives in two days' time. If I'm sending men to get her, I want to know what she can and cannot do. Know your enemy, sir. The first rule of war. You taught me that."

"She's not superhuman, Jones. This isn't some miracle drug

that Doctor Farrow has been concocting like some mad evil genius." Kane paused to ensure he had Jones' full attention. "But it is close."

Jones cocked his head to one side, a trait that annoyed Kane.

"Do you work out, Jones?"

"Yes, of course," he replied, with a subconscious glance at his body.

"How far can you run?"

"Before failing?"

"Yes," said Kane. "How far can you run before your legs collapse and your insides feel as if they're hanging by threads?"

"I've done a marathon, sir. I did it a couple of years ago," said Jones. "Aside from that, the army made me run every day."

"But to do that marathon, you had to pace yourself, right? You didn't just run flat out for twenty-six miles, did you? And even the army doesn't make you sprint until you collapse."

"No, of course not."

Kane nodded. "You lift weights?"

"Yes, sir," said Jones, with another glance at his arms. "I stay in shape. You know I do."

"And what happens when you hit the end of a session? You can barely lift your own arms, right? Your legs feel like jelly and your body screams for protein to repair the damage you've done."

"That's an accurate assessment, sir."

Kane nodded. "Chess," he said.

"Chess, sir?"

"Do you play?" said Kane.

"I've never really been one for board games, sir."

"Do you read, at least?" said Kane, unsurprised at the lack of intellect displayed by his second in command.

"Yes, sir. I read."

"And what do you read? Please tell me it's not the Beano."

"No. Books, sir. I like books."

"Good. What was the last book you read?"

"I don't know," said Jones, cocking his head once more and staring at the ceiling as he tried to remember the name of a book.

"Okay. Okay. Enough of the mental challenges, Jones." Kane pushed off the window sill and stepped back to his desk. He picked up his phone and scattered papers, then began to arrange them into a neat pile. "What if I told you that Doctor Farrow's creation could make you run a marathon flat out? No stopping."

"Sprinting?"

"Sprinting, Jones, from start to finish. And those training sessions when your legs feel like jelly and you can barely lift your arms? You could go for another hour at least."

"Respectfully, sir, that's not possible."

"Au contraire, Jonesy. You see, the drug is split into two separate chemicals. The first one, when taken individually, can push your body to the maximum. It finds those resources your body stores away, and when those are depleted, it'll eat away at things the body doesn't need and transform them into energy."

"Like what?"

"Like fat, Jones. Like tumours. Even muscle if you push hard enough. It becomes a living thing inside you, stealing resources from anything that uses your body's energy. If you push too hard, it'll start using the body's organs. That's what Farrow was testing."

"That's why three of the girls died?" asked Jones, his voice hushed as if they could be overheard and were disclosing secrets.

Kane nodded and glanced at him before lowering his eyes and steepling his fingers.

"They were on an early formula. Farrow has perfected it now."

"What about the second chemical?"

Pleased to move on, Kane looked back up at Jones. "What happens when you push too hard? If you're running and your body can't keep up?"

"I slow down."

"Why do you slow down?"

"I don't know. I guess my brain tells me to."

"What if that line of communication was blocked?" said Kane. "What if there was a drug that could push you harder than ever before and your brain was unable to receive messages telling it to stop? What if the harder you pushed, the greater the effect? The harder you'd run, the more energy you'd have. The more weights you'd lift, the easier it would become to lift more."

"I'd be superhuman."

"Not quite, Jones," said Kane. "But you'd be damn near unstoppable. You'd be in a self-fulfilling state. It's called SFS."

"Why did you ask about the reading?" said Jones. "I don't get what that has to do with it."

"Okay. Imagine this. You're pumped full of SFS. You've entered a state where every muscle in your body is running at full whack. It's not just your body that is heightened, your brain is a muscle too. You'd remember everything you've ever read, heard, seen, and smelled. Even the finest detail could be recalled."

"So we're talking about people with self-fulfilling states of energy essentially fuelling themselves, with no switch to turn them off, and who can remember the smallest detail. And we made that here?"

"Exactly," said Kane, leaning back in his chair and allowing himself a smile, despite the circumstances. "You're imagining what it would be like, aren't you? You're imagining how big those arms of yours would be. How fast you could run. How smart you'd become."

"It's hard not to imagine the possibilities," said Jones, running his hand across his shaved head, embarrassed by his selfish imagination.

"That's where you and I differ, Jones," said Kane. "While you are picturing how many girls you'd get and how they'd admire your body and possibly even your brain..." He leaned forwards onto his desk, linked his fingers and fixed Jones in his stare. "I'm imagining an army."

CHAPTER FOUR

Two men armed with automatic weapons dropped to the ground. Gabriella peered through the grass, her eyes flicking between the helicopter and the man she had thought was one of them. They took up defensive positions, scouring the field. A man wearing all black stepped down. His face was concealed by the grass but Gabriella recognised him, the way he stood with his back ramrod straight, as if he'd spent his entire life on military parade. He ducked low until he'd cleared the still-turning blades. Then he strode towards the jogger, who met him halfway to avoid drawing attention to Gabriella's hiding place.

Anxiety triggered a pulse of adrenaline through her body. She searched for an exit but saw only the road and more fields.

She wouldn't stand a chance.

The man in black showed the jogger a printed picture of Gabriella, gesticulating the direction from which she had run. The jogger seemed to remain calm with his arms folded across his chest. He appeared unfazed by the armed men who surrounded the chopper. The interaction seemed to take an age. Jones was asking questions, probably trying to trip up the jogger. But he responded only with shakes of his head.

Following the conversation was simple.

The man in black asked the jogger if he was sure he hadn't seen Gabriella.

The jogger confirmed with a shake of his head, while the man in black described Gabriella, holding his hand up at her approximated five-foot-six height.

The jogger shook his head.

The last question asked the jogger why he was covered in mud, with a gesture to his knees and running shirt.

From where Gabriella was hidden, the jogger appeared not to answer, only offering a shrug response and closing off the conversation.

The questioning finished with the man in black offering the jogger a card with a number to call if he saw someone of Gabriella's description. The jogger pocketed it without looking at the printed details then nodded, and the man in black signalled to both the pilot and the guards to wind it up and enter the helicopter.

Even when the doors had closed, and the rotor began to pick up speed, the jogger remained standing between the chopper and Gabriella's hiding place as if he was protecting her. He shielded his eyes, waiting for them to leave. Only when the helicopter had ascended, banked, and was well into its flight did the jogger turn and walk back to Gabriella. She stared at him with a mixed look of gratitude and uncertainty.

He stopped a few feet from the ditch, returning Gabriella's stare until she broke away. There was something in his eyes. A confidence. A history. A fearlessness.

"Who were those men?" he asked, removing his sweater.

"If I told you, you wouldn't believe me."

He tossed Gabriella the sweater and waited for her to pull it on before looking back. She tugged it down to her legs as far as it would stretch then gave him a grateful half-smile. Gabriella stood, but she said nothing.

The man pointed towards the beach road.

"If you go that way, you'll hit a town. It's about an hour's walk. Keep to the tree line and stay out of sight. You can keep the sweater," he said, then turned to leave.

"Wait," said Gabriella.

The jogger stopped but didn't turn. He took a deep breath as if he was aggravated. As Gabriella climbed from the ditch, the man remained facing the other way, defiant, as if nothing was going to change his mind.

"Aren't you going to ask why they're after me?"

"None of my business," he replied. "If you're mixed up in something, that's your business."

"They kidnapped me. I escaped. I don't know who they are. That's the truth."

"The men with the helicopter and armed security kidnapped you?"

"That's right."

"And you don't know who they are?"

"No."

"How long ago did they take you?"

"I'm not sure. A month maybe. They killed my friends," said Gabriella. She felt the tail-end of her sentence waver as the thought of Donna and the sound of her dying screams filled her mind. "They set dogs on us."

"Where?" he asked.

"I don't know. I've been running all night. I don't even know which direction. From Saint-Pierre, I think. But I can't be sure."

"Saint-Pierre is twenty miles away."

"I ran all night."

With visible reluctance, the jogger turned, giving Gabriella time to take in his strong features: a short crop of dark hair atop a lean face and piercing eyes. But she couldn't make out the colour.

"So who are you?" He asked the question like it was a duty he could do without.

"I'm Gabriella."

The jogger didn't reply.

"Gabriella DuBois," she said, hoping her full name might invoke some kind of response, some indication he would help her.

He looked as if he was going to respond, but instead, for the first time, he looked her up and down, sizing her up, until the stare became uncomfortable. Gabriella pulled the sweater down below her underwear.

"Two women are kidnapped. They escape. The captors set dogs on them, killing one. But the other one, somehow, manages to escape and run through the night, half naked. A private helicopter is sent out with an armed detail to find her?"

"That's right," said Gabriella.

"Then you're hiding something," said the man. "Kidnappers don't usually have helicopters at their disposal. Nor do they have an armed security unit."

"You have experience in such matters?"

The jogger didn't reply.

"You'll help me?" asked Gabriella.

Something in his voice had inferred that he might.

He looked back at the helicopter far off on the horizon and heard the series of barking dogs in the distance.

"No." His voice was void of both emotion and empathy. "I can't be involved."

"Just help me get somewhere safe until dark," she pleaded. "Then I'll move on. Please."

The man didn't reply.

"Please," said Gabriella. "If I stay out here, they'll find me.

Do you hear those dogs? They have found my trail. I know they have."

The man didn't reply. He checked the sky again to make sure the chopper wasn't returning then turned back to her. He was going to say yes. Gabriella could sense it. She bit her lower lip in anticipation.

"The next town is an hour's walk. I'd get moving if I were you."

"Wait," said Gabriella.

The man stopped but said nothing.

"You didn't tell me your name."

He turned to face her.

"It's Harvey," he said. "Harvey Stone."

CHAPTER FIVE

Steaming hot water rained down from the shower, filling the small bathroom with steam. Leaning on the wall with both hands, Harvey closed his eyes and let his head hang low, allowing the water to run across his skin.

The farmhouse he'd bought several years previously was his only possession, save for his beloved motorcycle. It was quiet, clean and simple, and exactly what he needed to escape the convolutions of his criminal past. Surrounded by his own few acres of land and the adjoining forests, it was a small pocket of peace where he could live out his retirement. The simple lifestyle required manual labour as he had to maintain the building. A cord of wood was stacked on one side of the house and his days were spent repairing the roof, painting the windows and tending the small plot of land. There was no television in the house and no radio, only his laptop and his mobile phone, which was ringing when he emerged from the bathroom wrapping a towel around his waist.

"Melody?" he answered.

"Hey, big man. How's France?" said Melody, unable to disguise her smile even over the phone.

"Quiet."

"Just the way you like it then?"

"Something like that," said Harvey. "How's London?"

"Cold and damp. Everyone's getting ready for Christmas. You should see Oxford Street this year. They've done a great job with the decorations."

"Sounds nice."

Harvey stepped over to the kitchen door and peered out at his small plot of land, making a mental note that he'd need to cover the small vegetable plot that Melody had started during the summer. In the reflection of the glass, his house seemed to have translucent trees across the walls, and the glow of the log burner shone like an orange window in the centre of his land.

"Are you sure you don't want to come and spend Christmas here with Reg, Jess and me?" asked Melody. "I could do with someone to keep me warm."

"We spoke about this already, Melody," replied Harvey. "I'm better here. Besides, I'm not really a Christmas type of guy, am I?"

"Oh, I don't know. I could imagine you dressed up in a little Santa hat. Maybe some tinsel?"

"You know I can't. I'm better off here alone. Things happen whenever I go back to London."

"Only because you let them, Harvey."

"Well, however it happens, it happens. I'll stay here and keep the farmhouse going. You enjoy yourself, and when you come back, we can spend some time together. How does that sound?"

"Like a weak excuse for not coming to see your friends for Christmas. You know we invited Tyler too?"

"They will understand. Tell them I'm sorry."

"Really? The famous Harvey Stone is saying sorry?"

"Well," said Harvey, "not sorry. But they'll understand why I can't come to London."

"So what are you going to do on Christmas day?" asked Melody.

"Sit by the fire. Go for a walk. I don't really know. The same as usual, I guess."

"Don't forget to cover the vegetables. It'll be cold down there by now. Have you done it already?"

"It's on my list."

"You have a list now?" said Melody. "What's on it?"

"It's a short list," said Harvey.

"So tell me."

"Cover the vegetables."

"And?"

"Sit by the fire."

"And?"

"Go for a walk."

"Is that it?"

"It's enough to keep me busy," said Harvey. "What's on your list?"

"Shopping. Drinks with Reg and Jess. More shopping. And I might meet up with some old friends."

"So you won't be sitting by the fire?"

"Reg doesn't have a fire."

"And you won't be going for a walk in the forest?"

"It's London, Harvey."

"So I guess you won't be covering the vegetables either then?"

"Only with olive oil before we put them in the oven."

"Doesn't sound so relaxing."

"Is that your sense of humour coming through again?"

Harvey didn't reply.

"You should relax more, Harvey," said Melody. "I'm liking

this funny side of Harvey Stone. Will he still be around when I get back?"

"That depends," said Harvey.

"On what?"

"How much time I get in front of the fire," said Harvey, still peering through the window. A light rain had started to fall, leaving wet dots on the small patio. He watched the drops as Melody spoke. The gaps between each dot grew smaller until the entire area was wet and small pools of water formed on the uneven surface.

"Am I keeping you?" said Melody.

"No," said Harvey.

"Well, I should go anyway. Jess is cooking up a roast for tonight. I think she's practising for Christmas day."

"A roast dinner?" said Harvey, imagining the spread. "I'd come just for that."

"So why don't you?" said Melody, sounding hopeful. "What have you been eating?"

"Fish."

"And?"

"Vegetables."

"Are you sure I can't tempt you? All your friends will be here. Are you really going to let them down just because you're afraid to leave the house?"

"I'm not afraid, Melody."

"So come then. You can make it if you leave today."

"Melody, don't push it."

"Why not? I'd like to spend Christmas with you for once as well. I miss you, Harvey. We all do."

Harvey sucked in a long breath, then exhaled and fogged the window.

"So that's it, is it?" said Melody. "You need to snap out of whatever cloud you're on, Harvey, and have a think about the people that care about you. Trust me, you don't have many. So if I were you, I'd be trying to hold on to whatever friends I had."

"It's lucky you're not me then, Melody," said Harvey, stepping across to the small lounge. He held the phone between his shoulder and his cheek, pulled open the glass door of the log burner, and placed four small logs inside.

"So should I call you tonight?" asked Melody. "I don't want to tear you away from your fire."

"Call if you want. I'm sure I can find the time," said Harvey, closing the small glass door and watching the flames take hold of the fresh fuel.

In the reflection of the glass panel, his kitchen appeared to be ablaze behind him. He watched for a moment as the flames grew higher and the logs settled into place.

"I love you, Harvey Stone," said Melody. "I don't want to fight. Not at Christmas."

"I'll talk to you later," said Harvey.

He dropped the phone from his shoulder into his hand then tossed it onto the couch. He stood and stared down at the log burner, feeling the warmth through his towel. Then he took a fire iron from the bucket of brass tools on the brick fireplace. Dropping to a crouch once more, he opened the burner door and buried the tip of the iron deep into the coals. Then, when the tip was hot enough, Harvey closed the door, stood, and turned to face the room.

"You've got three-seconds to show yourself."

CHAPTER SIX

The hard soles of Cassius Kane's service shoes clicked against the pristine, painted, screed floor of his purpose-built research and development centre, a U-shaped, brick building in the grounds of a disused factory. Behind him, Jones walked beside Doctor Farrow, a tall, lean man wearing a white lab coat and thick glasses, with a thin layer of hair pulled across his bald head.

"The subjects escaped from observation room three, sir," said Farrow. "It's just here on the right."

Ahead of Kane was a glass door. It was wide open, revealing a room with two gurneys inside and a small trolley containing a tray of syringes and a tray of vials full of prototype SFS. A thick plastic-coated cushion material covered the far wall and the floor was spongy underfoot, made of self-levelling rubber. To one side was a glass panel that allowed the staff in the adjacent control room to monitor the subjects. The door was six-inches thick with a similar cushioned material on the inside. Inside the frame, a large electro-magnet aligned with a steel plate to keep the door closed. Only those with an access card could swipe entry and exit to and from the room.

"So this is the observation room?" asked Kane.

"Yes," said Farrow. "It's one of three identical rooms."

"And the other rooms?" said Kane, peering along the corridor.

"All the observation rooms are identical, sir," said Farrow. His voice betrayed his attempt to regain Kane's confidence. "Only I and my staff have access cards. I've retracted all other access cards until we can bridge the design flaw."

"The design flaw?" said Jones. "But it was you who designed this entire facility, Doctor Farrow."

A bitter exchange of hatred passed between the two men in the guise of locked stares and tight lips.

"Let's keep it professional, boys," said Kane, as he walked across the room and peered into the control room. "There's no sign of a forced exit. No damage?"

"Nothing, sir," said Farrow.

"Jones, how would you get out?" said Kane. "If you were trapped in here, how would you make your escape? Maybe you could offer us an insight into the criminal mind?"

Taking the elevated compliment with all the grace of a bulldog, Jones ran his hand along the inside of the door, then did the same with the frame.

"And they had no implements?" said Jones, directing his question to Farrow.

"None at all. What you see is what you get. We like to reduce the distractions until we need them distracted. If we want to see them run, we bring in a treadmill. If we want to measure their strength, we bring in resistance machines. Nothing is left lying around."

"I don't see how they did it," said Jones. "Someone had to open the doors for them. My men don't have access cards."

"It was the night shift, Mr Jones," said Farrow. "There was nobody here to open the doors for them except the duty doctor."

"And can I presume the duty doctor was observing them?" said Kane. "Being as they were in the observation room?"

"Yes. They were being observed. Both subjects received a dose of undiluted SFS several hours earlier and were being monitored for deterioration."

"Deterioration?" said Jones.

"A comedown. Cold turkey. Whatever you want to call it. All subjects using the older prototype, the diluted mixture, without having a way of working the drug out of their system, experienced severe symptoms."

"Such as?" said Kane.

"Cold sweats. Fever. Cramps. Diarrhoea. Some hallucinated. One girl tried to tear her own eyes out a few weeks ago," said Farrow. "Her heart gave out before she could manage it fully and she died with her eyeballs hanging from her face."

The statement caught the attention of Kane and Jones, who stared at Farrow with incredulity.

"And you gave these two girls an undiluted batch?" said Kane.

"We had reason to believe the dilution was sending mixed messages. You see, you can take the drug, but it'll have no physical effect at all unless you give it stimulation. Otherwise, the drug will work itself out of your body, leaving you with trace elements. That's why they were getting withdrawal symptoms. We need to be able to administer the drug to hosts for everyday use. The vials in the storeroom are diluted; they are just prototypes. They'll do the job but the withdrawals will be heavy and the effects are less potent. If you're looking for long-term use, the undiluted version provides unmatched results."

"How do you stimulate the drug?" asked Jones.

Farrow glanced at Kane, who nodded his approval at disclosing the information.

"Adrenaline," said Farrow with a smile. "Imagine you have a

small army of men, highly trained and each and every one of them with this dormant drug inside them. And then something happens. Something forces them into action. The tension rises. Perhaps they're in battle. Perhaps they're performing a robbery of some kind. The adrenaline kicks in, triggering the SFS and the host fires into life. The rest, as they say, is history."

Jones nodded thoughtfully as if he was considering the possibilities.

"But if they were in the observation room, surely somebody was observing them? Where are they now?"

"The morgue, sir," said Farrow.

Both Kane and Jones raised their eyebrows in surprise.

"Doctor Harold Goldsborough," said Farrow. "He was one of my best."

Again both Kane and Jones stared at the doctor with questioning expressions.

"He swallowed his tongue. We found him on the control room floor. He didn't stand a chance."

"Did you just say he swallowed his tongue?" said Kane.

Farrow nodded.

"How does that have anything to do with how the two girls got out of here?" said Jones.

"It doesn't. But it explains why he didn't try to stop them or raise the alarm," said Farrow.

Kane ran his finger across the glass as he began to pace the circumference of the room. He stopped beside the door and nodded at Jones, who followed him, blocking Farrow's exit.

"You say only those with an access card can open this door from the outside," said Kane.

"There're no manual locks or handles," replied Farrow, with a growing suspicion of what was about to happen.

"And the undiluted SFS, would you call it a finished product?"

"I still have some testing to do," said Farrow. "But I'm quietly confident."

"And where is the undiluted SFS, Doctor Farrow? I want to see the finished product."

"We only made three batches," said Farrow. "We gave two to the test subjects."

"Well, one of them is dead and the other is missing," said Kane. "Where's the third batch?"

Farrow averted his eyes from Kane's stare and studied the floor.

"Farrow?" said Kane. "Where's the undiluted SFS?"

"I need some more time. I just need to run some more tests," said Farrow. "To be sure, you understand?"

"Farrow, I'll ask you one more time," said Kane. "Where is the vial of undiluted SFS?"

"She stole it," said Farrow. "It was missing when I found Doctor Goldsborough this morning. But I can make some more. I just need time."

Kane's hands flexed then bunched into fists. He locked his arms behind his back then stepped outside into the corridor, followed by Jones, who blocked the exit and pulled the door closed behind him.

"Where are you going?" said Farrow, seeing what was happening. "I can make more."

But it was too late. Just as Doctor Farrow launched himself at the door, the magnetic lock kicked into place. All they heard was a dull thump masked by three layers of steel and two layers of padded cushioning.

Kane moved to the control room followed by Jones. They could hear everything the doctor was saying through the internal microphones. On the control desk, among sliders, knobs and switches, was a round, green button marked with the letters MIC.

"This one," said Jones, seeing Kane search for the microphone.

Kane pressed the button with his index finger and it illuminated, green beneath his skin.

"The door works well," said Kane. "I should congratulate you on your design."

"This isn't funny, Kane," said Farrow. He slammed his hand against the glass. "You get me out of here. You'll never find her without me."

"Oh, I'll find her," said Kane.

"The tests aren't finished yet," said Farrow. "There's still a lot to do."

"Yes, you're right, Doctor Farrow. But, as you mentioned, we still have tests to run."

"So you need me?" said Farrow. "Let me out and let me finish the job."

"Oh, I'll need you alright, Doctor Farrow," said Kane with a smile.

CHAPTER SEVEN

Crouched in the kitchen behind the centre island, Gabriella prepared to defend herself. A trickle of warmth fed into her bloodstream and she felt her eyes dilate.

From nowhere, an iron poker swung around the corner where she was hiding. Gabriella ducked, rolled and bounced to her feet, swiping a knife from the block on the counter as the poker slammed against the wooden door.

"I told you I can't help you," said Harvey. His earlier nonchalant expression remained but anger was also shining through.

"I've got nowhere to go," said Gabriella. "I just need a place to hide until the sun goes down. That's all I need."

There was a calmness about Harvey Stone that was rare in men. He dropped the fire iron back into the bucket with the fire tools, then he let his head fall back, and rolled his neck as if he enjoyed the release of tension.

"You've got three seconds to get out of my house," said Harvey. "You've had all the help I can give."

"Just a day," said Gabriella. "That's all I need."

"Three," said Harvey, stepping forward, his eyes finding Gabriella's and locking on tight.

"Don't do this," she replied, holding the knife in front of her but backing away to give herself room to fight.

"Two," said Harvey. He took another step, forcing Gabriella to step back out of the kitchen area. Sliding a knife out from the wooden block, he spun it in his hand then extended his arm with the point of the blade aimed at Gabriella's face.

"Last chance to get out alive," said Harvey, collecting a dish towel with his other hand.

Gabriella glanced at the kitchen door and then back to Harvey.

"You wouldn't hurt a girl, would you?"

"If someone breaks into my house and threatens me with a knife, you'd be surprised at the things I would do. Have you finished stalling for time?"

"Just let me stay," said Gabriella, offering him her best sorrowful look and lowering her knife in a gesture of peace.

As quick as a flash, his knife cut through the air before Gabriella's eyes. She leaned back while returning the attack with a lunge to his torso. But Harvey twisted, arching his back, then delivered a left jab to Gabriella's face. The blow stunned her but triggered a fresh release of chemicals.

Three jabs with her blade were blocked, dodged and avoided by Harvey with a control that was, in Gabriella's mind, almost an art. She dropped to one knee to dodge a series of swipes and lunges from Harvey then slammed her knife down towards Harvey's foot. But he was light on his feet, switching stance in time to deliver a knee to her face. Reeling from the blow, Gabriella staggered back. Through her tangled mass of hair, she saw Harvey approaching fast.

She ducked and weaved to avoid two swipes of Harvey's knife, returning with her own, which he caught with the towel.

Then he wrapped it around her hand and twisted until she dropped her knife. Somehow, he managed to twist her over his back and launch her across the room.

Landing on her back on a wooden coffee table, which exploded with a crack of splintered wood, Gabriella rolled and got to one knee in time to see his oncoming punch. She leaned back, and felt the rush of air as Harvey's arm swung past and missed her by fractions of an inch. Then, grabbing a handful of his groin, she squeezed as hard as she could through the towel that was wrapped around his waist.

To Gabriella's surprise, he didn't cry out or retreat. He stared down at her, his lips tight as he fought to control the pain. His strong hand found Gabriella's neck, returning the squeeze with an animal-like strength. For a long moment, the two shared a battle of the tightest grip, and no matter how hard Gabriella tried, the tightness on her neck became overwhelming.

But she couldn't let go. Something inside her pushed harder. With her free hand, she punched out at Harvey's gut. But the man was like stone. The blows had no effect except to tighten his grip further.

A darkness crept in at the edge of Gabriella's sight. She continued to punch and continued to squeeze. Something inside forced her to try. But without oxygen, her efforts grew weaker.

The final punch Gabriella delivered was feeble. The squeeze she had on him softened to nothing, and her hand dropped to the floor to support her toppling weight. She looked up at him, his eyes black, his stare neutral, offering neither a look of compassion nor hatred.

As the envelope of darkness closed on her sight like black curtains and a rush of cold blood swept through her body from her toes to her head, Gabriella heard Harvey utter a single word.

"One."

CHAPTER EIGHT

Using a small hatchet, Harvey broke down the smashed coffee table into smaller pieces for the fire. He stacked them on the dry pile beside the log burner, burying the hatchet into a log. Then he moved into the bedroom to dress.

He found a pair of his usual black cargo pants and a white t-shirt then pulled on his tan boots and leather biker's jacket. He slipped his phone into his pocket then gave the room a quick glance and took a mental snapshot, a habit taught to him by his mentor.

In the kitchen, he filled a glass of water, found a straw in the drinks cabinet where Melody stored alcohol, then strode over to the dining table, where, bound to a chair by her arms and legs, Gabriella sat. Her head was hanging low and her eyes were closed. Only her restraints held her upright on the chair.

Half a glass of water splashed onto her face woke her with a start.

Her skin had turned white. Dark rings were forming around her eyes and her pupils were dilated, showing only a thin trace of her brown eyes. Harvey dropped the straw into the glass and held it up for her to drink.

The re-hydration did little to wake her. Though her eyes had widened, she stared at the floor with her mouth hanging open and a sweat on her brow that gave her skin a sickly sheen.

"Here's what's going to happen," said Harvey, placing his Sig on the dining table beside the glass. "I'm going to give you some clothes. You're going to freshen up, and then we're going to go for a ride. I'll drop you at the police station. Then you're on your own."

The girl offered no response. Her eyes closed and she let her head fall forward again.

A hard slap across her face woke her once more.

"You need to wake up, Gabriella."

But again, the girl just stared at the floor.

Harvey snatched his knife from his belt, slit the bindings on her wrists and ankles, and then hoisted her over his shoulder. He walked to the bathroom, lowered her to the shower floor, and set the water to cold before turning the shower on full.

Within five seconds, Gabriella was wide awake and scrambling at the wet shower walls in a confused state. Another five seconds and she was hurling abuse at Harvey, slipping on the tiles trying to get out. In five more seconds, she was out of the shower, shivering and hugging herself, until Harvey turned the water off and threw her a towel.

He stepped outside into the room, grabbed a few of Melody's old clothes, then returned to the bathroom and dropped them on the floor.

"Get dressed," said Harvey, then shut the door to give her some privacy.

A few minutes passed, which Harvey spent standing in the kitchen with his eye on the bathroom door wondering if Christmas in London with Melody, Tyler, Jess and Reg would have been easier. Then the door opened. Gabriella emerged looking refreshed and clean, wearing a pair of Melody's track bottoms and one of Harvey's white t-shirts, which hung from Gabriella's small frame like she'd borrowed her big sister's clothes.

She stopped in the hallway, her bottom lip sucked into her mouth and a sorrowful look in her eye.

"There's a pair of running shoes by the door. They should fit. You can have them," said Harvey.

"Merci," said Gabriella, as she made her way past Harvey, giving him a wide berth.

"Call it a parting gift."

She stooped to pull on the running shoes but staggered, unsteady on her feet.

From a distance, Harvey watched but refused to help. It was as if the girl was drunk. Even when she stood up straight, the blood rushed to her head and she had to use the door frame to steady herself.

"I'll be okay," she said when she saw Harvey watching.

Harvey didn't reply. He was enjoying the silence and the thought of peace and quiet.

"How far is the police station?" asked Gabriella.

"Twenty minutes," said Harvey, then gestured for her to leave with a nod of his head.

He gave the house another quick glance, making a mental note of the room, then locked the doors. The girl staggered a little in the fresh air, hugging herself for warmth. As Harvey pushed open the garage door, she peered inside, her eyes blood-shot and dilated.

"You'll need this," said Harvey inside the garage, and he tossed Gabriella a helmet.

"You do not have a car?"

"Coming from the girl who doesn't have shoes or clothes of her own?"

"I'm sorry. I didn't mean to offend you," said Gabriella. "It's just, well, it's cold."

Harvey eyed the girl who had just broken into his house and tried to kill him. She averted her eyes, apparently embarrassed by her comment.

With a sigh, Harvey removed his Sig from his jacket and tucked it into his waistband. He fixed his knife to his belt then slid out of his jacket and tossed it to her. Then he turned the key in the motorbike's ignition. It started on the first turn of the starter and idled with a low rumble.

"Have you ever been on a bike?" asked Harvey as he climbed on.

A long slender leg in ill-fitting track pants slid over the seat behind him and Gabriella's hands found Harvey's torso.

"There's a lot of things I hadn't done until today," she replied, her French accent becoming clearer.

"Is that right?" said Harvey, pulling his helmet on and sliding the visor down. "Like what?"

"Running from a pack of dogs, being hunted by armed guards in a helicopter, breaking into a house, and attacking a man with a knife. To name a few."

Harvey turned on his seat with one foot on the ground. She stared back at him through the open visor and shrugged.

"Just saying," she said.

"Hold on tight. Lean when I lean and keep your mouth shut," said Harvey. "And if you try anything stupid, men in helicopters will be the least of your trouble."

"So how do you think they got out?" asked Jones, as he and Kane stepped from the control room, closing the door to quieten Farrow's weak threats.

"It's interesting. I worked it out as soon as I learned how Doctor Goldsborough died," said Kane, letting his number two struggle with the answer for a moment. Kane delighted in demonstrating his superior brain power. He walked with his hands behind his back, a method to improve his posture with the added benefit of appearing relaxed even in the most trying of times. "The girl convinced him to do it."

"The girl? But she was in the locked room."

"You heard Farrow's complaints when we were in the control room. Did you hear him banging on the glass? Did you notice how clear his voice was?"

Jones nodded.

"Imagine. It's the middle of the night, and all you can hear are the seductive tones of a bright young female who is just a few feet in front of you. Maybe she let him see a little skin. Maybe she gave him a show. The doctors have it wrong. To them, the observation room is a window into the minds of the test subjects. But you heard him say it. If the body doesn't trigger the adrenaline, the drug waits. Dormant. Until withdrawal kicks in. The same goes for the brain. It's a muscle. Given the right stimuli, who knows what a person is capable of when the drug kicks in. For the right mind, that pane of glass is a window into the mind of whoever is sitting in the control room, late at night, alone, with just two pretty girls to look at."

"You mean, like a superior intelligence?"

"Exactly. All it would take would be for the girl to get the doctor talking. She'd be searching for a crack in his armour. A way in. But when she found it, with the right questions and feminine persuasion, who knows what she could get the doctor to do?"

"You think she convinced him to swallow his tongue?" said Jones. "Using just words?"

"Using her mind, Jones," said Kane. He stopped at the lab room where, on the white tables inside, sitting in neat rows, sat hundreds of vials of deep red liquid. The vials were in batches of five in plastic containers. "You see, Jones, the drug was designed to enhance every aspect of human performance. It takes brain power as well as sheer brawn and determination to win a war, you know?"

"So by giving her the drug but removing the chance of exercise or adrenaline, the drug concentrates on the brain?" asked Jones, struggling to understand.

"Yes. If the human body isn't active. For example, when you're at home watching TV, your brain is still working. It's the most active muscle in the human body," said Kane. "Even yours, Jones. The energy has to go somewhere."

"That only explains how she killed the doctor. How did she get out?"

"I think I know the answer to that too," said Kane, nodding

at Farrow down the corridor, who was pressed against the glass, staring at them.

"You think Farrow let her out?"

Kane nodded.

"Why would he do that?" said Jones.

"You want to know what I think?" said Kane. "I think Farrow fell for the girl's charm. He's weak. He made a mistake and he's covering his tracks."

"You think the girl convinced him to let her go?"

"I don't know, Jones," said Kane. "But I do know that Farrow's usefulness has come to an end."

Jones stared back at Farrow, who looked at them, trying to work out if he'd been rumbled.

"We need to find her before the prime minister arrives," said Kane. "He'll be driving into town at six a.m. By that time, I want the girl dead and I want your men in position. Is that clear, Jones?"

"Farrow mentioned withdrawal symptoms. How dangerous is this girl?"

"She'll be weakening. She'll be begging for a fix. Lure her out with a fix of the cheap stuff," said Kane, gesturing at the rows of prototype vials in the adjacent room. "Do whatever it takes. But do not come back here without her and the finished product that she stole."

Jones nodded.

"In thirty-six hours' time, the French prime minister will be making his way to Saint-Pierre for his annual holiday on his yacht. This is our chance at redemption. It might be the last one we get. If we fail, we'll live the rest of our lives in hiding, and I don't know about you, Jones, but I'm tired of living in hiding. I'm tired of disgrace. I want the world to see how strong we are."

"We only have twenty men, sir."

"You're right," said Kane, as he stared through a window at

the rows of vials in a temperature controlled room. "But twenty highly trained men pumped full of SFS will be a formidable force."

"Charlie-two, this is Victor-one," said a tinny voice over Jones' radio, which was clipped to his belt. "We have a positive ID on the girl."

The attention of both men was caught. Jones reached for the radio.

"Victor-one, this is Charlie-two. Go ahead."

"The dogs picked up her scent. We traced it to a small farmhouse on the coast. But there's no sign of her."

"Do you think she's got help?" Jones asked.

"I don't know, sir. It's hard to say. The trail ends here."

Kane took the radio from Jones and held it up to his mouth.

"Victor-one, this is Charlie-one."

"Sir?"

"Search the property. Find me the missing vial. Charlie-two will enlist the help of the local police. She can't have gone far."

"Copy," said Victor-one. "Will that be all, sir?"

"No," said Kane. "Destroy the house. Leave no trace."

CHAPTER TEN

"Is this it?" asked Gabriella, as Harvey pulled the bike to a stop on the beach road.

They sat two hundred yards from the police station, which was a single-floor, whitewashed building with shuttered windows and two weather-beaten, wooden front doors. The grounds were un-tended with long grass on both sides of the dirt track and fruit-bearing trees spilling their produce onto the ground below.

"What was you expecting? This isn't London or Paris. It's the French coast. Nothing happens here."

Outside the police station were two old Peugeot police cars and a black SUV with mud spattered up the sides of the paint-work. The Peugeots were parked in the shade beside the building. The SUV looked out of place as if it belonged to a visitor who had just stopped without parking and left the car to make a statement.

"So you're just going to leave me here?" said Gabriella, feeling a wave of nausea climb to the back of her throat, then recede when she swallowed.

Harvey didn't reply.

"Can you take me to the door at least?"

"The ride ends here," said Harvey. He revved the engine once, a single blast of the exhaust to demonstrate his impatience.

"Okay, okay. I got it," said Gabriella, as she slid from the bike.

She pulled off the helmet and let her long hair hang free. But the show didn't distract Harvey. He remained with his visor down and his eyes set on the door of the police station as if he expected to be rushed by the men inside at any minute.

"Do you have a history with them?" asked Gabriella, feeling her cheeks whiten; sleep beckoned.

Harvey shook his head.

"There's more to you than meets the eye, isn't there, Harvey Stone?" said Gabriella, fighting nausea with deep breaths. "I get the impression that you've tucked yourself away in that little farmhouse for a reason. You're hiding from something."

Harvey snatched the helmet from her hands, leaned back, and dropped it into the top box.

"Jacket?" said Harvey.

"Are you really going to leave a girl all the way out here with nothing but a t-shirt and pants?"

Harvey didn't reply.

"I guess you are," said Gabriella. She slid the jacket from her arms. "And they say chivalry is dead."

"Are we done?" asked Harvey, pulling his jacket on and connecting the zipper.

"I guess we are," said Gabriella. "I'd love to say it was nice meeting you-"

Before Gabriella could finish her sentence, Harvey dropped the bike into first gear. He checked the mirror and accelerated off onto the quiet beach road, leaving her to watch him ride away with just the glittering reflection of the Mediterranean by his side and a dark and stormy sky above.

"Goodbye, Harvey Stone," Gabriella said to herself, watching him fade to a tiny dot at the end of the road. She turned and began the short walk to the police station, going over what she planned to say in her head.

The building was small, a one-story cube with only a few small windows to keep the inside cool. It sat on a piece of wasteland, a baron collection of hard-packed gravel that allowed only the most resilient of weeds and grasses to climb their way into the sun. Behind and to one side, in stark contrast to the moon-like surface of the police station grounds, was the edge of the forest. Gabriella felt as if the land surrounding the police station had succumbed to the negative energy and corruption that grew like wildfire inside the building. It was, in Gabriella's mind, tainted land.

A single policeman sat behind a single counter that offered no bulletproof glass to shield him from an attack. Only an old electric fan sat with him, either to keep him cool or keep the flies away. A line of eight old wooden chairs ran across one wall. But Gabriella doubted that any more than two or three had ever been occupied at any one time.

The cop behind the desk followed her with his eyes as she approached. He sat with one leg folded over the other and a newspaper resting on his lap. Judging by the man's waistline, he hadn't seen much heavy action in recent years. A man's laugh came from the room behind him. There was an office maybe and perhaps a cell for rogue, drunk tourists. A single door behind the counter was its only exit.

"I'd like to report a kidnapping," said Gabriella. "Do you speak English?"

The cop just stared up at her from his seat. He allowed his eyes to wander to her chest before they returned to meet her stare. Making a show of closing his newspaper, he sat forward, leaned on the desk and collected a pen from a stationary pot, which, Gabriella noted, held just one pen.

"Quel est votre nom?" said the cop.

"Anglais?"

But the cop just stared back at her as if the thought of speaking English offended him.

"Gabriella," she said.

Again, the man stared up at her, waiting for a full response.

"Gabriella DuBois," said Gabriella. "D.U.B.O.I.S. DuBois."

"Date de naissance?"

"Did you hear what I said?" said Gabriella. "I'd like to report a kidnapping. I don't have time to-"

"Date de naissance?" the cop repeated, cutting her off.

"July fifth."

"En Francais."

"Le cinq juillet."

"Annee?"

"Quatre vingt onze."

"Bien," said the policeman, placing his pen back into the empty pot. He sat back and linked his fingers across his ample stomach. "Comment puis-je t'aider?"

"These men..." she began. Then she felt a warm sting of tears welling in her eyes and held onto the chair for support. Still, the cop stared at her, offering little assistance. She took a breath. "They kidnapped..."

But as she began to tell her story to the lazy cop behind the counter, the men's voices in the back room grew louder.

"I ran all night," said Gabriella.

But the voices. She singled out one in particular then stared at the door in disbelief.

"That voice."

"Madam?" the cop prompted her.

But Gabriella began to step backwards, moving away from

the desk, away from the cop. Even before the door handle turned, she knew who would step through the frame.

"Madam," called the cop, standing from his chair, confused by her reaction. "Où allez-vous?"

Three men, all bearing smiles, emerged from the back room. But the look on the desk officer's face and his raised voice had caught their attention.

The first man, a senior policeman with a gut larger than his deputy's, switched his confused look between Gabriella and the second man, who was wearing black pants and black boots, and cocked his head to one side.

"You," said Jones.

"No," said Gabriella, shaking her head. She bumped into the door, struggling to open it.

"Get after her," shouted Jones.

Man number three leapt into action.

Barging through the doors into the bright daylight, Gabriella looked left then right and found an opening in the forest. Behind her, as she ran, the doors crashed open and the third man gave chase. Tears leaked from her eyes and streamed across her face, pushed back by the wind. With her arms pumping as hard as they could, Gabriella prayed for the warm lick of whatever it was they had injected into her to rush across her muscles.

But nothing came but fatigue.

A gunshot rang out. The bullet found the bark of a tree and ricocheted off with a high-pitched whine. But Gabriella kept running. Soon, the only sound she could hear was the dull beat of her heart. She focused on one step after the other, leaping over logs and streams until the trees grew so dense she had to slow to cut a path between them.

Thick bushes sat at the feet of tall pines. The ground was a carpet of dry pine cones and scattered with leaves of autumn colour. Stopping behind a thick trunk, Gabriella calmed her heart and listened to the movement around her, forming an image in her mind of her hunter.

The heavy footfalls slowed to a stop. She imagined the man with his gun held out before him, sweeping the rows of trees for a sign of her. As the footfalls came closer, Gabriella prepared herself. The muzzle of the gun emerging from behind the thick pine trunk was the sign she needed.

With two hands, she reached out, twisting the gun and disabling the man's hands with his finger stuck in the trigger guard. A shot fired off and a small pile of leaves exploded on the ground beside her. The first blow the man threw was with an elbow. With his hands stuck on the gun, it was all he could manage, along with a sweep of his legs to knock Gabriella off balance.

But Gabriella was ready for the move. Using every ounce of energy that remained in her tired body, she ducked from the elbow and fell forward, pulling the man down as he swept his leg across. He came down hard on top of her, but momentum kept them rolling until they came to a stop with Gabriella on top, one knee on each of his shoulders.

She eased her knee forward onto his neck, squeezing his windpipe. With his hands still locked on the gun, Gabriella gave everything she had to close the man's airway, pulling his arms up and away and her knee down, hard on his throat.

The choking sounds and rustle of dead leaves fell quiet and the silence of the forest resumed. The man's hands fell limp, allowing Gabriella to release the gun.

A single shot to his head confirmed he was dead.

Breathless from the exertion and tension, Gabriella fell sideways to the ground, lying beside the man she had just killed.

Tears formed in her eyes and the harder she fought them, the more they formed until she relented to the emotions that had built up over the past two days. She curled into a ball and wept. Alone in a forest with nowhere to go and no-one even looking for her, she pitied herself. Even the birds in the treetops ceased their singing. The occasional branch flicked as a squirrel leapt to another tree. But no other sound followed.

Until, someplace far off, somewhere behind many trees and across a carpet of dead leaves and dried pine cones...

That voice called out.

Being a man of healthy routine and good habits, Harvey parked his bike in the detached garage, turned it around and killed the engine. He stepped off the bike, pulled off his helmet and slipped it into the soft helmet cover. Then he pulled the drawstring tight and hung the bag with the helmet inside on a single hook on the wall.

He entered the house through the back door as he always did, and scanned the room. It was a subconscious glance rather than a thorough investigation. Practice had taught him to leave items on surfaces perfectly square with their surroundings. Any movement or variation would stand out and catch his eye.

The iron fire tools had been moved.

Standing in the doorway, he studied the fire iron from fifteen feet away, thinking back to the fight he'd had with Gabriella. Had he moved them? Or hadn't he returned the iron to its place? But his confidence in his own methods far outweighed his doubt. Any discrepancy in the iron's position would have been noticed when he left the house with Gabriella.

With one quiet and smooth motion, he pulled the gun from his waistband and armed it, releasing the slide as quietly as possible. Even from the doorway, he could see the door to the bathroom in the hallway was slightly ajar. Another sign.

He stepped into the room, closing the kitchen door behind him, and walked through the hallway.

With the gun aimed at chest height, Harvey snatched the door open.

But nobody was there.

He glanced into the bedroom. The wardrobe had been ransacked. The drawers had been pulled out and emptied onto the floor. The contents of every box and bag was strewn across the bed.

A flash of light pulsed behind his eyes. Inside Harvey's gut, something stirred. The familiar feeling of his inner beast opened its eyes.

A dull thud came from the kitchen. It was the sound of the kitchen door closing.

"Gabriella?" said Harvey, trying hard to control the rage growing inside him.

But no reply came.

A shape passed by the kitchen window, quick and dark. Standing in the bedroom, Harvey traced the runner with his Sig. A flash of black against the bright sun behind, as the intruder passed by the living room window. Harvey continued to track him from the hallway. Then, as the muzzle of the gun lined up with the bedroom window, he fired.

Glass shattered and fell to the floor, and the moans of the intruder squirming on the ground came through the broken window.

Rolling his neck from side to side, feeling the click of bones, muscle and the release gases in his joints, Harvey made his way outside.

He slid the Sig into his waistband, stepped outside the house, and found the man lying on the ground beside Harvey's wood shelter, a small wooden lean-to frame he'd built the previous summer to keep his supply of wood dry. Inside the lean-to was the neat stack of firewood Harvey had been maintaining, along with an axe and a hatchet.

With one hand on the man's collar and the other on his belt, Harvey hoisted him into the air and slammed him into the wall of his house. The intruder's back bent across the wood pile. Fuelled by rage, Harvey held the man in black high above his head with his toes scratching the concrete ground. He slammed the man's face into the brickwork over and over until he could hold him no more, and let him drop to the ground.

A boot to the man's ribs rolled him onto his back, where Harvey could study his bloodied face. But he didn't recognise the man with one swollen eye, a broken nose and a claret-stained beard.

"Who are you and what are you doing in my house?" said Harvey, with his boot on the bullet wound in the man's shoulder.

But the man failed to respond. He made no effort to talk. Instead, he moaned at his injuries and stared up at Harvey with his one good eye.

"I'll ask you again. Who are you?" said Harvey.

But the man only smiled. The beginnings of a laugh came out but it was drowned in a cough thick with blood.

Hoisting the man to his feet, Harvey forced him against the wall inside the lean-to. He pulled his knife from the sheath on his belt, and put the blade against the man's throat, before searching his jacket and finding a wallet.

There was a European driver's licence with the name Frederick Shaw.

"Tell me what you're doing here," said Harvey, tossing the wallet and the licence to the ground. "You're not a burglar. You're looking for something."

No reply came.

"You came to the wrong house, Freddie," said Harvey. "You just pissed off the wrong guy."

He dug his thumb into the bullet wound, savouring the man's face twisting in agony. Spittle flew from Freddie's mouth as he fought the urge to scream. So Harvey dug harder, searching inside for the taut feel of tendons until he heard the scream he was anticipating.

The scream came and Freddie's knees buckled.

"You're going to tell me what you're looking for," said Harvey.

But still, he received no response other than a dry smile and a weak, bloodied laugh.

Harvey grabbed the man's arm, lay his hand flat on the wooden frame of the lean-to and, with one slick arc of his arm, he stabbed the blade through the man's hand, fixing him to the wood. A growl came from the very depths of Freddie. His breathing was short and shallow as if he were hyperventilating.

Harvey collected the hatchet from where it hung between two four-inch nails. He ran the blade across Freddie's shoulder as if deciding where to place the first cut.

Freddie's eyes opened wide, fearful of the hatchet and the lunatic who wielded it. It was a sign Harvey had seen a hundred times before a hundred confessions. He dropped the blade to the man's elbow.

"Elbow or shoulder," said Harvey. "Your choice."

The confident arrogance had vanished from Freddie's demeanour. He searched Harvey's eyes for a sign of weakness, a sign that he wouldn't go through with it.

But Harvey offered no such sign.

"I'll decide then, shall I?"

Harvey swung the hatchet back, but just as it reached the apex of the swing, Freddie spoke.

"The girl."

Harvey stopped. But he held the hatchet high, mid-swing. "What girl?"

"The girl that came here this morning."

Harvey didn't reply.

"We know she came here. Our dogs picked up her scent."

"Who do you work for?"

But Freddie just laughed. This time, it was loud and with renewed confidence.

Harvey completed his swing of the hatchet and buried the blade into the man's shoulder.

A wild scream rang out, and as Harvey lined up for his second swing, the agonised yelp evolved into another laugh. It was the laugh of a madman.

Freddie closed his eyes, laid his head back, and smiled up at the sky.

It was only then that Harvey noticed the wood pile. The top row was missing four logs, something Harvey almost never let happen. Only one row was taken inside at a time. Never one or two logs. Never half a row. Always a full row.

Freddie caught Harvey staring at the wood, and once more, his laugh filled the small space in the lean-to.

An image of the living room came back to Harvey.

He'd opened the kitchen door.

The fire irons had been moved.

The open bathroom door.

The blazing fire.

The logs should have burned down to coals. But there was a blazing fire.

As the realisation of what Freddie had done hit Harvey, Freddie erupted into uncontrollable laughter. Harvey stepped back and looked across at the house.

Smoke had begun to billow out of the windows and orange flames licked at the curtains.

The beast inside Harvey woke from its slumber. A surge of power pulsed behind his eyes. Sharp talons of the beast gripped his insides and, in a rare state of uncontrolled anger, he swung the hatchet back and aimed at Freddie's chest.

But it was too late.

The side of the house exploded in a shower of bricks, splintered wood and angry flames.

CHAPTER TWELVE

"It's just you and me, Doctor Farrow," said Kane, as he lowered himself into the seat and released the microphone button. Farrow's hands slid from the glass and hung limply by his sides. Somewhere on his face was an expression of hate, camouflaged by wonder, intrigue and a lack of understanding.

"Why?" said Farrow. "Why have me create all this and then moments before we finish, you destroy it all?"

"I'm not destroying it, Doctor Farrow. I thought that much was clear."

"If you kill me, you won't stand a chance," said Farrow. His voice had lost its urgency, as if his heart had resolved to his new prison. He spoke in gentle tones. "Only I know how to finish the project."

"The project *is* finished, Doctor Farrow," said Kane. He laid his hands on his lap and stared back at the doctor, offering him a look of compassion and disappointment. "Tell me straight. Where's the undiluted SFS?"

"I told you, I don't know. She must have stolen it when she escaped," said Farrow. But his expression betrayed his own deceit.

"Don't take me for a fool," said Kane.

"You're wrong. I've been nothing but faithful to you," snapped Farrow. "Even when you erupted into your little tantrums, shoved people around and set unrealistic expectations, who do you think stood by you? I defended you when the rest of the scientists and technicians threatened to leave. Who do you think kept this project alive? And now you repay me with this? A glass prison?"

"Be careful, Mr Farrow," said Kane, and he smoothed his lock of grey hair back into place.

"No. No, I damn well won't. If this is how you treat the people that help you, then I'll have nothing more to do with you. I'll have nothing more to do with the project. You can't use it. It's still untested. We still have weeks of research to do."

"The drug works, Doctor Farrow. We've seen it time and again. How much longer do I have to wait?"

"The drug works during physical activity, yes. But what about the dormant hosts? You saw what the girl did. Who knows what else she's capable of? We need to test it. We need to research and we need to make adjustments to the formula. You can't just inject people with it as it is. Not in the real world. There's too much uncertainty. And what is it you plan on doing with it anyway? You never did say. You can't sell it to the military. The research would never stand up."

"I'm not selling it to the military, Doctor Farrow."

"So who?" said Farrow. He began to pace the room. "Just let me out. Let me finish the job."

"Did I ever tell you about the time my father locked me in the cellar, Doctor Farrow?"

The doctor stopped pacing. He stared through the window, incredulous at the remark.

"What does that have to do with this? You're killing people, Kane. If this gets out into the wrong hands, there'll be chaos."

"I was an only child, you see. We lived on an old farm. It was a dream of my father's, I think, to have all that land. All that space. My mother went along for the ride. Back then, they did that, didn't they? Wives. There was no equality. If the woman spoke up against her husband, she'd be beaten. At least in our household, that's how it was. You see, my father was quite mad, I think. He was never diagnosed, but the signs were there, in hindsight. And me, a boy with all the time and space to exercise my curiosity as boys do, I was fascinated by the circle of life. How the birds ate the seeds my father planted, no matter how much it infuriated him." Kane smiled at the memory of his father's temper. "Then, through some kind of magic, the droppings of those birds would spread the seed. Somehow, through the miracle of life, that seed had sustained that little bird, given it energy and all the things it needed to live another day, and still, it had the power to bring more life, growing a new plant wherever that little bird happened to drop it. Quite fascinating. Don't you think, Doctor Farrow?"

"I'm a scientist," replied Farrow. His voice was low and calm as he pictured the little boy in Kane's anecdote.

"So I trapped one," said Kane. "You know the trick? A box held up with a stick and a piece of string. I sat there all day waiting for one to come along. And I nearly gave up too. But it's amazing what a little willpower can do."

"You caught one?" asked Farrow.

"I wrung its neck in my tiny hands, just as I'd seen my father do with the chickens. I felt the life leave its tiny body and I held it up to see it in the fading sunlight. I marvelled at how light it felt. How delicate life is. I sneaked back to my room and used a small kitchen knife to open it up. How wonderful life is, Doctor Farrow. It's a miracle how all those tiny organs fit into that little body."

There was a pause as Kane relived the moment when his

life had changed. But, feeling Farrow's eyes on him, silently waiting for the next part of the story, he continued.

"Curiosity got the better of me, I'm afraid. It wasn't long before I was opening up the feral cats on the farm. I was fascinated by the intricacies of their bodies, but naive to think that my parents wouldn't notice the smell of their rotting corpses in my cupboard."

"Your father found them?" asked Farrow.

"My mother found them. But being the devoted wife she was, she went straight to my father. She was fearful I was turning into a monster."

"And were you?"

"No," said Kane. "I was never a monster, Doctor Farrow. I was just a boy who was fascinated by the physical body. My father locked me in the cellar for three days straight with no food or water. No sunlight. Only the rats to keep me company. That's where it all began, Doctor Farrow. So when you talk about your research and what our little creation can do to a man's mind, I already know. I already know the possibilities of the human mind. I realised it on the seventh day of being locked in that little cellar. The curious rats with their tiny claws and teeth woke me every ten minutes. And the darkness, Farrow, darkness like you've never experienced before. They say your eyes adjust to the dark after time. But not when that darkness is total. When you're so far underground that your fingertips are bleeding from scratching at the walls and the door. Your forehead is swollen from trying to end it all, just to stop the incessant rats and torturous squeals and bites. All you want to do is say you're sorry. Seven days, Doctor Farrow, that's how long it took. When my body was at its weakest, my mind was broken, and death hung over me licking his lips, that's when I found it. That's when I found the strength to get out. That's when I became the man I am now. With nothing but a few meagre slices of stale bread that I had to share with the rats and a few cups of water from the drain, I found the strength to break free."

"You escaped?" asked Farrow.

"I did more than escape, Farrow. You never saw a boy so alive, so strong and fearsome."

"That's why you want the drug? That's the basis of all this research?"

"I know, Doctor Farrow, that the human body is capable of so much more. Instinct protects us. But what if it didn't? What could man be capable of if the measures that nature gave us to harvest energy, to feel fatigue, and to protect ourselves from ruination were removed? I know, Farrow. I know what they are. I know that just ten men with unlimited power, led by a man such as myself, would be unstoppable."

"You're as mad as your father, Kane," said Farrow. "You'll kill them all. All this will be for nothing. Let me help you. Let me finish the research."

"Oh, you're going to finish the research, Doctor Farrow," said Kane, taking delight in the relief that washed over his face. "In the absence of another suitable test subject, you're going to be my final experiment."

CHAPTER THIRTEEN

"I'll find you," called Jones.

That voice.

"I gave you a chance once before and you blew it. You chose to run."

Dead leaves beneath his feet crunched as he circled the dead body on the ground. Fifteen feet away, Gabriella hugged the trunk of a pine, not daring to move.

"The truth is, Gabriella, you need us. What are you going to do when it runs out? What are you going to do when your body aches for more? When you can no longer function without it? Doctor Farrow told me all about the symptoms."

His words elicited a desire in Gabriella's body; a bead of sweat formed on her brow. The skin on her back burned as if a fire roared in her flesh. Her throat, as parched as the desert sand, seemed to shrivel and crack like the leaves beneath her feet.

"What are you going to do, Gabriella?" His rough London accent conveyed the charmless smile of a man who held all the cards. "I have what you want right here. Do you want me to ease your pain? I can do it, Gabriella. I can make you strong again."

A shuffle of leaves scattered and his voice quietened as he

moved away. Gabriella rested her forehead against the bark of the tree. She stared at her hand. Her fingers twitched as if electricity pulsed through her veins. Her peripheral darkened and no matter how many times she blinked away the tears, her vision remained a blur.

"I'm leaving now, Gabriella. The choice is yours. If you want help, if you want what I have, then you come and find me. I'll be waiting."

A fatigue, stronger than ever before, came over Gabriella, weakening her legs. She clung to the tree but her fingers failed to grasp the bark. A wave of nausea washed through her body. Her burning skin and cold sweat found the forest breeze and she fell to the forest floor, breathless.

"Wait," she called out between gasps of air, using what felt like every ounce of remaining energy in her body. She squeezed her eyes closed as a rush of blood swelled behind her eyes. Then she crawled to the tree and lay against it as sleep seeped into her mind like dark molasses.

The crunching of leaves stopped.

"Show yourself, Gabriella," called Jones. "Show me you're not armed."

"I am armed," she called, and she felt the rise of acid at the back of her parched throat. "But I can't run any further."

"What about the vial that Farrow gave you? That's right, Gabriella, we know all about Farrow and the finished product."

"I don't have it."

"You used it already?" said the man. "No. I don't believe that for a second. You'd be high as a kite by now."

"I've hidden it. Somewhere safe," said Gabriella. "Somewhere you'll never find it. If you kill me, it'll be gone forever."

"Very clever, Gabriella."

"It's my insurance. Give me a hit and I'll tell you where it is," said Gabriella. She spat the putrid acid from her mouth. A string of thick liquid hung from her lip, but she no longer had the energy to care. "I just need one more hit of the prototype to help me walk."

"And then what?" said the man. "You take a dose and run again? Is that it? What about when that runs out?"

"It looks like you're the one with choices now, Jones. Option one," she called, recalling the choices he had given her the previous night. "You give me a hit of the prototype in your pocket. I walk out of here and tell you where to find the undiluted SFS."

"That's risky," said Jones. "Not much of an option. What's option two?"

"I put this gun to my head and you deal with the consequences."

CHAPTER FOURTEEN

The dust was still settling but the fire had exhausted anything combustible by the time Harvey came around. The roof of the garage laid on top of him. It was a single sheet of corrugated asbestos burdened with the weight of loose bricks and timbers pinning him to the ground.

He flexed his fingers and toes before trying to move his arms. Then he found room for his legs to move. But with nothing solid within reach, there was no purchase to push or pull himself out from the debris.

A small gap in the rubble to his right allowed a slither of sunlight to reach his face. He turned his head, seeking fresh air and feeling the weight of the roof on his chest as it rose and fell. But the stale, acrid air of fire smoke and dust was all he found.

He tried to roll, forcing the asbestos sheet up just a few inches, enough to make room for his body to shift onto his front. A wound in his leg screamed out at him, and the familiar warm trickle of blood cooled on his skin. With the smallest movements of his toes against the concrete, he worked his way toward a hole in the rubble, clearing debris to widen the gap as he crawled. Harvey's injured leg trailed behind, limp like a dead companion being dragged from the battlefield. With just his elbows and one foot, Harvey scraped, pulled and pushed until, at last, his head emerged through the hole in the ruins.

To force his arms through the gap meant the full weight of the roof crushed his chest. Eventually his hands, searching blindly in the open air, found a timber to hold. With a final pull, he wrenched himself free of the rubble.

Harvey rolled to one side, holding his damaged leg off the ground. Looking down, he found a shard of timber sticking from his thigh. His pants were torn and soaked with blood. He pulled the tear wider, exposing the wound, and reeled with pain as he inspected the damaged flesh.

With gritted teeth, he growled loudly as he worked the wood from his leg. Then, when the shard came free, he rolled onto his back, breathing deep and long, controlling the pain.

It was only when the initial sting of the injury had passed that Harvey opened his eyes, wiped them with the sleeve of his jacket and dared to look at what remained of his house. The entire side wall had blown out. The lack of support had collapsed the roof, which had fallen into the house and destroyed everything Harvey owned. The blaze from the explosion had burned through the ancient roof trusses, leaving just three half-standing walls and a pile of bricks and tiles.

Deep inside Harvey, another fire raged.

A brick moved close by then fell to the concrete floor followed by a shower of dust. A hand appeared from the far side of the debris pile, followed by an arm, coated in dust and blood. Freddie fought to scramble free of the debris, dislodging a pile of roof tiles that slid and crashed to the ground.

Rolling to his good leg, Harvey pushed himself onto one knee, wincing at the stab of pain in his thigh. He found a length of old window frame that had been ripped out of the house by the blast. Two long, twisted, rusty nails protruded from one end.

With the help of the timber, and by keeping his leg straight, Harvey managed to get to his feet. Then he hopped, dragging his foot behind him, toward the noise.

Half-buried under a pile of roof tiles and broken bricks, Freddie clambered free. Blood dripped from his forehead and neck. His leg was twisted at an unnatural angle and dragged behind him as Harvey's did. But Freddie's showed a glint of white bone through the broken skin.

Harvey swung the timber and buried the nails into the man's shoulder, eliciting a scream, long and loud. With gritted teeth and fighting to control the anger raging inside him, Harvey dragged Freddie away from the rubble. Then he dropped down onto one knee and rolled him onto his back, where he stared at Harvey with the same defiant amusement he had shown before.

"Tell me who you work for and I'll end it now," said Harvey, easing his own leg straight to stem the bleeding.

But the man merely coughed a spray of bloodied mist.

"And if I don't?" said Freddie, his voice choked with blood.

"I'll break every bone in your body."

But Freddie said nothing, forcing a smug smile between rasping breaths.

Finding a broken brick close by, Harvey took it in one hand, and without warning, he slammed it down onto the man's arm, crushing the bone against the concrete. Freddie's head shot up, but with Harvey kneeling on his chest, all he could do was growl and spit as the pain took hold of him.

"I'll ask again," said Harvey, adjusting the brick for a better grip. "Who do you work for?"

The intruder began to hyperventilate. His eyes forced shut and from deep inside him, a noise emerged, somewhere between a growl and a high-pitched whine.

Harvey brought the brick down on his other arm, feeling it crack. He held the brick in place for a moment, pushing the flesh against the shards of sharp bone and pinning the man down by his throat, who thrashed and tried to buck Harvey off his body.

But still, despite the sobs, whines and panting, the man refused to talk.

Reaching back, Harvey dropped the brick, took hold of the intruder's twisted leg by the ankle and held on as bone found nerve, and pulses of energy sent the man into spasms. His back arched, and as Harvey twisted the leg further and further, feeling the sinew stretch and tear, the man finally caved with a scream like a child. Blood leaked from his mouth. It spattered across his face and, as he lifted his head at Harvey, growling like a wild dog, it filled the gaps between his teeth.

Harvey raised the timber, resting the two sharp and bloodied points of the rusted nails on the man's forehead. Then he grabbed the brick from the ground.

Their eyes locked. The intruder stared at Harvey, pleading with his eyes to end it.

"Every man breaks at some point," said Harvey, his tone calm and soft. He spoke as a father might when sharing a nugget of wisdom with his son. "Most men will talk at the very fear of pain. Some men will wait a little longer, testing to see how far I'll push them. Others will hold out until they stare death in the eyes. Then they face the last decision they'll ever make."

"You're sick," spat Freddie, his throat thick with blood and his voice hoarse from screaming.

"The truth is, most men are weak. Most will cry. It doesn't matter how big they are. They'll cry like the day they were born at the very thought of the pain they might endure. You've done well, Freddie. You've lasted until the end," said Harvey, eying the two nails as they formed tiny dents in the man's forehead. "But this isn't the end. If you're thinking that all of this will be over in a few moments, if you're thinking you only have to hold on for a short while, think again, Freddie."

"Just do it," said Freddie. Then he lowered his voice as he faced his destiny. "Just finish me."

"I can make it stop," said Harvey, his voice quiet but loud enough to be heard above the panting. "Just say the words and it'll all be over."

"You'll never stop him," said Freddie. "He's too powerful."

"Power? Do you want to see power?" said Harvey. A flash of blood pulsed behind his eyes. He raised the brick high above him, locked eyes with the intruder, and felt the body tense beneath him. "You asked for this."

"Kane," said Freddie. "Cassius Kane."

Harvey stopped with the brick held high above his head.

"Where do I find him?"

A tear rolled from Freddie's eye, leaving a trail of pink skin in its wake, bright against his grimy face.

"Talk to me, Freddie. Where do I find him?" said Harvey.

But Freddie didn't reply.

He stared at the sky, still and silent. The rasping breaths stopped. The grunts as he fought to control the pain throughout his body silenced.

Harvey lowered the brick in his hand. He removed the wood with the two nails from Freddie's forehead and tossed the makeshift weapons onto the debris. But only when he climbed to his feet and began to hobble away did he heard a sound.

He turned and faced the dead man.

A radio on Freddie's belt crackled into life.

"Charlie-one, this is Charlie-two. Target is recovered. I'm bringing her in."

CHAPTER FIFTEEN

"Take the syringe, Doctor Farrow," said Kane. "You know what to do."

The doctor's eyes shifted from the stainless steel tray of loaded syringes on the trolley to Kane, who sat in the control room behind the glass. His feet rested on the desk and his hands laid folded on his lap as if he were watching a movie.

The show was just beginning.

"No," said Farrow. "I'm not a lab rat. I'm not one of your kidnapped test subjects. I am Doctor Jeremiah Farrow. I'm one of the most respected experts in my field."

"And now you're going to demonstrate what you can do, Doctor Farrow," said Kane. "I want to see the very limits of your wonderful creation. And who better to show me than the creator?"

"You can't force me," said Farrow. "Bring me one of your prisoners."

"You are my prisoner, Farrow. Do I need to remind you that you killed three of them and let two escape? So now, it's just you."

"I didn't kill them. You can't put that on me."

"There's five syringes on that tray, Doctor Farrow. On my command, you will inject the first syringe," said Kane. He flicked the power on the video camera and hit record. "The final test, Doctor Farrow. Are you ready?"

"And if I don't?"

"Oh, you will. One way or another," replied Kane.

He leaned forward and pulled a slider back on the complex control panel.

"What are you doing?" said Farrow, seeing his movements.

"Oh, I'm just giving you a choice, Doctor Farrow. I'm not an evil man, as you know."

The hum of the ventilation fans slowed then faded to silence.

"The ventilation," said Farrow. "What have you done?"

"I would suggest perhaps remaining as calm as you can, Doctor Farrow. You're aware, I presume, how much oxygen the human body requires?"

"Yes, I'm aware," said Farrow, eying the ventilation louvres at the top of the walls.

"Given the size of that small room, I'd say you have approximately an hour to live. Now, I'm happy to sit here and watch you suffocate. But what a waste that would be, Doctor Farrow. I'll turn it back on when you inject the first syringe."

"You're a cold bastard, Kane," said Farrow. "After everything I've done for you?"

"Time's ticking, Doctor."

Farrow unbuttoned his cuff, holding Kane's amused gaze in his own bitter stare.

"That a boy," said Kane with a smile, and released the MIC button.

Snatching the first syringe from the tray, Farrow prepared the injection. He released the air from the chamber, tapped the syringe to make sure no air bubbles remained, then worked his arm muscles to identify the vein.

"You never know," said Kane, more to amuse himself than spur on the doctor, "that drug with a brain like yours, you could become a *real* genius."

But to Kane's surprise, the doctor needed no more spurring on. He found the vein with the point of the syringe and administered the drug with no hesitation.

"All the way, Doctor," said Kane, watching with delight.

The syringe was pulled from the doctor's arm, and he held it up for Kane to see the empty chamber. Then he dropped it into the tray with a metallic clink.

"How do you feel?" asked Kane.

"No different," replied Farrow. "Do I get some oxygen now?"

"Sure." Kane pushed the slider up to the bare minimum until the fans kicked into life.

"So what now? Do you want me to run like the test subjects?"

"No, Doctor Farrow. I do not want you to run. I want you to stand perfectly still. I want you to think about everything you ever learned. I want you to reach into the corners of your mind and open the gates."

"You're quite mad, Kane," said Farrow. "You know that's not how the drug works."

"It worked for the girl."

"It worked for the girl because she was angry, because she'd been locked up for a month with all the time in the world to devise a plan. You want to see me escape? Do you really want me to convince you to swallow your own tongue, Kane?"

"No, Doctor Farrow. No. I do not want that. Although, it would be fun to see you try. No, Doctor Farrow. I want something quite different." He flicked his eyes to the stainless steel tray and back to Farrow. "I want to break you."

"Break me?" said Farrow.

Kane pulled down the dial for the oxygen feed.

"The next syringe, if you please, Doctor Farrow."

CHAPTER SIXTEEN

"How do you feel?" asked Jones, as Gabriella removed the needle from her arm. "Are you ready to walk?"

She stared back at him, her mind clouded with foggy memories of the previous day and uncertainty along whichever path she chose.

"Like I just woke up," replied Gabriella. Then she raised the gun at Jones as he took a step towards her. "No closer."

"You got what you want. Tell me where the vial is," said Jones.

"I'll tell you where the vial is when I'm somewhere safe, or you'll shoot me here and leave my body for the rodents."

"So let's walk." Jones pointed with his gun in the direction of the police station. "Ladies first."

"Are you going to shoot me in the back?" said Gabriella, as she made her way out of the forest, feeling the drug flow through her bloodstream and bringing with it a new lease of life.

"Not yet," said Jones, following her. "You try anything and I will."

"And the missing vial?"

"I'll take my chances with that one."

"So tell me," said Gabriella. "If you're so smart, why do you work for Cassius Kane? I mean, the way I see it, the men all report to you. You're the one they respect. You're the one they follow. Not him. He's just a paycheck. Am I right?"

"You don't know what you're talking about," replied Jones. "Keep walking."

"I'm just making small talk. But I guess you don't really have what it takes, do you? You don't have that vision. All leaders have a vision, you know?"

"I've got a vision alright. I've got a vision of you lying face down in this forest with a hole in the back of your head big enough to put my fist in."

"And there it is. That, right there, is why you will never be the boss."

"I can lead. I've got a vision."

"Yes. But to Kane, you're just a hired hand. To Kane, you're dispensable," said Gabriella.

She stepped across the stream she had jumped earlier when she had been running from the man she'd killed. The familiarity of the place, however fleetingly she had passed through it, came back to her with clarity. It was like she was walking a path she had walked a thousand times.

"You don't know Kane like I do," replied Jones. "With what he's got planned, we will be rich men. Our names will be cleared. Sure, I could start my own firm. I could take my men with me. They're loyal enough. But why would I do that when Kane can offer such a bright future?"

Ducking beneath some low hanging branches, Gabriella emerged and waited for Jones to follow. He came through behind her with the gun raised. In the distance, she heard the faint rumble of a lorry passing along the quiet beach road.

"Because you're weak," said Gabriella.

"Stop right there," said Jones. He stepped closer, ramming

the muzzle of the handgun under her chin and forcing Gabriella's head back.

"I know what you're doing. I know what you did to Doctor Goldsborough. You won't get me with your mind tricks. No more talking, or I'll cut your tongue from your pretty little mouth. Do you understand me?"

"So much emotion,' said Gabriella. "Just do it. Just pull the trigger."

"No more talking."

Gabriella laughed as Jones shoved her away.

"You need me alive. You're weak, Mr Jones."

"Move," said Jones.

"There's no need for the gun," said Gabriella. "I've got what I want for now."

"Just walk."

"I'm walking. I'm walking," said Gabriella, as she ducked beneath another low branch, pushing it forward out of her way. She took a breath and waited for the perfect moment.

"And stop talking," said Jones, as he followed her through the gap.

With the gun raised once more, he came through the trees and stood up straight just as Gabriella let go of the branch.

The thick bough pinged back at exactly the right height, catching him square in the face and triggering the adrenaline that Gabriella had been teasing into play. Once more, her feet and legs no longer felt like her own. The strides she took seemed long and endless. Jones' shot, which sang out behind her, ricocheted off the trees. The clarity with which the path lay out before her was a stark contrast to the blur she experienced from withdrawal on the way into the forest.

The white police building showed through the trees on her left, and to her right, the road beside the forest was as clear as day. She leapt a final ditch before breaking from the trees and landing with both feet on the tarmac road.

A screech of tyres to her right. Then the silence that ensues before impact.

Her instincts ablaze with sensitivity, she stepped sideways, turned, and braced for the blow.

But it was too late.

CHAPTER SEVENTEEN

The small coastal town of Saint-Pierre was a maze of back streets that encircled a small marina, which provided berthing for the wealthy to moor their yachts and enjoy the fine restaurants and bars. To one side of the marina was a small fishing port where local fishermen could unload their catch to sell in the famous Saint-Pierre fish market. The rush of traffic in comparison to Harvey's sleepy village was enough for Harvey to consider turning back.

But there was nowhere for him to go.

An image of the smouldering ruins of his house clung to the forefront of his mind and a familiar feeling stirred inside him, in the very pit of his stomach.

He pulled over beside a café where a few locals enjoyed coffee and cigarettes at small tables placed in a long row on the footpath. He raised his visor and caught the attention of an old man.

"Hospital?" he said, and shrugged, the international gesture for not knowing.

"Anglais?" said the old man. Then he mumbled some

French with accompanying hand signs to indicate that Harvey should turn right, and shouldn't ask any more questions.

Harvey nodded his thanks, pulled his visor down and entered the traffic. A set of lights had created a small tailback, but Harvey weaved through the cars then sped to the front of the queue on the wrong side of the street. Seeing a gap in the traffic, he kicked down into second gear and tore up the road.

Harvey slowed for a junction and his heart sank.

In the traffic on the opposite side of the road, two men stared at him from inside a black SUV.

It jumped into life as the driver pulled a U-turn. The junction ahead was blocked with cars so Harvey made his way along the outside on the wrong side of the road. The SUV driver followed, spanning the centre line and causing the oncoming cars to swerve out of its way.

They were closing in fast when Harvey ducked into the traffic, weaving at a crawl between the cars waiting for the lights to change.

The SUV driver's window opened and a spray of automatic fire whistled through the air above Harvey's head. He opened the throttle, revving the engine loudly. With cars either side of him just inches from his hands on the handlebars, he forged a path between the two lines of traffic.

The SUV followed on the opposite side of the road, creating havoc as cars swerved and honked their horns. The man with the gun continued to lay down fire in bursts of three, stopping only to change magazines when needed. At the front of the queue of traffic was a busy junction with the marina on Harvey's left and another turn on the right. The SUV drew up level with him. The automatic fire stopped; another magazine change.

Harvey chanced his luck. He tore across the front of the SUV into the right turn and merged with the stream of oncoming traffic. Wheels spun as the SUV followed. A glance in Harvey's mirror showed the huge SUV towering above the small European cars, swerving between them like a raging bull.

A maze of narrow alleyways cut through the rows of small, white-washed houses. Harvey dropped his knee, leaned into the turn, and accelerated into an alley. He put as much distance as he could between his bike and the SUV. But they followed. The driver sent the car sideways to make the turn. Then it straightened and stormed into the alley behind Harvey, knocking over garbage bins, smashing through anything that stood in its way, and leaving a trail of destruction in its wake.

Sirens sounded close by. As Harvey burst from the alleyway, across a road, and into the next alley, he caught the flash of blue light on the road parallel to his right. He slowed. At a cross junction of alleyways, he took the next left. It was a dead end.

Behind him, the roar of the SUV's engine grew louder.

Around him, the whine of police cars grew closer.

With high walls to his left and right and a chain link fence in front of him, Harvey turned the bike, dropped one leg to the ground and pulled the handgun from his waist.

The SUV skidded to a halt, blocking Harvey's exit.

The first shot Harvey let off hit the front left tyre. The second smashed the side window. And as the passenger fought to change magazines, Harvey planted the third shot into his neck. The driver crunched the car into reverse and spun the wheels, leaving a trail of thick tyre smoke. Dogs barked, disturbed by the action, and a German Shepherd jumped at the fence to Harvey's left, teeth bared. It snarled at Harvey, barked once, and then offered a low growl that diminished along with its anger. The dog returned to all fours then sat on its haunches and cocked its head, waiting for Harvey to respond.

Instead, Harvey kicked the bike into first. As the road ahead cleared of tyre smoke, he burst through, firing at the car as he passed. But despite the punctured tyre, the driver gave chase. The SUV filled Harvey's side mirror, slewing from side to side and filling the alleyway with its mass.

The exit to the road was ahead. But as Harvey kicked down into third to speed across into the next alleyway, two police cars skidded to a stop and blocked the exit. With the SUV picking up speed behind him and the road ahead jammed, Harvey was trapped.

He slowed then stopped twenty yards from the police. He heard the SUV slow behind him as the bare alloy rim scraped against the concrete track.

Behind him, a car door opened and a heavy boot stepped down from the SUV. But Harvey kept his eyes on the police ahead who were climbing from two small Peugeots, guns in hands.

Scenarios played out in Harvey's mind. The driver of the SUV had an automatic weapon, drove as if he'd been trained to drive, and wore military issue boots just like the intruder, Freddie. The two policemen each had a handgun, were overweight, and couldn't hit the side of a bus if it was parked beside them.

"Stone," called the driver of the SUV. Harvey put the distance at thirty yards and recognised the accent as English. But he didn't turn. "You have something of ours. Let me have it and you can go."

Harvey didn't reply.

"Don't do anything stupid," said the driver.

His voice was nearer now, as if he was closing the gap.

Harvey revved the engine. As expected, the two policemen cowered behind their cars and re-aimed their weapons.

"Put the gun down," said the SUV driver, his voice even closer.

Harvey dropped the gun to the ground.

"That's it. Put your hands in the air. Nice and slow."

Harvey raised his hands then rolled his head to the left. He felt the click of his joints, and then did the same to the right. Taking a deep breath, he waited. His eyes gazed past the cops and he saw, in the distance, a single building taller than the rest of the town. The hospital.

The moment the man's hand grabbed Harvey's wrist, he sprang into action. Twisting the man's arm backwards with one hand, Harvey whipped his knife from his belt with the other and slashed across the man's gut.

He stepped back in shock at the speed of which Harvey had attacked him. One hand on his stomach held the two flaps of skin together as blood seeped out across his arm. The other raised the automatic rifle at Harvey. The man's mouth was open, aghast at the wound. The rifle began to shake and even as he dropped to one knee, he fought his trembling hand, trying to squeeze the trigger. He fell forward onto his face and a three-round burst fire dotted the two police cars, sending the policemen diving to the ground for cover.

Harvey jumped back onto his bike, revved the engine once, kicked it into first, and shot into the next alley, leaving the two policemen cowering on the ground and the man in black fighting for his life.

CHAPTER EIGHTEEN

"The last syringe, if you will, Doctor Farrow," said Kane, as he watched the doctor pacing the room.

The doctor ignored his request. He lifted one of the two gurneys into the air and slammed it into the glass wall with little effect. Then he staggered backwards, drunk on adrenaline and fuelled by his own creation.

"Come now, Doctor. Just a little more medicine and it'll all be over," said Kane.

Through the speakers built into the control panel, the raspy breathing of Doctor Farrow could be heard as the oxygen ran low. The doctor staggered forward then dropped to his knees, one hand clutching his throat, the other feeling the thick, blue vein protruding from the side of his head.

"I need air," said Farrow.

"And I need results, Doctor Farrow," said Kane, his tone sharp and his impatience evident. "The last syringe, Doctor Farrow. Then I'll give you all the air you want."

A shaky hand reached onto the stainless steel tray and felt for the last remaining syringe.

"That-a-boy, Doctor Farrow," said Kane. He dropped his feet from the control panel and sat forward with interest.

But the doctor's shaking hand failed to grasp the syringe. His fingers fumbled and the syringe fell to the floor, where, on his hands and knees, the doctor searched for it. He moved his head from side to side as if only the very centre of his vision provided the clarity he needed to see; his peripheral was a mass of blur.

"A little to the left, Doctor." Kane watched as Farrow found the syringe and worked his elbow to produce a vein. "There you go. Nice and slow."

With a practiced hand, the doctor arranged the syringe. He searched for Kane through the window, but his eyes, blackened and dilated by the drug, failed to focus on anything beyond the sheen of the glass.

"In it goes," said Kane, like he was convincing a child to eat the last of his greens.

But the doctor, panting for breath, sat with his knees splayed, all willingness to live gone from his eyes. Shifting the air control slider forward a fraction of an inch, Kane teased the doctor with a blast of cool air then pulled it back and heard the fans slow to a stop.

"That's all for now," said Kane. Then he turned to the doorway as Jones stepped into view. "You're just in time for the show."

Jones glanced into the control room. He saw the upturned gurneys and the suffocating doctor poised with the syringe held above his arm.

"It's time, Farrow," said Kane, and he released the MIC button.

"It's time for what?" asked Jones.

"You'll see," replied Kane, without removing his eyes from the doctor. Farrow touched the needle to his skin and pushed the tip onto his vein, making a new hole beside four others.

"Squeeze," Kane whispered. "Show me what you've got, Doctor Farrow."

In just a few seconds, the plunger reached the bottom of the chamber. Weakened by the lack of oxygen and control over his body, Farrow fumbled to pull the needle out.

"How many?" asked Jones.

"That was number five," said Kane, who continued to watch as the doctor got to his feet.

"What's happening to him?" asked Jones, wide-eyed.

The doctor staggered to his feet with his mouth open and pointed to the vents high in the walls.

"There's an energy inside him like you never thought possible, Jones," said Kane. "He's had so much of the prototype that he no longer needs adrenaline to trigger its effects. Communication to his mind from his limbs and organs are numbed. He'll feel no pain. He's lost control of his senses, including the ability to talk, hear, smell and, as far as I can tell, see."

"He looks drunk," said Jones.

"It's similar, Jones. Right now, the drug is searching for any usable energy inside his body. His internal organs are being eaten and his blood is thick with the most intoxicating drug known to mankind."

"Adrenaline?" said Jones.

"That's right. Let's give him some air, shall we?" Kane slid the slider forward to full. Above him, the fans kicked into life and the doctor raised his arms in welcome at the cool breeze.

"Tell me about the girl, Jones," said Kane. "Are you sure she's dead?"

"Like I told you over the radio, she was hit by a bus. I stayed until the ambulance took her away."

"And do we have a problem?" asked Kane.

"No," said Jones, captivated by the doctor, who was shuffling across the floor towards the control room window. "No, she won't be a problem anymore. I radioed Sierra team to pay the hospital a visit to make sure she doesn't get a second wind."

"I was referring to the missing vial."

Jones was silent. He stammered then quietened once more.

"Jones?" said Kane. "Where is the vial?"

"Gone."

Kane turned to face his number two.

"Gone? How can it be gone?"

"She said she hid it somewhere."

A loud bang against the glass caught both men's attention.

"Where did she hide it, Jones?" said Kane, eying Farrow.

Another bang. The doctor peered into the control room. His dark eyes searched the room, and his tongue hung from his open mouth, dry and lifeless. He slammed his forehead into the window. Then he stared at Kane with his eyes an inch from the reinforced glass.

"She said she gave it to some guy for safekeeping."

Another bang on the glass. A web of angry, red arteries had begun to form on the doctor's forehead.

"And did you get this man's name?" asked Kane, as the doctor prepared for another attack.

"No. But Foxtrot destroyed his house as you requested," said Jones, hoping the positive news would counter the negative.

"And?" said Kane, more interested in Farrow's behaviour.

"He searched the house for the vial. Found nothing."

"I'm guessing there's more?"

"The man is Harvey Stone," said Jones. "Foxtrot found some ID. He's just some local guy."

Farrow's third head-butt split skin. A spatter of blood remained on the glass as the doctor pulled away.

"Good. Make sure Foxtrot one is rewarded for his work. At least someone is switched on."

"Not possible, I'm afraid, sir," said Jones.

Kane's head remained forward, but his eyes swivelled to find Jones taking a step back.

"Stone killed him, sir."

"Find him," said Kane. "Find him and kill him."

CHAPTER NINETEEN

A surge of acid bile rushed from Gabriella's stomach to her tongue; she rolled onto her side, opened her mouth and let it fall to the floor.

The familiar warm tingle in her fingertips ran up her arms like the last reach of the incoming tide. A pulse of blood rushed through her body, leaving her pale skin prickling as she sucked in a lungful of air and rolled onto her back. A throb inside her head kept time with her heart, which began to increase as consciousness crept over her.

Behind her eyelids, a bright light shone. It was enough for her to keep her eyes closed and let the pounding throb acclimatise. She lay back, controlling her breathing, as images from before unconsciousness flashed across her mind.

The trees.

The man.

She gasped when she thought of the man she'd killed, and her hands flexed in response.

Then that voice.

Jones.

The road, the horn and then...

She sat up as her last memory came back and she gasped for breath.

The bus.

But there was no pain.

She eyed her surroundings and found that she was sitting on a gurney in a white room. The clothes she'd been given by Harvey Stone were piled on a small chair to one side.

"No," she said. "I can't be back here again."

Darkness crept to the edges of her vision, a hint at the sickness that was to follow.

Voices in the hallway were muffled by the door but clear in Gabriella's mind as her enhanced senses focused.

Two men.

Wearing boots.

Not doctors.

She pulled the sheet from her body and slid her legs off the bed. An angry, purple bruise ran from her chest to her thighs, six inches wide with yellow around the edges.

An image of the bus moments before it had hit her flashed across her mind. As if to confirm her memory, a dull throb pulsed once in the centre of the bruise.

There was no pain as her feet touched the linoleum floor, only trepidation.

The voices grew louder. As Gabriella pulled on her clothes, the crackle of a two-way radio confirmed her suspicion. She snatched back the curtain that surrounded her bed and found a window with a view of the Mediterranean, a road, and a few small buildings. She counted the five floors to the ground but couldn't remember the lab being so high.

Or the bed having curtains.

A touch of the door handle teased her heightened senses in time for her to launch a chair at her visitors, which the first man took square in the face. He stumbled back as Gabriella tried to smash the window.

But it was stuck.

The second man barged into the room, stepping over his friend, and pointed his handgun. He raised the radio to his mouth, keeping the gun on Gabriella.

"Charlie-two, this is Sierra-one. Asset has been located. She has a pulse."

He stared at Gabriella, keeping his distance as if she was some kind of wild animal. The radio crackled into life.

"Sierra-one, this is Charlie-two. Good work. Terminate the asset."

He smiled at Gabriella.

"Copy that, Charlie-two," said the man into the radio. "With pleasure."

Three sidesteps was all it took for Gabriella to close the gap. She reached up, twisted the handgun, and two shots found the white plastered wall. Using her momentum, she planted her shoulder into the man's stomach, driving forward until they both slammed into the wall.

But the move hadn't earned her any time. The man returned the attack with a left hook to Gabriella's face while his gun was pinned to the wall above his head. The blow rocked Gabriella, but no pain found its way to her brain. Instead, she responded with a head-butt that flattened the man's nose. A second blow cracked his eye socket. But before she could deliver the third, the first man rose beside her and slammed the butt of his pistol into her face.

The shock knocked her across the bed, where she rolled and hit the floor. She slid beneath the curtains, searching for a weapon. But the two men moved fast. They snatched back the curtains and tore them from the rails then closed in either side of the gurney. One man on the right. One man on the left.

In Gabriella's heightened mind, possibilities flashed by. Take the bigger man on the right and escape through the door. Take the smaller man on the left, kill him fast, and then deal with the bigger man one-on-one.

She stepped toward the window, the sunlight blinding her. But as her vision returned, a shape appeared behind the two men that changed everything.

CHAPTER TWENTY

The hospital was a small five-story building painted white to match the surrounding neighbourhood of whitewashed houses and shops. A single entrance for ambulances was at the end of the short curved driveway. In a spot marked for emergencies only was a black SUV identical to the one Harvey had seen outside the police station and in the alleyway.

Harvey parked his bike on the pavement and entered the building. The nurse behind the reception glanced up at him, noticed the blood on his leg and the dust on his jacket, and tried to catch his attention. But seeing the sign above her head that read *traumatisme* with a number five in a small blue circle beside it, he moved toward the two small elevators without needing her help. He stepped inside as the doors were closing, just catching sight of the security guard who had been summoned by the receptionist.

The doors opened with a weak ping. One day a long time ago, it may have been loud and sustained but had tired from years of relentless use. Harvey stepped out into the corridor. He glanced left and right. To his right was a nurse's station. To his left were a few small, private rooms. Harvey turned left, peering into each one as he passed. Each of the doors were closed except one at the end of the corridor. Behind it were the unmistakable sounds of a struggle taking place.

Harvey stepped into the doorway.

Two men had trapped Gabriella, each one approaching from either side of the hospital bed, moving with caution and closing her in against the window. Collecting a fire extinguisher from the wall in the hallway, and with no hesitation, Harvey slammed it into the back of the larger man's head. He fell to the floor with ease. The smaller man to Harvey's right stepped back to raise his weapon. But Harvey threw the fire extinguisher at his head then shoved the bed toward him, crushing him against the wall.

"Shut the door," said Harvey to Gabriella, who jumped into action. "Lock it."

A single twist of the gun disarmed the man and broke his index finger. Harvey released the magazine onto the floor and held the weapon out for Gabriella, who took it without question.

Men began to bang on the door and shout in French. But Harvey ignored them. He dragged the bed out of the way and hoisted the smaller man to his feet. The man wore the same uniform as the intruder at Harvey's house and the man in the alley: a simple black shirt with epaulettes, black cargo pants and black military boots.

Harvey slammed the man's head into the wall.

"Cassius Kane," said Harvey. "Where can I find him?"

But the man said nothing. He stared at the floor as if he hadn't heard the question.

Three more times Harvey slammed the back of his head into the wall.

"Kane," he said. "Tell me where I can find him."

"You won't find him," said the man.

His eyes were squeezed shut and his hands reached up to hold the back of his head. But Harvey caught hold of his right hand, twisted his wrist and pushed it over the man's head until he felt the crunch of his shoulder joint dislocating, followed by a satisfying scream of confirmation.

The men outside began to force the door.

"They're going to break through," said Gabriella. "Merde."

"Block the door," said Harvey.

"But we will be trapped."

"We'll use the window. Just block the door."

"The window is locked. I tried it already," said Gabriella, as she pushed the bed to the door and tucked the metal frame beneath the handle.

Harvey grabbed the man by his collar.

"This is your last chance. Where can I find Kane?"

The man smiled up at him, dazed from the blows to the back of his head. Then he spat in Harvey's face. But his laugh soon faded as Harvey lifted him from the floor, turned, then launched him head-first through the fifth-floor window.

The window shattered and shards of glass rained down to the ground below.

"Are you crazy? We are five floors up, Monsieur Stone," said Gabriella, leaning against the bed with all her weight as the men outside tried to force their way into the room.

Harvey peered down at the ground below. The man's body lay spread-eagled on the concrete. A pool of red was forming by his head. A woman screamed and two nurses ran to his aid. To Harvey's right, along the outside of the building, there was a narrow ledge in the brickwork, level with the bottom of the window frame, and another level with the top.

He ducked back inside the room.

"Are you coming or staying?" he asked.

"What?" said Gabriella, eying the door and then Harvey,

who stood with his foot on the window ledge ready to climb through it. "Why are you doing this? Why are you helping me?"

"The man that kidnapped you, what was his name?"

"Cassius Kane," replied Gabriella.

"Can you take me to him?"

The effort against the outside of the door increased, and the entire frame began to shift in the wall as a fire axe attacked the door.

The radio in Harvey's pocket, which he had stolen from Freddie, crackled into life once more. So did the radio on the belt of the large man who'd received the fire extinguisher in his face. But this time, instead of the tinny voice with the London accent, it was a well-spoken man, mature and with an air of authority.

"Sierra-one, come back," said the voice.

Harvey looked across at Gabriella, who held the bed against the door as the axe broke through the wood. Two security guards peered through the splintered hole. Harvey pulled the radio from his pocket.

"Sierra-one, come back. This is Charlie-one."

"Is this Cassius Kane?" said Harvey, then he released the push-to-talk button and waited for the response. He remained calm and composed despite Gabriella's frantic efforts to hold the door.

"You must be Harvey Stone," said Kane after a pause. "You're becoming quite a nuisance, Mr Stone."

"Ditto," said Harvey.

"You have something that belongs to me."

Harvey didn't reply. He looked up at Gabriella, who said nothing but stared wide-eyed at the radio.

"Why don't you bring me what's mine and you can go about your life?"

Harvey stared at the girl, who pleaded with her eyes and shook her head.

"Do you know where to find him?" asked Harvey.

Gabriella nodded.

A crowd was gathering around the body on the ground outside and the door splintered again as the axe came through once more, widening the hole as two more men fought to get into the room.

But Harvey remained calm, considering his options.

"You're making a big mistake, Mr Stone," said Kane. "You don't know who you're dealing with here. Bring me what's mine and you walk. Enough blood has been shed."

Harvey depressed the button on the radio, silencing the static.

"Negative, Kane," said Harvey. "It's you who doesn't know who you're dealing with. You just destroyed everything I own. I'm coming for you, and I won't stop until I kill you."

CHAPTER TWENTY-ONE

"Who is this man?" asked Kane, and he threw the radio across the room. "He's clearly not just some local guy."

"He's taken down five of my men," said Jones, as Doctor Farrow planted his head into the glass. Blood leaked from several wounds on his forehead, and he gazed like an old drunk through the window at Kane and Jones. "Local police won't help anymore. They say it's too hard to explain a murder in the town in broad daylight. If there's more trouble, they'll be forced to get involved and make arrests."

"Cowards. They're just afraid because the prime minister is on his way. Any other day of the year and they'd be lining their corrupt pockets."

"We're on our own, sir," said Jones. "And either this guy has help, or he's-"

"He's what?" snapped Kane.

"I don't know. Ex-military? Special forces?"

"Jones, do I need to remind you that you have a whole team of ex-special forces men and this guy is picking us off like they're old grannies."

"I'm aware of my team's capabilities, sir," said Jones.

"But you're not aware of *his* capabilities. Know your enemy, Jones. The first rule of war."

"We can't find anything on him, sir," said Jones. "We've checked the police databases. We even had the local police check Interpol."

"Military?" said Kane.

"Nothing, sir. He doesn't exist."

"So who killed five of your men?" said Kane. "Who is it that has my vial? I want him dead, whoever this Stone is. I want his head on a stick and I want my vial back."

As if in response to Kane's mention of the vial, the doctor head-butted the partition once more, his breath fogging the bloodied glass.

"We're doing everything we can, sir. I've got all teams out looking for him."

"All teams? And what happens if he chews through those like he has the rest?"

Jones remained silent, unable to find a suitable answer.

"When the prime minister drives into Saint-Pierre, I want all bases covered. If we can pull this mission off, we'll be set for life. We'll have every government on the planet bidding for our services."

"I'll pull three teams, sir," said Jones. "Alpha team, Bravo team and Tango team. Alpha team will cover the entrance to the town. Bravo team will monitor the ambush site. Tango team will be the eyes in the sky in the tower."

"You're missing the point," said Kane. "Without the vial, even if we do pull this off, we have nothing to make us stand out from the crowd. We'll just be another rogue team of hired guns, and if Stone carries on the way he is, we won't even be a team. It'll be you and I standing there with our dicks in our hands begging for work."

"We don't need the drug, sir. I'm sure we can pull this off."

"Of course we can pull it off, Jones. It's not exactly a difficult mission. But I offered the men a future. I offered them a chance to clear their names, a chance at success and honour. That's what soldiers fight for, Jones. Honour. And in return for honour, they offer loyalty. That's how it works, Jones. That's how the system has functioned since the Romans and it's no different now."

"Loyalty isn't a question, sir. Every one of my men is loyal to a tee."

"Apart from the ones that Stone has hit already?"

Jones said nothing in response. Instead, he cocked his head to one side. Kane's lip curled at the mannerism he had always detested.

"Presuming we have enough men to pull off the mission, presuming we are successful, and presuming we get the vial back then we might just have a future, Jones. We might be able to offer the men a taste of honour. And they might, in return, offer us prolonged loyalty. Presuming the stars align and the heavens shine down on us, we might just get another job. And if I'm right, Jones, which I often am, we'll take that vial, and we'll make enough of it to last a lifetime. Our men will be unstoppable and everyone will be calling us. And you know what that means?"

"Money?"

"Blank cheques, Jones," said Kane. "That's when we get to write ourselves a blank cheque. What's that, Mr President? You're having trouble with the Columbians and their drug enterprise? Don't you worry. We'll take care of it. Oh, hello, Mr Minister of Defence. You need a village taken out in deepest, darkest Afghanistan and you can't send your boys in because you don't have one-hundred-percent proof it's full of terrorists? Don't worry. Our boys will take care of it for you. The same will happen with the United Kingdom, that very same country that trained us and nurtured us from young boys into the men we are now. The same country that took the best years of our lives, and took the best we had to give, then tossed us aside with shame after one simple mistake. You watch, Jones. If we can pull this off, you watch those bastards come crawling when they can't launch an attack because of some bullshit peace deal they made fifty years ago. When they're so tied up in the politics they can't see the wood for the trees, we'll be the ones they come to, Jones. We'll be the ones they call for help. And who knows? When that time comes, I might even offer them a free deal. A coupon, if you like. We'll go in and sort out their mess. We'll clear up what they can't. In return, we'll have our dirty, dishonourable discharges relinquished. Every one of your men will walk the streets with his head held high, Jones. Can you imagine that? Imagine the honour. Imagine the loyalty."

"It's a dream I have every day, sir," said Jones.

"Good," said Kane. "You keep dreaming of it. But let me tell you something. If you and your boys don't get me that vial, and if you and your boys don't pull this mission off tomorrow morning, it'll only be a dream. Nothing more. We'll all be downtrodden, disgraced scum for the rest of our lives."

"Understood, sir," said Jones.

"Stand to attention when I'm talking to you, Jones."

Snapping into life, Jones' right leg came up, bending at ninety degrees. His right boot stamped down beside the left. His chest stood out with pride. His back held ramrod straight and his arms fixed to his sides with his thumbs pointing down the seams of his pants.

"Do you understand the mission, soldier?" said Kane.

"Yes, sir," barked Jones.

"What are your primary objectives?"

"Find the missing vial, sir, and complete the mission with no fatalities."

Kane nodded. He stood from his chair, face to face with Jones, their eyes aligned.

"And how do you plan on achieving this, soldier?" said Kane.

"Destroy Harvey Stone, sir."

CHAPTER TWENTY-TWO

"You're coming with me," said Harvey, leaning in through the window. "Pass me the gun."

Gabriella followed his instruction and handed him the dead soldier's gun. Harvey took it. As Gabriella climbed up through the window and dared a glance down, he opened fire on the door.

"What are you doing?" said Gabriella, ducking out of the way.

"Buying us time," said Harvey.

"Well, now what?" said Gabriella. "I'm guessing you have a plan?"

Harvey looked right along the tiny ledge then back at Gabriella.

"This is all I've got," replied Harvey. "Don't look down."

The words triggered a rush of blood to her head. Gabriella felt the warm tingle of SFS strengthening her fingertips.

Harvey waited, half in and half out of the window, staring at her when she opened her eyes.

"What are you waiting for, Monsieur Stone?" she asked.

That seemed to be all the encouragement Harvey needed.

He edged along the tiny ledge to the corner of the building. Gabriella followed. Her foot stepped off the window sill and onto the narrow ledge just as the door crashed open inside the room. Two men in black uniforms burst through the broken window and peered out in disbelief. One of the men raised his weapon; the shot found the bare concrete wall as Gabriella slipped around the corner.

A steel fire escape ladder stood fixed to the building. The narrow ledge finished eight feet short of it.

"We have to jump," said Harvey, his fingers gripping just an inch of brickwork. The toes of his boots were turned sideways for maximum support.

"You first," said Gabriella, feeling another surge of energy, clarity and focus. It was as if only the ledge and the jump existed. The shouts and calls from the people on the ground were held at bay by her mind and drowned out by SFS.

With almost no hesitation, Harvey leapt from the ledge with his arms stretched out. His fingers just managed to grab onto a handrail while the rest of his body slammed into the steel framework. He slipped down, and just as Gabriella thought he would fall, he caught himself.

A thick drool of sticky blood leaked from a gash in his leg.

"Are you okay?" called Gabriella, as Harvey pulled himself onto the steel platform. He rolled to his feet and prepared to help her, his face masking his certain pain.

Gabriella pushed off with her right foot. Her left leg extended. Her foot found the framework and her hands clamped onto the handrail. She swung once to allow her momentum to disperse. Then, on the return swing, she hoisted herself over the handrail and landed beside Harvey who was crouched with his arm ready to catch her.

"Let's go," she replied, and stepped past him to the ladder.

A single gunshot rang out. The bullet pinged off the steel

framework above. A large man in a black uniform was leaning out of a fourth-floor window, gun poised to fire again.

Gabriella slid down the ladder with her feet and hands on the sides of the rails. Harvey dropped to one knee, aimed and fired, sending the man back inside.

Matching his speed, Gabriella landed on each landing as Harvey landed on the one above her. By the time she reached the ground, a crowd had gathered to watch the spectacle. Mobile phones were recording the dramatic video. Harvey dropped down beside her, limped, grunted, and dropped to the ground, clutching his wounded leg.

"We need to get you out of here," said Gabriella.

"You need to show me where to find Kane," he replied.

"But your leg. You need to get it looked at."

Harvey didn't reply. He stood, took a breath, and searched around him at the faces of the crowds that were snapping shots as if they were celebrities. He grabbed Gabriella's hand and made his way to the front of the hospital, barging through the crowd. Gabriella followed, hiding her face from the phones. This time, Harvey didn't hand her a helmet. Nor did he give her any instructions. He started the engine, waited for Gabriella to climb onto the bike, then roared off across the manicured lawn into the heavy traffic.

The black SUV swung onto the main road behind them as the driver fought to hold the turn with all four tyres screeching. He locked onto Gabriella and Harvey, and accelerated hard.

Gabriella tapped Harvey on the shoulder and leaned into his ear.

"They're behind us," she called.

Harvey glanced into his mirror, saw the SUV approaching, and then turned suddenly into a side street away from the marina and up a small hill. The SUV followed with speed. Harvey slowed the bike until the SUV was just a few seconds away then jammed on the rear brake, sliding the bike around to face the car head on.

He flicked up his visor, raised his weapon and aimed, finding the accelerating SUV along the short length of the handgun.

The driver's head became clear through the windshield.

Still, the SUV accelerated towards them, now only one hundred yards away.

"Monsieur Stone," said Gabriella.

Her weight shifted as if she was preparing to jump from the bike.

Harvey fingered the trigger, letting the steel bed into the first crevice of his index finger.

"*Monsieur Stone,*" said Gabriella once more, as the vehicle closed in at forty yards with no intention of avoiding them.

Harvey squeezed the trigger.

One shot killed the driver.

The SUV turned, slammed into the line of parked cars and flipped. All four wheels left the ground and the huge car completed a full roll before it crashed down on its roof, embedding its front end into the windshield of a parked van. Shopkeepers emerged from their doorways and passers-by fled to spectate from a safe distance.

The carnage came to a stop.

Broken glass fell to the tarmac road.

A hand appeared through the gap where the windscreen had been.

The passenger of the SUV crawled from the broken window and fell to the ground in a heap among the glass. His face was a bloodied mess. Harvey kicked down the bike stand and dismounted. He limped over to the man, gun in hand and oblivious to the spectators or the approaching sirens.

Gabriella remained on the bike. She watched as Harvey stood over the man on the ground.

"No, Monsieur Stone," she called.

But it was too late.

Harvey raised his gun. Aimed. Pulled the trigger.

Harvey returned to the bike and shoved the gun into his waistband. "You and I need to talk." He stood in front of Gabriella with his hands on his hips. "What does Kane want with you?"

"Who knows?" said Gabriella with a shrug. But she knew it was not convincing. "Are you going after him?" she asked, in an effort to steer him away from the truth.

"He destroyed everything I own," said Harvey, then he climbed onto the bike.

"I can help," said Gabriella.

"And why would you do that?" said Harvey, kicking the bike stand back up.

Gabriella hesitated, but Harvey waited for her response.

"He's planning to kill the prime minister."

CHAPTER TWENTY-THREE

Sirens in all directions wailed across the small town, growing louder as the net closed in on Harvey and Gabriella.

"It's Kane," said Gabriella, "he's paid the police off."

"We need to go."

Harvey climbed onto the bike as a police car came screeching into the road from the marina. As Gabriella slid on behind him, he kicked into first gear, opened the throttle and spun the rear wheel, holding the front brake until the bike had turned a full one hundred and eighty degrees to head out of the town. Open-mouthed onlookers were buried in the tyre smoke, and only the shrill whistle of the sirens cut through the roar of Harvey's bike.

They breached a small hill at the edge of town, only to find two police Peugeots waiting for them and parked in a V-shape blocking the road ahead. With the police car behind them approaching fast, Harvey tore into an alleyway at full speed. Both sides, the backs of houses opened up into small courtyards, and ahead, tall pines marked the edge of the town and the start of the forest.

Bursting from one alleyway without stopping, they sped

across the road and into another. Gabriella tapped Harvey on the shoulder and leaned into him.

"They are behind us, Monsieur Stone. Two police cars and another big black car. What should I do?"

"Hold on tight," said Harvey, as they approached the end of the last alleyway.

He slowed the bike to make the turn at the end onto the road then opened the throttle and headed back towards the town.

"Are we trapped?" said Gabriella.

Harvey didn't reply.

He cut through the traffic on the marina road, and used the opposite lane to put some distance between him and the men in black. The wind rushed past, stinging his eyes, and the biting cold gnawed at his hands. Still, the black SUV followed, bullying the oncoming traffic out of its way.

Harvey slowed once more, preparing to turn onto the road out of town after completing a full circle of Saint-Pierre. A large lorry nosed into view, turning toward Harvey's speeding bike.

The black SUV roared up behind them, its grill inches from Harvey's back wheel.

Harvey pulled his weapon from his belt and steered into the path of the lorry.

Seeing Harvey's maneuverer, the lorry driver pulled on the horn, the anger on his face clear even from two hundred yards away, and turned the steering wheel hard to avoid a collision.

The SUV nudged the back of the bike.

Harvey accelerated away at the last minute, aiming his gun with one hand as he passed the turning lorry, and firing a single shot into its off-side tyre.

The shift in weight along with the driver's hard turn sent the lorry leaning over. As Harvey braked hard to make the turn out of town, a quick glance in his mirror showed the toppling lorry and the SUV that buried itself into it. Speeding police Peugeots followed a few seconds later.

Once out of town, Harvey made for the forest, where he stopped the bike in a copse of trees atop the tallest hill for miles around. Behind them, at the foot of the hill, Saint-Pierre lay sprawled across the valley between the two surrounding mountains that met the sea. The noises of the sirens continued in the distance. But Harvey and Gabriella's escape had been successful.

"Tell me everything you know," said Harvey, as he checked the magazine in his Sig and found just one round remaining.

Stepping off the bike, he stumbled on his injured leg. He grimaced but held the pain inside.

"I have told you everything, Monsieur Stone," said Gabriella, eying his leg. "They kidnapped me, I escaped, and now they want me back."

With one smooth movement, Harvey caught her by the throat with his freezing hands, pulled her from the bike, and slammed her against a tree.

She stared at him in defiance until he plunged his knife into the bark beside her head.

"Don't take me for a fool, Gabriella," said Harvey.

With eyes wide open, she stared back at him. She was searching for something, buying time to think of a lie.

"Who is Kane?" said Harvey.

"He's a madman."

Harvey didn't reply.

"He is ex-military, British, I think. An officer. Or at least he acts like one."

"And his men?"

"They are all ex-military. All rogue. Shunned by the services with dishonourable discharges."

"What did they do?"

"I don't know. Something bad. In Afghanistan. It was covered up but they were discharged. Now they work for whoever offers the biggest paycheck."

"And they're planning to kill the French prime minister?" asked Harvey. "How do you know this?"

"I overheard," said Gabriella, shrugging.

"And how is Kane planning on killing the prime minister?" asked Harvey.

"Every year, the prime minister spends Christmas on his yacht with his family. It's his tradition."

"But he'll be guarded. That's not an easy mission."

"Cassius Kane is a criminal genius," said Gabriella. The words came from her mouth with a look of distaste. "As much as I hate to admit it."

"So how's he going to do it?" asked Harvey.

"He has developed a drug. He may only have a few men, but with the drug, they will be unstoppable. We have to stop them, Monsieur Stone."

Harvey released his grip a little, but still held her against the tree.

"That's why they wanted me," she continued. "They used me as one of the test subjects."

"A what?"

"A lab rat, Monsieur Stone," said Gabriella. She blinked away the tears. "They killed us one by one, testing the drug, adapting it a little, then testing again until it did exactly what they wanted it to do."

"And what *does* it do?" asked Harvey.

"It gives you superpowers," said Gabriella, her French accent thick and romantic with the idea.

Harvey didn't reply. He stared at her with disbelief.

"You don't believe me?" said Gabriella.

Harvey shook his head.

"How do you think I escaped from a high-security facility? How do you think I killed those men myself? Me? How do you think I survived being hit by a bus, Harvey? And how, god damn it, do you think I climbed out of that hospital with you?"

"The drug," said Harvey.

"Yes, Harvey. Have you ever felt the power of adrenaline? Have you ever felt its release into your blood stream and felt your power grow?"

"Often," said Harvey.

"Imagine if that adrenaline was amplified. Imagine if your body felt no pain. Imagine if your senses were heightened to an animal-like state."

"And Kane thinks he's going to take over the world?"

"No, Harvey, not the world. But he'll be unstoppable. Think of what a government could do with a drug like that. How much would they pay to have Kane's men do what a government is not allowed to do?"

"And that's why he wants you back?" said Harvey. "Because you know all his plans?"

"Well, yes and no. He wants the vial I stole," said Gabriella, offering a cunning smile. "His men will be more powerful than any men in any army. All communications between the muscles and the brain are blocked. Your body is far stronger than you know, Harvey Stone."

"A drug like that would be worth a fortune on the black market," said Harvey.

"In the right hands, a drug like that could stop many wars," said Gabriella. "But it's worth far more if only Kane's men have access to it."

"I can't be involved in all of that, Gabriella," said Harvey, and he released her from his grip. He stepped away and looked out over Saint-Pierre.

"Do you still want to kill him?" said Gabriella, her voice soft.

He felt her step up beside him and tracked her movements as she took his hand in her own, then lowered her head to kiss it.

"Where's the vial now?" asked Harvey.

A bead of sweat fell from Gabriella's brow onto Harvey's hand.

"I have hidden it," she replied.

Harvey removed his hand and stuffed it into his pocket.

"Hidden it where?" he asked.

"The safest place I know," said Gabriella. "But his men are still strong. He has a prototype."

"Kane took everything from me," said Harvey. "Drug or no drug, I'm going to kill him."

"Then I will help you," said Gabriella.

"I don't need help," said Harvey, relaxing his grip and stepping back from Gabriella. "Just tell me where to find him."

With both hands nursing her throat, Gabriella moved away from him and stopped at the edge of the hill, gazing across the valley at the town of Saint-Pierre.

She turned her head back to face Harvey.

"I will tell you where to find him," said Gabriella. "But first, you must help me stop the assassination."

CHAPTER TWENTY-FOUR

Eight men stood in a single rank in the courtyard outside the research and development centre as the first drops of rain announced the onslaught of a winter storm. Each man had polished boots, shiny buckles and pressed black uniforms. In front of them, their leader, Sergeant Jones, stood with his hands crossed behind his back and his feet shoulder-width apart. He stared straight ahead. Not one man moved a muscle.

Kane watched them through the doors. His chest swelled with the pride of a father.

He pushed through the double doors, stepped out into the evening, and marched to the front with one arm swinging. He came to a halt in front of Jones, performed a right turn, and stared at his second in command.

"Squad, attention," called Jones.

The entire squad brought their right legs up to ninety degrees and then back down in unison to stand beside the left boot. Their arms moved to the side of their bodies, thumbs pointing down, chins up, and fearlessness etched onto each of their faces.

Jones raised a salute, his arm rigid and perfectly square with his body.

"Thank you, Sergeant," said Kane, returning the salute. "At ease."

"Stand at ease," barked Jones.

The squad reversed their move, returning to the more comfortable position with their hands behind their backs and feet shoulder-width apart.

Kane eyed his men, admiring their chiselled features, strong bodies and the determined looks on their faces. He turned to the left, moved his hands behind his back, and paced to the front of the squad. Then he stopped in front of the first man, the tallest and broadest of them all.

"Name," said Kane.

Without moving his eyes, the man stood to attention then replied in full volume, "Bravo-one, sir."

"Are you ready, Bravo-one?" said Kane, his voice low but clear.

"Yes, sir."

"Do you know what God has in store for you tonight?"

"Victory and honour, sir."

Kane cocked his head at the reply, surprised and impressed.

"Good. At ease," said Kane.

The soldier returned to the at-ease position.

Kane continued his inspection, eying the men's boots, belts and uniforms as he passed. He stopped at the last soldier in the front rank, a squat man who appeared as wide as he was tall.

"Name?"

The man stood to attention with precise movements, showing the result of years of training.

"Alpha-two, sir."

"Alpha-two," said Kane, "which way around did you enter this world? Feet first or sideways?"

"Head first, sir," replied Alpha-two.

"Is that right?"

"I wanted to see where I was going, sir," replied Alpha-two.

"That's always a good idea," said Kane. "Tell me, Alpha-two, who do you follow?"

"I follow you, sir."

"Just me?"

"And Sergeant Jones, sir."

"Who?"

"Charlie-two, sir."

"And what about your squad?"

"I don't follow them. I stand beside them, sir."

"Good answer," said Kane. "And God? Where does he stand?"

"He carries me, sir," said Alpha-two. He allowed himself a smile, but then corrected himself.

Kane nodded. "At ease, Alpha-two."

The soldier returned to the at-ease position.

Kane strode straight-legged to the front of the squad, letting his heels click on the concrete with each step. He stopped, eyed Jones, and then stood silent for a while; it was a method of finding weakness in the squad. Uncertainty caused the weakest of men to shuffle, a natural movement he'd picked up many years before his own dishonourable discharge.

When he spoke, he projected his voice with authority. It was loud enough to be heard, clear enough to be understood, but quiet enough to ensure that each man strived to hear him.

"I have never been so proud," began Kane. "I have served in Afghanistan, Europe, and all over our Queen's empire, and never before have I rested my eyes on such capable men with such strength and determination."

Each man remained still, their eyes facing forward, accepting the compliment in silence.

"You all know what we have to do tomorrow morning. You all know the dangers. In eight hours from now, the prime minister of France will arrive here in Saint-Pierre. All hell will break loose. You *will* remain calm. You will *not* stand down. We will be *victorious*. Is that understood?"

"Yes, sir," said the squad in unison. Their voices echoed off the walls of the courtyard then faded as each man waited for Kane to resume his speech.

"Some of you may not survive. I wish I could sugar-coat it. But it's a fact. You'll be up against some of the most patriotic, determined and ruthless individuals you ever came across. But that's what they are: individuals. They're not an army. They're not like you. They don't have your training, your strength, and they don't have *this*."

Kane produced a single vial of prototype SFS and held it up for all to see.

"For six months, you've all been guarding this place, and for good reason. What I have in my hand will transform you. You think you're strong now? You think you're ruthless? Hard? Unstoppable?" Kane continued to hold the vial of red liquid high in the air, and met the eyes of each man as they stared at his hand. "No. You're wrong. But once you're charged with this, once this chemical finds its way into your blood, and the rush of battle hits you, nothing will stop you. I know the feeling a man gets when he puts his life on the line, as do all of you, when adrenaline takes over and you're so fired up you charge into battle screaming the Lord's name."

He paused to make sure he was holding their attention.

"This little vial is just a prototype. We have a stronger, more potent version. But even this tiny vial contains enough SFS to fire that adrenaline into action. It's just like flicking a switch. Each one of you will have the strength of ten men. Only then will you be unstoppable. Only then will you be the men you've been striving to be. When we win this battle, your names will go down in history. Not for the so-called crimes that we once committed, not for the infidelities that tarnished us and led us into the shadows, but for the honour you all deserve."

He paused once more to admire the looks on each of their faces: confidence, bravery, loyalty and trust.

"Tonight, gentlemen, you are Kane's Army. Who are you?"

"Kane's Army, sir," they replied, louder than before.

"Again?"

"Kane's Army, sir."

"And what do we want?"

"Victory, sir."

"Good," said Kane, allowing the noise to settle. He stood once more in front of Jones, coming to attention by bringing his right leg up and then stepping down beside his left.

"Squad, attention," called Jones, and the squad followed suit, their heels clicking on the concrete with unified perfection.

"Tonight, gentlemen, we have strength on our side. We have cunning. And we have God carrying us on our path to victory."

He met Alpha-two's eyes as the words left his mouth.

"Tonight, gentlemen," Kane continued, passing his gaze across his men, "we make history."

CHAPTER TWENTY-FIVE

"Take off your pants. You are no use to anyone with your leg like that," said Gabriella.

"I'll be fine," said Harvey. "I've had worse."

"Harvey Stone, do not take me for some kind of feeble, little girl. Tonight we will face Kane's Army and you are losing blood faster than your body can create it. Take your pants off and lie down on the ground."

Harvey didn't reply.

"That's an order, Monsieur Stone."

"I don't do so good with orders."

"So I gather," said Gabriella. "I don't do so good with partners who are bleeding to death. If you want to know how to find Kane, lie down and let me look at your leg."

Harvey dropped to the ground and peeled his cargo pants away from his thigh. The dried blood had stuck to his skin and the movement opened the wound further as he pulled the material free.

"There's water in the panniers," said Harvey, gesturing at the two boxes either side of the bike's rear wheel.

Gabriella fetched the bottles of water then slapped Harvey's hand away from his leg.

"Lie back," she said. "This will sting a little."

She ran her fingers around the five-inch wound on Harvey's thigh, nodding when she saw that the mouth-shaped ends had begun to heal. Her practiced eye confirmed no sign of infection. So, using her slender fingers to hold the wound open, she washed the cut with the cool water. Beneath her hands, Harvey's body tensed when the water splashed onto his pink flesh then eased as his body grew accustomed to the pain.

"How you doing up there?" she asked, as she gave the wound another careful check.

Harvey didn't reply.

"Give me your knife," said Gabriella.

Harvey's head raised from the ground, a questioning look on his face.

But Gabriella didn't respond to his lack of trust. She held out her hand.

"Knife."

With reluctance, Harvey pulled his knife from the sheath on his belt. He caught her eye, communicating some kind of warning, then spun the blade and offered her the weapon handle first.

Quick as a flash, and before Harvey could complain, Gabriella grabbed a handful of his t-shirt and cut a long strip from the hem. She was halfway through the cut when she met Harvey's eyes once more. This time, he offered the nearest she would get to an apology for not trusting her.

"You need to raise your leg," said Gabriella. "On three, you're going to rest your leg on mine. Don't bend it. I don't want the bleeding to start. Are you ready?"

Harvey blinked but didn't respond.

"One," said Gabriella. Then she lifted his leg onto hers before he had the chance to tense his muscle.

"Where did you learn to count?" asked Harvey.

"At military school."

"You were in the military?"

"I was a medic," said Gabriella, remembering the times she had used the *count to three* trick on other patients.

"Why did you leave?" asked Harvey.

"Would *you* fight for your country, Harvey Stone?"

"I'm different."

"How are you different? You're British?"

"Yes. But I..." Harvey paused before he said too much.

"You're what?"

"I'm just different. That's all you need to know."

"I don't need you to tell me you're different, Harvey. I knew it when I first saw you."

"When you were hiding in a ditch?" said Harvey. "Not very military, is it? Unless the French do things differently to the British?"

With a tug of the make-shift bandage, Gabriella pulled the two ends tight, watching as Harvey's face showed no signs of pain or discomfort.

"You're done," said Gabriella. She jabbed at Harvey with the knife before spinning it in her hand and offering him the handle. "You didn't even flinch. I could have killed you right here."

"If you were going to kill me, you would have done it long before you dressed my wound," said Harvey, as he pulled his cargo pants up.

Gabriella gave his body a farewell glance then met Harvey's eyes as they caught her in the act. She handed him a bottle of water, a silent gesture, acknowledging that she meant no harm. Then she sat down beside him and looked out over the town of Saint-Pierre as the first evening lights turned on.

"Is this why you brought me here? For the view?" said Harvey.

"It might be," said Gabriella. "Or I might be trying to seduce you."

The comment caught Harvey's attention enough to raise an eyebrow.

"Why don't you seduce me with Kane's plans?"

"Are you playing hard to get?"

"I'm playing impossible to get."

"The best guys always do," said Gabriella. She tried to stand, but she dizzied and fell back to the ground, steadying herself with her hands on the grass. A fresh wave of nausea washed over her.

"What's wrong?" asked Harvey.

"Nothing," said Gabriella. "It will pass, I am sure."

"Is this the effects of the drug?" said Harvey. "You don't look unstoppable right now."

"I said it will pass," said Gabriella, a little sharply.

Harvey didn't reply.

"Do you see the church tower?" said Gabriella, wiping her eyes and swallowing the acid at the back of her throat.

"West of the marina?" Harvey replied, with one eye on Gabriella.

"Yes," said Gabriella. "Two-man sniper team. From there, they'll see the entire armed procession coming into town. That's the fall-back plan. Do you see the row of buildings on the east side of the marina where the police cars blocked our escape?"

"Low-rise. What are they? Shops?"

"Restaurants," said Gabriella. "The procession will drive straight past them. One two-man team will take out the rear guard vehicles."

"What will that do?" said Harvey. "Why not take out the front vehicles?"

"He wants them to run. There's a protocol when you're guarding the prime minister. The security detail will be small. They will try to get the family out of the town. But if there is only one way out and it is blocked by Kane's Army, they will have no choice but to continue to the marina."

"Two men plus two in the church tower? He'll need more than that. How many men does he have?"

"Less than he did before, thanks to you," said Gabriella. "The final two-man team will ambush them from the fish market. They'll close in as he approaches with the first team bringing up the rear. The prime minister will have nowhere to go."

"Who's ordering the hit?" asked Harvey.

"No-one knows but Kane and the man with the cheque book," said Gabriella. "My guess would be the resistance."

"The resistance?" Harvey felt a smile creep across his tired face.

"The resistance is still strong, Monsieur Stone. They are angry. Too long have they waited in the shadows."

"And what do you get out of this?" said Harvey. "If you don't want to fight for your country, why are you doing this?"

"That's easy," said Gabriella. "I get Kane off my back, for one. But perhaps more importantly, I get to do something significant. It's not every day you get to save your country, Harvey."

"And if we fail?" asked Harvey.

"If we fail and the prime minister is killed, the country will fall. The revolution will destroy us."

"So there's a patriot inside you somewhere?"

Gabriella considered her response. She lay back and let the cold sweat run its course then rolled onto her side to face him.

"I am not a patriot, Harvey Stone. I am just a girl who longs for peace and a simple life. That is all."

CHAPTER TWENTY-SIX

"I don't know how much longer I can hold on," said Gabriella.

Harvey slowed and pulled the bike into a side street one block away from the fish market. He killed the engine then let his mind adjust to the silence before stepping off, searching high on the rooftops for black uniforms against the night sky. But he could only see the dark clouds of a winter storm.

The sound of a body slumping to the ground behind him caused Harvey to spin.

Gabriella lay with her face on the concrete, unable to move. She gave a little moan as Harvey reached beneath each of her limp arms and pulled her out of sight against a whitewashed wall.

He sat her up, loosened the top that he'd given her earlier that day, and felt for a pulse.

It was racing.

He placed his hand against her forehead and felt the burn of fever, damp to the touch but moist with a layer of cool sweat.

"Gabriella," whispered Harvey, checking left and right. "We need to move."

But Gabriella didn't respond.

Her head rolled to one side, and a line of thick saliva crept from her open mouth, forming a string that reached the ground. Seeing an alleyway between two boat yards, Harvey scooped her up in his arms, found a dark corner between two bins and lay her down out of sight.

"Gabriella, wake up," said Harvey, and gave her face a gentle slap.

She moaned and opened her eyes. The dim light caught the moist tears that formed and rolled across her face.

"What's wrong with you?" whispered Harvey, aware that Kane's men would be close by.

"I need something," said Gabriella.

She reached out a shaky hand to cling to Harvey's jacket.

"You don't need anything, Gabriella. Get yourself up. We've got work to do."

"I can't," replied Gabriella, letting her hand slip from Harvey's jacket and fall to the ground. "Go on without me. I just need to rest."

"This is what the drug does?" asked Harvey.

"I'm sorry," replied Gabriella, her body tensing as if every muscle in her body called for the drug. "Go on without me. I'll be here."

"What can I do?"

But Gabriella didn't respond. Her eyes closed and her head fell against the wall. Her shallow breaths and racing pulse were the only indication of life.

"Gabriella, what can I do?"

Again, she offered no response.

Harvey checked the street to the left and right. A few Christmas lights adorned the windows of whitewashed houses. The bare roads waited with open arms for the prime minister's arrival. Only the trees that rocked in the growing wind gave sign that the scene wasn't a picture postcard.

Leaving Gabriella in the shadows, Harvey made his way along the road, keeping to the pockets of darkness. The first drops of the approaching storm dotted his leather jacket, leaving black holes in the dust.

The aroma from the fish market hit Harvey before he saw the building. Two cats stopped in their tracks then fled when Harvey dropped from the chain link fence. He remained crouched, watching for movement or light, but found none. A single black SUV was parked beside the main building, which Harvey gauged to be the size of half a football pitch.

Approaching from the shadows, Harvey stepped up to the car. It was empty. But the front was still warm. Droplets of rain fell onto its glossy paintwork, landing with the sound of tiny tapping fingers.

Then, loud and alien in the night, a metal bar slid across the two sliding doors beside the car. The right hand door to the main building screeched into life. Harvey threw himself against the wall as a curtain of light spilled across the ground, illuminating puddles of rain that had already begun to form on the rough concrete.

A man stepped out and exhaled, taking a breath of fresh air. The smell of old fish met Harvey's nostrils stronger than before. Dressed in the familiar black uniform and black boots, the man turned his face up to the rain to refresh himself. On a strap around his neck, an MP-5 hung behind his back, and a handgun was fixed to his chest.

He pulled a cigarette from a pack then stuffed them into his breast pocket before flicking open a zippo lighter. The flame cast a dancing orange light on the man's rough skin then vanished as he slapped the lighter shut and pocketed it.

Harvey took a single step toward him.

But the man's radio broke the silence.

"Alpha-two, this is Alpha-one. Come back."

A plume of thin, grey smoke vanished into the air as he pulled his radio from a pouch on his belt.

Harvey crept through the shadows behind him.

"Alpha-two receiving," replied the man.

"How are you feeling, Alpha-one?"

"I haven't taken it yet. Have you?"

"No, not yet. I'm not one hundred percent sure about injecting myself if I'm honest."

"Same," replied Alpha-two. "I'll use it when I have to. When is the attack due?"

"I have no idea. But keep your eyes peeled. Charlie-two says the boogeyman is out there tonight."

"The boogeyman or Santa Claus?"

"The boogeyman, Alpha-two. You're on the naughty list. Remember?"

"How could I forget?" said Alpha-two, taking a long pull on his cigarette. "I'm out back. It's all clear. I think the smell will keep him away."

"Get back inside. Control your zone. Charlie-two seems to think this guy is good."

Alpha-two exhaled a cloud of smoke, looked left and right, and then raised the radio to his mouth.

"I guess he's on the naughty list too then?"

"Back inside, Alpha-two. Over."

Alpha-two dropped his cigarette to the ground beside the car. It landed with a hiss before the man crushed it beneath his boot. He turned and stopped in his tracks as Harvey pushed the tip of his blade under the man's chin and up into his mouth.

Wide-eyed, Alpha-two inhaled his last breath as he tried to push Harvey's hands away. But a single kick sideways into the man's knee took him down onto the wet ground. Harvey knelt on his chest, released his knife and eased the man's suffering with a slash across his throat.

CHAPTER TWENTY-SEVEN

"Six hours, Jones," said Kane. "Six hours until the prime minister arrives and we become the most celebrated men in France. Are we ready?"

"The men are in position, sir," said Jones.

The sound of footsteps on the steel mesh mezzanine walkway that ran around the perimeter of the pharmaceutical factory was percussive in the open space. Bright lights hung from the white painted ceiling, illuminating the glass vials and casting monstrous bloody shapes across the smooth, white worktops.

"Six months, Jones. Six months of watching those scientists day after day, failure after failure, excuse after excuse. And we finally have it. Nothing can stop us now."

"What about the girl?" asked Jones.

"She'll come crawling back. She's been dosed with SFS for the past month. Her body needs it. She can't live without it."

"And Stone?" said Jones. "The man has taken out three teams already. He'll come for us here and we don't have the men to stop him."

Kane pushed off the handrail where he'd been leaning,

looked across at his number two, and smiled the smile of success.

"Follow me, Jones," said Kane, as he descended the steel staircase. "There's something I want you to see."

On the wall beside a pair of double doors was a large exit button. Jones hit it and the electric doors opened. A loud electronic alarm sounded to alert anybody in the factory that someone was entering.

The doors opened into a small cleaning chamber; as soon as the electric doors closed behind Kane and Jones, it clicked into action. A loud hiss from above indicated that air was being sucked out of the room. Tiny jets on the walls issued clouds of chemically enhanced steam that sanitised a person's clothes on entry and exit. A blast of fresh oxygen cleared the air and another set of doors opened along with the sound of another loud electronic alarm.

With his hands behind his back, Kane enjoyed the tap of his heels against the painted concrete floor in the long corridor. He savoured the lines of glass-walled observation rooms, control rooms and cells, where the test subjects had been kept like dogs.

Like a king overlooking his kingdom, Kane admired his creation. But as he stepped up to observation room three and stared down at the ruination that Doctor Farrow had become, Kane felt his power grow a little more. Just like Frankenstein pulling the switch and seeing his collation of dead body parts twitch for the first time, Kane recognised the monster he had created.

"Is that Farrow?" asked Jones, peering through the glass with a look of both disgust and intrigue.

"It *was* Doctor Farrow, Jones," replied Kane, admiring his work. "I don't know what you'd call it now."

"How many doses has he had?"

"Five," replied Kane. "Five doses of SFS in under five hours.

It's the most anybody has ever survived, even if it is the prototype."

"You call that surviving?" said Jones. "Is he even human anymore?"

As if on cue, a hand slapped against the reinforced window. Its outline was traced by a cloud of breath that fogged the glass.

"I don't know what you'd call it now," said Kane, feeling the corners of his mouth rise with success. "But God help anyone who stands in its way."

CHAPTER TWENTY-EIGHT

A crack of thunder dragged Gabriella from her slumber in a panic. Her body shook with the cold, aching for something she knew would kill her. But still, one more hit was all she would need.

Another rumble in the black sky above and the sound of rain like white noise hissed at her from every direction. A single flash of lightning lit the night. Its bright fork reached down and struck the earth somewhere far away behind the unmistakable silhouette of the fish market.

It was a sign.

The fish market was large and plain. It was the only building with lights on along the street save for the flashing colours of Christmas decorations that brought cheer to a world far removed from Gabriella's mind.

She rolled to her side and pushed herself up to one knee. Then, using the wall for support, she stood. A rush of blood rocked her and a surge of nausea rose from her stomach; burning acid seeped into her mouth until she bent, vomited, and spat the acrid remnants to the wet ground.

Her feet moved of their own accord. Her hands crept along

the wall to her side, keeping her from falling. Her vision blurred at the edges; just a plain white, square building focused in its centre.

Somewhere inside that place was everything she needed.

The chain link fence rattled when she fell against it then supported her as she pulled herself along and sought a way through. A gate, a hole or a break.

But she found no such entry.

Another flash of lightning struck simultaneously to the thunder that cracked, angry and deep, above Gabriella. Her body began to climb up the fence while her mind still wondered at the sky. She rolled over the top and fell to the ground in a daze, unhurt. Then, like the first land creatures, she crawled across the wet ground, weak and with an unrelenting hunger.

She clambered onto a motionless body in black. Her fingers pried open his pockets. Her hands felt the seams of his clothes, bloodied from the slash across his neck. But she found nothing and fell back to the ground. Something stabbed at her arm.

A shard of glass.

Fingering the wound, she plucked the tiny glass fragment from her skin, feeling its smooth surface. Then she recognised its tight curve.

With a gasp, she dropped the glass and began searching the wet ground, but found only the remains of a broken vial, which had been crushed by a boot. Its contents had spilled onto the rain-soaked ground and been washed away to a nearby drain.

The ache in her heart weighed heavy as she closed her tear-filled eyes and lay down staring up at the sky.

Bright fluorescent light flickered through the open factory door, lighting Gabriella's face in flashes of anguish mirrored by the distant lightning. She rolled to her side and stared through the gap. The view offered her little more than rows upon rows of white, shiny benches stood on a shiny, white, tiled floor. A shadow rose against the furthest wall then shrank again as if a rat had ventured into the open, scurrying toward a lamp, then retreated back to the safety of the cold, dark corners.

Gabriella crawled closer, rising to her feet, then peered inside.

At one end of the building were huge shutter doors, where the fresh fish would be unloaded from the boats. Giant hooks hung from thick chains on beams that would lift the cargo to be sorted, cleaned and then sold.

A single drop of water fell from someplace high, perhaps a leak in the roof. It landed on a bench, where a seller would display his fish, facing out towards the customer with his mouth open and blank wide eyes staring at a palm full of Euros.

Blank, wide eyes.

Gabriella knew the empty stare.

She'd seen it in the girls with whom she'd shared the past month of her life. They'd been pumped full of chemicals and forced to run until the only way for their bodies to survive was to shut down the very organs that kept them alive.

The blank stare.

The blank stare of her father while batons continued to beat him even after all life had slipped away. Strong hands had pulled Gabriella off him, where she lay protecting his body. But not for her own safety. Instead, crazed uniformed men had rained down blows on her instead.

The crack of bones echoed in the empty space. A rattle of chains responded. Gabriella spun. Her feet scraped against the screed floor, answering the crack with the squeak of rubber.

Blinking the blur from her eyes until a fragment of focus formed, she made her way toward the shutters, the shadows and the crack of bones. Accompanied only by the rasp of her breath and the sound of her hand brushing along the benches, the noises guided her in her semi-blind state.

A dark, glossy shadow formed between the two shutter doors, a spreading blemish seeping out on the white tiled floor. Its black fingers found the joins between the tiles and ran between them, spreading the word of darkness.

A finger of the spreading shadow touched Gabriella's running shoe. Then it split to run around each side of her foot. She stepped away, horrified at the sticky blood. But something touched her shoulder. Startled, she spun, and came face to face with a tongueless man. He stared back at her in the flickering light with soulless eyes wide with fear.

Moving away from the atrocity, Gabriella fought to calm her breathing. She slipped in the puddle of blood and fell to the floor. But she continued to scramble away backwards on her hands, searching around her for the culprit in the shadows.

But curiosity drew her attention to the dead man. She stared in awe at his lifeless form. A hook had been buried into the back of the man's skull; the chain above from which it hung was taut.

She crawled closer.

The body swung back at her touch then rocked forward.

Blank with wide eyes.

CHAPTER TWENTY-NINE

The flickering light cast flashes of monstrous shadows as Gabriella fumbled her way around the rows of benches. The girl who had demonstrated rare strength and courage now appeared feeble in Harvey's eyes. He was driven on by something far more powerful than her drug, which had only proven to grip her and render her unconscious.

She jumped at the touch of the body and slipped in its blood.

Harvey remained curious and hidden in the shadows.

Scrambling to her feet, her bloodied hands searched the corpse, ripping open pockets and dropping items onto the sticky floor until she found what she was looking for. She stopped and gasped.

As if she'd discovered some long, lost treasure, Gabriella pulled her hand from the pocket with a tenderness contrasting the frantic searching she had performed moments before. Cupping the item in both hands, she held it up to the light as if her disbelief required a visual inspection and confirmation.

Between her finger and thumb, Gabriella held a vial containing a dark, red liquid.

Seconds later, she began another search of the man's pocket. She found a small pouch and set to work. She ripped open the flap. The rasp of Velcro was sudden and violent, and lost to the incessant pitter-patter of rain outside, on the roof, and against the steel shutter doors.

A practiced hand prepared the syringe with surprising speed, but her haste and shaky fingers dropped the vial onto the bench. It rolled away from her.

"No," she whispered.

Seeing the vial pick up speed, Gabriella headed for the end of the bench. She dropped the syringe, pushed past the swinging body, and reached for the vial. Missing her aim, she slipped in the bloody puddle. She clung to the surface as her feet danced then found grip on a dry tile.

But it was too late.

The vial teetered on the edge of the bench, teasing Gabriella as she stood frozen, not daring to move in case she tipped the balance and sent the vial crashing to the floor.

"Stay," said Gabriella.

Her voice was a low whisper. She spoke as if the vial would hear her command. Reaching across the bench and sliding across the smooth surface, her hand then raised like the head of a cobra, poised, ready to strike and trap the vial.

The fluorescent light above her buzzed with electricity. The vial toyed tentatively with Gabriella's state of mind, daring her to make her move.

She struck.

The light blinked off and on.

And the vial fell into Harvey's hand.

Gabriella slid to the floor as if the hunt had taken every last morsel of energy, leaving her without hope. The tears began first, silent as if Gabriella mourned the loss of a friend. Her weak grip on the bench released and her knees buckled as if the weight of the loss was too much for them to bear.

She sank to the floor.

Harvey stepped from the shadows.

"Get up, Gabriella," said Harvey.

His voice startled her. She fell back onto her hands and scrambled away from him through the blood.

A crack of thunder outside tore through the night. She pushed back against the bench and pulled her knees up to her chin.

The light flickered off.

Harvey moved closer, watching her head twitch left and right. Her eyes blinked for focus then stared at the darkness and blurred shadows.

"Who's there?" said Gabriella.

Harvey didn't reply.

"I said, who's there?" said Gabriella, louder than before, as if her aggression would elicit a response.

She pushed herself to one knee, held onto the bench and stood, peering around for movement.

"How bad do you need it?" said Harvey.

He moved through the darkness as she placed the voice and stared into the shadows.

"How bad do you need a fix?" he asked.

But Gabriella couldn't reply.

"Are you dying?" asked Harvey.

"I don't know," said Gabriella, her voice low and weak, and her eyes glistening in the half-light. "This is the longest I have been without it. My body is shutting down. I can feel it happening inside me. It's like small pieces of me are turning off."

"You're weak," said Harvey.

"He did this to me," said Gabriella. "He made me this way."

"Why don't you come and get it?" said Harvey, stepping into view holding the vial out for Gabriella's poisoned mind to find.

"Give it to me, Harvey."

"You can have it," said Harvey, as Gabriella's hands reached forward onto the floor.

Her legs straightened behind her, raising her body as a leopard might prepare to attack. Gabriella inched forward, hand over hand, footstep by footstep, until she stared up at Harvey like a wild animal, only a pounce away.

"You want it?" asked Harvey.

He opened his hand and held it out an arm's length away from Gabriella. Her eyes followed the vial, her body tensed, and her breathing slowed.

She struck, snatching at Harvey's palm. But he closed his fist around the vial, reached down with his free hand, and took hold of Gabriella's neck, gripping tight and lifting her into the air before slamming her into the shutters.

Gabriella's nails scratched at Harvey's face. Her feet kicked out at him until he slammed her once more into the shutters to silence her. Gabriella's top lip retracted, exposing her teeth in a snarl. A visceral growl emerged from her throat.

She spat in Harvey's face.

"Give it to me," said Gabriella, panting and struggling to breathe through Harvey's grip.

Harvey leaned in close, searching her dilated eyes to see if the blackness held any sign of colour.

"You're going to take me to Kane," said Harvey. "You do that for me, and you can have as much as you need."

CHAPTER THIRTY

"Bravo-one, come back," said Jones, as he paced the courtyard, searching for the best radio signal. "Bravo-one, come back. This is Charlie-two."

Kane leaned against the door under the porch canopy with a cigarette in his hand, eying his second in command as he fought to maintain an expression of control and composure. Yet Jones stomped around in the rain, his anger and frustration getting the better of him.

"Alpha-one, come back," said Jones. "I repeat, Alpha-one, this is Charlie-two. Come back."

A surge of static crackled through the radio's circuitry then faded.

"Problems, Jones?" asked Kane, as he exhaled a cloud of smoke and watched the atmosphere dilute it until nothing was left but the tainted scent.

"Nothing I can't handle, sir," replied Jones, raising the radio to his mouth once more. "Tango-one, come back. Tango-one, this is Charlie-two. Talk to me."

"He's out there," said Kane, before a crackled voice came over the airwaves.

"Charlie-two, this is Tango-one. Copy."

"Sit-rep?" said Jones.

"Nothing to report. I have a clear view of the marina, the yacht, and most of the town. It's all quiet on the western front."

"Tango-one, have you got eyes on the fish market?"

"Charlie-two, copy. That's a positive. I have eyes on the fish market. Not a creature is stirring, not even a mouse."

"Drop the Christmas jokes, Tango-one. Do you have eyes on Alpha team?" said Jones, then glanced back at Kane.

"Charlie-two, this is Tango-one. No visual on Alpha-one or Alpha-two. Nothing to report, Sarge."

Jones stared up at the sky, squinting as the rain drops bounced from his face.

"You're worried, Jones," said Kane, as he flicked his cigarette butt across the courtyard, watching the little orange ember spin then disappear in a hiss when it landed in a puddle. "I've seen that look before."

"I'm sending in Bravo team," said Jones. "Alpha team are the strike force. The fish market is the perfect place for an ambush. I need comms with them."

"You're also leaving the door open," said Kane. "If Stone is in there, he'll escape. Isn't it better to contain him?"

"All units stand by," said Jones into the radio.

Jones glanced up at Kane then lowered his eyes to the ground.

"We've got a few hours before the prime minister rolls into town, sir. I'm nine men down, and I've lost contact with my strike team. Stone or no Stone, I need my strike team in place and I need comms."

"Do you think Alpha team can take him down?" asked Kane.

Jones nodded. But it was not the nod of a confident solider

sending his men into battle. Instead, it was the nod of a man hedging his bets and playing the odds.

Pulling his packet of cigarettes from his pocket, Kane removed the last one then crushed the empty pack and tossed it to the ground.

"How well do you remember that night?" asked Kane.

Jones looked back at him. His face was only half-lit by the spotlights on the roof of the building and rain dripped from his nose.

"Afghanistan?"

"Is there another night you have in mind?"

Jones shook his head. "I relive that night at least three times a week, sir."

"Three times a week?" said Kane, in surprise. "I think about it every day."

"Have you thought about seeing a counsellor?" asked Jones. He didn't smile at his own joke, even though both men knew the idea was out of the question.

"I remember when we got the call over the radio," said Kane. "I remember your face, and that was the first time I ever saw you falter."

"With all due respect, sir, I'd have to contradict that statement."

"Permission denied, Jones," said Kane, and stepped into the rain. "Your decision that night cost men their lives. Your failure to make the call at the right time killed my men, the army's men. Your decision earned us all a discharge."

Kane put his hands behind his back, held his chest out, and walked behind Jones. His second in command remained resolute, facing the doorway. He was always the model soldier.

"Stand up straight, man," said Kane.

Jones stood to attention. "Every decision we made in that hell-hole cost men their lives, sir," he said. "That was our night to lose lives. It was an ambush. You know as well as I do that we'd have lost every single man if I hadn't made a decision at all."

"Quite right," said Kane. "Quite right indeed. That's why I stood by you. That's why, regardless of the friends and comrades we all lost, the men out there tonight stood by you, because you made a decision."

"Innocent people died, sir. That's a fact I'll live with for the rest of my life. But fifteen good soldiers came home."

"They slaughtered a village, Jones."

"They were hiding militants," he replied. "They may not have had AK-forty-sevens in their hands, but they were hiding the men who did."

"That's not how the Queen's army works though, is it, Jones? That's not standard operating procedure."

"Standard procedure would have killed every single man on our squad. My decision saved a handful of them and we completed the mission."

"And that handful of men are out there right now, Jones. They're facing a lunatic who is pulling your team apart. What are you going to do about it?"

"We're going to take him down, sir."

"But what about the prime minister?" said Kane. "What about the mission?"

Jones hesitated.

"Tick-tock, Jones. The prime minister is on his way here now and there's a madman picking your men off. What's more important? Your men or the mission?"

"My men, sir."

Surprised by the response, Kane stopped his pacing, but allowed Jones to continue.

"Without my men, there is no mission," said Jones. "Without my men, all this would be for nothing."

"So what are you going to do about it?"

Jones didn't reply.

"It's time for SFS," said Kane.

"They don't need it, sir. Not yet. I can't risk them hitting withdrawal before the prime minister arrives."

"That's your call, Jones. But remember, if you make the wrong decision again, I might not be so..." Kane hovered, searching for the right word. "Forgiving. Do you think Alpha team can take him down without SFS?"

"I have every confidence in them, sir."

"Then do it," said Kane. "It's decision time."

Jones turned on the heels of his boots to face Kane. He held his stare in an effort to convey a renewed confidence in his decision. Then he raised the radio.

"Alpha-one, this is Charlie-two. Come back."

Silence was broken only by the flow of static.

"Alpha-one, this is Charlie-two. Come back."

"Charlie-two?" came the reply.

"Alpha-one, respond using radio protocol."

"I don't really know about protocol," said the voice. "But you're running out of men, Charlie-two."

CHAPTER THIRTY-ONE

The wide, leather seat of the black SUV sucked Gabriella from a world of pain, cramps, cold sweats and nausea as her muscles begged for a sharp stab into her skin and the release of SFS. She slipped into a world of soft, blurred dream-like visions as if she was standing giddily on a precipice. One step forward would snatch her from everything she knew, a world where trees grew tall and carpets of green lined the earth beneath the summer sun. One step back would dismiss the unknown that beckoned her forward, coaxing her with flashes of potential happiness and the faces of those she had sworn to avenge.

Revenge seemed so far away.

With barely the energy to raise her arm and guide Harvey Stone, she mumbled directions whenever she swayed back to reality. Then she sunk into the warm arms of the soft seat once more to search the darkness for another glimpse of her father and brother.

Just one more glimpse of their faces. One more word from their mouths. The sound of their voices.

The dashboard lights faded and the outline of Harvey's taut face melded into the darkness that enveloped her vision once more. Gabriella embraced the tightness in her chest and the grip on her stomach as memories span around her like an old film reel, spliced with desire and longing.

She saw her father working his garden in his favourite tan corduroys, braces and a white under-vest. His paunch was on display like a trophy. He was unashamed, a man who had raised two children, faced the trials of life, and emerged on the other side with just a bloated tummy for a wound. Gabriella stepped from the house, lifted a hanging grape vine from the archway that divided the garden, and stepped through into her father's vegetable patch. It was his pride and joy. Rows of shallots and carrots, romaine lettuce and leeks, cauliflower and zucchini were bordered by trellised walls of berries and grapes. Butterflies danced from flower to flower and the song of the birds hung on the breeze that tickled the tops of the fat apple trees beyond the garden.

He leaned on his garden fork, fanning himself with his cap, and smiled at Gabriella as the summer sun shone across his tanned skin. He opened his arms as she approached, welcoming her in for one of those long, tight hugs, his hands stained with the rich soil and his warm eyes following her every step of the way.

But the smile faded.

His face twitched.

The mud on his hands turned red when he raised them to his face. A baton came down, striking his flesh and breaking his bones. The garden was gone, replaced by a busy Parisian street. The tall walls of grapes and berries morphed into lines of men in helmets with riot shields and batons. The bright flowers in Gabriella's memory that her father had so lovingly planted and nurtured became the bright vests of the angry, the upset, the beaten and the trampled. The wandering smoke of the smouldering compost blended into clouds of tear gas.

Her father's face faded away, hidden with each strike of the batons and every kick of the heavy, black boots that stamped on Gabriella's memories. She'd tried to pull the men off him but they were too strong for her. She'd tried to cling to her father's bloodied clothes, but his corduroy pants slipped through her hands and he disappeared into the cloud of tear gas, leaving only a bed of memories.

Inside Gabriella, a seed of hate had taken root. Its gnarled and twisted fingers had violated the deepest parts of her mind, leaving nothing but the bitter taste of revenge.

The memories faded away as consciousness emerged from the darkness. But no matter how hard Gabriella fought it, the lights on the dashboard became clearer. The outline of Harvey Stone's face became defined. The incessant rain on the windows and car roof hissed like white noise.

"You're back," said Harvey. He glanced across at her before returning his attention to the wet road. "I'm going to need some directions soon."

But slumber still held Gabriella with a single, bony finger. Unfinished thoughts and memories amalgamated into a bizarre reality. That man wasn't Harvey; that was Francis, her brother. It was Christmas time, long ago, when they were driving through the night for Gabriella to see the Paris lights.

"Remember, Gabriella, you must not tell mother or father about this," Francis had said. "It is our little secret."

Curled in the passenger seat of her brother's car, Gabriella had dozed. The rolling fields and endless railways made it seem as if they hadn't travelled a single mile, despite a full night of driving.

"I won't tell them," said Gabriella. "Will we see the Eiffel Tower?"

"We will, and you will marvel in its beauty, Gabriella."

"And the Notre Dame? Will we see the Notre Dame?"

"Never again will you find such beauty in something so grotesque, little sister."

"And will there be Christmas lights at the Champs-Elysees?"

"Brighter than the stars in the sky, Gabriella," said Francis. "Go to sleep. We will be there in a few hours. I will wake you."

Sleep had welcomed her into its warm, outstretched arms with the promise of everything she loved. A blanket had covered her and tucked beneath her arm was Antoine, a fluffy, blue rabbit with one eye and a broad smile, always a smile.

A strong hand had gripped her and wrenched her from sleep, pinning her down so she couldn't move. Blinding lights turned the woken world white. The thump of rotor blades just meters from the roof of the car pounded her ears like the beating of her heart, heavy in her chest.

"Hold on, Gabriella. Don't be scared," said Francis. "This is going to be a little rough."

She woke with a start, sucking in air. For the first time, she saw the dashboard clearly and vividly. A hand pinned her to the seat. Harvey's face was so defined even in the meagre light beyond the window.

"Hold on, Gabriella," said Harvey. "This is going to be a little rough."

CHAPTER THIRTY-TWO

Two guards in black uniforms stepped into the road and opened fire as soon as Harvey slid the SUV into the driveway of the old factory. Bullets shattered the windscreen and punctured the engine block. A violent hiss of angry steam burst from the front of the car, obscuring Harvey's view. But he planted his right foot and aimed at the two men, who continued to fire, unafraid of the two tons of car that accelerated towards them. Crouching with his head low and peering above the dashboard, Harvey felt the car slam into the two bodies. One of them was forced beneath the wheels, lifting the car to one side with a sickening bounce. The second guard rolled onto the bonnet. His face was a bloodied mess as he clung to the wipers and raised his head to stare through the shattered glass at Harvey.

Holding on with one hand, the man began to punch through the broken windscreen, ripping his skin with each blow. Unde-terred, he continued to force a hole, making it larger and larger. Harvey accelerated harder, weaving from side to side to shake the man from the car. But he held on with ruined hands and rare tenacity.

At the end of the driveway, a small complex of buildings

issued the only light in an otherwise black landscape. The buildings on the left and right formed the sides of a U with a central building behind connecting them to form a central courtyard. Aiming the car at the end of the left building, Harvey dropped down into third gear. He gave everything the car had as the guard continued to hammer his way through the glass.

Seeing Harvey's intentions, the man doubled his efforts, sliding his body around and bringing his heavy boots into play. The heel of a black boot burst through the glass and kicked at Harvey's face. It retracted for another kick and the guard maneuvered for better purchase.

But it was too late for him.

The front wheels hit the curb stone and lifted the car into the air. The rear wheels followed, sending the vehicle soaring inches from the grass border and smashing into the end of the building. It powered into the laboratory from the outside.

Rows of benches blocked the car's path, but it bounced on the laboratory floor, continuing the momentum and ploughing through anything that stood in its way. The benches, dozens of glass vials and various pieces of lab equipment scattered across the floor.

A set of double doors stood at the far end of the lab. The car hissed and moaned with the effort, but Harvey forced it forward, smashing into the doors and wedging into the gap.

The engine died with a blast of angry steam.

A hiss of gas blasted from the walls.

The guard fell from the front of the car.

"What have you done?" said Gabriella, trying to force the car door open, but finding herself trapped. "You're insane."

But there was no time for discussion.

Two men dressed in black stepped into the corridor in front. They ducked through separate side doors then peered around the corners, releasing a three-round burst of gunfire each, which dotted the front of the car.

"We need to go," said Harvey. He raised his leg to kick the remains of the windscreen out from its frame. "Now, Gabriella. Move."

But she didn't follow.

Harvey rolled from the front of the car and clambered into the doorway of a sample room just as more bullets peppered the car. He pulled his knife from his belt; it was his only remaining weapon. With his back against the wall, he waited with his eyes closed, calming his breathing and listening for the approaching guards.

The heavy boots on the linoleum floor came in waves of five. First one set then the other. Harvey pictured the two men running five steps, stopping, and then dropping to a crouch to provide cover for the next man to progress forward.

A flash of movement came from inside the car. Then nothing. Harvey strived to see through the steam that billowed from the grill, but saw nothing. He peered into the corridor.

The first guard stepped into view, his attention focused on the car, searching through the billowing steam for signs of life. A jab of Harvey's knife to the man's throat sent a spurt of blood across the floor. His partner opened fired. Harvey pulled the dying man in front of him and rushed the second guard using the twitching body as a shield.

The guard hesitated. Instinct prevented him from shooting his partner. The force of Harvey and the body colliding with the guard sent him reeling backwards and through a glass wall into a small office. As the shattered safety glass rained down upon the two men and the body, Harvey began an onslaught of violent punches into the guard's face and throat.

But each blow seemed only to anger the guard. His strength seemed to increase the angrier he became until he forced

Harvey up with two powerful hands on his throat. Dragging Harvey to his feet, he slammed him into the wall. Harvey continued to punch, finding the sweet spot every time. But each well-placed blow angered the guard more and more until, tired of the charade, he threw Harvey across the room like a rag doll. Harvey crashed onto a wooden desk, breaking it in half, and landed in a pile of splinters on the floor.

But there was no reprise.

The man was unstoppable.

He stepped into view, kicking away the remains of the desk, and grabbed Harvey once more by the throat with a grip like iron. Bright lights sparkled in Harvey's vision. A darkness formed at the edge of his sight. As the guard dragged Harvey from the office, Harvey's boots struggled for purchase on linoleum floor. He knew that the man's steely grip was squeezing the life from him.

Then a burst of glass and the roar of something wild and new filled the space.

The man's grip released Harvey, dropping him to the floor where he rolled onto his front, clutching his throat. He stared up at the source of the distraction.

But even Harvey was unprepared for what he saw.

A man with his forehead caved in, the skin of his face shredded, and his naked torso, stripped of clothing, pulsing as if his body played host to something far wilder than mankind, rose to stand. He emitted a scream so unnatural and inhuman that Harvey squeezed his eyes closed at the intrusion and lay perfectly still.

The guard began to backtrack as the disfigured man took a single, unstable step. He appeared to sniff at the air, then grunted in delight at the fear his sense found. The ruined man took another step, then another, finding his flow and balance. As momentum built, he began to run. He passed Harvey in a flash of anger, his bare feet leaving a trail of blood.

The SUV lodged into the wall blocked the guard's exit. Scrambling, the terrified man found his partner's rifle lying dormant on the floor. He turned and fired.

But it was too late.

The ruined beast of a man collided with the guard, pinning him to the front of the car. He reached for his prize, gripped the man's head in both hands, and smashed his skull into the bonnet until it broke with a sickening crack.

Stunned by the events, Harvey began to move away. He rose to his feet with no sudden movements and stepped backward, creeping further into the building. But, as if enhanced senses alerted the ruined man, his head snapped around to face the corridor. His tongue, half-chewed, licked his lips. And his eyes, wild and red with blood, met Harvey's.

Harvey returned the stare.

The blood-soaked creature took a step towards Harvey.

CHAPTER THIRTY-THREE

Staring through a pair of double doors, Kane grinned as Doctor Farrow dropped the remains of Zulu-one and set his deranged sights on Harvey Stone, who was backing away along the corridor.

"Now we'll see the real power of SFS," said Kane. "Even if it is just the prototype."

The doors rattled as Stone tried to pull them open. But Jones slid his MP-5 through the handles, blocking his escape. Stone's angered face appeared at the small window then vanished behind a fog of breath. As the condensation faded, something hard and heavy slammed into the doors, and loud, feverish grunts accompanied the dull thuds of viscous beating.

"How long do you think he'll last?" asked Jones, standing beside Kane and watching with the same enthused awe as Harvey Stone and the drug-fuelled remains of Doctor Farrow rolled away from the doors along the corridor, locked in battle.

"I'm surprised he's lasted this long," replied Kane.

Harvey rolled on top and forced his thumb into Farrow's eye socket. But the move only antagonised the doctor. A surge of power threw Stone to one side, where he rolled to his feet in time for Farrow to launch another attack. The pair slammed against the glass wall of an observation room. From Kane's viewpoint behind the safety doors, he saw the glass panel flex with their weight. The two men, locked in a wrestle, pulled each other to the floor, grappling for control.

Farrow found himself on top.

The punches came hard and fast with no clarity as to which was Farrow's leading arm and which was his trailing follow-up punch. Each blow rocked Stone's head from side to side, and with each hit, he weakened a little more.

But there was more to the man who, over the last two days, had taken down Kane's Army one by one. There was a resilience uncommon in any man Kane had ever seen before. He had a tenacity so pure and raw, Kane couldn't help but admire him as he watched the battle play out.

"He won't get up," said Jones. "Nobody can withstand that."

But from their viewpoint, they saw calmness come over Stone. He no longer appeared to fight back. Instead, he absorbed the blows, either waiting for death to take him or his opponent to tire.

"That's it," said Jones.

Stone lay motionless on the bloodied floor, and Farrow rose, searching for a new victim. His eyes fell on Kane and Jones staring at him through the two small windows in the doors.

"Stone is done," said Kane.

"We have a much bigger problem," said Jones.

Farrow's eyes remained fixed on Kane's. His ruined body pulsed as the muscles beneath his flesh tensed and relaxed with the high volume of SFS. A flap of skin hung from Farrow's face. Tiny shards of glass were embedded into the wound and his fractured skull revealed a sickening sight.

"Farrow's tiring," said Jones, re-securing his MP-5 in the

door handles. "The SFS must be wearing off. We need to get to the bunker."

"No," replied Kane, his eyes wide with both disappointment and admiration. "Look at him, Jones."

But Jones was backing away from the doors, pulling his handgun from the holster fixed to his chest. "Move away, sir," he said. "If Farrow comes through, I'll take him down."

The tiny round window in the door darkened with Farrow's shadow. His face appeared at the glass. Torn skin revealed his rear teeth through what was once his cheek. His caved forehead seeped dark, red blood in thick gloops that hung from his brow. And his eyes, redder than any eyes Kane had ever seen, stared deep into his own.

Farrow's hand appeared in the second window pane. The doctor's once soft, gentle skin was now stained with blood. His once slender, precise fingers, the instruments of his profession, were curled, gnarled and tense, and ready to crush anything they gripped.

"Sir, move back," called Jones. "I can take him from here."

But Kane was in awe. He approached the window, stopping inches from Farrow's face, holding his gaze with wonder and fascination. Kane raised his hand, laying it flat against the glass and meeting Farrow's tensed, splayed fingers one for one.

"Sir, don't do it," said Jones. "He's wild. Move back. Let me take him out."

"No," said Kane, snatching his head to face Jones, whose face dropped at the sudden anger. "Lower your weapon, Jones."

But Jones remained with his weapon aimed at the glass.

"I said lower your weapon, Jones," said Kane. "That's an order."

He turned to face Farrow once more, who offered Jones a spiteful glare then returned to meet Kane's eyes, and softened. His head cocked to one side, and his face grimaced as he forced his tense hand flat against the glass, connecting it with Kane's.

With his free hand, Kane reached into his pocket, retrieved the small vial of prototype SFS, and held it up for Farrow to see. The effect was immediate. Farrow's unblinking eyes widened further. A snort fogged the glass and he began scratching at the door, pushing the wood until it bowed.

"Open the door, Jones," said Kane.

"Absolutely not, sir," replied Jones. "You've lost your mind."

"I said open the damn door," replied Kane, and pulled his weapon on Jones. "Now."

Jones glanced at the wall switch that released the electromagnetic doors, then at Farrow, whose ruined face pressed against the glass watching Jones' every move, and then back to Kane, who held his weapon high with a finger poised over the trigger.

A battle seemed to take place inside Jones' mind as he fought between what he knew was right and everything he'd been taught about respect, trust and loyalty. He took a breath and raised his arm to hit the switch. But at the last minute, he turned his weapon on Kane.

"Sir, I respectfully decline," said Jones, holding his head high.

"You'll open that door if it's the last thing you do," said Kane.

Farrow banged against the glass window.

"Sir, I cannot."

Kane shifted his aim from Jones' chest to his head.

Farrow banged against the door.

"Last chance, Jones."

The doors cracked as Farrow slammed against them; the wood bowed and flexed with his weight.

"Sir, you've lost your mind."

Both men opposed each other, fingers teasing the triggers, in a silent battle of courage until, at last, Jones lowered his weapon.

"For a moment there, I thought you'd forgotten who you were talking to," said Kane. "Drop it."

Jones tossed the handgun to the floor.

"Now open the damn door," said Kane.

Jones stepped forward to the doors, staring at Farrow eye to eye through the glass. He slid the MP-5 from between the handles, pulled the cocking lever, and flicked the safety off.

Bloodshot eyes tracked Jones to the emergency release button on the wall.

The doors flexed as Farrow pressed against the wood.

"Go on, Jones," said Kane.

With the MP-5 raised against Jones' shoulder, he nudged the door release with his elbow.

The doors crashed open and slammed into the walls. Jones stepped back, finger fixed to the trigger, and Doctor Farrow stepped through, sniffing at the air. Soft grunts came from his throat with each rapid breath. His eyes twitched and the muscles on his lean body tensed then relaxed as if on a perpetual cycle. He eyed Jones and took a step forward.

"That's it, Farrow," said Jones, taking a step back. "One more step and I'll put you down like a dog."

But instead of rushing Jones as Kane thought he would, Farrow turned his head sideways, studying the greying man who stood before him.

Farrow let out a cry, opening his mouth as far as his ruined jaw would allow.

Standing his ground, Kane reached into his pocket and removed the little vial of red liquid once more.

Farrow silenced.

"You want this?" asked Kane. Farrow snatched at the vial.

But Kane saw the move coming and snapped his hand away. "Now, now, Doctor Farrow, remember your manners."

Farrow retracted his hand like a child, but followed the vial with his eyes like a dog with the promise of a bone.

"Farrow," said Kane, pointing to his own face. "Eyes up here."

Farrow tore his eyes from the vial.

"You want this?" said Kane.

Farrow grunted in confirmation, his jaw muscles so tense, they allowed for no articulation of pronounced words.

Kane glanced across at Jones who was frozen in horror, and then back at Farrow.

"Kill," said Kane.

CHAPTER THIRTY-FOUR

Frozen with fear and facing death, Gabriella lay curled on the passenger seat with her feet against the dashboard as a deranged guard clung to the bonnet and tried to force his way through the windscreen. Harvey aimed the car at the building. Her eyes wandered to Harvey, and somehow in all the chaos she admired his control and tenacity. She reached out a hand and rested it on his shoulder, pushing the sickness to one side as the anticipation of feeding her hunger grew.

But the chance of satiating her thirst and her focus faded when the engine suddenly roared and Harvey pushed himself back into the seat. Then came a sense of weightlessness, a peace where time slowed and nothing mattered, until the front of the car smashed through the wall and chaos ensued.

Even as bricks and glass showered down onto the car, Harvey forced an entry through the row of lab benches, pushing further into the building despite the grinding, smoke and strong smell of fuel.

"We need to go," said Harvey. He raised his leg to kick the remains of the windscreen out from its frame. "Now, Gabriella. Move."

She feigned sickness, exaggerating her incapacitation by curling into a ball and closing her eyes.

"Stay here," said Harvey, and climbed through the space where the windscreen had been.

Harvey hadn't even hit the floor before gunshots sang out in the corridor ahead. Gabriella pushed the chair back and climbed into the rear of the car. She lay out of sight, peering through the rear window at the carnage in the laboratory.

Furniture had been toppled and dozens of vials had smashed onto the floor, forming a puddle in the middle of the room.

Her stomach twisted at the sight as if some monstrous hand squeezed her insides.

She scanned the wreckage for something. Anything. And gasped when her eyes found what she'd been looking for.

Glass shattered in the corridor in front of the car and the grunts and groans of men fighting, furniture being destroyed, and tempers flaring masked the heavy click of Gabriella opening the rear door.

But the sickness still lingered. Despite the thoughts of replenishing her body with another dose, and the joy as she pondered the feeling of it running through her veins, her legs failed to carry her weight.

Inch by inch, Gabriella crawled across broken glass, her body aching and sleep tugging at her consciousness, pulling her mind from the tray of syringes ahead and the single unbroken vial. She reached out, stretching as far as her weakened body would allow, feeling the taut muscles in her stomach pull. The weight of her arm was too heavy to hold. Her fingers fumbled for the tray but pushed it further away. One more shuffle across the floor and she reached it, tipping the tray over to spill its contents onto the floor.

Gabriella lay on her side. Her weak and shaking hands

caused the plastic hygiene wrapper to slip through her fingers. She tore at it with her teeth then spat the plastic away.

A scream, wild and savage, echoed from the corridor as she pulled the protective tip from the needle and plunged it into the vial. Nothing else existed as she watched the red liquid fill the syringe chamber.

Something huge crashed into the front of the car. Gabriella's heart jumped into gear as more agonised screams illustrated the scene in the corridor.

A vein, thick and blue, stuck out from her arm as if her body craved the offering, presenting itself to the needle. Her hands, weak and uncontrollable, fumbled with the syringe, and her eyes, laden with the weight of revenge, used every ounce of her energy to remain open.

The needle pierced the skin. The hot feeling as it found the vein and worked its way inside brought a grimace to Gabriella's numb face.

But the warm, tingling sensation as the drug worked its way into her bloodstream raised a sigh of relief from Gabriella's throat. It travelled to the far end of her toes and fingers. Almost immediately, the pain in her side subsided, the dull ache of her huge bruise faded, and her muscles found a new source of life.

Another scream came from the corridor. Heavy pounding like fists on wood. As Gabriella's senses recovered, an image formed of the scene.

A wave of nausea washed over her as she stood, and a rush of blood filled her head with blinding effect. She grasped for the support of a nearby bench, but misjudged her reach and fell to the floor, dizzied.

Climbing to her knees, she rose, slow and steady, controlling the movement, and stepped over to the middle of the room. Through the open rear door of the car in the corridor, she saw Doctor Farrow, enraged and pinning Harvey to the floor. An endless barrage of fists rose and fell, causing dull, hard thumps of bone on bone. Harvey was powerless.

As if sensing her observation, Harvey raised his head. His cold eyes found hers and, for a brief moment, there was an understanding. Then the doctor's fist came down once more and slammed Harvey's head to the floor.

For a second, her body reacted. Her heart began to race. She stepped forward as if she might reach him in time.

But she stopped.

And as the punches rained down on Harvey's body and SFS flowed through her veins bringing a renewed strength to her tired muscles, the darkness outside beckoned.

She whispered a silent thank you to Harvey and stepped outside into the rain.

CHAPTER THIRTY-FIVE

An electronic buzzer announced the opening of doors followed by a tiny click as the electromagnet locked them into place. Then came a hiss as the air stabilised and finally an extractor kicked into life.

Harvey moved his leg, wincing at the wound that Gabriella had dressed as the dried blood ripped from the material of his pants. His tongue slipped between his lips but found only split skin beneath a layer of dried and crusted blood. Breathing through his nose was close to impossible due to the sharp ends of broken bone that pierced his flesh.

A glass-walled room enclosed Harvey. It was featureless save for the single solid wall with a glass observation window.

Slow footsteps clicked on the linoleum floor.

Harvey opened his eyes, expecting to find himself bound to the gurney he was lying on by ropes or handcuffs. But only the pain in his bruised body stopped him from jumping up and throttling the old man who stepped into view. The man held his hands behind his back with his head upturned as if pondering where to begin.

Kane stared down at Harvey, smiling with inquisitiveness, as a cruel child might when pulling the wings off an insect.

Rolling his neck to one side, Harvey waited for the satisfying click. But his bruised shoulders complained. Even his breathing, which was extremely shallow, hurt like never before.

"Good evening, Mr Stone," said Kane. His voice was clear but dulled by the sound control built into the room.

Harvey didn't reply.

"You're quite the fighter. Most men would have given up with a beating like that. But I am glad you decided to drop by. And I'm glad you decided not to give up on life just yet, Harvey. Can I call you Harvey?" said Kane, leaving no gap for a reply. "You've become quite the thorn in my side."

"You haven't exactly brightened my day, Kane," Harvey mumbled painfully.

"Well, before you get any good ideas, I might remind you that it's feeding time for Doctor Farrow." Kane leaned in closer to Harvey and lowered his voice. Then he opened his hand to reveal a vial of red liquid identical to Gabriella's. "He'll do anything for a fix."

Harvey didn't reply.

"Do you know what this is?" asked Kane, as he stepped over to the glass wall and peered at the wreckage outside.

"I've seen what it does," said Harvey, and gestured at Farrow.

"Why don't we start from the beginning? I'm assuming Miss DuBois put you up to this?" said Kane, ignoring Harvey's flippancy.

Harvey didn't reply. Instead, he locked onto Kane's stare, watching every move, twitch and gesture.

"Would you like something for the pain, Harvey?" said Kane with a smile. "I've got just the thing."

"I don't need anything."

Harvey swung his legs from the gurney and looked around the room.

"Such strength," mused Kane, turning his back to stare back through the glass wall. It was a power move to assure Harvey that Farrow would prevent any attack he was planning. "A man like you would be unstoppable with a little help from me. I could make you rich, you know?"

"I don't want your money," said Harvey, finding his lips dry and his throat scratched with thirst.

"We all have our price, Harvey. There isn't a man I've met in all my years on this earth who wouldn't break his moral code for a fee."

"You haven't met me before."

"My loss, Mr Stone. But I'm sure we'll make up for lost time," said Kane, and offered Harvey a wink in his reflection. "So, where were we? Oh yes. Am I right in assuming that you were coerced into this little enterprise by our friend Miss DuBois?"

"I have nothing to do with her," said Harvey.

"But you do know of her?"

"She broke into my house."

"Your house?" said Kane, feigning ignorance.

"The one you burned down," said Harvey. He felt the jolt of something inside him, like the flicking of a switch as his anger flared, and then subsided.

"I hope you can see how devoted I am to the cause," said Kane. "I've put everything I have into this little enterprise and nothing will stop me now."

"What's the cause?"

"Honour," said Kane, without any hesitation. "Plus, it would be nice to clear my name along the way. It got a little tainted in my younger days. I'd like to leave this world with some kind of legacy, something the world can remember me by, not just my mistakes. You know how it is. People have a tendency to remember the bad and forget about the good."

"Does it matter what other people think?" asked Harvey. A single bead of sweat formed on his brow then began its slow journey down his face before nestling in the two days' growth on his skin.

"I bet you've done some bad things, Mr Stone. I bet there's more to you than meets the eye. The funny thing is, when we searched the databases, Harvey Stone doesn't seem to exist."

"You researched me?" said Harvey, then coughed as burning acid reflux warmed the back of his throat.

"I tried. There's no shame in knowing who you're up against, is there? Know your enemy, Harvey. The first rule of war. Now, in my experience, there are two types of man with your talent and no record. But I can't decide which you are."

Harvey spat on the floor, taking deep breaths and directing his thoughts to an escape.

Kane watched with curiosity, his head cocked to one side and one eye semi-closed, as if he was reading what Harvey was thinking.

"What are my options?" said Harvey. "I'll tell you if you're right."

"Men like you don't exist for a reason. The government keeps you secret. They've invested too much into you. Training. Knowledge. Secrets that will go with you to your grave."

"Or?" asked Harvey.

"Or you're a bad, bad man, Harvey Stone. You've done terrible things that can never be known and you're destined for a life underground. That's why you're out here. That's why you're so upset about your crummy little house. Because it's all you had and all you'll ever have. You so much as raise your head in a crowd and someone out there will take it off, tick a box, and walk away with just another brown envelope. You're a notch on a hit list and nothing more."

Kane allowed a small pause for his two theoretical summaries to digest.

"Why don't *you* tell me which one you are, Harvey? The good news is that I admire both," said Kane. "There's no prejudice here. So, tell me. Who is the *real* Harvey Stone?"

Kane turned back to face the glass wall. His cruel expression softened into a picture of admiration while Harvey took a breath to reply.

"I've got some bad news for you, Kane," said Harvey, as he pushed himself from the gurney and stood for the first time, his bruised bones screaming for some kind of reprise. He found Kane's reflection and fixed his stare. "I'm just a guy who's going to kill the man who burned down his house."

"It's a pity. We would have made a great team," said Kane, with an audible and theatrical sigh. "I suppose Miss DuBois is out to scupper my plans right now, is she?"

"I'd say your plans are well and truly scuppered, Kane," said Harvey.

"How so?" said Kane. "The prime minister is a few hours away, and I still have one man in the field. Plus I'm not too long in the tooth to get my own hands dirty, you know?"

"Who was it Kane?" said Harvey. "Who's paying you?"

"Now, now, Harvey. A good businessman doesn't reveal his sources."

"And what's next? A life on the run?" said Harvey. "Honestly, it's not what it's cracked up to be."

"And why would I run, Harvey?" said Kane. "We'll be heroes."

"If you kill the prime minister, Kane, that's it. You'll have every contract killer in Europe after you, and you can't run forever. They'll hang you by your balls."

"Kill the prime minister?" said Kane, unable to contain a crazed laugh. "Mr Stone, I am not going to kill the prime minister."

"So why are your men placed strategically across the town?" asked Harvey. "Armed to the teeth and preparing for a battle?"

"We're not planning the prime minister's assassination, Mr Stone," said Kane, as he stepped toward Harvey. "We are here to save him."

Harvey didn't reply.

"So where's Gabriella, Harvey?" said Kane, his voice serious and his tone flat and cautious. "I imagine she's comatose somewhere, withdrawal getting the better of her."

"She's gone," said Harvey.

"Gone?" replied Kane, his voice rising as temper reddened his face. "Gone? Do you realise what you've done, you meddling fool?"

Harvey didn't reply.

His thoughts returned to his conversation with Gabriella on the hill, about how Kane was planning the attack, about her military days, and how highly she had spoken of the resistance.

"So it seems your usefulness has expired, Harvey Stone," said Kane, seeing the realisation hit Harvey like a slap in the face. "And my work is still incomplete. So I'll bid you farewell."

Kane moved across to the doorway, where he turned and looked back at Harvey. Then he moved his attention to Farrow.

"You know what to do, Doctor Farrow," said Kane, then pulled the door shut.

Kane appeared on the far side of the glass wall. Harvey limped away from the gurney to face Farrow head on.

But a tiny light appeared in the corner of Harvey's vision.

A flash of steel where Kane was standing.

A flickering orange flame.

And a sickening smile as Kane dropped a lighter into the pool of fuel.

CHAPTER THIRTY-SIX

From the rise of the hill in the pouring rain, the fire burned bright against the dark sky and black forest, which filled the valley like a slow moving river in the night.

With one hand on the open door of the SUV, Kane turned and surveyed the sleeping town before him, revising his plan for the prime minister while the citizens counted down the hours to Christmas.

A single road entered the town, dotted with the large villas of the rich until the rows of terraced houses began. Tourist-fuelled restaurants sprawled out from the marina, a catchment for the cruise ships that docked in the port each week.

Obscured by shadows, two alleys sat either side of the road where the terraces began. It had been the perfect place for Bravo team to close the doors. But somewhere in those alley-ways, they had been cut down by Stone, leaving the doors wide open.

A distant crack of thunder grew in volume then faded like the grumbling of a bear.

A flash of lightning silenced it; the light formed a snapshot of the town on Kane's retinas.

At the foot of the main road, the largest rooftop in the small town sprawled from the dockside to the core of the community. All routes led past the fish market. With exits to all corners of the town, it had been the perfect place for an ambush.

But somewhere inside lay the corpses of Alpha team, Kane's best men. His eye twitched at the thought. But the inferno that filled the night behind him satiated his anger.

The entrance to the marina was accessed by two gates at the far end of the town. In his mind's eye, Kane imagined the prime minister and his family with their motorcade driving past the fish market and through the gates. Kane's last man would be scanning the scene through the telescopic scope of his high-powered Diemaco from the church tower.

He raised his radio to his mouth, searching the dark town for the tall steeple.

"Tango-one, this is Charlie-one. Come back."

But only static returned through the radio's tiny speaker. The signal boost from the research facility would be down, and the distance from the hill to the church was too great for the radio waves to travel.

"Tango-one, this is Charlie-one. Come back."

But still, there was no reply.

Climbing back into the car and running his hand through his wet, grey hair, Kane fired the engine into life, killed the lights, and rolled into town, all the while searching the sides of the road for DuBois.

It was just an ordinary night in the alleyways where Bravo team had been stationed. The black SUV, identical to Kane's, was still parked close by. There was no sign of the bodies of his men. Kane stopped the car and searched the alleys.

Tucked into the shadows, Bravo-one stared lifelessly up at the sky, his mouth ajar and frozen with an expression of fear.

Bravo-two was lying close by. The rain that pounded his dead flesh was insufficient to wash the blood from his open neck.

Kane examined the bodies and removed all identification. Then he searched the road left and right and tried the radio once more. His proximity to the church was now much closer.

"Tango-one, this is Charlie-one. Come back."

But no reply came.

Kane cruised to the fish market. The five hundred yards required little more than a tickle of the heavy SUV's accelerator. Gravity finished the job, and he rolled to a stop beside the building, leaving the lights on and the engine running.

Heavy rain thundered onto the roof of the long building, drowning out all other sounds save for the low rumble of the storm that hung in the sky above, reluctant to pass by.

The car park was empty, except for the dark corpse that lay on the ground. The body was lit by a flickering light from inside the two sliding doors. Kane stood over Alpha-two and peered into the building. Rows and rows of benches, worn from years of local fishermen selling their catch to tourists and restaurants along the coast, stood proudly in the flickering light.

But at the far end of the space in the loading bay, a grisly form swayed back and forth, hanging lifeless from a block and tackle. A steel hook was buried deep into the back of Alpha-one's head. Strings of blood hung from the body, visible even from afar.

Once more, Kane collected the identification of the men he had served with, the men he had been proud to fight with, and the men with whom he had shared a common disgrace from the country they'd served for most of their adult lives.

He added the IDs to those of Bravo team, and placed them inside his breast pocket. Then he stepped back out into the rain. Three flashes of lightning lit the sky. The first captured Kane's attention. The second allowed him to take in the scene. The third drew his focus to the tallest landmark in the town.

"Tango-one, this is Charlie-one. Come back," said Kane into his radio, half in and half out of the SUV.

Silence.

He stared up at the steeple at the far end of the dockside road, which framed the marina as if holding the town at bay from the welcoming Mediterranean Sea.

"Tango-one, this is Charlie-one. Come back."

He dropped the radio into the inside pocket of the car, climbed in, and closed the door, shutting out the noise of the rain on the fish market roof. The little green LED at the top of the radio lit up. It was faint, but bright enough to catch Kane's eye.

"Charlie-one, I have you in my sights."

Kane froze at the sound of Gabriella's voice. The green LED blinked on once more.

"One wrong move, Monsieur Kane, and I'll put a hole in you big enough to park the prime minister's yacht."

"DuBois, you don't know who you're messing with," said Kane over the radio. "You're playing with the big boys now and you're in way over your head."

"Au contraire, Monsieur Kane. I know exactly who you are. I knew about you and your plans even before your imbecile friends captured me. It is you who is ignorant of who *I* am," replied Gabriella. "Do you honestly think that a cretin like Jones could catch me, Gabriella DuBois? I think not."

"Are you trying to tell me you planned on us kidnapping you?" said Kane with a laugh and a single exhale of disbelief. "You could never have known what we were planning."

"Unless we had someone on the inside, Monsieur Kane," said Gabriella. "Someone who had access to all of your plans."

"Would this someone possess the knowledge to create SFS too, Miss DuBois?"

"The knowledge, yes. But alas, we lacked the funds."

A smile, raw and vengeful, found Gabriella's lips as Kane hung his head.

"Farrow was with you all along?" asked Kane.

"You should have done your research, Monsieur Kane.

Farrow was a good friend, as devoted to France as you are devoted to power. But now your power is gone. Your time has passed. In fact, you can count the hours of your remaining life on those stubby little fingers of yours."

She placed the radio resting on the ledge. Positioning herself with her back to the church bell, Gabriella took three deep breaths to control the tingling in her fingers. She flexed her hand then fingered the trigger.

In her sights, the only movement was the wash of wind-blown rain that fell diagonally across the marina.

"I have played your games for long enough. I am no longer your laboratory rat, Monsieur Kane. Now *I* am the master, and you will do everything I say, when I say so."

"You'll die for this, DuBois," said Kane. "No more games. No more small talk. When I'm finished with you, you'll wish you had died in the lab with your dirty little friends, twitching on the ground while their organs failed and their bowels collapsed like the dirty little French whores there were."

A rush of blood dizzied Gabriella. It was enough to elicit a smile but faint enough for her to bring it under control with a few breaths of the cold air. It was too early to peak.

"And who will do such a thing?" said Gabriella. "Your men are all dead. All that remains of Kane's Army is a sad, pathetic old man."

"It isn't over yet, DuBois."

"No," said Gabriella. "No, you're right. In one hour, the sun will rise, and the prime minister and his motorcade will drive into Saint-Pierre, safe in the knowledge that Kane's Army has secured the town."

She paused, giving Kane time to imagine what was in store for him.

"In two hours, you will be dead," said Gabriella. "But in the eyes of the French people, you will be a hero. If I were you,

I would let that little thought carry you through to the morning."

"We have a very different understanding of the word hero, DuBois."

"Remove the keys from the ignition," said Gabriella, maintaining control of the situation. "Try to run and I'll cut you down."

The interior light of the SUV flashed on. Kane stepped out into the rain, closing the door behind him. He stared up at the church tower.

Through the rifle scope, Gabriella met his stare. The crosshairs met in the centre of his chest. She adjusted her aim, finding his forehead. She imagined pulling the trigger. The spray of red mist. His body as it crumpled to the ground.

Kane raised the radio to his mouth. "Now what?"

Gabriella returned the rifle to aim at his chest, the largest target with the most devastating result.

"Toss the keys into the boat yard," replied Gabriella. She watched him throw the keys, keeping sight on him at all times. "Are you armed, Monsieur Kane?"

"You can see me. Why don't you tell me?" replied Kane.

"You have a handgun under your jacket on your left side. Remove the gun."

Kane did as requested. As any man with military experience might, he felt the weight of his handgun with a practiced hand.

"How many rounds?" asked Gabriella.

Kane looked up at the church again as if he was surprised that she saw the movement.

"A full magazine," he replied.

"Good," said Gabriella. "Although you will need only one."

"You're running out of time, Gabriella."

"Au contraire, Monsieur Kane. It is you who is running out of time," said Gabriella, enjoying the power she held over the man who threatened everything for which she had lived. "Kneel on the ground."

Even from a thousand yards, Kane's outrage was clear. He stared up at her with his arms outstretched as if questioning her sanity.

"Do it, Monsieur Kane."

"You're out of your mind, Gabriella. There is no more time for games."

Adjusting her aim to the right, Gabriella fired once. The headlight of the car smashed. She returned her aim to Kane.

"Next time it's your knee," said Gabriella. "Now kneel."

Kane bent one leg, held onto the wet ground for stability, and then bent his other leg and knelt on the hard concrete.

"Is this it?" said Kane. "Is this how I die?"

"No, Monsieur Kane. This is how you repent. Close your eyes and turn your face to the rain."

The distance was too far to see, but with his face upturned to the skies, Gabriella assumed that Kane's eyes were closed.

"Now, Monsieur Kane, put the gun to your head."

There was no movement for a second, save for the cocking of Kane's head to one side as he struggled to comprehend the instruction.

"You heard me correctly," said Gabriella. "Place the gun to your head."

Kane did as requested.

"Repeat these words after me," said Gabriella, her voice calm. She closed her eyes and gave thought to those that had fallen in the battle, grateful to reach the end.

"Claudia Deseille," said Gabriella.

No reply came.

"I have only one headlight left, Monsieur Kane. Do I need to fire another warning shot?"

"Claudia Deseille," spat Kane, then lowered the radio.

"Monica Deux," said Gabriella.

"Monica Deux," said Kane. He exhaled the words as if he understood what Gabriella was trying to do and felt that the recital was needless.

"Estella Bouchard," said Gabriella.

"Estella Bouchard."

Pausing to allow Kane to reflect on the names he'd recited, Gabriella opened her eyes and found him in her sight. He was ready to die. He had accepted death long before he'd stepped foot on a battle field.

"Donna Almeida," said Gabriella.

She felt the pang of SFS release into her blood like a hot coffee on cold teeth.

Kane remained silent, as if saying the name and reaching the end of the recital would instigate his end.

"Monsieur Kane, say her name," said Gabriella. "Donna Almeida."

"Donna Almeida," said Kane. The voice cracked from interference over the radio and the broken tones of a guilty man. He straightened his posture, kneeling tall and proud, waiting for the bullet.

A tear formed in Gabriella's eye and she cleared her throat of emotion, holding the push-to-talk button down on the radio, but saying nothing.

The one movement she allowed him was to hang his head in shame.

"Thank you, Monsieur Kane," said Gabriella. "Are you ready to die for your honour?"

CHAPTER THIRTY-EIGHT

The lack of airflow in the glass-walled room combined with the fire that raged in the corridor outside encouraged a layer of sweat on Harvey's skin that soaked into his clothes. Farrow slid down the rear wall to the floor. All anger and aggression for Harvey had dissipated, leaving just the shell of a drug-fuelled man whose body had entered into self-destruction.

Tall flames licked at the corridor ceiling, angry and unrelenting in their efforts to chew through anything that stood in their path, demonstrating to Harvey and Farrow what lay in store for them when the glass gave way.

"How long will it last?" said Harvey.

He paced along the length of the glass and stood beside the control room window. The control room still sat in relative peace and darkness, its conditions untainted by the blaze of orange that crept along the corridor outside.

Farrow stared back at him, offering an expression that conveyed an acceptance of death.

"Can you talk?" asked Harvey. But Farrow slumped further, his broken mind and dying body clinging to the cool wall. "Farrow," said Harvey, crouching before him, "we have to get out of here."

Farrow stared back at him. He raised a hand and touched Harvey's swollen face as if ashamed of what he had done. His red eyes moistened and a tear formed in the corner of each eye.

Farrow shook his head then turned his face against the wall.

"Farrow, how long will the air last?" said Harvey, grabbing Farrow's shoulders and losing control of his anger.

The aggression roused the forlorn man from his semi-slumber. He flinched at the touch of Harvey's hand and, in an instant, gripped him by the neck, holding with an iron-like grip despite Harvey's attempts to break free.

Climbing to his feet, Farrow dragged Harvey up and across the floor to the control room window, where he slammed him into the glass.

"Don't you see?" said Farrow, with more of a breath than articulated words. "We both die here."

Harvey pulled at the man's hands with everything he had, but to no avail. The grip seemed to strengthen with Harvey's efforts.

"I'm dying," said Farrow. "I can feel my body failing."

"There's time to get out," gasped Harvey. "There's time to get Kane."

"Die with me here before the fire consumes us both," said Farrow, as if his offer of death was some sort of compensation for the beating he'd given Harvey.

"Stop, Farrow," said Harvey, struggling to suck in the thinning air. "Don't do this."

But Farrow increased the strength of his grip, pinching at Harvey's windpipe and slamming him into the glass.

With only seconds of strength left, Harvey began an onslaught of punches.

But no matter how hard Harvey punched and kicked, the

blows failed to halt Farrow's efforts. He slammed Harvey into the wall, pressing his face against the control room window.

Harvey's hands fumbled for Farrow's face. His thumbs found the soft eye sockets and forced an entry, pushing the eyeballs back until Farrow screamed and squeezed Harvey's throat, closing off whatever gap remained.

Deeper and deeper, Harvey forced his thumbs inside the sockets. He pulled at the sinew inside, finding taut nerves that seemed to electrify Farrow. But still, the man held onto Harvey's neck. A thick sweat glazed Farrow's skin. As the two men grappled, each of them pushing the other closer to death, bright lights danced in Harvey's vision. A darkness enveloped his sight and the beat of his dying heart thumped like a bass drum inside his chest.

Without warning, a pane of the glass wall exploded from the heat and vacuum of air.

Angry flames licked at the walls around them both, searching for fuel. They found Farrow's tortured body.

He screamed and released Harvey, who pulled his hands back to cover his face from the searing heat. Harvey fell to the floor, gasping for air. His fingers searched for something to grip on the smooth linoleum floor to pull himself away and find somewhere cooler.

The flames receded, finding no air to fuel its rage, and the next pane of glass cracked from top to bottom as the heat overwhelmed the glass.

Harvey dragged himself to his feet, his raspy breath sucking in as much air as it could. He pulled one of the big heavy gurneys closer then lifted it, holding it high above his head. Then he hurled it at the control room window.

Nothing happened. The gurney bounced back and fell to the floor at his feet.

Then the glass partition became a wall of raging flames as

the fire closed in, trying to enter the control room. Inside, the ceiling had begun to smoulder and thick smoke rolled through the top of the doorway.

Seeing his last chance of escape become engulfed in flames, Harvey pulled the gurney up above his head once more, stepped back, and smashed it into the window with everything he had.

Nothing happened. His attempts were too weak to scratch the glass. He struck the glass three more times. But the oxygen in the air had grown too thin. Harvey dizzied. He rested the end of the gurney on the floor, leaning his weight on it while sucking in empty air.

Through the control room window, flickering orange crept into view, finding new fuel in the untouched walls and ceiling.

Harvey dropped to one knee, unable to hold his own weight.

A hand gripped Harvey's shoulder.

Instinct sent the signal to his brain to defend himself and strike out, but his body was starved of oxygen. He let go of the frame and braced for the final blow that would finish him.

But no blow came.

The gurney was wrenched from Harvey's grip. He toppled and fell to the floor. The bright lights that had danced across his vision in wondrous circles now succumbed to the darkness that was closing in. The pain in his chest, like stabs of a blade, grew stronger as his lungs sought fresh, clean air but found only thick, black smoke.

The next partition of the glass wall shattered. The flames erupted as if rejoicing at their invasion and reached out across the ceiling.

The control room window was framed with a mix of fiery reds and oranges. Harvey turned his face to the floor, seeking a layer of air as the room prepared to collapse.

Harvey closed his eyes.

Another bang sounded, louder than the first. Glass shattered behind him as more of the glass wall gave in, and a rush of heat filled the room, fighting for the same sparse oxygen as Harvey.

Farrow screamed, wild and angry. The yell evolved into a growl that culminated in a final smash of glass. Harvey rolled, peering through one eye in time to see the gurney disappearing through the control room window.

A hand, strong but gentle, pulled at Harvey's arm. He tried to fight back, but there was nothing left. Even as Farrow pulled him to his feet and lifted him, Harvey's fingers searched for a weakness, the eye, the ears, anything.

A breeze touched Harvey's face. It was weak, but it was there, fractions of a degree cooler than the hot air that was suffocating him. He opened his eyes as Farrow held him up to the window, trying to pass him through the gap into the control room.

Hope reared its head.

He sensed a taste of oxygen, faint, but enough to tease Harvey's dying body.

But as Farrow leaned through the hole, pushing Harvey to safety, the ceiling above them collapsed. Burning timber and ceiling fixtures dropped into the room, landing on Harvey and Farrow, and pinning Harvey to the ground with its burning dead weight. Intense heat singed Harvey's face and hands. Smoke stung at his eyes like hot sand. There was nowhere to turn, no refuge from the blaze.

With a roar of sheer power and animal strength, Farrow threw himself through the flames and fell to the floor. He pulled the burning debris off Harvey, who rolled to his knees and clambered back to the one remaining wall that wasn't ablaze.

Harvey pushed himself to his feet and shielded his face from the intense heat. But through the flickering flames and heat haze, he saw Farrow crouching in the collapsed doorway.

The man who had been so close to death just ten minutes before, whose body had entered into self-destruction mode, began to stand.

The timbers across his back found skin with a hiss that was audible above the crackling destruction of wood. He growled once more. It wasn't a roar of anger. It wasn't a cry of pain. It was the final growl of a man who was sacrificing his life in repent.

Timbers fell around him, scorching his melting skin. His hair took flame and lit his anguished face. But he rose to full height, creating a small gap in the flaming debris for Harvey to escape.

As the flames danced across Farrow's ruined face, his pain-filled stare found Harvey's eyes. No words were needed. There was no time for sorrow.

"Now," Farrow cried.

He squeezed his burning eyes closed and let out one final scream of spent energy and frustration.

With just fractions of a second to spare, Harvey threw himself between Farrow's legs into the corridor. He rolled to where the fire had yet to reach. A cool stretch of linoleum lay beneath a layer of cool oxygen.

Harvey rolled to his feet and reached into the fire, fumbling to pull Farrow free.

But it was too late.

As Harvey's outstretched hand touched Farrow's melting skin, the rest of the control room ceiling and walls gave way. Harvey leaped for the safety of the unburned stretch of corridor. He turned to witness a frenzy of flames rush across the debris pile in a victorious dance of orange and red with Farrow beneath it, his sins repented.

CHAPTER THIRTY-NINE

"How does it feel?" said Gabriella over the radio.

Kane sighed and hit the push-to-talk button. "Do you think this is the first time I've had a gun pointed at me?"

"A man like you? No. I imagine there have been many men who have had you in their sights," said Gabriella. "But rest assured, this will be the last."

"And if I pulled the trigger now? What would you do then?"

"I would do nothing. My plan would continue and you would die, shamed, as you are now," said Gabriella. "Don't you see, Monsieur Kane? I am offering you a chance to redeem yourself, to clear your name. I am offering you a chance to save France and all she stands for."

"Why would I care about France?"

"You would be a hero. I've seen how you wear those medals on your chest, regardless of your disgrace. You have no honour. Men like you seek glory whatever the cost."

"You don't know anything about me, Gabriella," said Kane. "You were just a lab rat, a disposable lump of meat in the palm of my hand."

"Lower the weapon, Monsieur Kane."

Kane glanced up at the tower in the distance.

"I said lower it," said Gabriella.

He lowered the gun.

"Now get up and walk."

"Where am I walking?"

"To victory, Monsieur Kane," said Gabriella. "When the prime minister arrives, you will be standing there waiting for him. He will see you, so he can recognise your infinite leadership skills and the quality of Kane's Army."

Kane said nothing. He just stared up at the church tower.

"But your success will be short-lived. You will die. But whether you die a hero or the disgraced fool you are is up to you," said Gabriella. "Now walk."

Kane began the long walk, following the path the prime minister's small motorcade would be taking in the morning. He splashed through puddles of rain water and considered his defeat. What would it mean to the men that had died for him? Killed while fighting for their names to be freed from their tarnished state. Failure now would seal their fate.

"Are you going to tell me how you pulled this off?" said Kane. "Surely now is the time to gloat."

"We've known about your plans for some time," said Gabriella. "We have spies everywhere and we are all willing to die for France."

"All of you?" said Kane. The statement invoked a conscious thought that held the faces of his men at bay. "Who's all of you?"

"Donna," said Gabriella, "Claudia, Monica, Estella. We were all against you. There are others, as I'm sure you will know. We are willing to die for our beloved France. Not even the vile tactics of a disgraced British military officer could stop us."

"So it's true," said Kane. "You are resistance."

"Yes. If you have to categorise us, if your analytical mind must place us, then we are the French Resistance. Too long have we hidden in the shadows. Too long have we been forced underground. We fight for France. We fight for everything she stands for."

"I don't see any others," said Kane. "Does the future of France rest on the whims of one stupid girl and her idiotic fantasies about right and wrong?"

Gabriella laughed, admiring Kane's confident officer-like gait from afar.

"The prime minister will be here in thirty minutes," she said. "He will arrive unannounced to spend a private Christmas with his family in his yacht. It is the perfect opportunity for an assassination. Am I right, Monsieur Kane?"

"Yes," said Kane.

"The French government knows this. But to install a security detail would bring too much attention to this small town. Would it not, Monsieur Kane?" said Gabriella. "People would talk. They would wonder why the military walked their streets. The prime minister's visit would be all over the national newspapers. It would be an invitation for many nationalists to come and vent their anger at the man who is bringing France to its knees."

"People often pay no attention to what is in front of their faces, DuBois," said Kane.

"And that is why Kane's Army were hired, a team of highly trained men who can patrol the streets without raising an eyelid. Am I correct, Monsieur Kane?"

"That's about the size of it," said Kane. "Is there a point to all of this?"

"So let me finish my summary," said Gabriella. "Let me explain what this stupid girl and her idiotic whims of what is right and wrong has accomplished. Behind you, at the entrance to town, is the perfect place for Bravo team to secure the town of Saint-Pierre. No escape. Am I right, Monsieur Kane?"

"Yes."

"And the fish market beside you is the perfect place for an ambush, so it must be guarded. I'm sure you found Alpha team by now."

"Yes," said Kane, remembering the hook in the back of Alpha-one's head.

He crossed the street with the dockside on his left and the church ahead on the right overlooking the small town.

"And from the church tower of Saint-Pierre, Tango team can see the whole town. He was your last resort, was he not, Monsieur Kane?"

"Yes," said Kane. "So what?"

"So now, when the prime minister drives into the town, there will be no Bravo team to lock the doors behind him. There is no Alpha team to prevent an ambush. And there is no Tango team to overlook the town. There is just you, me, and the prime minister, Monsieur Kane."

"Why are you doing this, DuBois?" said Kane.

"For my love of France. For freedom and for revenge," said Gabriella. "We will both be heroes. The only difference is that I'll be alive to enjoy my glory."

Kane stopped at the edge of the dockside. Dark, inky water lapped against the concrete. The Mediterranean Sea beyond the port was pale with white caps merging in the wind. The rows of vessels, from small fishing boats to sailing yachts, rocked back and forth with the ebb and flow of the storm-driven water.

"So how is this going to work?" said Kane.

"The best plans are always the simplest, Monsieur Kane. The plan differs from your own only in the final act. You will wait where you are. The prime minister will arrive and you will be greeted. You will be thanked and complimented on the excellent security, leaving you to escort him and his family to his yacht."

"I'm gaining his trust?" said Kane.

"Yes, Monsieur Kane. The prime minister will allow his family to board the yacht. His staff will carry their bags and the prime minister will board the boat last. The moment he turns his back, you will fire a single shot into the back of his head. Your name will forever be tarnished in the eyes of the military. But, Monsieur Kane, in the eyes of France, you will be a hero."

"And if I don't?" said Kane, with an exhale. "If I don't pull the trigger?"

"Ah, Monsieur Kane," said Gabriella. "If you do not kill the prime minister, the consequences for you will be beyond your wildest imagination."

Three pairs of headlights appeared at Bravo checkpoint. They passed by unhindered and cruised into the town. Bravo team did not close in behind them.

The first and last cars were both police Peugeots. The middle car was a sleek, black saloon. The motorcade continued down the hill to the fish market, which they passed without incident. Alpha team were not surveilling the area for an attack.

The cars drove on, washing through a long rain puddle, maintaining the thirty-kilometres-per-hour speed limit despite having one of France's most prominent targets on board, despite the town being deserted on Christmas Eve, and despite the apparent lack of security.

The three cars pulled into the marina, took a wide half-circle and stopped beside the yacht's boardwalk, where Kane was standing to attention.

"It is show time, Monsieur Kane," said Gabriella.

The two policemen in the first car remained seated, but the passenger door of the saloon opened and a man in a suit appeared. He glanced around at the empty space and nodded at Kane before approaching him.

"I have your eyeball in my cross-hairs, Monsieur Kane," said Gabriella. "If you try anything stupid, you will die a failure and a disgrace. Blink twice if you understand."

Kane blinked twice then offered his hand to the prime minister's chief of security.

"Mr Kane?" said the man.

"Good morning, Monsieur Berger," replied Kane.

"The area is secure? I haven't been able to reach you. We agreed on open communications, did we not?"

Kane nodded. "Apologies, Monsieur Berger. It must be the storm." Kane waved his hand at the sky then opened his palm out to catch a few drops of rain. "It's been playing up all night."

Berger studied Kane as if reading him with a trained eye.

"Is everything okay, Monsieur Kane?" asked Berger. "You seem a little distracted."

"I'm fine," said Kane. "It's been a long night, that's all."

"And your men? Where are your men? You promised me a minimum of three teams. Yet nobody stopped us on the way into town. I saw no men at the agreed check point. Where are they, Monsieur Kane?"

"I promised you security, Mr Berger. That you cannot see my men is a testament to their skills."

"Very good, Monsieur Kane," said Berger, offering a nod with a hint of suspicion. "Is there anything I should know? Were there any incidents at all?"

Berger continued to examine Kane, waiting for an answer. But Kane remained silent.

"Monsieur Kane. I asked you a question," said Berger. "Is there anything I should know about?"

"Charlie-one, this is Tango-two," said Gabriella through the radio. "All clear, sir. Nothing to report."

Through the scope, Gabriella saw Berger raising his eyebrows.

"Nothing to report, then?" said Berger.

"Nothing to report," said Kane, snapping out of his daze.

The two men met in a stare. Berger's inquisitive eyes searched for a hint of disbelief. Kane's blank stare offered nothing in response but a seed of doubt and a flavour of fear.

"Very well, Monsieur Kane. Let's get this over with," said Berger.

He turned, gave the small marina a thorough visual examination then stepped over to the saloon and opened the rear door. He retrieved a black umbrella from the parcel shelf and popped it open in time for a tall man in a casual sports jacket, cream pants and boat shoes to step out. The prime minister buttoned his jacket, collected the umbrella from Berger, and held out his hand for his family to follow. A small boy climbed outside then turned and waited for his mother, displaying the mannerisms of a well-educated young man rather than the average boy who might have run to the gangway and onto the boat.

The first lady of France followed, her smile barely weakened by the harsh wind and incessant rain. She stood beside her husband, who passed her the umbrella, then she took the boy's hand. The prime minister extended his arm, allowing his wife and son to board the yacht. Then, as two staff carried two cases aboard, he shook Berger's hand. He turned to board the boat but stopped when he saw Kane. His eyes flicked between the two men as if requesting an answer to an unspoken question.

"Sir, may I introduce Monsieur Kane," said Berger, his voice hinting at a bitterness or reluctance to make the introduction.

"Keep your cool, Monsieur Kane," whispered Gabriella.

"Anglais?" said the prime minister.

"Yes, sir," replied Kane.

The prime minister offered his hand to Kane, who hesitated, then reached out and shook it.

"Our journey was uneventful. I believe we have you to

thank, Monsieur Kane," said the prime minister. "We were expecting the journey to be a little bumpy."

"Enjoy your Christmas, sir," replied Kane, and offered him a weak smile.

The prime minister nodded. "And you," he replied. Then he nodded his approval at Berger and turned to board the boat.

"Are you ready, Monsieur Kane?" whispered Gabriella. "Glory and honour await."

"Sorry, sir?" said Kane as the prime minister placed his foot on the gangway.

He turned to face Kane, his hand on the rail.

"Now," said Gabriella.

"There is just one more thing," said Kane.

He raised his weapon as Gabriella's first shot entered the side of Berger's head.

A single shot sang out in the night. It came from a high powered rifle from the church steeple above where Harvey stood with his hand on the ancient door handle.

The incessant wind that tore into Saint-Pierre from the sea bit into the burns on his face, but eased when the cool church air touched his skin. At the east end of the church was a door either side of a raised platform, where Harvey assumed a choir would stand. The door to the left had been built into the curved, stone wall. The tower rose above it, disappearing into the vaulted ceiling and beyond.

The tiny echoes of Harvey's boots seemed to wake a thousand years of memories that whispered in the shadows, the eaves and the galleys. He stopped at the wooden pew closest to the chancel and, for the first time in his life, he sat down in a church.

There was no lowering of his head in prayer or thoughts of those he had loved. Just a rare peace. A peace he had sought for too long.

No thoughts of God crossed Harvey's mind as he marvelled at the stories told by the stained windows. But he felt a curious understanding, perhaps more than ever before, about the solace others found in prayer.

The space held a thousand years of births and deaths, weekly prayers, and sorrowful confessions, and there Harvey sat for the tiniest fraction of time. Another thousand years of births and deaths would follow, although they would be stained by the violence Harvey was about to bring to the peace.

An apology formed on Harvey's lips, as soundless as it was subconscious and prominent in his mind. The memories that stared down at him from the lofty shadows of the vaulted ceiling seemed tangible. It was as if he could touch them, or if he spoke, be heard by them.

Or be seen by them. His actions might be judged by the presence of peace itself.

Shadows buried the aisles to each side of the nave and concealed Harvey's approach. But still, the eyes of memories bore into him, teasing his conscience with reminders of the purity he was about to taint with the blood of man.

He stopped at the door to the tower with his hand against the wood. Something was watching him, something more than the memories of happiness and peace that filled the ancient space. Eyes drilled into him. Unafraid.

Lowering his hand, Harvey remained still, his senses alive in his new surroundings.

As if acknowledging Harvey's awareness of his presence, a figure, robed and silent, stepped from the darkness with the confidence of a man who knew no fear and held the greatest power in his heart.

In a silent exchange of questioning expressions, the priest conveyed an understanding of Harvey's purpose. He nodded. The movement of his head was almost imperceptible in the dark church. Only the motion of the glints of his eyes were clear.

Harvey turned the ancient handle and pulled the door,

which opened with surprising ease. No creaks or groans broke the silence. Only the first cold, stone steps of a narrow curved staircase presented itself before the priest spoke. His voice was old and cracked like the ancient timbers that sheltered them both from the storm.

"Prenez la mort de cet endroit," said the priest.

"Anglais?" replied Harvey in a whisper, finding his throat parched and his own voice cracked.

Long robes fell over the priest's feet as he moved closer to stand in front of Harvey, fearless with his God by his side. He reached out a folded arm, the long sleeves unfurling to reveal a thin, weak hand that rested on Harvey's shoulder.

"Take death from this place."

The staircase, narrow and curved, led clockwise with walls that threatened to squeeze Harvey the further up he climbed. It was as if the church itself knew that death had crossed its threshold. He turned sideways, taking soft steps and listening for a sign.

Narrow windows, empty of glass and as wide as Harvey's fist, adorned the baron walls with each sweeping turn. One was home to a pair of pigeons, who neither saw nor heard Harvey approach or move past them as they perched on the ledge, their heads buried in plumes of thick feathers.

At the top of the staircase, the dim, morning light revealed an old wooden door, framed by a stone arch no higher than Harvey's shoulders, and much narrower.

A soft tuneful murmur came from the far side of the door. It was the hum of a song that sounded familiar, along with the aroma of one-thousand-year-old stone and dust.

Harvey lay his hand against the painted wood and closed his eyes, picturing the scene on the far side of the door.

The image in Harvey's mind showed a bell hanging from the centre with a narrow walkway around the edge. There would be large open windows below the pitched roof offering a three-hundred-and-sixty-degree view of Saint-Pierre.

The sweet, tuneful humming had ceased and a silence ensued that offered Harvey small teases of the tiniest movements.

"Are you ready, Monsieur Kane?" said Gabriella.

Harvey ran his finger along the grain in the wood, his eyes closed, picturing the scene. In his mind, he placed Gabriella to the left, her back to the door and her focus on Kane.

A strong wind touched his burned face with the hint of a sting. But it also allowed him to orient his position in relation to the sea.

"Now," said Gabriella.

CHAPTER FORTY-TWO

A spray of red mist covered Kane's face. He spat the iron taste from his lips, holding the prime minister in his sights along the length of his handgun.

The police cars burst into life. All four doors opened and all four policemen began to wave their guns, searching the boat yard for the source of the shot.

The second shot burst through the chest of the policeman closest to the prime minister.

The prime minister froze to the spot. His eyes were wide, his mouth hung open and his legs shook as he was unable to hold himself still.

"Tell the prime minister to step off the boat, Monsieur Kane," said Gabriella over the radio.

"Step away from the boat, sir," said Kane.

The remaining three cops turned their guns on him.

Gabriella fired another round that severed the neck of the lead cop. He dropped to his knees, choking on his own blood.

"Toss the guns into the water," said Kane. "Or the prime minister is next."

Two splashes confirmed the policemen had obeyed the order.

"You're making a big mistake," said the prime minister. "I'll see that you die for this, Kane."

"Please, sir, step off the boat."

"I knew we couldn't trust a bunch of hired guns," the prime minister continued, as he stepped away from the boat. "You will die for this."

Kane gestured with his weapon for the prime minister to move past the cars and into the open ground where, he knew, DuBois would be able to see him through her scope. But in the distance, above the wind and the rain, the sound of approaching stomping feet began to grow louder.

"Remove your headset, Kane," said Gabriella. "I wish to talk with the prime minister."

Kane did as instructed, pulling the cable from the radio and tossing it to the ground, then he held out the radio. But the prime minister was transfixed on the sight of a hundred or more people marching in unison toward the marina. The dark shape of their mass and the volume of their boots formed a terrifying image. The policemen began to step back towards the water's edge, their worried faces a picture of fear and uncertainty.

"Monsieur Prime Minister," said Gabriella. Her voice sounded tinny through the small speaker, but her confidence carried through despite the incessant wind that blew off the sea in a growing rage and rocked the smaller boats moored in the marina. "You will, no doubt, be questioning your decision to employ the services of Monsieur Kane. And you would be correct to do so."

The prime minister turned to look at his yacht. Through a small port hole, he saw his wife staring down at him and holding her son close with a look of terror on her face.

The mass of people stopped at the gates of the marina, blocking the exit. A single man's voice began to chant. The crowd replied with audible anger.

"Monsieur Prime Minister, do I have your attention?" said Gabriella.

Kane held the push-to-talk button down for the prime minister to reply.

"You have my attention. Who am I talking to?" said the prime minister, shouting to be heard above the chanting crowd one hundred yards away.

"My name is Gabriella DuBois, Monsieur Prime Minister."

The prime minister's eyes flicked from the yacht to the mass of people at the marina gates, and then to Kane.

"You are Gabriella DuBois, sister of Francis DuBois? The infamous leader of the French rebellion? He was a traitor to France."

"My brother was not a traitor, Prime Minister. He was a patriot. He died for what he believed in, and his blood has stained your hands for long enough."

"He was a traitor, DuBois," said the prime minister. "He died because he was a threat to France and all we stand for. You and all these people, is this it? Is this the sum total of your so-called rebellion?"

"We prefer to call ourselves La Resistance," said Gabriella. "And we are many, many more than what you see."

"The resistance died with World War Two, DuBois. The resistance had honour. They fought for the nation and its people."

"You're correct, Monsieur Prime Minister. Look at the crowds in front of you. They are the people. It is they who suffer at your hands. We fight for our nation. Only this time, instead of ridding France of its Nazi occupation, we are disposing of the corrupt, selfish government. The time for change is long over-due. The time for action is now. If you want your family to survive, you will do everything I say. Do I make myself clear?"

"My family?" said the prime minister. "Leave them out of this, Miss DuBois."

"I will try my hardest, Prime Minister. But do you see my friends at the gates? They are angry. Something must be done to save this country from the turmoil you have created. A new government must be empowered, a government that recognises France and *all* its people as great, not just the wealthy minority. A new balance must be found, and for that to happen, I am afraid, you must die."

As if on cue, a rumble of thunder rolled across the sky. Two great flashes of lightning lit the marina and the mass of angry rebels who waited at the gates.

"Monsieur Kane, I am now talking to you. I have you in my cross-hairs," said Gabriella. "It is time."

Kane sighed and hung his head. Rain fell from his nose and chin. For the first time, his boots felt like lead weights, gripped by fear and indecision. He stared back at the church tower.

"Monsieur Kane, I will explain. The prime minister and you have two options. Are you hearing me? Do you understand? Tell me you understand, Monsieur Kane."

He raised the radio to his mouth, hit the push-to-talk button and spoke through his choked throat. "I understand, DuBois."

"Option one," said Gabriella. "You will raise your weapon to the prime minister's head and pull the trigger. The crowd before you will rush in and raise you up. You will be a hero. You will be on the front page of every newspaper across the world."

Kane's stomach rolled. He blinked away the rain drops that disguised his tears.

"And option two?" said Kane.

"You fail to kill the prime minister. The resistance will storm the marina and may God help anybody who stands in their way."

CHAPTER FORTY-THREE

Standing from her position behind the tower wall, Gabriella rose and outstretched her arms. The resistance could see her figure in the dim morning light. Her crowd roared in response, and the chanting began again with renewed vigour, awaiting her command.

She held out her hand, palm facing out, and the crowd below faded to silence. Only the hissing of rain hitting the ground and the rushing of wind off the sea could be heard.

"The fate of the prime minister's family resides with you, Monsieur Kane," said Gabriella over the radio. "It is time to decide."

Below, standing in the centre of the marina with the Mediterranean Sea behind him and a hundred rebels in front, hungry for blood, Kane raised his weapon and aimed at the prime minister's head.

A woman's scream cried out from inside the yacht. It was carried by the wind to Gabriella's ears, raising a smile on her tired face. She lifted the rifle to her shoulder and found Kane in the scope, his head a perfect fit between the cross-hairs.

Kane mouthed an apology to the prime minister, who

dropped to his knees with his hands behind his head. But he remained resolute with a straight back, a proud man who would die for his family and stare at his killer with open eyes.

"Now, Monsieur Kane," said Gabriella, "or I will order the attack."

But Kane's hand began to shake. He supported the weight of the weapon with his left hand, but still, the muzzle wavered.

The angry crowd tensed. The atmosphere was electric amongst the rain-soaked bodies who fought their way to the front of the group to be the first to get their hands on the man who was destroying their country.

"Now, Kane," screamed Gabriella.

But Kane lowered the weapon.

He stood staring wide-eyed at the prime minister, who was shouting at him to pull the trigger, to save his family.

Kane shook his head.

He dropped the weapon to the ground.

The prime minister glanced back at his family.

And Gabriella gave the signal for the charge.

CHAPTER FORTY-FOUR

A surge of people stormed through the gates of the marina. Their chants turned to battle cries. The rhythmic stomping of their feet, which had percussed the initial negotiations, gave way to a flood of heavy boots that charged at the prime minister and Kane.

"May God be with you all," said Gabriella, and lowered the radio as a wave of bodies engulfed the two men.

Gabriella lowered the rifle to the floor of the tower.

Harvey stepped up behind her.

"For you, my brother," she whispered.

But her sentiment was lost to sudden confusion as, from nowhere, bright spot lights lit the riot on the ground below. She searched the skies for the source of the lights as a familiar sound became clear, carried to the church tower during a brief lull in the wind.

The scene below grew brighter. Then, to Gabriella's despair, two military helicopters shot past either side of the church tower, banking hard to come to a hover above the rioting crowd.

Cries of anger rose up from the battle below and the fighting intensified.

"No," screamed Gabriella, leaning from the tower into the wind and the rain. "Finish them."

The side doors of the choppers opened and two ropes dropped from both helicopters.

Gabriella fumbled for the rifle behind her, but found nothing.

She turned to look and pressed her neck into the blade of Harvey's waiting knife. But before he could react, she arched backward, rolled, and sprung to her feet.

"Monsieur Stone, you're just in time for the fun," said Gabriella, keeping the huge church bell between them.

Keeping Gabriella in sight, Harvey followed her around the bell, the narrow walkway no wider than the length of his boots.

Below the bell, a pitch-dark chasm fell to the depths of the church. Behind Harvey was a drop to the ground of Saint-Pierre, where the cobbled streets below would break every bone in his body.

But Gabriella moved with feline grace, stepping forward then back, taunting Harvey and laughing at his clumsy attempts to follow her.

With his free hand, he tossed the rifle from the tower, where it landed without a sound on the street below.

"I can't let you do this, Gabriella," said Harvey. "You lied to me."

"You would never have helped me if you had known the truth, Harvey," replied Gabriella, backing away around the narrow circular walkway.

Matching her step for step, Harvey followed her, watching her feet below the rim of the bell.

He shoved at the giant bell, but the weight was too great and the swing too slow to make an impact. The deafening chime of the huge, hollow bronze filled the tiny space and Gabriella's feet danced to one side.

Harvey lurched to grab her, but she slipped away as the bell receded. He followed, using the short dwarf wall to stop him from falling over the edge. But Gabriella was too fast and nimble.

Using the momentum of the bell, she forced it toward him on the return swing. Harvey dove to the stone floor as the bell swung over him. He searched the walkway opposite for Gabriella as the swinging bell sang its song, loud and proud for the entire town to hear.

But she wasn't there.

He jumped to his feet, sidestepped the deafening bell once more, and edged around the walkway.

But there was no sign of her.

Behind him, a helicopter turned its spotlights on the church tower and banked towards them.

"The fun's over, Gabriella," said Harvey. "You can't escape from this."

A short burst of automatic fire caused a series of tiny explosions in the church's stonework. Harvey dropped to the floor once more as the gunfire tore into the wall behind him. He peered over the parapet wall to find a man in military fatigues preparing for another burst.

The helicopter banked as the pilot sought a new angle, but as Harvey stood, Gabriella swung from the rafters above. Her feet caught him square in the face, forcing him backward into the low parapet wall.

Gabriella dropped to the floor in front of him and began an onslaught of punches that connected with Harvey's already bruised body, never landing in the same place twice. The first rocked his head to one side. The second caught his solar plexus, winding him. He bent forward, sucking in air as the third blow, an uppercut, sent him reeling backwards.

The reprise allowed him time to block the next round of punches. Seeing a gap in Gabriella's attack, he lurched forward and smashed his forehead into her face.

She spat blood from her mouth, and smiled as the downdraft from the rotor blades ripped at her clothes and sent her hair waving in all directions. As the gunman opened fire once more, she ran at Harvey. Her shoulder slammed into his gut and her feet scrambled on the stone floor for purchase, forcing him back further and further until there was no more walkway and the back of his legs found the low parapet wall.

His knees buckled as another burst of gunfire pinged off the still swinging bell. Gabriella screamed, giving everything she had and forcing Harvey over the wall.

His hands found nothing to hold.

A sickening feeling rushed from his gut to his mouth as his feet left the stone floor and the empty space swallowed him whole.

The touch of stone as his hands found the parapet wall.

The jolt of his body.

One hand slipped off the smooth stone and fell away.

His boots scrambled for a foot hold, dangling from the tower.

And Gabriella rose up with raw malice in her reddened eyes, fury coursing through her veins, and her arms raised high above her head, poised to send Harvey to his death.

Through the fog of rain, a wave of angry faces burst through the gates of the marina.

The battle cry roared.

The prime minister glanced back to his family. Then, standing, he prepared to meet his fate.

"Get on the boat, sir," said Kane, grabbing his gun from the wet ground. He moved to stand before the prime minister, forcing the man behind him with his arm. Then he opened fire on the surging crowd of rebels.

The first two men dropped to the ground, their bodies trampled underfoot by the following masses, who seemed to swell with anger the closer they got.

Shoving the prime minister backward, Kane emptied his handgun into the crowd. The few that fell were swallowed by the rebels that rose over them like a wave, closing the distance.

"I said get on the damn boat, sir," said Kane to the prime minister, who was frozen to the ground with shock. "Get on the boat and get out of here."

Kane threw the gun at the storming crowd, turned, and shoved the prime minister away.

The prime minister was transfixed at the crowd of surging rebels. He walked backward with slow steps, his eyes flicking from Kane to the crowd and back at his family.

"Run, sir," shouted Kane.

He turned to face the crowd, planting his back foot into the concrete. He opened his arms and, as the first helicopter tore across the sky above the marina, the mass of rebels engulfed him, lifting him from the ground.

Blow after blow found Kane's body, rocking his head from side to side. Heavy boots connected with his back, cracking a rib that stabbed into his lung. The stamp of another foot snapped his leg back. The rounded face of a bat crushed his groin then raised into the air for a second blow.

Bright lights danced above him like angels, thundering overhead as consciousness faded in and out like the tide of the sea across broken rocks, revealing the world in all its glory then smothering it for the forces of the world to do its damage.

Black shapes fell from the bright lights.

Gunfire ripped through the night.

Kane was hoisted into the air. Vicious hands clawed at his skin and pulled at his hair as Kane approached his final battle. Death hung above him in the form of an enticing hand urging him forward.

The bat found another rib, issuing a spurt of blood from Kane's mouth. As his head fell back, his eyes fell upon the prime minister who stood leaning on the handrail of his yacht some fifty metres from the dockside.

The angry crowd hurled rocks and abuse at the boat. But those that dove into the sea were cut down by the angels from above.

For the smallest fraction of time, before the angry hands of the rebels grabbed onto his arms and legs, Kane thought he saw the prime minister offer him a smile in a shared moment of understanding. All was forgiven. The drug, Afghanistan, the murders. All of it. Every wrong decision he'd ever made.

The slate had been wiped clean.

Honour was finally his.

And as the rebels tore his body apart, the cost of his honour was death.

CHAPTER FORTY-SIX

A burst of gunfire ricocheted off the bell.

Gabriella lunged, knocking Harvey. His hands gripped the wall, but the smooth stone offered little purchase. One of his hands fell away, leaving him hanging above the street below.

She raised her arms high, summoning all of her strength. With her back arched, she let out a scream, wild and furious, as she struck to bring Harvey's knife down onto his own hand.

But Gabriella's attack was stalled mid-strike.

Three burning hot stabs of lead punched three holes into Gabriella's flesh.

The chopper maneuvered to gain a better angle.

Her attack faltered then faded away.

She dropped the knife to the stone floor.

A single shot found the flesh of her leg while two more rounds buried themselves in the stone wall.

And suddenly, everything was real.

Her father in his tan corduroys and under-vest, leaning on his garden fork, displaying the paunch with pride.

The clear profile of Francis' strong features against the

window of the car as he reached across and pulled the blanket over her.

Then the heavy boots and batons with the crack of bones and teeth and the image of her father lying in a pool of his own blood. The police moving on to find some other protester's family to destroy.

And the whomping of the helicopter overhead, shining bright lights into the car.

A gunshot.

The windscreen cracked.

More gunfire, forcing Francis off the road to Paris, where they rolled, flipped and bounced along the tarmac. Soft, wild grass had caught Gabriella in its arms when she'd been thrown from the rolling car. It left her conscious enough to see the wreckage come to a stop and Francis' body bury itself through the shattered glass.

Harvey's straining eyes stared up at her as she fell forward onto the parapet wall.

The ground below became a blur of shiny, wet cobbles in the half-light of the morning as her weight carried her over the edge.

Weightlessness as if she hovered above her memories.

A light, bright and mesmerising. She reached for it with both hands.

The ground below with its welcoming open arms.

But a strong hand found her wrist.

Her body jerked to a standstill and her feet swung in the air like lead weights that pulled her down.

She opened her eyes as a rush of wind from the chopper blades spat dust into her face, stinging like a thousand bees.

Above, Harvey looked down at her, pleading with her to hold on to his hand.

But her power was gone, her strength diminished.

The bright light worked its way across the stone wall of the tower once more, lighting Harvey Stone like he was a fixture of the structure, a gargoyle, devoid of comedy, or anger, or fear.

Three shots sang out like the beat of a drum, the finale of a sick masterpiece. Three more rounds tore through her skin, smashing through bone and organ.

The gunman in the helicopter positioned for the final shot, signing to the pilot to turn, who was fighting the heavy wind and rain.

The time was close.

She met Harvey's eyes staring down at her from above.

He was calling to her, but the deafening beat of the helicopter swallowed all sound save for the voices of her family who called for her to join them.

Her mouth opened but the words were lost to gunfire.

Harvey screamed at the gunman.

His hand slipped further. He was hanging by the fingers of one hand with Gabriella hanging from the other.

She could feel his strength crushing her wrist.

His power was etched on his straining face.

She shook her head at Harvey Stone. The gunman fired his final shots, loosening Gabriella from Harvey's grasp as she fell into the open arms of her father.

CHAPTER FORTY-SEVEN

Aching muscles groaned at Harvey's weight as he hauled himself over the parapet wall then slumped to the floor, numbed by fatigue. Heavy winds forced the onslaught of rain sideways into the tower, as if it cleansed Harvey of recent events.

A momentary lull in the thundering rotor blades allowed him a reprise. Sleep crept in before reflections of the past, the present and the future could take root. Instead, the cool stone floor and patter of rain on his face allowed him to slip further into the slumber.

A hand, gentle but firm, touched his shoulder, triggering Harvey's defences.

But the darkness had him in its grip.

He lay still, open to a blade across his throat, offering himself to be cut wide open.

But no blade appeared.

The hand touched his forehead.

"We must go," said the voice of an old man, his tone urgent and hushed.

But the command faded away to thoughts of Melody, his house, and sheer silence.

Another set of hands joined the first; they gripped his shoulders and hauled Harvey to his feet.

The priest and another man, both robed and equally cautious of the circling helicopters, each took an arm to support Harvey's weight and led him to the staircase. Using the curved wall for support, Harvey descended, urged on by the priest behind, and his momentum controlled by the man in front.

The high, vaulted ceilings greeted Harvey once more, and though the daylight had been dim outside, it seemed to sing through the stained glass windows of the church.

"There's no time. They will come for you. I know a secret way out," said the priest.

He coaxed Harvey forward. The other man waited at an open door, his eyes flicking to the main entrance at the far end of the church. The priest caught the attention of his friend.

"Jacques, we will take the tunnel. Make the arrangements for Monsieur Stone's escape."

"D'accord," replied Jacques, and held the priest's gaze in a silent goodbye.

"Hold them for as long as you can," said the priest.

Nodding, Jacques walked towards the main entrance as the brakes of a car squealed to a stop outside. Voices of authority barked orders in French.

Jacques turned to face Harvey and the priest.

"Go now," he said. Then he caught Harvey's eyes. "Peace be with you."

Harvey tried to read between the lines on Jacques' face; sincerity, gratitude, fear.

Harvey replied with a nod, catching the glint in the man's eyes, then followed the priest as the church doors burst open and the sound of heavy boots echoed through the vaulted ceiling.

Lit only by the burning flame of a single torch, the two men made their way down to the very pit of the church. The staircase opened out into a larger space with arched alcoves featuring stone effigies of strong faces and bold stances that cast shadows as the flame passed by. In the ceiling, a circular opening offered a glimpse of the daylight high above. Harvey stared up at the underside of the giant bell.

"Hurry," said the priest, stopping at the entrance to a dark tunnel. "This way."

The torch flame lit the arched, stone ceiling, but faded before the end was in view.

"Can you walk?" asked the priest, securing his robes tight. "It is quite some distance."

Harvey didn't reply.

Instead, he followed the flame as heavy footsteps began to echo behind them.

They followed a series of bends, long and sweeping, as men's voices entered the tunnel. Bend after bend, the two men pushed on with their pursuers close behind. Twice, the priest stopped to help Harvey, who limped with one hand holding the wound on his leg and the other clutching his bruised ribs.

But try as he might, Harvey's broken body refused to push faster than a slow limp. They stayed one bend ahead of the men behind them until, at last, daylight lit the arched exit ahead. The priest doused the torch in a pool of rain water then broke through a tangled mass of leaves and roots. He held them high enough for Harvey to limp through after him then dropped them to cover the tunnel once more.

Shielding his eyes from the bright sunlight, Harvey followed the priest, who pulled him along with more strength than Harvey expected. The ground was soft underfoot and waves crashed close by. As Harvey's vision returned, he saw a wall of rocks to his right and the sea to his left. In the distance, the town of Saint-Pierre enjoyed the calm that follows a Mediterranean storm.

The wind had fallen. The sun had risen high. The grey sky that Harvey had stared up at from the top of the church tower had been replaced with a crisp sheet of blue, dotted with stretching fingers of white clouds that seemed to reach across the sky forcing the storm on to somewhere else.

Standing beside the rocks were two local, teenage boys, grinning from ear to ear and speaking in French too fast for Harvey to understand. They leaned on Harvey's motorcycle and beamed with pride.

"My bike," Harvey said, and turned to face the priest.

"Do not take me for a simple priest, Monsieur Stone," he said, dismissing Harvey's surprise as he walked through the soft sand. Then he gave a cautious glance back to the tunnel. "You must go. It is not safe for you. Follow the beach west and stay close to the rocks. When you are clear of the town, you will find the beach road."

Harvey pulled his injured leg over the seat. The key was in the ignition where he had left it. He pulled the clutch, turned the key, and tickled the throttle.

The engine caught on the first turn of the starter.

"Sir?" said Harvey, unsure of what to call the priest. "Thank you."

The priest appeared to relax a little. He stepped up to Harvey, placed his hand on his shoulder, and looked him in the eye with the same confidence Harvey had seen the first time they had met.

"Do not thank me, Monsieur Stone," said the priest with a smile. "France is grateful to you."

The voices in the tunnel grew louder as the men approached the exit, excited by the sight of sunlight.

"But I fear not all of France understands what you have done," said the priest.

"Is that the military or the prime minister's security?" said Harvey, gesturing to the tunnel.

"It is the police. They will be looking for somebody to charge to cover their own corruption. If they catch us, you will never see the light of day again. They are not good men."

"Will you be okay?" said Harvey.

"I will hold them," said the priest, his smile broadening. "I have God on my side. Now go, and may God be with you, Monsieur Stone."

The tangled mass of climbers and leaves burst apart and three men in police uniforms forced their way onto the beach, blinded by the sun.

With a twist of the throttle, Harvey kicked the bike into first gear, spun the back wheel, spraying sand over the men, and then tore along the beach. In his mirror, Harvey saw the men, angered and outraged at Harvey's escape, and the priest standing with the peace and confidence of a man with God by his side.

Ahead of Harvey lay a stretch of coast, long and unbroken. Bright sunlight gave the wet sand a mirror-like appearance and the glistening Mediterranean Sea offered the peace that Harvey had sought for so long. The all-terrain tyres on his motorcycle tore across the surface of the hard, wet sand, and the wind that rippled across his skin brought a new lease of life. A new direction.

He slowed to a crawl then navigated a small track that led up to the beach road where he stopped beside a small junction. A sign pointing left directed him to the village of Argeles, where Harvey would find the ruins of a once loved farmhouse, and the burned possessions of a man who owned very little.

Ahead was the French network of motorways with its offerings of Europe, peace and solitude. London called to him with its promise of seeing Melody, Tyler, Reg and Jess. Their faces hung at the forefront of his mind.

It was Christmas Day. He imagined they would be drinking coffee by now and perhaps exchanging gifts over breakfast. He wondered if they would be thinking of him. He wondered if they understood why he sought peace.

Riding slow to savour the memories, Harvey rolled the short distance along the narrow lane to where his house once stood. The fire had consumed most of the wooden beams and only one wall still remained. The roof tiles and broken bricks were strewn across the debris, smothering any indication that the house was once somebody's home.

Pulling the bike to a stop, Harvey stepped off and began a slow walk around the perimeter of the ruin, kicking the bricks to one side and stopping on occasion. Sometimes he thought he caught a glimpse of a photo sticking out from beneath the rubble. But he knew that no photos had survived.

He stopped beside the small vegetable patch Melody had tended. The plastic sheeting had melted from the blaze to reveal six neat rows of soil like a miniature ploughed field, all devoid of life. The green leaves of the hardy, winter vegetables had singed to wafer-thin, black images of leaves, frozen in time until Harvey touched them, and they crumbled to ash.

A tiny flash of green caught Harvey's eye.

Buried under the cremated vegetables, a sole survivor stood proud. Its leaves flicked in the wind. Harvey pulled at the root, easing the carrot from its nest. It was only half-formed, but it was all that remained.

The sum total of Harvey's life in France.

He tossed the carrot onto the blackened remains of his house and thrust his hands into the pockets of his jacket. Then he rolled his neck from side to side, waiting for the satisfying click.

But his hand found something hard and alien.

He worked his fingers into a hole in his jacket pocket he didn't know existed and fumbled until he pulled out the object.

He held the vial between finger and thumb up to the sunlight, rolling it back and forth, and staring in wonder at the red liquid.

In front of him were the ruins of his house and the remains of one dead man, one of many strewn across the town of Saint-Pierre. Harvey thought of Farrow. He thought of the guards that had died.

And all for one tiny vial of deep red liquid.

He shook his head in disbelief then let the vial fall into the palm of his hand. He rolled it back and forth, admiring the red light on his skin as the morning sun shone through the glass.

Then, taking one last look at the cause of his ruin, he dropped the vial to the ground and crushed the glass beneath his foot.

CHAPTER FORTY-EIGHT

A blanket of dark grey cloud hung low in the sky, so heavy it seemed as if it would crush the many couples, joggers and dog walkers beneath its weight. Standing alone on the bridge, Harvey watched the endless flow of water rush beneath him. The evening lights blinked on one by one. Their reflections in the water multiplied and fragmented.

Like broken glass.

Harvey stretched, rolling his neck from side to side and bending his legs, which were stiff from the two-day ride.

A few dots of rain found his face, inciting memories of the church tower. His hand felt his bruised ribs then lowered and touched the tender wound on his leg. In his mind, Gabriella fell from his grip.

A look of peace upon her face.

He leaned on the handrail and peered out across his city.

"I'm home," he whispered. But the sentiment failed to raise a smile.

He pushed off the railing and limped towards his bike, then hoisted his leg over and started the engine. Leaving his visor up for the cool air to rouse him for the final mile of his journey, he rolled onto the road and slipped into the light Boxing Day traffic.

At a set of lights, he came to a stop beside a bus. He could have squeezed through the gap to the front, but he had neither the energy nor the desire to lead the pack of vehicles. On the bus, sitting at the window, a man in a heavy Kashmir coat was reading a newspaper. The headline caught Harvey's eye. The traffic began to move. At the next corner shop, Harvey stopped to buy a copy and tucked it into his jacket to finish the journey.

Harvey stopped the bike in a small car park. He felt the familiar sense of relief when a long journey comes to an end and the engine shudders to a stop. Pulling the paper from his jacket, he climbed off the bike and leaned against it. The pages caught a few drops of rain that smudged the ink, but it mattered little to Harvey, who was interested in one article only.

French PM saved from assassination plot.

The sub-heading read: *La Resistance is dead.* The article described a heroic attempt to foil a plot to kill the French prime minister by a retired British army officer. There was no mention of Kane's dishonourable discharge. The reporter described the rebellion group as frustrated French citizens who were reviving the infamous French Resistance, but had only served to taint the title. The prime minister had pushed an emergency panic button to alert the French special forces, who arrived on the scene to find more than one hundred rebels attacking the PM and his family. Major Cassius Kane was killed defending the PM and forty rebels were killed in the attack.

The attack was led by Ms Gabriella DuBois, sister of Francis DuBois, the rebel leader who was killed a decade previously in a government-led attempt to eliminate rebel forces. The father of Ms DuBois was also killed less than a year ago during the angry protests that caused riots and closures of France's motorway network.

Ms DuBois was killed in the attack on the prime minister, which happened on Christmas morning. French police are looking for a man who escaped the scene and helped the Special Forces bring down Ms DuBois. The French prime minister has offered the unknown man, who wears a black leather jacket and rides a motorcycle, a reward to come forward. No other information about the vigilante is known.

Harvey closed the newspaper then rolled it up.

He pushed off his bike and limped towards the building, a small, three-story apartment block.

Flower beds lined the pathways and small areas of well-kept lawns filled the spaces between them. At the doors, Harvey was presented with a number pad to ring at the apartment. But he hadn't even raised his hand when the door burst open and Melody flung herself into his arms. He caught her and staggered back on his injured leg.

"I knew you'd come," said Melody, burying her face into his jacket and pulling herself against him, squeezing his bruised ribs. "Everyone will be so pleased to see you."

She pulled away and looked up at him, letting her eyes wander over his body. He tried to stand straight but his leg wouldn't allow it. Melody's smile faded. She said nothing but examined Harvey's posture, torn clothes and tired eyes.

She caught sight of the newspaper tucked inside Harvey's jacket.

"Did you grow bored of sitting beside the fire?" she asked, her eyebrows raised. A smile returned to her face.

Harvey shrugged.

"I hear they're looking for a man in a black leather jacket who rides a motorcycle," said Melody, and moved in closer for another kiss.

She pulled away and raised an eyebrow once more in question, but failed to contain her grin.

Harvey didn't reply.

The End.

STONE FACE

CHAPTER ONE

"One click of that button, Herman," said Lucas, as he tugged at the small growth of hair he was cultivating on his chin. "That's all it takes."

Herman Hoffman held his head in his hands, squeezing his ears to stop Lucas' taunting voice. The green light from the computer screen was bright in the dark room and, on the screen, monochrome cars sat in lines of traffic while pedestrians fought a perpetual battle for pavement space without breaking momentum.

"I can't," said Herman. "You can't make me do this. It is not right. It is inhuman."

Lucas raised his hand to Herman's face, stroking his skin and caressing the outside of his ear.

"I think we both know that's not true, dear Herman," replied Lucas, and twisted Herman's face towards the closed door on the far side of the room. "How do you think the lovely Martina would feel about that? What do you think she will say when I tell her that her poor dear Herman has failed?"

"Stop it," said Herman, covering his face with his fingers, and peering through the gap at the door. "Just stop it all."

"She thinks you're a failure anyway, doesn't she, Herman? Why else would she do what she did? Why else would she fall into the arms of another man?"

"You don't know that. You have no proof."

A vein, blue and thick, stuck from Lucas' left temple, and his eye twitched twice, followed by the left side of his mouth as if in reply.

"I have all the proof I need, Herman," said Lucas. "The unexplained late nights, the missing money, and let's face it, when was the last time she kept you warm at night?"

"That's none of your business," said Herman.

"Well, I'm making it my business. If you can't be a man and stand up for yourself, perhaps I should. You're not going to let people walk all over you, are you?"

Herman stared at the door.

"No," said Herman, after a pause.

"So be a man, Herman," said Lucas with a grin. "Show them who's boss."

"Does it have to be this way? Surely there must be some other way."

"No," spat Lucas. "It must be this way and it must be now. Strike while the iron is hot, Herman. All you have to do is hit the button on that remote and your journey to becoming a man will begin. Albeit, a little late in life."

A tightness began to squeeze at Herman's chest. His eyes watered, stinging from lack of sleep.

"You do want to be a man, Herman?" said Lucas, running his hand through the tight curls of his dark hair, admiring his reflection in the window. "Do you want people to remember you as the man who stood up for himself? Or do you want people to remember you as the man who failed? The man who sobbed and wept and watched while his brother stood up for him?"

"But there's so many people down there," said Herman. "There's so many innocent people."

"Innocent?" said Lucas. His mocking tone accentuated the word. "Innocent? Herman, you have so much to learn. Every one of them down there is guilty of something. Every one of them deserves punishment in one form or another. And it'll be you who delivers that punishment, Herman. It's nearly time. Are you ready?"

"No," said Herman. "I can't do it."

"So then, I must make a man of you myself," said Lucas, still admiring his own reflection. His voice quietened. "But you must decide who is first."

Dropping his head to his hands once more, Herman pulled at his hair, letting it run between his tight knuckles. Tears fell to the carpet and a low, monotone grumble grew from the back of his throat.

"Tell me," said Lucas. "I am losing my patience and the window of opportunity is closing."

"How can I decide?"

"Shall I decide for you?" said Lucas, allowing anger to slip into his tone. But then he caught it and softened his words. "Who should die first? Dear little Sam?"

"No," said Herman.

But Lucas continued his musings, regardless.

"He wouldn't even know it was coming. His neck would snap in my hands like a Christmas turkey, Herman."

"Stop it. How can I decide?"

"Or perhaps the marvellous Martina should go first?" said Lucas. Then he stopped and stared at his reflection again in wonder at his own imagination. "I might even have some fun with her before she goes. Now there's a thought."

Herman raised his head from his hands. The emotion was

gone from his face, leaving nothing but anger and hatred in his eyes.

"You wouldn't," said Herman.

Lucas smiled at him.

"Oh, but I would, Herman. It's not hard to imagine what she looks like beneath those slutty dresses she wears when she goes to see her fancy man, her bit on the side."

Herman's voice lowered. He stood from the desk with his back to the door and stretched his arms out to defend his wife and child from the monster that plagued his mind.

"If you lay one hand on her, Lucas," he began.

"Oh yes," said Lucas, exaggerating his nonchalance.

"If you touch one hair on her body."

"There he is," said Lucas, stepping forward. "That's the Herman I wanted to see."

"Get away from me," said Herman. "Leave us alone."

"All you have to do is hit the button, Herman."

Herman brought the phone up into the dim light and stared down at the green call button, imagining the lives that would change if he pushed it.

"That's it," said Lucas, glancing at the screen and then his watch. "That's it, Herman. It is time."

Herman studied the phone as if seeing it for the first time.

Behind him, the door handle squeaked as Lucas pushed it down.

"I can't," said Herman, as Lucas pushed the door open to reveal Martina tied to the bed, her eyes wide and pleading. But the gag in her mouth prevented any sound other than a high-pitched muffle to escape. Sam was sitting on the floor. His hands were bound to the bed frame and a hood had been pulled over his face.

"So then, I'll decide," said Lucas, his voice dropping to a whisper. He stepped across the threadbare carpet to where

Martina began to thrash against her restraints. He turned to face the window and let a serious look of hatred wipe away his delight.

"Stop it," said Herman, pleading with Lucas to stop the torment.

Lucas flicked at Martina's hair with his index finger then ran it down her face to her chest.

"No," said Herman. "Just stop it."

But Lucas' wandering hands were already exploring Martina's rigid body.

"Okay. Okay," said Herman.

Lucas looked up to the window, his hand pausing mid-action.

Martina stared at her husband. A look of dread filled her eyes.

"I'll do it," said Herman, holding the phone in the air.

Lucas smiled.

"So you've become a man, my dear Herman."

With his eyes locked onto his wife's in a look of apology, Herman pushed the button.

CHAPTER TWO

The driver's door of a silver saloon opened and a middle-aged man wearing a cheap suit eased himself out of the car. He straightened his tie, checked his reflection in the car window, then closed and locked the door. The indicators flashed on once simultaneously with the sound of the locks clunking into place.

"Are you ready for this?" said Melody, as she killed the engine of her little Mazda.

"How hard can it be?" replied Harvey.

"Just be nice to him," said Melody. "Don't scare this one off."

Opening the passenger door, Harvey climbed out, stretched his neck and nodded at the man, who made his way towards them with a smile that faded when he caught Harvey's eye. He diverted to Melody, his smile returning at half-mast.

"Miss Mills?" said the man, offering his hand to Melody, and then to Harvey who watched him walk around the car. Feeling the sharp end of Melody's stare, Harvey shook the man's hand. "I'm Jeremy. You found the place okay?" he asked. His thick eyebrows lifted as if two giant caterpillars on his face prepared to fight.

"It was easy enough," said Melody. "Thank you so much for

meeting us at short notice. We were keen to get the paperwork signed."

"It's no bother at all, really," he replied, offering a warm, practiced smile. "I really do think you'll enjoy living here. If you're looking for character and space, you can't really go wrong with Wimbledon. Are you familiar with the area at all?"

He stopped at the gate to hear Melody's response.

"Well-" said Melody.

"Yes," said Harvey, looking up at the windows of their new, rented house. "We know the area well enough. Shall we do the paperwork inside?"

Holding his hand out for the man to enter first, Harvey waited then followed the others into the house, ignoring Melody's warning stare.

"The place has been empty for a few weeks, but I'm sure it'll air out. It's fully furnished, as you know, so it's ready to move in," said Jeremy.

"Good," replied Melody, "because right now we're staying with friends. We'd like to start the new year in our new home."

"A fresh start?" asked Jeremy. "Nothing beats starting a new year in a new house with new habits. Out with the old and in with the new, as they say," he finished. But his humour failed to raise a smile on Harvey's face.

"Is there an inventory?" asked Melody.

"Yes, of course," said Jeremy, and laid his case on the kitchen work surface. He ruffled through some paperwork, muttering to himself.

"I'm going to take a look around," said Harvey.

"And leave me to do the boring stuff?" said Melody with a smile. "I'm joking. Go. Look around."

Harvey slipped out into the hallway and stepped into the living room. Large bay windows offered a wide field of view into the street outside. A large TV had been placed in the corner of the room in front of a leather sofa and two armchairs.

The high standard of finishing had been continued upstairs. The front bedroom, which was the largest of four, offered an en suite bathroom, a large king-sized bed and built-in wardrobes. Generic artwork of city life tastefully dotted the walls. The bedroom also featured a bay window with a window seat comprising of three purpose-made cushions to allow the occupant of the room a place to sit and watch the world go by.

Harvey didn't sit. Instead, he let his eyes roll across the Mercedes and BMWs that lined the street, noting how the South West suburb differed from the East London he'd known as a child, where the working class drove used cars. Only the wealthy could afford Jaguars and higher-end vehicles, such as his foster father who relished in the turning of heads as he cruised along the narrow streets.

The main bathroom was at the far end of the upstairs hallway. A built-in shower with a glass cubicle large enough for two or three people overlooked a roll top bathtub. The sunlight through the opaque glass fragmented across the gleaming white surface.

The back bedroom looked out onto the modest garden with a view of the side street where the line of high-end cars continued. Harvey noticed the long, unkempt grass and poor condition of the house behind, like a stain on an otherwise very affluent street. And in the distance, Wimbledon Common broke the pattern of houses and streets with its tall trees and seemingly endless green.

The front door closed and an excited Melody ran up the stairs calling Harvey's name.

"In here," he said, and continued to gaze out of the window.

Melody sidled up to him, sliding her arm around his waist.

"We should celebrate tonight," she said. "Our new home together."

But her eyes followed his gaze.

"Jeremy offered that house to us as well," said Melody.

"It's up for rent?" said Harvey, surprised at the condition. "It looks terrible."

"It's cheap in comparison to this place but would need a lot of work. It would suit someone. Just not us."

"I'm done decorating and renovating, Melody," said Harvey. "I need to settle in and relax."

"I'm sure we can manage that," she said, pulling him around to face her and closing the gap between their lips. "I think we should have an early night."

"I'll get the bags from the car," said Harvey.

"I'll pop a bottle of wine," replied Melody. "Then tomorrow, I have a full day of sightseeing planned."

"Sightseeing?" said Harvey. "Where?"

"London, Harvey. Do you know I've lived here all my life and haven't visited half the tourist places?"

"Do we have to see them all in one day?" said Harvey.

"No, but today is the first day of our new life together. I want it to start exactly how it will continue," said Melody, gazing out of the window at Wimbledon Common in the distance. "I want it to start with a bang."

CHAPTER THREE

Three photos were laid on the table in front of Detective Inspector Reilly. He turned them away from himself for the benefit of his suspect, Abdullah Nakheel, who sat opposite with his ankles cuffed to the chair legs and his wrists cuffed behind his back.

"You see this?" said Reilly, jabbing the photo with a shaky index finger. "Do you recognise her?"

Nakheel stared back at him through swollen eyes, but said nothing.

"Your wife, Nakheel," said Reilly. "Do you know where she is?"

But still, Nakheel remained silent.

"I can tell you, Nakheel, that she is not in the same location as this girl," said Reilly, resting his finger on the face in the second photo. "Your daughter, Fatima. Or indeed, your second daughter. In fact, we have gone to great lengths to ensure that neither your wife nor your two daughters are together. They are being kept in various government facilities across the city, and I can assure you that if you do not start to cooperate, they will suffer far more pain than you have done."

A tell-tale twitch of Nakheel's broken top lip betrayed his silence. The movement, barely discernible, was caught by Reilly to use as a guide for further questions.

"Now, Nakheel, we have less than five minutes before the guards remove you. I'll schedule another interview in twenty-four hours. During that time, you will undergo more pain than I can imagine and great lengths will be taken to ensure your discomfort. But, rest assured, that whatever you endure, your family endures too."

Reilly checked his watch and pulled his sleeve down to allow Nakheel a little more time to think.

"Three minutes," said Reilly. Then he nodded at his colleague, DS Cole, who stood to one side and slid a single piece of paper onto the desk along with a black marker. "Write the name down. You don't even have to say it out loud, Nakheel."

He nodded at the guard to uncuff Nakheel's wrists then turned back to face the man he'd been hunting for more than six months. But even as the cuffs were unlocked and the man's arms were released, Reilly knew he wouldn't pick up the marker. Nakheel grimaced at the touch of the guard, squeezing his eyes closed to refrain from crying out with the pain throughout his broken body.

"Think of your family, Nakheel," said Reilly, softening his tone. "Have you any idea what will happen to them? Your daughters and your wife, alone, in a strange place." Reilly shook his head in disbelief. "How could you do that to them?"

The dried blood that bound Nakheel's lips released as he opened his mouth for the first time, defiant yet on the verge of a physical breakdown. He rested his bruised right arm on the desk. His left, which was turning a deep violet from the multiple fractures, hung loose. The pain was evident in Nakheel's expression, poorly masked by fatigue, at the thought of his two young daughters in a similar room with similar people in some other place.

"Your country," Nakheel began, his voice cracked, dry and no more than a whisper. "Your country is weak. You cannot hurt my family. You have too many rules."

The statement changed everything. Nakheel stared across the desk at Reilly, confident in the protection the United Kingdom would offer.

"Cole," said Reilly.

"Sir?"

"Leave the room."

"Sir? I thought I'd-"

"Leave the room now, Cole," said Reilly, his tone sharp and impatient. "That's an order."

Brown eyes, set in deep ravines and cracked from the sun, studied Reilly's features, who shared the same weathered skin around his eyes, but which was a result of the beating cold wind and his own sins that kept him awake at night.

The door closed, leaving just Nakheel, Reilly and the guard who, at the slight nod of Reilly's head, stepped into action. He pulled a cord around Nakheel's neck and closed off his air supply.

Cuffs rattled against the chair and scrambled on the smooth concrete floor. Nakheel's one good arm shot up to defend himself, but the guard was strong and Nakheel was weakened by sleepless nights, regular beatings and malnourishment.

Reilly studied him, admiring his spirit and his fight to survive. So often, Reilly had seen men endure far more than he thought he ever could, which gave question to the strength of some men surpassing that of ordinary men. Or were they the ordinary ones? And men like Reilly, who would crumble at the horrific, tortuous procedures, were just weak?

Angry and gargled moans from Nakheel's throat sent spittle

from his mouth as he fought for his life. Reilly checked that Cole had truly gone then pulled his hip flask from his pocket and unscrewed the lid, allowing Nakheel to watch him enjoy a drink while he died a slow death.

A flick of Reilly's eyes as he replaced the hip flask into his pocket was enough to tell the guard to ease off. From his pocket, Reilly produced one more photograph and lay it on the desk beside Nakheel's daughters.

The cord was removed from Nakheel's neck and the guard's firm hand dragged his body forward in the chair to look at the new photo.

"I'm sure you recognize him, Nakheel," said Reilly. Then he paused for the image to work its magic. Only Nakheel's rhythmic panting could be heard. A long bead of drool hung from his lip and touched the photograph.

Tears followed.

"Your son, Nakheel," said Reilly. "I didn't want to show you the photo, but I'm afraid you need to understand where you are and who you are dealing with."

With his good arm, Nakheel raised his hand and touched the face in the photo.

"He died in this very facility, Nakheel," said Reilly. "It's a shame we've only just found you. I would have let you watch."

Reilly stood from his chair and walked to the side of the dark room, away from the heat of the single bulb that hung above the desk. With a handkerchief, he wiped the thin layer of sweat from his brow, allowed himself another drink, and felt the warmth ease the shaking in his hand.

"Right now, Abdullah Nakheel, you are in a place that does not exist. You see the man behind you? He doesn't exist. And the men that come for you in the night to offer you their boots?" said Reilly, shaking his head. "They don't exist either. Your son is missing. Nobody knows where he is. His body will lie untended until the smell becomes too foul then it will be discarded like trash."

Allowing a pause to add weight to his words, Reilly watched as Nakheel's eyes traced him in the dark. His expression had changed.

"So please do not think for one second that you have the safety of the British legal system on your side, Nakheel, because right now, you're missing. And your family? They're also just missing. That's all."

He stepped from the shadows to reveal his serious expression to Nakheel, who followed him with new curiosity. Then, leaning close to the man who held the key to every Islamic sympathiser in London, Reilly whispered, "We don't exist."

Then he smiled at Nakheel.

A bang on the door broke the tension that Reilly had worked to build, and Cole took a single step inside.

"Sir," she said, her voice urgent and her sharp eyes flicking to the cord in the guard's hand and the red ring around Nakheel's neck. She handed Reilly a small piece of paper with three words written in block letters.

Reilly looked back at Nakheel, who let his head hang low.

"Take him away and make arrangements to relocate his family," said Reilly to the guard, and he saw the prisoner's brow raise in panic. Nakheel lifted his head in slow realisation of what was to come. "Maybe it's time we showed him how serious we are."

Reilly turned to follow Cole from the room, but just as the door was closing, a dry, weak and broken voice called out.

"Wait," said Nakheel.

CHAPTER FOUR

"Oh, you're good at this, dear brother," said Lucas, watching the computer screen as connections were made, encrypted and locked in place. "You're a technical genius."

"It's nothing," said Herman, his voice as quiet and humble as ever.

"Are you thinking about the bomb?" said Lucas.

Herman hung his head, shamed by the devastation he'd caused.

"It's just taking care of business, Herman," said Lucas. "That's the way you need to think of it. You're making sure everyone knows that you're not a coward."

Herman nodded and blinked away a tear.

"Have some confidence, Herman. Look at what you've done. How did you learn all this anyway?" said Lucas, fascinated by the way the screen had been divided into squares, each one showing a different CCTV camera.

"I..." began Herman. Then he paused and hung his head again. "I'd rather not say."

Lucas felt his jaw hang open then a smile curled the corners of his mouth like a snake with two tails. "You learned all this for your dirty little secrets?"

"Stop it," said Herman. "I don't want to go there."

"But, Herman, do you realize the power you have?" said Lucas, exciting himself with imaginings of what could be. "Can the signal be traced?"

"No. Well, yes. But it would take time," said Herman, reddening at the praise. "The signal is encrypted and diverted across Europe. The cameras are set to change at intervals, which means by the time they trace it here, the video feed would have changed and they'd have to start the trace again."

"You're a whiz," said Lucas. "That's the word. Like that kid at school. Do you remember him? The kid with the curly hair and glasses."

"I'm not a whiz," said Herman. "And besides, it didn't stop me being found out."

"But you learned, right? You learned how they found you before?"

"Of course," said Herman. "I have a trigger on a virtual firewall that will cut the feed if they manage to keep the signal alive, or if the feed doesn't change."

"See? You should be proud of what you can do, Herman. In another life, you could have gone places doing this stuff."

"In another life. Maybe," said Herman, and turned away from his brother's stare in the reflection of the computer screen. "I'm scared of getting caught. This is serious stuff, Lucas."

"With your computer skills and the things I learned during my little foray at Her Majesty's pleasure, there's no way we'll be caught. Besides, their eyes will be elsewhere. Every policeman in London will be out for him."

"But he'll be out for us," said Herman, his voice rising in both pitch and volume. He stood from the chair and faced the wall, turning his head sideways to find Lucas in the mirror, staring back at him with pure malice.

"I told you to watch your tongue, Herman. I told you to let me handle it. All I need is for you to do what I tell you. I don't need your cries. I don't need your worries. All I need is for you to listen to what I say and do exactly what I tell you. Word. For. Word."

Herman sighed and faced the wall.

"Do you understand, Herman?" said Lucas.

Herman nodded.

Lucas' frown relaxed, smoothing the pale skin on his forehead and softening his eyes.

"Come now, dear brother. Let's not argue. We've started it now and nothing can stop us."

But Herman remained silent.

"Herman, come," said Lucas. "We have things to do, people to see and places to go. It's going to be such fun. How will we find him?"

Breaking from his downtrodden slump, Herman stepped across to the computer table. He collected a tablet and placed it inside Lucas' rucksack.

"I can find him on here," said Herman. "I can remotely access the computer from the tablet. We can follow him without being seen."

"A whiz," said Lucas, winking in the mirror.

"Lucas?" said Herman, ignoring the compliment. "Can I ask you something? But don't be mad. I...I just need to know."

"Ask away, Herman," said Lucas. "I won't be mad, whatever you ask."

Herman pulled the rucksack onto his shoulders then pulled his hood up over his head. He checked the mirror to see how much of his face the hood covered then pulled it tighter.

"If he does see us, do you think he'll recognize us?" said Herman.

"My dear brother, if he does see us, it'll be too late for him."

"But what if he does sees us and he does recognise us? What will he do?"

"Would you like to do something before we leave?" said Lucas, averting the question.

Herman glanced at the computer desk then back at his own reflection. "You mean?"

"Yes, dear brother. Do it."

Taking the single pen that lived alone in the little, square, wooden pen holder on the desk, Herman opened the notepad. With a grubby index finger, he traced the list of names down until he found the one he was looking for.

"Say it out loud," said Lucas. "Say the name."

"Patrick Gervais," said Herman, pronouncing the name with as much clarity as he could muster.

"He'll never humiliate you again," said Lucas. "Say it."

"You'll never humiliate me again, Patrick Gervais."

"Good," said Lucas. "Now put a line through his name, and tell me who's next."

Herman let his finger slide across the notepad to the next name.

"Daniel Frost," he said. But the strength had gone from his voice. He glanced up at the bedroom door, picturing Martina inside and the times they had shared.

He pictured her with Daniel Frost and his emotions began to stir.

"Let's get on with this," said Lucas, sensing his brother's loss of strength. "Time's a ticking, dear brother, and our Mr Frost has a price to pay."

CHAPTER FIVE

"Stop," said Melody, and Harvey heard her stop in her tracks.

He turned to face her, glancing around for the cause of the outburst, and then gave her a questioning look.

"Come here," she said, smiling as she checked behind her, lining herself up with the infamous Trafalgar Square lions. She raised her phone in front of her face. "Come on, Harvey. Get in close."

"You want a photo?" said Harvey.

She thinned her lips at him, a sign there was no use in arguing.

He leaned into her and looked at the camera, but couldn't raise a smile. Beyond the phone that Melody held in the air, a security camera panned around and stopped when it reached where they stood.

The photo was taken, and Melody linked her arm through his and pulled him along.

"Come on," she said. "This is our day and there's so much I'd like to see. I can't believe I've lived here most of my adult life and have never been inside the National Gallery."

Standing beside her, Harvey eyed the people around them.

Office workers and construction workers cut through the square heading in all directions. Tourists wrapped in scarves and gloves huddled close, both for the warmth and the safety against pick-pockets. A steady flow of double-decker buses moved through the heavy traffic. To one side of the square, a small lorry was parked and workers were beginning to build the barriers around the lions and other statues in preparation for New Year's Eve.

A crowd of people surged past. Harvey stepped out of the way and bumped into a woman who was rushing behind them. Melody apologised but the woman kept on walking, her head lowered to her phone.

He found another security camera in the opposite corner of the square. It panned when he moved and stopped when he stopped.

"Looks like we made it in time for rush hour," said Harvey, as three police cars with flashing blue lights cruised around the square, the lead car blazing its sirens. "Although they don't look like they're in a hurry."

"They're tightening security for New Year's Eve," said Melody. "I imagine the gas bomb yesterday shook them up a bit."

"It hasn't deterred the tourists," said Harvey, eying a group of teenage girls. One of them screamed as a pigeon flew past her head, to the amusement of her friends.

"How would you control them then?" asked Melody.

"Control the tourists?" said Harvey, gesturing at the hundreds of people around him.

"No. How would you control the terrorists who planted the gas bomb? How would you stop them? Millions of people are going to be standing here two nights from now. How would you keep them safe?"

Harvey smiled. "I'd go home and put my feet up," he replied. "I told you, it's dangerous outside."

"Oh, come on," said Melody, unimpressed by his response.

"I'm serious, Melody. I'm tired of all the drama. I just want to relax."

"Is the one and only Harvey Stone getting old?" said Melody, taunting him with her tone. She wrapped her scarf around her face and tucked the ends tight inside her jacket.

Harvey's smile faded.

"I'm just tired, Melody," said Harvey, and then grimaced as the group of girls nearby all began to scream and the pigeons flew around their heads.

"It'll quieten down," replied Melody, as the ever-present flock of pigeons took off.

The police sirens faded, leaving just the sound of the scurrying pigeons, which caught Harvey's attention. He tracked the nervous birds across the heads of the crowd, watched them circle once and then return to the feeding frenzy in the square, disinterested by the sirens.

"Shall we go inside the gallery?" said Melody. "It's getting busy here already."

But as she said it, a man knocked into Harvey in the bustling crowd. Harvey turned to watch him walk away. He was carrying a small rucksack and his face was hidden by a green hood that had been pulled tight against the cold.

"Leave it," said Melody, with her hand on his arm. "It was an accident."

But Harvey continued to watch him walk away through the crowd, sidestepping through people to the annoyance of a group of girls who called after him.

Harvey tracked his every move, waiting and watching.

"Harvey, come on," said Melody, tugging on his arm.

But Harvey remained where he was.

And then it happened.

The green hood turned. A pale eye found Harvey, offering a glimpse of one side of the man's face. Then he turned forward, put his hands in his pockets and worked through the endless stream of people.

Harvey made his move.

"Harvey?" said Melody, calling after him.

Turning and twisting through the traffic, Harvey side-stepped into spaces, cut between people, and moved others out of the way, his eyes focused on the green hood.

Melody was behind him, urging him to stop. But he had to know.

The crowd thinned at the edges, allowing Harvey to move fast. He ran into a space and scanned the area where he'd seen the hood last. Melody caught up with him and pulled on his arm.

"Harvey? What's got into you? I nearly lost you in the crowd."

Harvey didn't reply.

"Who is it?" said Melody, following Harvey's eyes as they passed over each and every person in sight.

A flash of green hood passed between a group of people. The face stared at Harvey then turned out of sight when he caught Harvey's eye.

"Him," said Harvey, and began to run.

"Harvey?" called Melody.

The hood slipped out of sight onto the Strand so Harvey gave everything he had, pumping his arms and finding a route through a group of tourists. He burst around the corner but found no sign of the man. Jumping onto the top of a small set of steps by a doorway, he scanned across the tops of heads, searching the pavement and the road. Then, on the far side of the square, beside Charing Cross station, the hood turned back to look at him.

Car horns blared as Harvey darted across the road. A woman stepped back in surprise when Harvey vaulted a barrier and ran across the road into Villiers Street, a narrow side road that led down to the Thames embankment. The hood, always one step ahead, ducked into a side street and began to run.

With his target in reach, Harvey gave chase once again. Running down the centre of the road, he followed the hood into the side street and through the gates of a small park.

He stopped.

A homeless man lay on his bed of plastic bags and flattened cardboard boxes out of the way of the flow of foot traffic, seeking shelter from the wind between some bushes. He watched Harvey with blatant curiosity through the steam from a polystyrene cup. His eyes flicked to the right and back to Harvey just as Melody came to a stop beside him.

"What on earth is going on?" said Melody. "Who did you see?"

But Harvey didn't reply. His eyes were locked onto a man at the far end of the small park, who nodded once at Harvey, turned and climbed into a taxi.

"Who was that?" said Melody.

Memories of a thousand faces took pride of place in Harvey's mind. Each one, he discarded and discounted. Too old. The wrong hair. The wrong gender. The wrong age. Too big. Too small.

"Harvey, talk to me," said Melody. Her tone dropped to a warning.

But before Harvey could answer, before he could issue the words he knew she was dreading, he felt a vibration from his jacket pocket.

Harvey stopped.

He put his hand into his pocket. His fingers grasped a mobile phone, its tiny screen alight with a sickly, bright green and the words CALL ME in bold, black letters.

Harvey glanced at Melody, who had begun to look worried. His thumb hovered above the green button.

"Harvey?" said Melody. "What is going on?"

He didn't reply. He hit the call button.

The taxi turned a corner at the end of the road, leaving Harvey with a glimpse of a pale face with a cruel smile.

A silence hung in the air like time had stopped.

"Harvey?" said Melody, growing agitated.

He scanned the park, listening to the phone as the connection was made and a dial tone began. The homeless man stared back at him. Tourists crowded around a map of London. Commuters walked fast with their hands tucked into their warm pockets.

A rucksack at the foot of a statue.

An image of the green hood climbing into the taxi played back in Harvey's mind. The man wasn't wearing a rucksack.

Harvey removed the phone from his ear, staring at it as the pieces came together like some sick puzzle.

"Harvey," said Melody, "what's happening?"

"Run."

CHAPTER SIX

An armed, uniformed officer raised the red and white tape that closed off the crime scene. Detective Inspector Reilly removed his cigarette, flashed his ID card, ducked below the tape, and then stood on the other side, not waiting for Cole, who was busy on her phone. The sound of her heels assured him she had followed and her sweet-smelling perfume arrived moments before her.

"We're looking for Connor," said Cole to another uniform, who was guarding the entrance to Belvedere Road and waving a Hazard Area Response Team through in their van.

The shrill sirens blared once to scatter a group of slow moving tourists trying to reach the London Eye. The young policeman responded with a gesture behind him, where Reilly saw the man he was looking for. At the end of the street, beside the entrance to Jubilee Gardens, a man in a long, beige overcoat braced against the wind and held his phone to his ear, pacing across the street. He finished the call, agitated as Reilly approached.

"I don't want to hear it, Reilly," said Connor, raising his hand, palm out.

"Not my fault, Connor," said Reilly, raising both hands in defence.

"Where were you twenty-four hours ago when the bodies were being removed?"

"Questioning a suspected terrorist," said Reilly, leaving Connor no room for a comeback.

"I've seen too much today for you to come wandering in and taking over, Reilly."

"What's the damage?" asked Reilly, ignoring Connor's comment. "I haven't seen the CCTV footage yet. But I understand it was an explosive gas canister?"

Connor nodded. "Poisonous gas," he said in confirmation.

"Well then, it's terrorism and it's my problem. I don't make the rules, Connor," replied Reilly.

He eyed the scene in the park. The uniforms had done a good job of sealing the area off, and the only movement was men and women in white hazmat suits with full face protection.

"How bad is it?" asked Cole.

But the look on Connor's face said it all.

"You'll need to suit up," said Connor. "HART have cleared the area for more explosives, but we're expecting the area to be reopened shortly."

"How many?" said Reilly, dropping his cigarette to the ground and crushing it with his shoe.

Connor eyed the cigarette with a subconscious look of disapproval, and answered in a similar tone. "Dead?" asked Connor. "Twenty-three with eleven more in the hospital."

"Has the detonator been located?" asked Reilly.

"A rucksack was found. It's being examined."

"What about suspects?" asked Reilly.

Connor's brow furrowed. He stared at Reilly as if searching for the right words.

"Have you got any idea what we've just seen?" said Connor.

"Have you got any idea what twenty-three dead bodies looks like? Have you got any idea at all how hard it is to control your own anger when you're staring into the eyes of a poisonous gas bomb victim? Fighting for every breath. Knowing it may be their last."

"I'm sure it's been a very trying morning, Connor," said Reilly, nodding and trying to convey as much genuine sympathy as he could.

Continuing with his stare as if in total disbelief, Connor remained rooted to the spot, his hands clenched and his nostrils flared.

"Trying? You heartless bastard, Reilly," said Connor.

Reilly prepared himself. He turned side-on to Connor and positioned his rear foot for stability. The signs were all there. Emotions were high. As Connor's shoulder moved back, his lower lip disappeared beneath his front teeth in a grimace.

"That's enough," said Cole, her voice breaking the tension just enough for Connor to relax his arm. She nodded at the small park ahead of them. "Sir, the hazmats are being removed."

Leaving Connor with one final stare to make sure the punch wasn't swung, Reilly turned to the park. Two people were walking out, removing their protective head gear and breathing apparatuses. They stepped into a large tent that Reilly deduced to be some kind of hose-down due to the water that ran from it across the street.

A sickly feeling gripped Reilly's stomach. Standing outside the crime scene was bad enough and having the jurisdiction argument with Connor was tedious to say the least. But entering the scene and focusing on the source, focusing on the facts and making a plan took mental strength.

He puffed his cheeks and exhaled loud enough for Cole to hear.

"Shall we?" Cole asked. It was a suggestion to move Reilly

away from Connor with the subtle tact that she so often displayed.

Nodding at Connor, the two exchanged a look of understanding. There was no apology. The scene was stressful. The tension was high. And beyond their own personal disputes, people had lost their lives, while some still fought for them. They'd pick up the argument another day.

They approached the entrance to the park and flashed their ID cards at a man who was placing a used hazmat suit in a plastic container.

"You must be Reilly," said the man.

Reilly nodded.

"Jarvis," said the man, offering his hand, which Reilly shook. "The boss said you'd be coming."

"This is DS Cole," said Reilly, presenting Cole to his right. "You're HART?"

Jarvis nodded and cleared his throat.

"Are we clear to go in?"

"There's not a lot to see," said Jarvis. The lines of his face were deep as if they'd been carved into his skin. "No explosion damage and no sign of a device. It's like they all just dropped to the ground."

"Cole, get the CCTV sent across to HQ," said Reilly.

"The scene is clear. Whatever it was, there's no sign of it now."

"No residue on the bodies?" asked Reilly.

"The post-mortems will tell us," said Jarvis. "But it'll be a few hours before we get any results."

"No device and no explosion," said Reilly, verbalising his thoughts. "What are the symptoms?"

"Suffocation."

Reilly raised an eyebrow in question.

"They choked to death, sir. One minute they were all

enjoying their lunch or walking through the park. The next, they were fighting for their lives."

"The survivors?" asked Reilly. "They must have been far enough away from the source for the air to dilute the gas. What's the range of the gas?"

"Thirty feet." said Jarvis. "The dead were mostly found beside the memorial. The survivors were thirty feet or more away." Reilly opened his mouth to raise a question, but Jarvis, an experienced investigator, continued. "The memorial is clean," he said. "As is the children's play park, flowers and grass around it."

An image of what the scene of the play park may have looked like came to Reilly's mind, substantiating Connor's words and demeanour.

"CCTV is being sent across, sir," said Cole, pocketing her phone.

"Good," said Reilly. "Have Connor and his men keep this place locked down. I want a list of the victims and I want a name to every face that walked through this place in the last forty-eight hours."

"I'm on it, sir," said Cole, walking away and retrieving her phone again. It began to ring as soon as she lifted it from her pocket.

"You're an experienced man," said Reilly, turning his attention back to Jarvis. "In your professional opinion, would you say this was a planned terrorist attack?"

Jarvis shook his head, biting his bottom lip.

"Without seeing the device, sir, I wouldn't like to say," said Jarvis, taking on a grave expression. "But I do know this. In two days' time, two million people are going to descend on London for New Year's Eve, and if we don't find the culprit, we could have something far worse on our hands."

It was as if the wind had dropped to allow Jarvis to speak. It began again as soon as he'd stopped, while the two men stood eye to eye digesting the potential risk the comment alluded to.

The tension was broken by Cole, who stepped between them. "Sir?"

"Yes?" said Reilly, breaking his stare from Jarvis.

Cole's phone hand dropped to her side, along with the expression on her face.

"There's been another attack, sir."

CHAPTER SEVEN

"Honey, I'm home," said Lucas, as he closed the door to the apartment behind him and pulled his hood off his head.

His tone hinted at humour, but his hate-filled eyes maintained their cruel slant. He collected an apple from a bowl on top of a cabinet and clicked open his knife. The bedroom door creaked open at his touch to reveal the boy still sitting on the floor, hooded and bound, and his mother, gagged, bound and staring back at him with bright red eyes. Her mass of hair clung to her face, damp with sweat and tears.

"Hey," said Lucas, leaning on the door frame. "What have you been up to?"

The blade of his knife cut perfect circles of apple, two inches in diameter. He took three steps to the boy, still holding Martina's threatening gaze, and licked his knife clean. Her eyes widened as he approached her son, and with renewed vigour, she fought against her bindings. Then she stopped, breathless and red-faced.

Stooping to place the slice of apple into the boy's hand, Lucas lifted the hood so he could eat, then cut one more slice and placed it in his palm. The boy's eyes were swollen with tears, his nose crusty with dried snot and his mouth a mess of dribble. He looked up at Lucas. The whites of his eyes criss-crossed with tiny red arteries.

"It won't be long now," said Lucas. "Your daddy just needs to clear a few things off his list. Okay?"

The boy nodded, locking eyes with Lucas with the innocence of a child.

"What about you?" said Lucas, standing, stepping away from the boy and facing Martina. "Hungry?"

Staring back at him, unsure of what her response should be, Martina remained silent. Her nostrils flared once and her eyes blinked away the tears that began to swell.

Lucas placed the apple on the bedside table, beside a novel, which was opened and laid face down to hold the page, and a small digital alarm clock. It was the type that had a large button on the top for the owner to hit and silence the alarm and large green numbers on the display that cast an eerie, green glow across the surface of the table.

She stared at the knife then back at Lucas, watching him unzip his jacket. He slid it off and laid it over the arm of a small wicker chair in the corner of the room. Then he sat on the edge of the bed and turned to face Martina with his back to the door.

"I'm going to release your gag from your mouth," said Lucas. "If you scream, it'll be your last. Do you understand?"

She nodded then grimaced at his touch as his finger slid the length of her cheek and pulled the twisted bandanna out of her mouth. He held it for a moment to make sure she kept her end of the bargain then dropped it to her neck and reached for the apple.

"Hungry?" he asked.

"Can I feed myself?" she asked. "At least offer me that dignity."

"Dignity?" said Lucas, as he cut a broad, round slice of apple. "How much dignity did you give Herman?"

"Lucas, you can't-"

"Do you want the apple or not, Martina? I haven't come to discuss the weakness of my brother and your extra-marital affairs."

"Where's Herman? I want to talk to Herman."

"Oh, no. Herman isn't allowed in here. You know the rules. He's weak. You'll convince him to set you free with your fork tongue," said Lucas.

"So why are you here?"

"To keep you alive long enough to see you suffer," said Lucas, his tone flat and direct. He popped the slice of apple into his mouth and bit into it, chewing with his mouth open. "Oh, and to give you the good news."

"Good news?"

"Your man," said Lucas. "What was his name?"

"Herman," said Martina.

"No, not him. The toy-boy. What was his name?"

Martina shook her head in disbelief.

"Daniel, wasn't it?" said Lucas, cutting himself another slice.

"What about him?" said Martina, her words staccato, as if she sensed the sentence Lucas was preparing to say.

"We killed him," said Lucas, and winked at Martina, whose face seemed to drop as if every muscle had been replaced, leaving her jaw hanging. "Well, I say we, but honestly, it was all Herman. He really is getting some strength. You should be proud of him."

"You bastard," said Martina, her voice a deep breath of hate. She tried to continue an onslaught of abuse, but emotion grew the better of her, and her voice whined to a high pitch then faded into tears. Prevented from rolling onto her side by the bindings on her wrists, she turned onto her shoulder and let her thick hair cover her face.

"I thought you might say something like that," said Lucas, pulling her hair away.

"Leave me alone," she snapped, and jumped into life. But her restraints stopped her like a guard dog's chain.

"Let's just pop this back in then," said Lucas, and pulled at the gag. Her emotions elicited some resistance. But Lucas pulled back a handful of hair and held her head still to replace the bandanna. "There you go," he said, and tapped her on the cheek.

He stood from the bed, collected his jacket and dropped the apple into the boy's hands without saying anything. Then he pulled the door closed behind him.

"How is she, do you think?" said Herman.

"Never mind how she is," said Lucas, taking a seat at the desk. "I need you to focus. Do you feel the strength growing?"

"I don't know," said Herman. He glanced at the bedroom door and then back to the computer screen.

"I'm so proud of you, Herman. Just look at what you've achieved," said Lucas.

"Look at all those people," said Herman.

He reached up to touch the computer screen. His fingers traced the outline of a woman who had fallen to her knees with one hand clutching her throat and the other hanging onto her baby's pushchair, her weak grasp slipping further until she slumped to the ground. On the ground in full view of the CCTV camera, a dozen or more people were fighting for their lives, including two paramedics in green uniforms.

"Roll the camera back," said Lucas, checking his watch. "Twenty-five minutes."

The footage rolled back, showing the woman with the

pushchair standing in reverse. Tourists who were sitting beside the statue in the park popped up from the grass and sat talking.

A homeless man lying beneath a bush raised his head and rested it on his hand.

And Harvey Stone ran into the park backwards then stared at the mobile phone in his hand.

"There he is," said Lucas. "When you take him down, Herman, that's when you'll become a real man."

CHAPTER EIGHT

The doors of the train carriage seemed to linger for longer than Harvey remembered.

The noise of the crowds that followed grew, and as the first feet of the panicked stampede entered the tunnel, the doors closed with a hiss and the train jolted into action. Peering through the door as people banged on the glass of the moving train, Melody watched in dismay as the scared crowds grew larger, desperation etched on their faces at the realisation that yet another London bomb had exploded.

Then darkness, as the station fell away to the perpetual black of the tunnel.

The seats of the westbound train were empty save for a dozen people of various origins who all appeared to be traveling alone. The crowd outside was soon forgotten. Books were opened and legs were outstretched as the commuters enjoyed the less packed part of their daily journey. Newspapers covered faces and the noise through headphones was drowned out by the rumbling of the old train through the tunnel.

Only one man hadn't returned his attention to his paper. He

watched Harvey with inquisitive eyes that lay in the shadow of his long flock of thin, grey hair.

"What just happened, Harvey?" said Melody, moving close to be heard above the noise of the train. She gave a cautious look over her shoulder to make sure they couldn't be heard then waited for Harvey to respond.

But Harvey didn't reply.

"Harvey, this is too weird," she said. "How did you know to run?"

"Instinct," said Harvey. "It didn't feel right. He lured me there."

"Who was he? Was it him that gave you the phone?"

"He didn't give me the phone, Melody. He planted it when he bumped into me."

"So who is he then?" asked Melody.

"I'm trying to think," replied Harvey.

"Well, think harder," hissed Melody, leaning in closer. "It's him, isn't it?"

"Who?"

"The bomb guy from yesterday. They must be connected."

"Must be?" said Harvey.

"So there's two gas bombers now, is there? The odds are too small, Harvey."

"There could be three," said Harvey. "Or four or five. How do I know who's responsible?"

"Did you get a look at him?" asked Melody.

Harvey sighed and dropped to the seat nearest the door, gesturing for Melody to follow.

"Green hood, short jacket, jeans and black trainers," said Harvey.

"How about his face?"

"Just a glimpse. Not enough to place him."

"But enough to recognise him if you saw him again?"

Harvey shook his head. "I don't know."

Melody let out an audible sigh and sat back in the seat. "All those people in the park. Do you think-"

"I don't know what to think, Melody. Where exactly was yesterday's bomb?"

"Jubilee Gardens," replied Melody, as the train slowed for the next stop.

"The Southbank?"

"Right beside the London Eye," said Melody.

"Why would he attack there if it was me he wanted? I was at home with you."

"Whoever it was, they clearly tried to kill you, Harvey. You need to think hard who it could be," said Melody. "And how would he know you'd be in Trafalgar Square?"

"The cameras were following us. Well, me."

"What cameras?" asked Melody.

"In the square," said Harvey, trying to piece it together. "The security cameras."

"Why would the cameras follow you?" said Melody. "You don't exist. Remember?"

"I don't know. None of this makes sense," said Harvey, as the train rocked to a stop and the doors opened with a hiss.

"What's going on? We're not at a station," said Melody, looking from side to side out of the windows and into the dark tunnel.

"It's the security protocol," said Harvey. "They're shutting down the underground. We're being evacuated."

The other passengers closed their books and newspapers. Stretched legs prepared to stand and headphones were pulled from heads as each commuter carried a look of confusion.

And still the man with the long, grey hair stared at Harvey.

"We need to go now," said Harvey, keeping his voice low in the relative silence.

"No. We should wait until someone comes."

"We're on camera, Melody. If they can see us out there, they can see us in here too. We need to get out of here," said Harvey, obscuring his face from the view of the dome-shaped security camera fixed to the ceiling of the train. He stood and pulled Melody with him.

The man's eyes followed his every move as Harvey peered outside the train for signs of a torchlight or approaching rail staff.

The voice of the train driver came over the speakers.

"This is a security announcement. My apologies, ladies and gentlemen. We've been asked to stop here and walk to the next station. If you could please disembark and make your way to the front of the train."

"Just stay with the crowd, Harvey," said Melody. "We haven't done anything wrong."

The other passengers in the carriage stood and shared in the confusion, each of them finding Harvey and Melody staring back at them with guilt written all over their faces.

"Just follow the crowd," said Melody.

But as the passengers made their way towards the open doors at the far end of the carriage, Harvey turned back to Melody, pulling her close to him.

"No," said Harvey, as passengers from the other carriages made their way along the narrow raised footpath that ran along the side of the tunnel. "We need to get away from the cameras, and fast."

"And how do you suppose we do that?" said Melody, as a man reached out to help them down from the carriage. She waved him off. "I'm fine, thank you, sir. I'll wait."

"Follow my lead," said Harvey, keeping his voice low.

He jumped the small gap then turned and reached for Melody to help her across. But she was already beside him.

Slowing to let the crowd move ahead, Harvey checked behind him to make sure they were the last in the line. Then he stopped.

"What are you doing?" said Melody. "Keep moving."

But Harvey remained still, pulling them into the side of the tunnel and out of sight.

"We need to stay off the cameras," said Harvey.

"You're not making sense, Harvey," said Melody. "None of this is making sense."

"If he knew I would be in Trafalgar Square, he's probably watching me," said Harvey.

"So?" said Melody. "We need to get out of here."

"No, Melody," said Harvey, catching the faint light in the wetness of her eye. "If he's watching me, if he's planning another attack, I need to be as far away from crowds as possible."

CHAPTER NINE

For the second time that day, a uniformed police officer raised the red and white tape for Reilly and Cole to pass beneath it. Two vans were parked close to the gate at the end of Villiers Street beside the entrance to Embankment tube station, guarded by two armed police wearing protective head gear and breathing apparatuses.

Temporary barriers had been put up by the HART teams to funnel crime scene investigators into a large tent. Both Reilly and Cole entered the tent on the safe zone and emerged in the danger zone, fully clad in hazmat suits and breathing gear.

"This is ridiculous," said Reilly, hearing his own voice muffled by the full face mask. He opened his mouth to continue his complaints. But then two men in hazmats marked with a red cross on their sleeves carried a stretcher towards them from the small park. Parting to allow the paramedics through, Reilly and Cole both caught a glimpse of the man on the stretcher. His green uniform was distinct.

"Did you see that?" said Cole, when the paramedics had passed.

"Early responders," said Reilly, gesturing at two paramedic

motorcycles parked in the danger zone further along the road. "Poor sods didn't stand a chance."

"They must have run right into it," said Cole.

"Are you ready for this, Cole?"

"Let's get in there, sir," she replied.

They turned the corner, stepped through the park's gated entrance and stopped in their tracks.

"Oh my," said Cole.

"Let's let the paramedics do their thing," said Reilly. "We're looking for the device. Note the locations of all cameras and mark the kill zone on a map of the park. Sketch it if you have to. We can't help these people. But if we can find some kind of clue as to who and what this is, we might be able to stop this guy before he strikes again."

"Copy that, sir," said Cole.

She walked off towards the centre of the scene, leaving Reilly standing alone at the edge of the park, staring at the array of bodies that looked as if they had been arranged by a Hollywood set designer. He took a breath and felt his own exhalation on his skin, warm and moist. The next inhale was warm and stale like used air. He blinked away the heat in his eyes and tried to wipe them, but his hand hit the face mask and he dizzied a little. In an instant, his breathing grew faster. It was as if there was no oxygen and he was trapped in a box. He leaned on the park gate and doubled over, forcing himself to breath. But still, the hyperventilating continued.

His hands fumbled at the mask, but the gloves were restricting his movements.

He turned from the park, his hand finding the red plastic barriers that funnelled him into the white tent. But he wasn't even halfway there when he realised he wasn't going to make it. He had to get the mask off. He had to breathe fresh air.

Seeing him stumbling, a member of the HART team ran to his aid.

"Sir, are you okay?" she said.

Reilly stared through the mask, mouth wide open, trying to suck in the air. The woman began to lead him away, tugging at the breathing apparatus to check the valve was opened.

The inside of the tent was dark in comparison to the winter morning sunlight and Reilly's eyes struggled to adjust in time. Still fighting for breath and with the added blurred vision, his panic increased.

"Let me out," he said, in between raising breaths. "Get me out of this thing."

"Sir, calm down," said the lady who had come to his rescue. "Let's get you hosed off."

"No. Just let me out. I need air," he said, as his vision blurred almost in its entirety.

Two strong arms pulled him away and forced him beneath an open shower. The sound of rain against the hazmat material beside his ears added to his confusion and state of panic.

"Thirty seconds, sir, and you'll be out," said a man's voice. "You're nearly there. Just hang on."

But it was too much. First, one knee buckled and another hand supported him. Then the other knee gave way and he slipped from the grasp of his aid to the floor.

Voices, muffled with distance but loud with urgency, span around him. Darkness bore down on him and just a thin trickle of oxygen was extracted from each labouring breath.

Then, like a cool breeze washing across his naked body, his senses numbed.

Darkness closed in.

And there was silence.

CHAPTER TEN

"Stay with him," said Lucas. "Don't let him out of your sight."

"Oh, I don't know if I can do this," replied Herman, his stomach bunching into a knot. "There's too much evil. I can't do it."

"You can't do what, Herman?" said Lucas. "You can't find the man that destroyed your life? Or you can't push a few buttons to save the lives of your family?"

Herman stared at him in the reflection of the computer screen, his face a picture of misery.

"You know I'll do it," said Lucas. "The only reason they're still alive is because of you. Look at what you've done. Look at how far you've come."

Hanging his head with the fatigue and stress from two days of being locked in a tiny apartment, with his captive family and the blood of so many people on his hands, Herman began to weep.

"Oh, stop your crying," said Lucas. "We've got work to do. Where's Harvey Stone?"

"I don't know," said Herman.

"But you have access to every CCTV camera in London,

Herman," said Lucas, his voice softened and calming. "You told me you could do this. We can't stop now, dear brother." He raised his hand to the left side of Herman's face and traced the outline of a scar.

"Stop it," said Herman, and pulled his head away.

"We're doing this for you. Remember? We're doing this so you can live, so you can grow, and so your boy can remember his pa as a great man with power and strength, not the dirty little pervert who couldn't keep his hands to himself. Or do you want him to believe the picture the public paints of you?" said Lucas.

"I can't let my boy see me like this. I don't deserve to be a father," said Herman. "Maybe it's best if he-"

"If he what?" snapped Lucas.

Staring into the screen, Herman lost himself in a trail of thought that seemed to lead him by the hand through the images of London and to someplace cold, dark and lonely. It was a safe place, a place away from the taunting boys, the jeering crowds and the look of hate in every eye that jabbed at his very soul with their opinions.

"If he what, Herman?" said Lucas, snapping him back from his safe place.

He looked up and found his brother in the reflection of the screen. He opened his mouth, struggling to form the word, although he knew it and knew how to articulate it. But to speak it was alien. Inhuman.

"Dies?" asked Lucas, prolonging the noise and adding a sense of joy to the rising tail of his public school boy articulation.

There it was.

The word.

"Yes," whispered Herman, his voice more of a breath than a word. A short, sharp exhale followed like some part of his subconscious found a thin slice of humour in his thoughts and forced it through while his consciousness was numbed with the mental imagery. "At least then he wouldn't have to suffer as I have. At least, if he was dead, he wouldn't have to endure the agonising taunts from the boys. He wouldn't be the boy whose father is the pervert. He wouldn't be the boy that causes girls to huddle together when he passes like some contagious monster."

The final sentence fell from Herman's lips, leaving his mouth hanging open in memory of the words.

"At least he would die with the innocence he deserves," finished Herman.

"Snap out of it," said Lucas, his voice loud and his tone sharp. He slammed his hand on the desk to add weight to his command. "In two days' time, you'll be walking the streets with your head held high with your boy by your side. And you know what, Herman? He'll be holding your hand and looking up at his father as he walks beside you, trying to match your step. And he'll be proud, Herman, proud to be your son. He'll feel safe. And you know why? Because his father will be a man who will take care of him. His father will be the type of man who won't let anybody take advantage of him, who won't let anybody hurt him. Is that what you want, my dear Herman?"

The scene in Herman's head softened his expression. He closed his eyes and clung to the thought like a fist grasping at the cold morning fog. And as the last wispy trails of the dream vanished, he opened his eyes to stare at his brother in the reflection of the screen.

"Tell me, dear brother. Is that what you want?" whispered Lucas.

The question danced across Herman's mind between flashes of the dead lying on the cold, hard ground.

"Is that what I want?" he asked, confirming the question as his focus returned to the damp, dark apartment. "Yes. Yes, I want him to feel safe. I want him to hold my hand. I want him to match my steps, to keep pace with me. And yes. I want him to be proud of his father."

"Good," said Lucas, tracing the outline of Herman's ear with his finger. "So let us continue."

"Yes. Yes," said Herman with a new burst of life.

The energy brought a smile to Lucas' face. He opened the small notepad on the desk to the page marked with the lid of their pen.

"Who's next?" asked Lucas. "Look at the list, Herman. Tell me who's next."

A long, unmanaged fingernail trailed a list of names from top to bottom. A tongue eased from between Herman's lips. Then his face hardened as his finger came to a stop.

He looked up at Lucas, who stared back at him through the screen's image of people in white suits carting the dead and dying onto stretchers, but said nothing.

"Good choice, Herman, my dear brother," said Lucas. "Good choice."

CHAPTER ELEVEN

"Follow me," said Harvey, and he ran further into the tunnel, following the other passengers. He stopped and stood flat against the wall when they reached the station and began to file onto the platform. Melody crept up beside him and peered along the tunnel.

"What are we going to do?" said Melody, peering after the small, scared crowd edging their way along the tunnel.

"You're going to follow them," said Harvey. "Mingle with the crowd, get in a taxi, drive one mile then find another. Lose them, whoever it is watching us. Lose them."

"What? No," said Melody. "I'm staying with you."

"Listen," said Harvey. He turned from watching the passengers climb up to the platform to look at Melody. "Whoever this is, he knows where I am. And he's one step ahead. I need to get away."

"Where will you go?" asked Melody.

"I'll find him," said Harvey, and he met her stare. "I'll stop this."

"Harvey, no. That's how trouble finds you, Harvey. Just let the authorities deal with it for once."

"They've done a great job so far, haven't they?" said Harvey. "And what am I supposed to tell them? I used to work for an organised crime family and now I have someone trying to kill me?"

"Do you think it's someone from-"

"I don't know who it is, Melody. I have no idea. All I can do is get out of here and track them down. I can do it. I'll be okay. But if..."

He paused and turned away.

"If what, Harvey?" said Melody.

He sighed.

"If anything happened to you, I don't know what I'd do. You're the only solid thing in my life right now," said Harvey. "If I didn't have you, I'd have nothing."

Melody pulled him in close and hugged him. He felt her swallow and clear her throat.

"I'll make a deal with you," said Melody.

"What's the deal?"

"You get yourself out of here. Stay off the cameras and lose the tail. Then come find me and we tackle this guy together?"

"No. Melody, I-"

"I won't hear another word, Harvey," said Melody, as she pulled her jacket off and tied it around her waist. "If you're not going to the police, if you're doing this alone, then I come with you and that's final."

"And when we find him?" said Harvey.

"We take him to the police," replied Melody. "No guns. No weapons. We do this clean. We said we'd start a new life here. I'm not having it tainted just because you can't go to the police."

The words circled in Harvey's mind like vultures circling a corpse with their wings spread wide, hanging on the breeze. Then they closed their wings and descended to their prey.

"Okay," said Harvey. "Now go."

"Go where?" said Melody, as Harvey walked back into the tunnel.

He turned, took the few steps back towards her and kissed her hard, cupping her face in his hands.

"I'll find you," he said, then slipped into the darkness.

CHAPTER TWELVE

"Sir, can you hear me?" said a voice. It came to him like the voice of a faraway angel, bringing with it a warm breath that quelled the cold grip of his slumber. "Sir?"

A clicking sound, close to his face, moving from side to side.

Reilly opened his eyes to find dark shapes against bright white.

The clicking continued.

"That's it, sir," said the voice. "Take it easy."

The shape focused as if someone was adjusting the lens of a camera. The image brightened to reveal a pair of pretty eyes, soft in heart but with a hardened appearance behind glass.

"Cole?" said Reilly.

"I'm here, sir," replied Cole. "You had a giddy turn. You're okay. But we need a paramedic to check you over. Are you okay with that?"

"A paramedic?" said Reilly, still digesting his circumstance. "Where am I?"

"Villiers Street, sir," said Cole. "We were investigating the-"

"The gas bomber," said Reilly, interrupting her with his recollection.

"That's right, sir. You've been out for a few minutes. Just relax. We've asked one of the paramedics to pop over. He'll be here shortly."

"No," said Reilly, and rolled to his elbow.

"Sir, stay where you are."

"No, Cole. Let me up."

"Sir, you need to relax," said Cole, as a second lady bent to help restrain him.

"Just relax, Mr Reilly," said the woman. "I'm afraid I can't let you leave. We have to have you checked out. This is still a controlled zone and it's HART's jurisdiction." She turned to Cole. "Go get the paramedic. Tell them to hurry."

"No," said Reilly. "I'll wait. I'm okay."

"But, sir," said Cole, torn between the two instructions.

"Let the paramedics deal with the injured. I'm okay. I'll wait," said Reilly.

"I'm afraid I'm going to have to ask you to wear your oxygen mask, sir," said the woman in white. "If you breathed in-"

"I won't be wearing that, I'm afraid," said Reilly.

"But, sir, if you have inhaled the chemicals-"

"If I breathed in the chemicals, I wouldn't be talking to you now. And besides, if I did breathe them in and I'm dying, I won't be spending my dying breaths wearing that bloody thing."

The woman nodded at Cole, who relaxed and returned to Reilly's side.

"Help me sit up, will you, Cole?" said Reilly, as he pulled himself around to lean against a table leg. He nodded once more to the woman, reconfirming his position on the paramedic and the oxygen, and offering thanks for allowing him a little comfort.

"Do you remember what happened, sir?" asked Cole.

"I blacked out. The air. It was constrictive. I felt boxed in," said Reilly, struggling to end the words to say how he'd felt. "I felt like I was suffocating."

"Do you have any history of claustrophobia?" asked the woman, who still lingered nearby.

"No-one likes being trapped," said Reilly.

"But it affects some more than others," replied the woman. "It's nothing to be ashamed of."

"I'm not claustrophobic. It was the mask. It must be faulty or something. There was no air."

The woman in white stared down at him, her lips taut and her smile false. "I'm sure," she said.

Leaving the woman to surmise her own opinion, Reilly turned to Cole. "Did you find anything?" he asked, moving the topic of conversation away from his own weakness.

"A rucksack," she replied, reaching for her bag. "I've asked for the CCTV footage to be sent through while it's taken to the lab. Early inspections show it's a homemade device triggered by a mobile phone."

"How does a phone trigger the release of gas?" asked Cole.

"We can't be specific to this case until the bag has been examined. But typically, an incoming call will initiate the detonator by sending a current through the phone's circuitry, and the explosion will occur when the circuitry powers down, usually when the call goes unanswered. In the past, bombers speed up the process by programming voicemail to kick in after three or five rings. It gives them enough time to get away and avoids somebody intercepting the call."

"So he knows what he's doing then. Do we know what the gas is?" asked Reilly, glancing at the woman. "That might give us a clue."

The woman collected a notepad from a nearby table and flicked back a few pages.

"Early findings are showing it as a chlorine bomb. We found residue on the plants in the bomb's locale. The symptoms support this."

"The symptoms?" said Reilly. "People are dead."

"The symptoms of the survivors, Mr Reilly. We think another toxin has been added to the chlorine to increase its toxicity."

"What are the symptoms?" asked Reilly.

Taking a long breath, as if preparing herself to say the words out loud, the woman closed her notepad and leaned against the table.

"Those who were fortunate enough to survive all have inflamed respiratory systems. They are relying on permanent oxygen feeds. The survivors who were closest to the bomb when it released the gas are experiencing non-cardiogenic pulmonary edemas and may never see the light of day again."

"What's a pulmonary edema?" asked Cole.

"Fluid on the lung, which can be fatal by itself, but when you add the inflamed respiratory systems into the mix, they don't stand a chance," said the woman. She offered Reilly a grave stare. "It's just a matter of time."

"But in the open air, surely the effects are diluted?" said Reilly. "I mean, I can understand how that could be deadly in a confined space, but in the open?"

Nodding in agreement, the woman pushed off from the table and walked across to the front of the tent to stare outside.

"The gas release would be toxic for a few seconds, maybe ten, in these conditions. The wind is fairly strong and constant. But the cloud gas that would have been emitted would have been enough to affect people in a twenty-metre radius."

"So the survivors were all in that radius?" asked Cole, as she tapped on her tablet, scrolling through the images.

"We can assume so. The CCTV footage will give us a clearer picture," said the woman. "The poor souls in the centre of the gas release wouldn't stand a chance. Even if they ran, they would still have inhaled two or three lungfuls."

"And that would be enough?" asked Reilly.

"More than enough," she replied. "The effects would be instant. The body would react to the gas and inflame."

"So they suffocated?"

"The people that died on the scene would have, yes," she replied. "The survivors will die a much slower and more painful death."

A pause followed the statement as each of them processed the information in their own way.

"Sir, I found something. Look at this man and woman. Here," said Cole, turning the tablet to him.

"What's that in the guy's hand?" asked Reilly.

"A mobile phone, sir."

CHAPTER THIRTEEN

"There he is," said Lucas. "Do you see the confidence in his stride, Herman?"

Herman nodded.

"You're going to take him down. You're going to bring him to his knees. And when he's there, fighting for his life, he's going to ask why. He's going to question everything he ever did to deserve such suffering. Say it," said Lucas. "Say his name out loud."

Looking at the list, Herman found the third name down and thought of the misery the man had caused.

"Jasper Charles," said Herman, remembering the man he'd met as a boy and what he'd done.

"It's okay," said Lucas, seeing the memories unfold. "You're getting stronger with each one."

"I want to be there," said Herman. "I want to see it happen. Not on the screen. I want to watch him suffer in real life."

A warm joyous sensation grew from the pit of Lucas' stomach at the words. His top lip rose in a cruel smile, revealing his stained teeth. His tongue emerged to wet his lip then slid back into his mouth.

"Shall we? Shall we go and spectate?" said Lucas. He turned from the computer and stared out of the window, imagining the possibilities. "We could follow him and witness his final moments. How I'd like to stand over his body and remind him of the things he did to you."

"I just want to see from a distance. Far enough to be away from the gas, but close enough to see the look in his eyes."

"Oh, you'll be close," said Lucas. "You'll be close enough to hear his dying breath. Close enough to remind him of the terrible things he did. Tell me, Herman. Where do we find him?"

"He's a manager. In Chelsea. An Italian restaurant. A place called Via Venato."

"Sounds posh," said Lucas.

"It is. They have seafood and fine wines and pastas," said Herman, recalling the online menu.

"Was he hard to find?"

"No. The restaurant has a photo of him on their website."

"So he isn't hiding. He's unashamed," said Lucas. He turned back to the screen. "You'll deliver his surprise to the restaurant where there will be no escape. We'll need the van and paperwork. Delivery notes, you know, the stuff they sign."

"I'll have a clipboard," said Herman, his enthusiasm growing as the plan unfolded. "And a trolley with boxes."

"And a uniform," said Lucas. "That'll throw them off the scent."

"I can find out who their suppliers are and fake some delivery papers and a uniform."

"No. We take the supplier's van. We take their uniform. There can be no mistake. Can you hack their restaurant delivery system?"

"Of course," said Herman, with renewed confidence.

"You are such a talented boy, Herman."

"I'll get into the restaurant's system and find out who their suppliers are," said Herman.

"And then?" said Lucas, brimming with excitement.

"I'll hack the supplier's system and find out when the next delivery is."

"That's the ticket. I can see it now, Herman. Oh, how special will this one be? I can see you standing there while someone signs your papers. I can see him walking through those swinging double doors, full of pride and authority. That's when you do it. That's when you pull the mask to your face and watch him choke," said Lucas, drawing out the last three words, savouring the flavour of his brother's revenge.

The computer screen was split into four CCTV feeds. Every ten seconds, the feeds changed to another four cameras. Millions of people passed by in monochrome. Tourists clung to each other's arms and looked around in wonder at the ancient buildings. Workers hurried by with routine, a daily walk, a daily cycle, a daily drive. Beyond the tourists, workers, bicycles and cars, Lucas found Herman staring at him.

"You can do this, Herman," said Lucas. "You can really do this. It'll be your greatest yet."

"Yes."

"Just think of the beatings, Herman. Think of the shame, the humiliation and the torturous nights he put you through when you were just a boy."

"Stop," said Herman, hanging his head. "I'll do it."

"And when you do," said Lucas, "be sure to look him in the eye. Be sure to remind him who you are and wait for that moment. That moment when his pupils dilate. When his mouth opens just a fraction and the recognition sets in."

"And it'll be too late," said Herman.

"There'll be no escape," said Lucas.

"But what about Stone?"

"Leave Stone to me. We'll save the best for last," said Lucas. He stood from the old swivel chair beside the computer desk and strode to the window. "You're still learning. You're still growing. And with each name on that list, you grow a little more. But mark my words, Herman, Stone is out there somewhere. He has to surface soon. And when he does, we'll find him. You can track the phone we gave him."

"What if he throws the phone?" asked Herman.

"Oh, he won't. He's got nowhere left to hide."

"Do you think he'll come after us?"

"Almost certainly, dear Herman," said Lucas, and placed his hand against the cold glass window. "We've woken the beast."

CHAPTER FOURTEEN

The tunnel was devoid of sounds, save for the scurrying of rats, distant murmurings of trains being disembarked, and their passengers stumbling confusedly along the dark corridor.

Step by step, Harvey sought the raised platform, running his hand along the damp, brick wall to his right for guidance. The empty platform ahead offered little in the way of refuge, only bright lights, the smell of grime and the noise of a rolling drinks can being pushed along by the incessant breeze.

From the darkness, Harvey studied the platform. The exit tunnel, which was shiny with white tiles, snaked out of sight towards the station and escalators. Two CCTV cameras faced the exit from the platform.

Beside the exit was a set of double doors marked as staff only by a sign branded with the London Underground logo. Breaking them open would create attention.

Harvey ran the scenarios through his head. Whoever it was that was out to get him would find Melody and assume Harvey was close by. By the time they checked the surrounding stations, Harvey would be out and far away from the cameras.

He climbed onto the platform, tried the double doors and found them locked, as expected. So he took the exit tunnel.

The long bends seemed endless, masking any sign of the end. But the shiny white tiles echoed every sound, providing Harvey's only clue as to what lay ahead. The click of a door being closed echoed along the corridor. A rattle of keys followed and then came the sound of a man clearing his throat.

Harvey slowed his pace, listening for the man's approach, but he heard nothing.

He stopped.

Heels clicked on the tiled floor, growing louder.

A man's whistle, tuneful and relaxed.

Then a shadow on the curved wall began to grow like some monstrous demon rising up from the floor. With nowhere to turn but back the way he came, Harvey pressed himself against the wall. But the shadow grew larger still from the floor up the walls and across the arched ceiling.

And then a boot stepped into view.

It stopped.

Another rattle of keys and then the opening of another door with an audible squeak of dry hinges that played backwards as the door closed behind the man with the solid touch of heavy wood on wood.

Harvey moved forwards with slow, cautious steps, rounding the bend as close to the wall as he could. He found the door on his right and peered around the corner. An armed policeman travelled up the escalators with his arms resting on his weapon, rocking from his toes to his heels, in what Harvey could only assume to be a method of maintaining the circulation in his feet. The policeman disappeared from view, blocking the only exit known to Harvey.

Moving back to the door, Harvey listened for movement inside, but heard nothing.

The door handle, a brass knob that appeared to be several decades old, rattled at his touch and the squeak of the hinges seemed louder than before. Inside, he found a service passageway with electrical panels fixed to the white tiles at head height. A series of switches that Harvey presumed to be lights were fixed beside the inside of the door.

He closed the door behind him, easing it into place with practiced silence.

A man cleared his throat somewhere close. He was in the left passage, Harvey deduced with his head cocked to one side. The whistling began, allowing Harvey to place the distance. He was close by and tinkering with something. Harvey pictured the scene as the sounds came to him.

A small screw being placed on a metal container. Then another.

A metal panel being removed.

The whistling stopped. Concentration.

Harvey opened the panel on the wall to the right. A series of electrical breakers were sitting in four rows of fifteen. Each of them was marked with a small label that Harvey presumed to be electrical circuits. At the bottom of the panel was a single breaker, larger than the rest.

Harvey placed his finger beneath it, but hesitated, considering a plan that was formulating in his mind.

"Here, what are you doing in here?" said the old man, stepping from the service passage as he tucked a screwdriver into the breast pocket of his coveralls and pushed his glasses onto the bridge of his nose. "You aren't supposed to be in here. What are you doing?"

Harvey gauged the man to be in his late fifties. He wore a few days' growth and his wrinkled face was tanned with age beneath a flock of smooth, grey hair.

Placing a single index finger to his lips, Harvey gestured for the man to be quiet, conscious of the armed guard outside.

"Don't tell me to be-"

Harvey flicked the switch.

In an instant, the small passageway was plunged into total darkness. A hum of ventilation that Harvey hadn't previously registered fell silent.

"What have you done?" said the man, and stepped towards Harvey. His footsteps were loud enough for Harvey to guess his distance, reach out, place one arm around the man's neck, and cover his mouth with the other.

A green light above the doorway flicked once then shone a dim ghostly light over the room.

"I don't want to hurt you, old man," said Harvey. "But I will if I have to. Do you understand?"

A feeble nod beneath Harvey's grip.

"I just hit the main breaker. Is the station in darkness?"

Harvey loosened his hand.

"Just the emergency lighting, son," said the man.

"Good. Do you have duct tape?"

There was a pause. Then the man nodded and tapped Harvey's arm with the roll from his tool belt.

"Pull a piece off about eight inches long."

The man's eyes widened, but Harvey offered no indication of emotion through his blank stare. He took the length of tape from the man.

"I'm going to remove my hand. If you call out, you die. If you struggle, you die. Do you understand?"

The old man nodded once more.

"Give me the roll of tape."

He did as he was told.

"Put your hands behind your back."

"It's you, isn't it?" said the old man, as he did as instructed. "You're the one they're looking for."

Harvey pulled his arms tight then loosened them a little, to allow the old man some comfort, before wrapping a long length of tape around his wrists. Then Harvey pulled the tape across the man's mouth, tugging to make sure it was tight.

"Can you breathe?" asked Harvey.

The old man nodded.

"Are you in pain?" asked Harvey.

The man shook his head. The movement was barely discernible in the dim, green light.

"Last question," said Harvey, and released the tape from the man's mouth. "I need to get out of the station without being seen. Where the nearest exit?"

"Go up the escalators and turn right," said the old man. "Go through the double doors and you'll see a fire escape. It brings you out onto the side street."

"And the CCTV?"

"You just killed the lights to the entire station. CCTV won't pick you up until you hit daylight at the top of the escalators."

"Do you understand what I'll do if you're lying?"

There was a pause. Then the old man nodded.

"If anybody asks?" said Harvey.

"Just go, son. This place will be swarming with police in a few minutes," said the old man. "I didn't see your face."

"I'm sorry I had to do this," said Harvey, as he pulled the tape back across the man's mouth.

The old man appeared to be unafraid. He stared up at Harvey and watched as he opened the door, took a glance outside, and then ran.

CHAPTER FIFTEEN

"The faces on the left were all victims of the Jubilee Gardens bomb, sir," said Cole, presenting a series of printed photographs that had been stuck to a magnetic glass wall.

"The deceased?" asked Reilly, sipping at his coffee with one hand. His other hand turned a coin over in his pocket. It was his method of keeping his shaky hand away from the inquisitive Cole.

"The dead and dying, sir," replied Cole. "Any one of them could have been the target, if indeed there was a target."

"So the faces on the right-hand side are the victims of the Victoria Embankment Park bomb?"

"Precisely, sir," said Cole. "We're looking for any links between any of the people on the left with any of the people on the right."

"A common factor?" said Reilly, nodding his approval. He gestured at a large TV screen that was mounted on a trolley to one side of the rows of faces. A video had been paused on the optimal shot of the man with the phone. His features were clear and cold. "What about the man with the phone?"

"Tech are running facial recognition now," said Cole. "He's

not wanted by the police for anything. So they're running him against the database."

"And the girl he was with?"

"Same, sir," replied Cole. "Although her scarf covers most of her face. We should have answers soon. Until then, I'm working on the victims, starting with those closest to the bomb."

"Good," said Reilly. "So who do we have? Is there anybody that might have enemies?"

"These four here," said Cole, indicating the top row of four faces, "were closest to the Jubilee Gardens bomb. This lady's name was Rose Clare, a hairdresser from Lambeth."

"What was she doing there?" asked Reilly.

"We don't know yet. But she was found lying beside this guy," said Cole, moving to the next photo. "Patrick Gervais. An associate partner in an accountancy firm across the street from where the bomb went off."

"A couple meeting for lunch?" offered Reilly.

"Likely, sir. They were both unmarried," said Cole, moving to the next photo of a red-headed man with tattoos that crawled from his chest to his neck and a thick beard. "Anthony Robinson. Art director for a web design firm. His office was two minutes away from the park. His wife and child have been informed."

Reilly shook his head, inhaled long and slow, and gestured for Cole to move onto the last image.

"Jason McMillan. A mechanic from Essex. Visiting the London Eye with his wife and two children and had just left them to get a drink from a nearby shop when the gas took him down."

The pause was enough to not have to ask the question Reilly was avoiding.

"His children escaped without harm," said Cole.

"And his wife?"

"She died a few hours ago, sir," said Cole, her tone low and quiet. "She ran into the gas cloud to help her husband before the gas had fully dispersed. Her body just gave up."

A thick knot sat at the back of Reilly's throat. He swallowed, but still, it remained.

"Who does this, Cole?" asked Reilly. He stopped turning the coin and swapped the coffee to his other hand, aware that Cole had seen the shake. "We're not going to find the answer here in time to stop him striking again."

"There may be a clue, sir."

"There will be a clue," said Reilly. "But we don't have time. He's out there preparing to hit us while we're down."

"How do you know it's a he?" said Cole.

"I don't. I'm stereotyping. Not many women could do that to children," said Reilly.

"And how do you know it's one person and not a group of them?"

Reilly sighed. "I don't. I'm going with my gut."

"Based on experience?"

Reilly nodded. "It's a homemade device using chemicals available on the open market. No terrorist group has claimed the attacks and only a handful of people have lost their lives."

"A handful of people, sir?" said Cole, her face twisting with incomprehension. "We have forty bodies on our hands."

"I know it sounds callous, Cole," said Reilly. "But how many did we have after seven-seven? How many did we have when the IRA blew up the city and the docklands?"

"More. But still-"

"And each of those bombs were followed up with a call to the prime minister taking ownership for the blasts."

It was clear to Reilly that Cole wanted to hate him for his remarks. But her eyes softened, betraying her emotions.

"What we have here is a vendetta, Cole. You're right.

There's a clue in those names and faces and we need someone on it. But not you. Right now, we need to focus on that man with the phone, and whoever the hell he's with."

"Her face isn't shown. She's wrapped up in a scarf, sir. I think we'll have better luck finding him on the database."

"What about the phone?" said Reilly. "A call was being made. Maybe it triggered the bomb? Can we trace it?"

"Not after the fact, sir," said Cole. "Besides, it's probably a burner."

"And where does he run to?"

"Embankment underground station," said Cole. She lifted her laptop to control the video on the large TV and began to talk Reilly through their escape. "They take the westbound train, but they don't get far before the security protocol stops the trains and evacuates the passengers."

"After that?"

"They disappear."

"What's the next station after Embankment?"

"Westminster, sir," said Cole. "But they didn't show up. Same with the next two stations."

"Show me the girl again," said Reilly.

A few mouse clicks later, Cole had the picture of the girl up on the screen. She slowed the video to frame by frame then paused it on the clearest shot. The video was monochrome and pixelated.

"Now show me the passengers evacuating from Westminster station," said Reilly.

A few moments later, a video of Westminster station exit appeared on the screen. Passengers hurried through the doors, checking behind them. People clutched their bags and one woman with two children held them both close, trying to flag a taxi in competition with the other passengers.

"She's not here, sir," said Cole, selecting a new video. "Here's the platform where the passengers come out of the tunnel."

Sipping at his coffee, Reilly sat back on the edge of the desk and folded his shaking hand beneath his arm. Just as Cole opened her mouth to say something, he saw her.

"There," he said, standing and moving to the screen. Reilly pointed to the last passenger to climb from the tunnel. "This girl. This is her."

"Sir, she doesn't match-"

"It's her. Play it back."

The video reversed then played back frame by frame.

"Wait for it," said Reilly. "Here she comes. Look at her. Why is she only wearing a t-shirt in the middle of December? And look how she glances back for just a fraction of a second."

"You're right, sir," said Cole.

"Find me that girl," said Reilly. He tossed his polystyrene cup into the waste bin, walked across to the TV screen and jabbed at the girl's face. "We've got thirty-six hours before millions of people descend on London, and she knows something."

A row of warehouses backed onto a wide, concrete opening that was dotted with trucks and articulated lorries. Forklift trucks ferried goods from the lorries to the warehouses, while the drivers leaned against their rigs. Men in various coloured uniforms wheeled trolley loads of boxes to the smaller trucks.

"There's our truck," said Lucas, staring through the windscreen of their little car. "The green one with the back doors open."

"How are you going to do it?" said Herman. "We don't have to kill him, do we?"

"You leave the truck to me, dear brother," replied Lucas. "You need to focus on the job at hand. Run me through your plan."

"My plan?" said Herman. "I don't really have one."

"You know where to park the truck?"

"In the loading bay behind the restaurant."

"And then what will you do?"

Catching sight of the glint in his brother's eye in the rear-view mirror of their car, Herman looked at the truck three hundred yards away and lowered his voice, as if reciting a dream.

"I open the back of the truck, check the delivery notes for the right boxes-"

"That's important," said Lucas. "They'll be expecting the right boxes and they'll know what they look like. We don't want to cause suspicion."

"Right," said Herman.

"Carry on," said Lucas. "I'll play Jasper. Come on. It'll be fun."

"I wheel the boxes into the back door of the restaurant."

"Can I help you there?" said Lucas in a mock Italian accent.

"I've got a delivery," said Herman.

"You've got a delivery?" replied Lucas. "And what is it a delivery of?"

"Erm," said Herman, "I'd need to check the delivery notes. I don't really know."

"Fail," said Lucas, his voice loud in the confined space of the car. "You just annoyed the man. He's running a kitchen. He doesn't have time to mess around."

"But how do I know what I'm delivering?"

"You check the paperwork beforehand, Herman," said Lucas. "Let's switch. I'll be you, and you can play soon-to-be-dead Jasper."

Turning in his seat to see his own performance in the rear-view mirror, Lucas cleared his throat.

"Can I help you there?" said Herman. His Italian accent was weak and his voice trembled.

"Are you Jasper?" said Lucas, putting on his best London accent whilst flicking through a make-believe clipboard.

"Yes," said Herman.

"I've got three boxes of napkins, two boxes of sea salt, and a particularly nice crate of Vermentino. A gift from the boss," said Lucas, and winked in the mirror.

"A gift from the boss?" replied Herman.

"A new year's gift for his favourite customer," said Lucas, slotting into the role with ease. "He sends his regards, of course."

"Oh," said Herman, unable to think of a response suitable for the role play.

"If you just want to sign here, Jasper," said Lucas, and he imitated handing over the clipboard. "I'll show you a bottle."

He stopped and his London accent fell away to his usual harsh, monotone voice.

"That's when you do it," said Lucas.

"That's when I pull the mask out?" asked Herman.

"And deploy the gas," said Lucas. "He won't stand a chance. You'll stand over him while he suffocates and you'll get to see the panic in his eyes. You'll get to smell his fear, Herman."

"But what if I get it wrong?" said Herman. "What if I mess it up and he suspects something is wrong?"

"You won't, and he won't," said Lucas.

"And the wine. Where will I get the wine?"

"There is no wine, Herman," said Lucas, struggling to contain his impatience.

"But you said there was a box of wine."

"The box of wine is the gas, dummy," said Lucas. "There is no wine. But we need a reason to be delivering an extra box, don't we?"

"Right," said Herman. "I see."

The driver of the green truck slammed the door and pulled a wide U-turn across the concrete.

"But what about Stone?" asked Herman.

Lucas studied the driver as he passed then watched the truck fade into the distance.

"You leave Stone to me, my dear little brother," said Lucas. "You leave him to me."

CHAPTER SEVENTEEN

A kick to the handle of the fire doors sent them slamming back into the walls and a blast of cold air greeted Harvey in an instant. He scanned the area for police, but found only a side street devoid of people save for two taxis waiting for a fare near the top of the road.

He opened the rear door for the first cab and slid inside.

"Elephant and Castle," said Harvey, pulling the door closed as sirens began to wail nearby.

"I hope you're not in a rush, mate," said the driver, as he pulled out onto Westminster Bridge.

"Is traffic busy?" asked Harvey, feigning ignorance.

"Been another one of them gas bombs," said the driver. "Bloody nutters, they are."

"Is it the same guy?" asked Harvey.

"It must be," replied the driver. "They hit Jubilee Gardens the other day and now they've hit the little park outside Embankment station. Bleeding transport police have shut all the trains down. I heard it on the news."

"I'm surprised you're still working," said Harvey. "Isn't it safer to get out of town?"

"I am, mate. I was waiting for a fair to take me out of the city. The least I can do is help someone get home."

"Right," said Harvey, as another police car shot past in the opposite direction. "Do you think they'll catch this guy before New Year's?"

"I don't know, mate," said the driver. "I mean, how do you catch someone like that? It's sick, is what it is. Whoever is doing this must be an absolute nutcase. It's lucky most people are off work for the holidays. It could have been a lot worse."

"I agree," said Harvey, and peered out of the window. The traffic moved in one direction like a mass exodus lumbering from danger in a slow moving crawl to safety. "Have they said how many people have died?"

"Two dozen in the first bomb. Plus I heard there's more in hospital, but the chances of survival are pretty slim," said the driver. He shook his head and tutted. "What a world, eh?"

Harvey didn't reply.

"Drop me here," he said, when the taxi emerged from a back street close to Elephant and Castle junction. He pulled a twenty from his pocket, slid it through the gap in the glass and waited for the door lock to click off.

"Take care, mate," said the driver, as Harvey stepped out.

"You too," said Harvey, and closed the door.

The taxi drove off, leaving Harvey standing at the kerb watching the flow of traffic. A few miles from the attack, the people were less hurried, but anxious to get home. In less than two minutes, a second cab trundled along the bus lane. Harvey flagged him down.

"Where you going, mate?" asked the driver through his open window. "I'm only heading out of town."

"Clapham," said Harvey.

"That's good enough for me," replied the driver, and released the rear door.

The driver muttered under his breath at the other road users, leaving Harvey free to drop the innocent charade. He pulled the phone from his pocket, hesitated, and then hit the power button.

A few seconds later, the phone found a signal but sat dormant in Harvey's hand. He opened the messages, but found none. The list of recent calls contained only one number.

The taxi driver meandered through the back streets, crossed main roads and avoided the traffic the way only black cab drivers know how. They arrived on Clapham High Street, where Harvey tapped the glass partition.

"Anywhere here will be fine," he said, and slid another twenty beneath the glass.

The cold bite of the wind hit him as soon as he was out and he watched the taxi join the ranks of traffic.

Harvey walked to a side street to get out of the wind and noise of the main road. He found a doorway, which felt warm in comparison to outside, then pulled the phone again from his pocket.

He hit the button to bring up the recent calls, selected the only number that showed, and then hit the green button and waited for the ring tone to begin.

"Harvey Stone," said a timid voice. "Is it really you?"

CHAPTER EIGHTEEN

"We've got her, sir," said Cole. Her breathing sounded heavy over the phone connection. "Facial recognition gave us every-thing we need. Tech guys found her on social media and another search found that she's just rented a house in Wimbledon."

"Where are you now?" said Reilly, holding the phone with one hand, while his other hand struggled to tip a single tablet from a pill bottle.

"Out running, sir. I'll be back in an hour."

"You're running at a time like this?"

"It helps relieve tension, sir. You should come with me one of these days. You'll feel better for it."

A single pill fell onto Reilly's desk. He snapped the bottle closed.

"I'd only slow you down, Cole," said Reilly. "Besides, I have my own ways of dealing with tension. Whatever works for you."

"Can I speak freely, sir?"

Reilly closed his eyes and readied himself for another round of unwanted advice. "Of course," he said, and dropped the pill into his mouth.

"The answer isn't in a bottle," said Cole. "I know it's not my place, but-"

"That's right, Cole," said Reilly.

He paused, refraining from saying more and deepening the rift between them.

"Whatever works for you, sir," said Cole.

"So what's your plan?" said Reilly, moving the subject on. He raised the tumbler of whiskey to his nose, inhaled the sweet fumes, and then took a sip to wash the pill down his gullet.

"I'm assembling a team, sir. We've got the go ahead for a raid," replied Cole. "Armed support in case it gets ugly. Air support in case they run."

"They?" said Reilly. "You have them both?"

"We don't have a name for the male, sir, but we do have a face. She's pictured with him-"

"Don't tell me. On social media?"

"Yes, sir."

"Who'd have thought the answers to our problems would be lying amongst pictures of cats and people's dinners?"

"It's a digital world, sir," said Cole. The sound of her voice changed as if she accepted the she wasn't escaping the call and had slowed to a walk. "There's no escaping it now."

"For better or worse, Cole," said Reilly. "Talk to me about surveillance."

"I've got two teams already in place, sir. She's home alone."

"So you're hoping the man with no name returns in time? What if the surveillance scares him off?" said Reilly. "He might be watching from a distance for all we know."

"I said the same, sir," said Cole. "But word from the top is that they want a face to put out on the media before New Year's Eve. If this affects the New Year's celebrations, the damage to the UK reputation could be irreparable."

"That's a big risk," said Reilly. "We could lose this guy for good. He'd still be free to do it again. The consequences could be far worse than a damaged security reputation."

"True," said Cole.

"No doubt you have something up your sleeve?"

"The thinking behind it is that it'll draw him out," said Cole. "But we need more resources."

"We need every camera in the city manned until he shows up. But we won't get that," said Reilly. "I'll find out what resources we can get. As a minimum, I'll ask for a mile radius around the two attack sites."

"A mile? Sir, that's thousands of cameras and we can't be sure the next attack will be in the same area."

"No, but he's struck the same area twice. He could be targeting one particular person."

"I had the same thought," said Cole. "He might have missed his target the first time and lined up a second."

"In which case, he might never show his face again," said Reilly. "Or he could be a nutter. Plain and simple. An angry soul who wants the world to see how powerful he is."

"Statistically there's a target, sir," said Cole. "And that could break down into a religion, a company, a political opinion. Or it could be an individual."

"We haven't found any links between the victims yet," said Reilly. "So let's assume he has a target. We'll need to know if any of the victims had enemies, if they were up to no good or mixed up in something."

"That will take weeks, sir," said Cole. "New Year's Eve is tonight."

"That's my point, Cole," said Reilly. "We need to plan for the worst. I want every camera in a square mile radius around the attack sites manned. I want the girl taken underground. No public announcements. And I want a team digging up every bit of dirt on the victims. This is a war, Cole, and I don't intend on losing."

"No public announcements, sir?" said Cole. "The PM wants a face to show, a public enemy captured. If we don't have that, we could have bigger problems."

"Do we have a deadline?"

"Six p.m.," said Cole. "Six hours before the celebrations."

"By my watch, that gives us four hours to break her," said Reilly, and tipped the remainder of his scotch into his mouth.

CHAPTER NINETEEN

"Harvey Stone. Is it really you?"

Harvey didn't reply.

"I've been thinking about you," said Herman, holding the phone to his ear with his shoulder while he pulled the car into a parking spot a few hundred feet behind the green truck. "I've been thinking about you a lot."

Harvey didn't reply.

"Talk to me, Harvey, please," said Herman. "You're trying to place my voice, aren't you? You're trawling through that catalogue of obscenities in your mind, searching for a face to put to the voice. There's so much I want to say."

"Well, you found me. So say it," Harvey replied.

"Do you know how long I've been thinking about you, Harvey?" said Herman, tracing the outline of the steering wheel with his left hand, picturing Harvey's face.

Further up the street, the driver of the truck opened the rear doors, pulled out a trolley and checked his paperwork against the boxes inside.

"Longer than I've been thinking about you," said Harvey.

"You obviously want something. I'm not playing games. This call is over."

"No, no, no," said Herman. "Are you there?"

"I'm here," said Harvey, after a pause.

"If you could see the dreams I've had. Just you and me. Alone with nobody to get in our way. Nobody's attention to contend with," said Herman. "Nobody to hear the screams."

"Or I could just carry on with my life, ditch this phone and forget all about you," said Harvey.

A long blast of a car horn sounded in the distance and wind rasped through the phone's speaker.

"Could you, Harvey?" said Herman. "We've been planning this for a long time. You're outside right now, aren't you? You can't go home. Am I right? I'm right, aren't I?"

Harvey didn't reply.

"Let me guess. You made it out of the city and you're somewhere familiar. Somewhere where you know the back streets. But you can't show your face in case we find you."

"Are you going to tell me what you want?"

"You haven't even asked me my name yet, Harvey," said Herman. "Do you even care who I am and what you put us through?"

"It doesn't matter who you are. In fact, it's better if I don't know."

"Oh, we're so alike. We have so much in common. I'd love to get to know the real Harvey Stone. I'm sure you'd grow to enjoy my company."

"We have nothing in common. You tried to kill me once and failed," said Harvey. "I never fail."

"Hmmm, don't be so sure," said Herman, as the driver of the truck emerged from a small restaurant in South London. "It's a shame. I'd love to talk to you. I'd love to see inside your mind."

"So let's meet," said Harvey.

"I thought you'd never ask," replied Herman, glancing in the rear-view mirror and finding his brother's approving nod. "How about lunch? Somewhere warm. Or are you as cold-blooded as they say you are, Harvey Stone?"

"Name the place," said Harvey.

"Via Venato. Fulham. One hour," said Herman, as he pushed open the driver's door of his little car.

"Fulham High Street?" said Harvey.

"That's right. We made a reservation under the name of Harvey Stone," said Herman, smiling at his brother's genius. "We thought it best if we meet in public. I hope you don't mind, but you do have a bit of a reputation."

"And after that?" said Harvey. "Are you going to tell me what this is all about?"

"I'll explain it all over lunch," said Herman. "I have to go. I..."

"What?" said Harvey.

"I can't wait to see you, Harvey Stone."

He hit the red button to disconnect the call and pocketed the phone.

"Good work, Herman," said Lucas, as he slipped his Taser from his pocket. "That wasn't too hard, was it?"

"I remember him so clearly, Lucas," said Herman.

"Hold that thought, dear brother," said Lucas. "Just hold that thought."

The driver was just loading his little trolley onto the back of the truck and was about to jump down to the ground and close the rear doors when Lucas approached.

"Excuse me, sir," said Lucas in his finest broken English with a strong flavour of Germanic. The driver looked up and waited for Lucas to reach him. Lucas smiled the friendly smile of a helpless tourist, retrieved a folded map from his pocket and began to point. "I am trying to find the train station. I wonder if you may help me."

CHAPTER TWENTY

Harvey climbed from the third taxi he'd been in that day and closed the door. Three teenagers wearing skin-tight jeans, sweaters with sleeves that covered their hands and dark make-up around their eyes strolled past. None of them glanced at Harvey, each lost in the music that played through their headphones.

A father walked with his two children and their little dog, hurrying as if they were late for something. The children wore hats pulled down over their ears and thick coats buttoned up to their chins.

Steel shutters were pulled down over a few shop fronts, but most outlets were open, taking advantage of the holiday season. A clothes store advertising a fifty percent discount across their entire range had drawn the attention of two women who were looking through the window. One wore a black furry hat with her long blonde hair hanging over a tight leather jacket. The other wore a pair of knee high boots, tight jeans and was letting the cold wind keep her dark, curly hair from her face.

With bus lanes on either side of the road, there was no place for parked cars. Harvey studied the face of every man he saw.

An old man with a walking stick coughed into a handkerchief then resumed his slow amble. A tall man in a suit, talking into his phone, stood by the kerb. He finished the call and flagged the next taxi before disappearing.

An image of the man Harvey had seen in the park flashed to his mind. A slither of a face shrouded by the green hood. Distinctive eyes, pale like an albino, but lined with fatigue or memories.

Or suffering?

The face matched no man in view so he stepped over to a phone box. The exterior remained the classic red London phone box that was known across the world. But the inside had been upgraded with the latest technology.

The coin slot received a one pound coin. Harvey tapped the number from memory then waited for the connection to be made and the ring tone to begin. It lasted five rings then silenced.

"It's me," said Harvey.

"Are you safe?"

"I can't talk," he said. "I just wanted to know you're okay."

"I'm fine," said Melody. "I'm worried about you. Just who is this-"

"I made contact," said Harvey. "It's best if that's all you know."

"What are you going to do?"

"I'm going to finish this," said Harvey. "Stay low."

He replaced the handset and hung his head to rest on his arm, picturing Melody in their new home. She'd be cleaning the kitchen, seeking a distraction. The more she thought about what she'd seen and what might happen, the harder she would scrub, venting her anger and frustration through the grime.

A laughing child ran past the phone box, breaking Harvey's thoughts, then stopped and waited for his father to catch up.

Nearly ten shops down from the phone box on the far side of the road, Harvey could see the cream signboard with the words Via Venato. It was printed in black, scripted font as if somebody had handwritten the name of the restaurant on a napkin and declared it the company logo.

He checked the time then glanced at the people walking by.

No green hood.

No slither of face.

No pale eyes.

Keeping to his side of the road, Harvey made his way past the restaurant, scanning the customers inside with two swift, casual glances, as a shopper might. The restaurant appeared to be laid out similarly to every other restaurant Harvey had dined in. A selection of two and four seated tables stood against the windows with four seaters occupying the centre space and a handful of family-sized booths against the rear wall. A pair of double doors led to the kitchen out back. The restaurant was served by three waiters.

Continuing past the restaurant, Harvey ran the image of the lunchtime customers through his mind. An elderly couple had taken a two seater table by the window. Four men filled one of the four seaters, but were sitting casually with glasses of wine like old friends catching up over the holidays. A family were seated in one booth: husband, wife, and two children, one boy, one girl.

The perfect family.

Harvey crossed the street and doubled back, keeping to the roadside to maintain his view through the restaurant windows. Then, with a glance back over his shoulder, he entered the building and let the door close behind him.

The chat of the restaurant hit him like the friendly hug of a long lost friend, and a waiter approached, his eyebrows raised as if he was waiting for Harvey to talk.

"You have a reservation, perhaps, sir?"

"Harvey Stone," said Harvey, keeping his voice low.

"Ah, yes, Mr Stone. This way please," said the waiter, taking charge with his soft Italian accent. He pulled out a chair from beneath a two seater table in the centre of the window and waited as Harvey checked the room, the double doors, and then sat.

"May I take your coat, sir?" asked the waiter.

Harvey shook his head, met the stare of the elderly woman sitting across from him with her husband, and then averted his eyes.

Offering Harvey a small, cardboard menu, the waiter smiled and informed him that the soup of the day was pumpkin sage with Italian ham.

"Will you be dining alone?" said the waiter.

The question sounded easy to answer. But uncertainty clouded Harvey's thoughts. He opened his mouth to speak but hesitated.

Everything was wrong.

"Sir?" said the waiter, prompting him for a response.

Harvey stared at him, trying to match the face to the slice in his mind. But the waiter's eyes were dark and wide with almost sickeningly smooth skin surrounding them.

"Is everything okay, sir?" said the waiter. The repeated question attracted the stare of the two children in the booth to Harvey's right.

"I'll be dining alone," said Harvey, lowering his head and watching the inquisitive children through his peripheral vision as they grew bored and returned their attention to their food.

A rush of cold air swept across the floor as if a door had been opened at the back of the restaurant. He checked the room again. The customers. The elderly couple. The friends.

The perfect family.

He stood, knocking his chair back.

"Is everything okay, sir?" asked the waiter, as Harvey met the stares of each customer.

The hush of chatter fell to silence.

"What's he doing?" asked the little girl who had been watching him. Her question caused her parents to turn and stare.

The banging of a door in the kitchen and the murmur of voices.

"Sir?" said the waiter.

The silence continued.

The gap of light beneath the double doors flashed bright white, accompanied by a loud metallic crack.

Harvey felt his eyes widen and heart stop. He raised a chair above his head, preparing to hurl it through the broad glass window as the doors burst open and a man wearing kitchen whites staggered through, clutching his throat.

Harvey hesitated. Behind the chef stood the shape of a man holding a mask to his face. Even through the protective glass and thick yellow smoke, Harvey saw two pale eyes staring directly back at him.

"Sir, tech intercepted a call to Mills' house," said Cole, as she stepped into Reilly's office, sliding her phone into the pocket of her jacket. "No names. But it's him."

"Do you have a transcript of the dialogue?" said Reilly, glancing at the door in a silent gesture for Cole to close it.

"The call was short. Less than a minute," said Cole, as she pulled a sheet of paper from the blue folder in her hand and slid it onto his desk. She perched on the edge, clutching the folder to her chest, and waited for Reilly to read the transcript of the call.

"Seven lines," said Reilly. "Less than fifty words."

"I said it was short," said Cole.

He studied the dialogue once more.

"'It's me', he said," said Reilly. "That's confirmation he's not in the house."

"I've got the raid team on standby," said Cole.

"Good. Let's not blow this," said Reilly. "She asked him, 'Are you safe?'"

"Sentiment?" asked Cole.

Reilly nodded. "The social media photos of them together

support that. And in the fourth line, Mills states she's worried about him."

"'I can't talk'," said Cole, reading the next line out loud. "That suggests he knows he's being watched. But we've only just worked out who Mills is. So who's watching him?"

"It's the next line that intrigues me," said Reilly, picking up the sheet of paper from his desk and sitting back in his chair. "'I made contact. It's best if that's all you know'. He's protecting her."

"From us? Or from whoever else is watching him?"

"'I'm going to finish this. Stay low'," said Reilly. He turned in his swivel chair to look out of the window. The River Thames flowed past beneath the office and the London skyline appeared black and featureless against the blanket of grey sky. "He's going to finish it."

"What's he going to finish?" said Cole.

"And when did it start?" said Reilly.

"You're suggesting the first gas bomb wasn't the beginning of this?"

"Potentially," said Reilly, closing his eyes to picture the man and what his motives might be.

"He's going to finish it. Another gas bomb?" said Cole.

"Maybe the two gas attacks were failed attempts," said Reilly.

"Failed attempts on a single target?"

"What if he made the attacks public to disguise who the target is?"

"Because he knows we'd make the connection."

"Does that mean the victims of the first attacks were unnecessary?"

"They were just masking the motive."

"But this time he's going to try harder?" said Reilly. "The language he uses in the transcript, it's definitive."

"A bigger bomb?"

"More casualties."

"A bigger audience."

"New Year's Eve," said Reilly, dropping the sheet of paper to his desk and staring up at Cole. "Keep the surveillance on Mills. It sounds like he won't return until he's done what he set out to do. We need to move in and take her now. She's the only one who knows who this guy is, and the only way we're going to stop this is by knowing who he is and what his motives are. Who is she anyway? What's her background?"

"There's not a lot of information in the usual places," said Cole. "In fact, there's a huge gap in her whereabouts."

"How big is the gap?"

"Five years."

"What did she do before the gap?"

"Do you really want to know?"

Reilly allowed his expression to answer the question.

"Police," said Cole.

It was a response Reilly wasn't ready for. He sat forward, leaning his elbows on his desk and burying his face in his hands. "In London?" he asked.

"Yes, sir," replied Cole. "Exemplary career too."

"But then she vanished?"

"She didn't vanish, but her career did. There's no record of what she did. Just a P45 to close off her employment, and then nothing."

Pushing himself to his feet, Reilly sighed and strode to the window. "London seems so peaceful from here," he said. "So much history. So many secrets."

"Sir?" said Cole. "Are you feeling okay?"

"What did you do before you wound up here in counter terrorism, Cole?"

"Major crimes, sir."

"And before that?"

"I worked my way up through investigative support, sir," she replied. "Why?"

"Investigative support?" said Reilly. "Are you sure about that?"

"Do you have a problem with my methodology, sir?"

"Not your methodology, Cole."

"So what then?"

"When you ran a search for Mills, what did you do exactly?" said Reilly, letting his eyes trace the outline of the dark roofs against the grey sky.

"It was a standard search, sir," replied Cole. "I followed protocol."

"So break protocol."

"How?"

"Start by searching in the cracks. I'll get you clearance."

"The cracks, sir?"

"I would hazard a guess, Cole," said Reilly, "that Miss Mills was an exemplary police officer so she worked her way through the ranks. And finished up where?"

"Organised crime, sir," said Cole.

Reilly nodded his approval. "From there, she didn't just disappear, Cole," he said. "Nobody just disappears. The paper trail is harder to follow, sure. But nobody disappears."

"Are you saying she stayed in the force, sir?"

"Sharp girl," said Reilly.

"I don't understand. Why would her records stop?"

Turning from the window, Reilly stepped across to her and held out his hand. Cole handed him the blue folder, trying to gauge where he was going with his thoughts. He lowered his voice to a murmur, and leaned close enough for Cole to smell stale alcohol masked by peppermints.

"Let's just say that there are certain necessary operations the force doesn't associate itself with and therefore doesn't recognise."

"Dark ops, sir?" said Cole. "I wouldn't even know where to start searching for that."

"That's good because you wouldn't find anything," said Reilly.

"What if she's still in the force? What if she's working undercover?"

"You would have had a tap on your shoulder if you got too close, Cole," said Reilly. "A polite word in your ear to drop your investigations on Miss Mills."

"So if she's no longer active..."

"If she's no longer active, Cole," said Reilly, letting the folder fall to his desk with a slap, "it means she's super smart, highly trained, and she's somehow involved in the case."

A pause, as both Cole and Reilly processed the idea of what and who they might be up against, was broken by the door being pushed open.

"Sir," said Vaughn, a young officer, keen and green, who had popped his head into Reilly's office.

Reilly held Cole's eyes for a moment longer then turned his head to face Vaughn.

"I'm sorry to trouble you, sir. But there's been another attack."

CHAPTER TWENTY-TWO

Thick, yellow smoke hung in the air like a poisoned fog. The few screams of kitchen staff faded to gargled chokes, but even the sound of the dying soon faded.

All that remained was the sight of Harvey Stone.

Hands tugged at Herman's legs, pleading for help with waning strength. Bloodshot eyes stared up at him. They were wide, not with fear, but with the knowledge that death was seconds away.

And then recognition.

A hand released his leg and pointed up at Herman in disbelief, but the look weakened as Jasper Charles failed to inhale his last breath of air through his swollen throat and bleeding lungs.

The hand on Herman's leg relaxed and Jasper fell to the floor. Herman stared in wonder as the man tensed then twitched as if something inside him fought the battle to the end.

Bending to a crouch, Herman laid his hand on Jasper's head and met his eyes, feeling pity and sorrow.

Lucas' words played through Herman's mind in a whisper.

"It had to be," said Herman.

Jasper blinked, releasing tears that ran from his dying body, carving flesh-coloured lines in the yellow dust that coated his skin.

"You know what you did to me," said Herman, his voice soft, not cruel. He found sympathy for the man who had broken him. He also saw desaturated images of Jasper as a young man and Herman as a mere boy with a naivety that begged for guidance and confidence, not the sick games Jasper had played.

In Herman's mind, the two sat beneath the bridge in the local park. A small river flowed by and incessant rain dulled the view outside, cocooning them in that space. It was as if, beneath the bridge, they were safe, and to step outside through the mist of rain, they would enter a new world where their secrets could never be told.

But Herman's secrets were safe with Jasper. That's what he'd said as they sat on the cold, loose stones, reassured by Jasper's wandering hands.

"You shouldn't worry about what your parents will say," Jasper had said. "They treat you like a child. But look, look how much of a man you've become."

Herman had pushed him away as society had told him he should. But the rain outside and Jasper's persistence made him stay. Besides, he hadn't wanted to leave. Jasper had made him feel like a man, like a grown-up, and had shown him what grown-ups do, there beneath that bridge.

"You did this to me," said Herman, smoothing the hair on Jasper's head. "You made me who I am. You made me into a monster."

But Jasper's eyes no longer flicked in wonder and question at Herman's. They stared to nowhere, no longer instruments of sight but matter, matter that would perish, decompose and leave nothing but a stain on the earth.

"A stain on the earth," said Herman, out loud to himself. "That's what you made me. The things I did to those poor boys was all because of you. The things they shamed me for, the lives I ruined, was all because of you."

The sound of a door closing nearby broke Herman's thoughts, sending his memories scampering away to hide in the cold, dark corner where he kept the visions of the terrible things he'd done.

Safe. So that nobody could take them away.

He stood and glanced around at the bodies on the floor, bodies in white aprons, checkered pants, hair nets and chef hats.

Out front, a few cautious people peered inside. No longer hidden by the thick, yellow smoke, Herman stepped back to the door, remembering Lucas' words about the escape. As the first sounds of sirens approached, one man stared back at him, his eyes boring into him like daggers. Memories of a rainy night, of pain, of his own suffering.

But Lucas' whispered voice banished the thoughts back to the darkness.

"Run."

CHAPTER TWENTY-THREE

The steel legs of the chair burst through the pane of glass. The cool wind outside sucked at the yellow gas. Harvey tore the cloths from empty tables, sending cutlery, empty glasses and condiments crashing to the ground, and tossed them at the family of four.

"Cover your mouths and get out," said Harvey.

Two of the four friends remained seated and open-mouthed, too shocked to move. The other two edged towards the door, undecided as to the right thing to do and aghast at the kitchen worker who lay crumpled on the floor, twitching at their feet.

But it was too late for them. The yellow haze had found them and the first of them dropped to his knees, wheezing, wide-eyed and clutching the nearest table.

"Leave him and get out," said Harvey, and pulled the father of the family to his feet. "Get your family out and don't breathe until you're clear."

The frightened father gave him a grateful but unsure look, but Harvey hurried him along, pulling each family member from the booth, then shoving them to the door. With his shirt pulled over his face, Harvey ran to the old couple. The old man sat with his eyes closed, fighting for his last breath. His arms lay across the table, clutching those of his wife, who sat unmoving and staring back at him as the last of her life left her body.

"Move," shouted Harvey at the two surviving friends who were helping the family through the door. The last of them stopped to glance back at his two dying friends one more time. "Now."

Ripping a cloth from a table for himself, Harvey stepped over the waiter to the broken window. He sucked in a lungful of fresh air, glanced once at the gathering crowd and heard the approaching sirens. Harvey covered his face, turned, and walked through the double doors that were held open with the bodies of the kitchen staff. He saw the back door slam shut.

In an instant, Harvey gave chase.

Bursting through the rear doors, he tossed the table cloth to the ground and scanned the alleyway, just catching sight of the man he'd seen through the fog disappearing around a corner.

The world rushed by in a blur as Harvey's arms pumped harder than ever before, pushed on by the adrenaline that surged through his body. He turned the corner, taking it wide to maintain his speed, then ran into the road to avoid a group of people who spanned the width of the pavement. Behind them in the distance, the man ran across the street heading for a bright green railway bridge that crossed the road. Beside the bridge was a car tyre shop, its shutters down, closed for the holidays. As Harvey followed, the man leaped onto the bins outside the tyre shop.

Harvey closed the gap. He was seconds behind. As the man pulled himself onto the roof of the tyre shop, Harvey slammed into the wall beneath him, reaching for his ankle and missing by inches.

A police car screeched to a halt behind him. Harvey glanced

back, saw the officers climbing out of the car, then looked up to see the man's leg disappearing over the wall.

"Armed police," called the officer. "Stop or we'll shoot."

Time stopped for the briefest of moments. Melody's words sounded clear in Harvey's mind.

"That's how trouble finds you, Harvey," she'd said.

Harvey glanced back once more at the officers who were closing in, took a breath of fresh air, then pulled himself onto the roof and leaped across to the train tracks.

One hundred yards to Harvey's right, the man, who had ditched the uniform he'd been wearing and pulled his hood up over his head, ran along the trackside, turning for a nervous quick look back.

Large, grey stones lined the ground around the sleepers and tracks, and barely an inch of wall remained that wasn't adorned with graffiti. Then two hands appeared at the wall beside Harvey and the muzzle of a rifle followed.

Slamming his boot into the police officer's fingers, Harvey then leaped over and shoved him off the wall. His partner raised his weapon and aimed, but it was too late. Harvey was already on the heels of the man in the hood.

The stones crunched underfoot. They slipped and twisted at Harvey's ankles. Ahead, the hood was suffering the same problems. The chase slowed but continued. The tracks to Harvey's left gave off a soft hum and buzz of electricity, signifying an approaching train, warning him away from the tracks. Ahead, the hood ran on, doubling his efforts to escape Harvey.

But then he stopped. He turned back to face Harvey and, for a moment, he pulled his hood away, revealing the white skin of his face. And as the approaching train rushed past Harvey, the hood covered his face, and ran across the tracks.

Glimpses of the man climbing the wall and disappearing from sight through the momentary gaps between the train's undercarriages put the chase to an end. The train finished passing and Harvey stepped across the tracks, all urgency gone.

The man was nowhere to be seen.

Instead, the thumps of an approaching helicopter brought with it new dangers.

Behind him, several police officers and dogs had climbed the wall and were on his heels.

With nowhere to hide, Harvey continued to run along the tracks. Behind him, the barking of the dogs grew louder and the constant thumping of the helicopter's rotor blades seemed to add to the chaos. It wasn't until Harvey reached the bridge that spanned the River Thames that he saw his escape blocked by more police coming the other way.

He turned in time to see the handlers letting the dogs free. There were two dogs, both jumping on the spot, eager to run Harvey down.

The helicopter burst into view overhead, banked, and came around, level with Harvey. It yawed, bringing its opening side door to face Harvey. A man appeared, raising a rifle to his shoulder.

With the dogs closing in behind him, the police in front blocking his escape, and the sniper in the chopper taking aim, Harvey took his only option.

He jumped into the murky brown water that rushed past below him.

CHAPTER TWENTY-FOUR

The same officer that had lifted the red and white tape at Jubilee Gardens let Reilly and Cole through to the scene on Fulham High Street. Although he demonstrated professionalism, his face conveyed a deep-rooted anger.

"Do you see those cameras up there, Cole? Have the tech guys send the footage through as soon as possible. I want to see anyone who entered the building in the past forty-eight hours."

"I'm on it, sir," said Cole, pulling her phone from her pocket and moving to one side.

Three ambulances were parked at the side of the road by the rear doors and EMTs in green coveralls tended to two small children and two adults who looked to be their parents. The second ambulance had a young man wrapped in a red blanket, his face buried in his hands. His friend was standing close by, leaning against the vehicle, rolling a lit cigarette between his fingers, blank faced and red eyed.

An officer, deep in discussion with two others, glanced up and saw Reilly. Then he tapped the man in front of him and muttered something inaudible. The man raised his head, dropped some paperwork to his side and inhaled, his chest expanding as he prepared to greet Reilly.

"Connor," said Reilly, keeping his tone business-like and offering his hand. "Were you first on the scene again?"

"One of my unit was," said Connor, nodding at the officer who had let Reilly through. He shook Reilly's hand in what could be assumed as comradeship over manners, rank or jurisdiction.

"How does it look?" asked Reilly, taking a moment to gather his senses and get a lay of the land before entering.

A red mist formed over the whites of Connor's eyes. He turned away and cleared his throat. Giving Connor the time he needed to compose himself, Reilly studied the front of the building. Uniforms had taped off the area and blocked the street. A helicopter thundered overhead.

"Some guy ran from the scene," said Connor, seeing Reilly's eyes follow the chopper until it disappeared over the buildings. "They chased him onto the train tracks about five hundred yards that way." He gestured with his paperwork hand to indicate the direction.

"Did they get him?" asked Reilly, knowing the answer would be negative.

"No," said Connor, tight lipped and shaking his head. "Mad bastard jumped in the river. I got the news about two minutes before you showed up. It's a shame. I'd have loved to have got my hands on him."

"He's dead?" said Reilly, feeling a squeeze on his gut relax for a glorious second. "I presume we have river support out there?"

"It's three degrees," said Connor. "If the fall didn't kill him, the cold will. No doubt, we'll find his body downstream in a day or two and you'll be able to close the case off. Another roaring success."

Connor's bitter statement caught Reilly off-guard. He opened his mouth to say something, but paused.

"Sorry, Reilly," said Connor. "I shouldn't take it out on you."

"Don't apologise," replied Reilly. "This isn't easy for any of us. Thanks for doing what you've done here."

"We'll keep the area cordoned off. CSI are en-route. Just get in there and do what you need to do so these people can get back to their lives. With any luck, this is the last of it."

"What should I expect in there?" asked Reilly.

"Twelve dead," said Connor. "It's not pretty."

"And the device?"

"In a box in the kitchen. One of my guys did a pass through before he realised it was the gas bomber."

"So the gas has cleared?"

"You should still suit up, Reilly," said Connor. "Don't take any chances."

Nodding, Reilly made to leave. He glanced across at Cole, who had her hand on the shoulder of the man with the cigarette. The family at the first ambulance were all huddled together beneath blankets and the HART team were constructing a white tent on the pavement.

"Connor," said Reilly, stopping the man as he walked away. "Do me a favour and keep me posted on the body in the river. I'll have my hands tied up in there. I could do with the help."

"I will do," said Connor, and nodded his appreciation.

A senior member of HART crossed his arms and waved Reilly away as he approached.

"Five minutes, sir," he said. "It's a no go until then."

Diverting, Reilly walked past Cole, who needed no interruption, and stopped at the nose of the foremost ambulance. He leaned against the bodywork and stared into the broken window, wondering how it had all gone down. A couple held hands across a table but slumped in their chairs as if they held each other up. The doors to the kitchen were held open, but offered him little view of what was inside.

"Penny for them," said Cole, the heels of her boots growing louder as she approached.

Reilly turned his head away.

"How long until we suit up?" she asked, tapping on her tablet and swiping through various applications.

"HART says five minutes," replied Reilly. "Did you get the footage?"

"I got everything we need," said Cole, and handed him the tablet. A frame had been taken from the video and enhanced. Using his finger and thumb to expand the image, Reilly centred on a man's face as he entered the restaurant.

"Black leather jacket," said Reilly.

"Same boots. Same pants," said Cole. But her eyes were on Reilly's shaking hand, not the image on the tablet.

"And the same cold expression," finished Reilly, handing the tablet back to Cole. He pushed off the ambulance and stuffed his hand into his pocket. "Let's go."

"Sir, we need to suit up," said Cole, calling after him.

He stopped but didn't turn.

"We're not suiting up," said Reilly, and watched as she caught up with him. He waited until she was by his side and lowered his voice. "We're not going in."

"But, sir, it's the crime scene."

"And I'll tell you what we'll find. We'll find twelve dead faces that will haunt the rest of our lives. We'll see carnage and chaos, and we'll see panic and fear. But you know what we won't find?"

"The bomber?"

"Get the teams standing by, Cole," said Reilly, giving the restaurant one last glance. "We're taking Mills underground."

CHAPTER TWENTY-FIVE

Cold hands found hard rocks and numb fingers sank into soft mud.

The current tugged at Harvey's heavy legs, pulling him along for the ride, until his boots found purchase on the debris that lay beneath the treacherous water.

Unknown strength pulled him free then subsided and dropped him like the river might let trash fall to its bed.

He rolled to one side, felt the bitter wind against his aching body and, for a moment, let the darkness creep in. Long, black fingers muted his mind of anything but the warm arms of death, shrouding his vision and clouding memories that might sway his inner strength.

But there was one memory the darkness was unable to conceal.

One memory of two pale eyes beckoned him further. The memory gave strength to his legs and carried him through the mud to where a small wooden jetty, dark and stained by the river, reached into the water and provided shelter from the wind.

The tide lapped at the mud, boats cruised past, and with nothing but his muddied clothes for warmth and the growing night for cover, he climbed the concrete wall and dropped to the riverside footpath below, grateful for the holidays and sparsity of people. A small patch of grass nearby offered him a single tree with thick bushes at its roots, a place for him to wring his shirt, tip his boots and bang the mud from his cargo pants.

But the biting cold found him and sank its teeth into his flesh. With fingers trembling from the cold, he buttoned his pants, and his numb fingers tied his sodden boot laces.

He breathed into his hands, covering his face to bring some feeling back. Then, making sure nobody was in sight, he jogged on the spot, flexing his freezing feet and rigid joints before heading towards the streets in the distance.

A helicopter circled someplace far off, a street corner played host to a group of teenagers, and a car with four young men inside was parked nearby. The unmistakable thud of bass was clear in the early evening. A man leaned into the driver's window then the music stopped, and the boys on the corner silenced as Harvey grew near. Heads turned to watch him approach.

An electric window rolled down, releasing a thin cloud of smoke from the car and the tang of marijuana into the air.

"You got a problem, mate?" said the driver, his face masked by his hood and the shadows.

"Whose car is this?" asked Harvey.

"It's my car. And it's my street. So you best be on your toes, if you know what's good for you."

"I need to use it," said Harvey, checking the street left and right, but finding nothing but the street lights and lit houses.

"You what, mate?" said the driver. "Did you hear this guy, boys? Fool thinks he can walk up to me in my own street and take my car." He turned back to Harvey. "You best be on your way, fool. This is my street and I don't remember saying you could be in it."

"I didn't see a sign," said Harvey.

"Why am I going to give you my car, fool?" said the guy.

"Because you're selling drugs. You're probably carrying a knife and you probably have a record. You act tough, but deep down you know you wouldn't last two days in prison. If you were as tough as you say you are, you would be out of the car right now. But you're not. You're sitting in it because you're scared. So you have two choices."

"Two choices? Is that right, mate?"

"First choice. Give me the car, walk away and don't look back."

The four men began to laugh, and a joint was passed from the back seat to the driver, who took a long pull and eyed Harvey as he sucked in the thick smoke.

"Second choice," continued Harvey. "Stay in the car and I take it from you."

A siren in the distance grew closer then faded as it passed on the main road.

"You're not taking nothing, fool," said the driver.

"You've got three seconds before I make the choice for you. Leave the keys in the ignition," said Harvey.

"Fool, you have no idea who I am," said the driver, and his three friends began to chime in.

"Three," said Harvey.

"You stink, mate," called one from the back, inciting laughter from the foursome.

"Yeah, go back to the swamp, Swampy."

"Two," said Harvey, rolling his neck from side to side and waiting for the satisfying click from each side.

"Boy, you better be on your way and get off my street," said the driver, as the window began to wind up. His voice lowered with bravado but the fear was evident. "I'm not even wasting my time with you anymore."

"One," said Harvey, as the window closed fully.

The heel of his boot smashed through the glass and connected with the driver's face. As Harvey withdrew his leg, he leaned in and pulled the guy from the car. The driver dropped to the ground and scampered away, his voice high, panicked and embarrassed.

"You don't know who you're messing with, fool," he said, as he scurried backwards away from Harvey on his hands and feet.

Leaning into the car, Harvey addressed the other three young men, who were all sitting with their mouths hanging open, aghast at what they'd seen.

"Are you guys coming with me?" said Harvey. "Or are you getting out?"

In an instant, door handles clicked and the three men piled out, backing away from the car as if it was contagious, leaving Harvey free to climb in, engage first gear, and pull away.

He found the main road, recognised the area as Bermondsey, and made his way towards South West London, opening the windows to let out the smell of the joint.

In the centre console, a welcome surprise was waiting for him: a mobile phone in a shiny, plastic case, made to look as if it was gold-plated. Steering with his knees, Harvey popped out the SIM card and tossed it out the open window. He pulled the bomber's phone from his pocket and took out the SIM card, slotting it into the new device. The old, water-logged phone smashed on the street behind him as he joined the South Circular Road and settled in for the ride.

He was just five minutes from his destination when the new

phone began to play a rap song. The only number stored on the SIM card flashed up on the screen. Harvey hit the green button, pictured those pale eyes, and waited for the timid voice to follow.

"Are you ready to play a little game, Mr Stone?"

CHAPTER TWENTY-SIX

"All units standby," said Cole into the radio, as Reilly hit the accelerator and spun the wheels. "Mobile one, give me an update."

"No movement at the front," came the reply from mobile one, an unmarked van parked four doors down from the rented house. "But she's home. Lights are on and off."

"Is there any audio?" asked Cole.

"Not a peep," said mobile one.

"Mobile two, what have you got?" said Cole, using one hand to steady herself against the dashboard as Reilly navigated a series of parked cars on a tight street.

"Nothing worth talking about," came the reply. "A few lights turned on and off as she moved from room to room. But nothing out back."

"Good. We're fifteen minutes out. I need armed support covering all exits, and let's see if we can get some eyes in the sky."

"Copy that," said mobile two. "Switching to channel three."

"Where's mobile two located?" asked Reilly.

"In the house behind," said Cole, adjusting the radio to the broadcast channel and turning the volume down to quieten the sudden burst of activity. "The house is up for rent and we gave the agent a good deal on a short-term basis."

"Are you serious?" said Reilly, flicking his head to see her then turning back to the road. "What was the deal?"

"Give us the house for free or we'll report him for renting to illegals," replied Cole, and offered Reilly a smile. "The badge helped."

"It usually does."

"The house is an end plot. We've got mobile one covering the front and side, with mobile two at the back. Nobody has been in or out and what audio we've managed to get hasn't picked up a thing."

"Are you doubting your decision, Cole?"

"We need to be sure, sir," she replied.

"When it comes to terrorists, the rules are different. You have to understand that."

"Who are you referring to here?"

"I'm referring to them all, Cole," said Reilly. "Race, colour, religion, none of it matters. A terrorist is a terrorist. We're not dealing with drug dealers or petty thieves here. They need to be stopped as soon as the evidence is there, not a moment before, and not a moment after. Twice now, we've seen this guy at the scene of the crime and twice he's got away. This girl knows something."

"There're procedures, sir," said Cole.

"And see where your procedure will get you," said Reilly. "You'll need twenty-four hours just to get an answer from her."

"I thought the rules of engagement were different with CTU?"

"The rules are different, but the top brass is the same. In twenty-four hours' time, she'd have said nothing and you'd have the chief leaning on you to get an answer or let her go, worrying about a court case. That's not happening, Cole. Not with this one. I've seen too many bodies these past two days to let this go."

"He's probably dead anyway," said Cole.

"And how's that going to come across on national TV?" said Reilly, dropping into third gear to take a corner. "We failed to catch the man that brought panic, pain and misery to our nation's capital. But it's okay. We think he might be dead." He shook his head and undertook a car hogging the outside lane. "That's not happening, Cole. I want to know who he is or was. I want to know what all this is about. And I want to be able to stand in front of those cameras and make damn sure those people are safe."

"So you're taking her underground?" said Cole.

Reilly answered with his silence.

"And I'm supposed to go along with it, am I?" said Cole. "I'm supposed to risk my career because you don't want to tell people the truth. You'd rather break all the rules-"

Reilly slammed the brakes, dipped the clutch and eased the car to the kerbside, to the annoyance of the drivers behind him. He leaned across Cole and pulled the door handle. Then he pushed the door open.

"There it is," said Reilly. "There's your ticket out of this. I'm doing it my way and I'm getting results. If you're not okay with that, I won't judge. But I can't let you stop me."

"Sir-"

"We've spoken enough. If you're in, say so and we'll get this done. If you're not, get out. Call a cab. Expense it, if you like. But do not stand in my way."

The two locked stares and several car horns sounded. A driver passed by, glaring out of his open window, and hurled abuse at Reilly, who returned his attention to Cole.

She unclipped her seatbelt and was about to speak when her radio crackled into life.

"DS Cole, come back," said the voice.

Cole held Reilly's stare until he nodded for her to answer the radio.

"This is Cole, go ahead, dispatch," she replied.

"Uniforms picked up a man in his twenties in Bermondsey for possession."

"What does that have to do with the gas bomber?" said Cole, and lowered the radio to her lap.

"He said he had his car stolen from him," came the reply.

"What does he want? Time off?" said Cole.

"No, ma'am," came the reply. "The suspect reported the thief was a man in a black leather jacket, cargo pants and black boots who stank like the river. Thought you'd like to know, ma'am. The suspect is heading west on the south side."

Cole slammed the door, hit the dash switch for the blues, and pulled her seatbelt on as Reilly floored the accelerator and the screaming siren cut a path in the traffic ahead.

CHAPTER TWENTY-SEVEN

"I'm not into games," said Harvey.

"I think you'll find this particular game intoxicating," said Herman, running his hand along a hose that connected three small gas tanks to a small compressor. "I call it 'catch a killer'. What do you think? Think it'll catch on?"

"I think you're insane," said Harvey. "I think you're in above your head and you're scared."

"No. You're wrong," said Herman. "We're strong now. Stronger than ever."

"That makes two of us," said Harvey.

"Well then, now that we're all warmed up, it's your move. What are you going to do?"

Harvey didn't reply.

"You're wondering what your options are."

"You're weak," said Harvey. "I can hear it in your voice."

"No. You don't talk," said Herman. "Let me remind you who the boss is now. You had your turn. You took everything. And now it's my turn."

"So tell me what my options are then," said Harvey. "If you're the boss, show me."

"Option one," said Herman. "Save the pretty girl. Oh, and we must congratulate you. She's very pretty."

"She can take care of herself," said Harvey. "I doubt she's afraid of you."

"That might be the case," said Herman, sitting down in front of the computer screen. "But it's not me she should be afraid of. You're about to lose your only ally. Then you'll be all on your own, just like I was. Do you remember?"

"What's option two?" said Harvey.

"I can see you now," said Herman, struggling to control a fit of childish giggles. "I can see you in my mind's eye. You're sitting in the dark while every policeman in the city is looking for you. It's just a matter of time before they find you. But you don't care, do you? No. You're too strong for that. You're waiting for me to talk. A monologue perhaps? Well, how's this for you, Harv? You can sit there in the dark, giving my voice the freedom it needs to trigger a memory. Something to place my face. Something to complete the triangle. You know me. You recognise me. My name is on the tip of your tongue. All you have to do is reach out and say it."

He stopped and pictured Harvey with his eyes closed.

"Option two," said Herman, softening his voice, luring Harvey to him. "Forfeit the game and spend the rest of your life behind bars."

"I'm not playing games."

"Oh, but you are, Harvey. Don't you see? We've spent a long time devising this game. And we'll play it whether you like it or not. Five long years, Harvey, and every second of that time, we thought about you. We thought about what you might do. We thought about every twist and turn. And we thought about you, Harvey Stone, suffering for all those people you judged. Now it's your turn to be judged."

"What am I being judged for?" asked Harvey.

"Oh, that's a good question," said Herman, as he stood from his chair and pushed open the bedroom door, stopping at the threshold. Two eyes flicked open in the darkness and stared up at him from the bed at the far side of the room. "But if I told you that, the game would be too easy, and I'm not ready for that just yet. In twenty-four hours, millions of people will be flocking to the city. You have until then to solve the clues. You see, Harvey, while I pondered my misgivings, staring at the walls, I made myself a list. And guess who's on it?"

"I'm not biting," said Harvey. "You want me. You come and get me."

"It began as a list of six. But now there's only three. And when we get to one, it'll just be you and me."

"What do you want me to do? Rhymes aren't my thing," said Harvey.

"We want you to die, of course," said Herman. "We want you to suffer as we have. We want you to beg for your life, cry for mercy, and rain forgiveness on all the lives you have taken."

"I'm not the begging type," said Harvey.

"Then Harvey Stone will be responsible for London's worst atrocity in history. You'll never walk free again. You'll be hunted until the day you die." Herman paused. "Do you remember us, Harvey? Or were there so many that our faces blend into one?" he said, biting his lower lip. "I hope you can remember me. I do so want to see you die."

"So why not tell me who you are now and be done with it?" said Harvey.

"Time," said Herman. "The timing has to be perfect."

"So what now?" said Harvey, after a pause.

"Do you want a clue?" said Herman. "Find the place where long grass grows, between three trees and then you'll know."

Herman hit the red button to disconnect the call and

dropped the phone to his side, taking a deep breath to ease the adrenaline that raced through his bloodstream.

"You did good, dear brother," said Lucas. "You're growing stronger."

He stepped over to the bed and brushed Martina's hair from her face, ignoring the muffled objections. She stared up at him with all the murky hatred she could muster, her breath forcing the tape in and out of her mouth.

"Your time is coming, my dear," said Lucas. "Your beloved Herman is growing strong, and soon, all this will be a distant memory."

CHAPTER TWENTY-EIGHT

Killing the lights as Harvey turned into his street, he pulled the car into the first space he found, using the handbrake to slow to a stop to avoid the rear brake lights glowing red. He killed the engine, let his head fall back to the rest, and gathered his thoughts.

The conversation played over in his mind as he committed the words to memory. One sentence in particular played over and over, coming back to him clearly in that monotone voice.

"But it's not me she should be afraid of."

The street was still. Too still.

The scene of the bomb in the park played back in his mind. The hood. The chase. The park.

The camera.

He'd looked up at it.

And Melody.

The scene played back once more.

Trafalgar Square.

The photos Melody had taken.

The two of them together.

On social media.

The chase along the train tracks. It was Harvey they were after and Melody was the key to finding him.

They'd found her from the photos and were ready to strike.

He studied the street once more. It was early evening. The roads were quiet. Parked cars lined the kerb, BMW's and Mercedes, a sign of the area's affluence. Three hundred yards along the street, a single white van was parked between Melody's little sports car and an SUV.

A flicker of doubt stirred inside Harvey's gut.

He climbed from the car and entered the network of alleyways that ran behind each of the streets offering residents a rear entry to their property. He slowed to a walk when he neared the house and, keeping to the shadows, peered over the wall.

A light flicked on at the back of their house. Melody passed by the window. She stopped, held her phone up, and then dropped her hand to her side.

Disappointment or frustration?

The empty house behind was in darkness, a black stain on the street while the neighbouring houses glowed with the lives of families staying home in the warm before the New Year's celebration.

Harvey studied the empty house. The top rear windows offered little view inside. But just as he turned away, he caught a tiny flash of light.

A reflection on the window maybe?

Or a camera lens turning to scan the darkness and monitoring the rear of the house?

Harvey looked closer.

Once more, light flashed as the street lamp caught the end of the lens. He imagined the operative scanning the area with the camera on a tripod.

Seconds passed as Harvey stared up at the window from the shadows of the alley.

The flash of light again.

He began to count.

He focused on the window, nothing but the window.

Twelve seconds, and the light flashed once more.

He scaled the wall and dropped down to the soft grass below.

Ten, eleven, twelve.

He worked his way along the side fence, keeping to the thick hedgerow.

Ten, eleven, twelve.

He dropped to the ground and rolled beneath the hedge.

Ten, eleven, twelve.

He closed the distance to the back door of the house and flattened himself against the wall.

Nine, ten, eleven, twelve.

He forced the back door with the heel of his boot and slipped inside.

Only the rhythmic thud of his pulse in his ears sounded, and the warmth of the house found his damp clothes. The lights downstairs were off so Harvey made his way into the lounge and used the bay window's wide field of view to find the van parked along the street. The rear doors had been fitted with blacked-out windows, as had the side of the van that faced the house.

Using the sides of the staircase to avoid making a noise, Harvey crept up the stairs. A slice of bright light shone beneath the door of the rear bedroom. All other rooms were in darkness.

He placed one foot on the hallway carpet at the top of the stairs, stepped across and put his ear against the door.

Nothing.

Knowing the back bedroom would be monitored by the cameras in the empty house, Harvey stepped away from the door just as a fist came out of the darkness.

With one hand, he caught the arm, twisted it, and pulled it

up tight behind Melody's back, placing his free hand over her mouth and pulling her back close into his body.

"Shhh," he whispered, and felt her body relax when she realised he wasn't an intruder.

Harvey released his grip, motioning for them to go into the bathroom. He kept the lights off and ran the shower, using the noise to mask their whispers.

"What's going on?" Melody asked.

"The house is being watched," said Harvey, listening for any changes in sounds outside.

"What?" Her face screwed up in disbelief. "He knows where you live?"

"It's not him that's watching," said Harvey, putting his finger to his lips to keep her voice low.

"So who..." said Melody, then stopped as the realisation hit her. "No."

Harvey nodded. "There's an unmarked police van outside and a crew in the run down house behind."

"What do they want?" she said, glancing through the doorway to the front of the house. "We haven't done anything."

"They have us on camera running from the scene," said Harvey.

"We can explain that," hissed Melody. "We can turn this around."

"They also have me running from the restaurant in Fulham."

Her eyes widened, glowing in the dark. "What were you doing there?"

"I told you I'm going to stop this."

"Harvey," said Melody, a horrified expression creasing her perfect skin, "if they think you're the gas bomber, it won't be the police outside. It'll be special operations. Counter-terrorism maybe. And they won't be taking us to a nice police station for some gentle questioning. These guys don't mess around. They can make us disappear if they really have to. Just give yourself up. We can get you out of this."

"I can't. He's got something planned."

"I told you to let the authorities deal with it."

"By the time they realise it wasn't me, it'll be too late."

"Too late for what?"

"New Year's Eve," said Harvey. "I don't know what, but he's planning something."

"Planning what?" said Melody.

But Harvey just shook his head in response, unable to convey his whirling thoughts into a single intelligible sentence.

"What does he want?" asked Melody. "Is he trying to kill you?"

"Eventually," said Harvey. "It'll be slow and painful."

"So why the bombs?"

"He's got a list. The bombs weren't meant for me. He's working his way through a list of people. It began as a list of six. But now there's only three. And when we get to one, it'll just be you and me," said Harvey, reciting the words he'd committed to memory.

"He's killing everyone who ever wronged him?" said Melody, her brilliant mind digesting the information. "What if the bombs were designed to kill more than just the intended victim? What if the victims could all be linked to him and by killing multiple people, he could cover that link?"

"It's possible," said Harvey, as a loud crack of splintering wood came from downstairs.

They both spun to face the bathroom door.

"Come with me," hissed Harvey, as he reached for the window.

"No. You go," said Melody, and turned towards the hallway to peer outside as heavy boots stomped into the house downstairs. She stepped to the window, reached up and kissed him hard. "Find him and stop him. I'll do everything I can to help."

Harvey opened the window wide and climbed onto the ledge as the heavy boots banged up the stairs and men began to shout for Melody to get down on the ground. She glanced up at him as she dropped to her knees, her hands raised in compliance.

Harvey jumped to the ground below.

CHAPTER TWENTY-NINE

"Cuff her," said Reilly, as he reached the top of the stairs and gave Mills a long, hard stare. She stared back as if to ask why he was wasting her time.

"All clear, sir," said an armed uniform, as he appeared in the doorway to the bedroom cradling his rifle.

"No sign of him?" asked Reilly.

"He's not here," replied the officer.

"I want this place swept for explosives and gas, any sign at all that he's involved," said Reilly. He turned to Mills as the officer began to instruct his team. "Where is he? Where's your man?"

But Mills remained silent, replying with only a cold, hard stare.

"I'll find him, and when I do, he'll be in a whole new world of hurt."

Still, Mills remained silent, kneeling on the bathroom floor. Reilly flicked his eyes around the bathroom from the shower to the bath, and then to the open window.

"It's a bit cold to have the window open in the middle of winter, isn't it?" said Reilly.

Mills looked away to one side then returned her stare.

"Lock the place down. One mile radius," said Reilly, speaking to the officer standing in the hallway behind him. He continued to stare into Mills' very beautiful eyes then turned to find the officer still standing there. "Now. Roadblocks, air support and an officer on every street. He's close and he's on foot."

He stepped past Mills into the bathroom and leaned out of the open window, feeling the cool air on his face. Below him, the side street was bare, but the main road to the front of the house was a hive of activity. Spinning blue lights flashed across the rows of houses, curtains twitched and curious neighbours were standing at their garden gates, wondering what was disrupting their idyllic neighbourhood.

There was no sign of the bomber.

Reilly giddied as if his head had been rocked from side to side. He held onto the window ledge, feeling his slick, sweaty hands slide on the PVC.

"There's nothing here, sir," said Cole.

Her voice sounded distant as nausea took hold. Leaning forward out of the window, Reilly dry-retched then spat. The cold air on his sweaty brow sent a shiver through him.

"But we found the stolen car five hundred yards up the road. Sir?"

Breathless and unsteady on his feet, Reilly sank back to perch on the edge of the bath and rested his forehead in his hands, taking deep breaths to calm his rapid heart rate.

"He was here," said Reilly.

A warm hand found his shoulder, and Cole knelt in front of him.

"Sir?" she said, her voice a whisper in the spinning room. "I'll take care of this. You need to go."

"No," replied Reilly, aware of his slurred words. He swallowed hard, forced his eyes wide to focus and found Mills staring back at him from where she was kneeling on the floor.

"Sir, leave this to me," said Cole, squeezing his shoulder. "I'll get her processed and you can meet me at headquarters. Go see a doctor."

"You," said Reilly, pointing his shaking finger at Mills. "Where is he?"

Mills said nothing.

"Sir, let me get her processed. I can take care of it," said Cole, as Reilly stood from his perch and staggered a little, but used the wall to step past Mills into the hallway.

"What's his name?"

"Sir, let me take care of it," said Cole.

"She isn't going to headquarters," said Reilly, finding a clarity of vision in his anger. He bent his knees to crouch in front of Mills. "She's going underground and she's going to tell us everything she knows."

"Sir, she's one of us," said Cole.

"So she should know what to expect," replied Reilly, easing himself to full height. "Get her hooded and get her to the facility."

"First we thread the hose through here," said Lucas, as he fed the orange gas line through a series of small loops in a bag he had modified. "Then we pull it tight."

He tugged on the line and began to crimp a brass gas fitting to the end of the hose.

"Do you see this, Herman? You may have all the computer skills, but when it comes to delivering a slow and painful death..." He looked up at the computer screen on the far side of the room. "I learned from the best."

He gave the fitting one final squeeze with the crimping tool and set it down on his workbench.

"You don't have to do this, Lucas," said Herman. His eyes flicked to the bedroom door, enough for Lucas to notice. "We don't have to kill them."

"Dear brother, you're so weak. So innocent. There's so much you need to learn about life."

"I learned forgiveness," said Herman.

"And I learned revenge," replied Lucas, his tone sharp and cruel. "Forgiveness is for the weak. Forgiveness will weigh on you like a lead weight for as long as you walk the earth, dear brother. No. Revenge will raise your head up high. Revenge will see you standing tall and proud. That's what we need. That despicable wretch of a woman in there, no sooner than when you were out of the picture, she was hoisting up her skirt for all and sundry."

"But my son..." said Herman.

"Your son?" said Lucas. "Your son? Do you honestly think that, right now, that boy sees you as the man he calls his father?"

"But he doesn't know me," said Herman. "Not the real me."

"No. All he knows is that his father is a weak-minded fool who couldn't keep his hands to himself. All he knows, right now, is that his life on this earth was destined to end before it began because of you, his father. Oh no, Herman. When the last breath of air touches that boy's lips, he'll see how strong his father is. He'll wish he knew you. He'll wish his bitch of a mother hadn't opened her legs so readily."

"But we can let him go," said Herman. "The boy deserves a chance. He's seen nothing of the world. He wouldn't tell. I could look after him."

"You can barely look after yourself, dear brother. Look at you. You're wetter than a limp lettuce leaf," said Lucas. "No. We're going to create you a new beginning, Herman. A new life. Look at what you've achieved so far. Look at the list and how far you've come. Forget about the past. Look to the future, dear brother. Think of how bright and glorious the world will be when everybody who ever wronged you is gone, and there only exists freedom. New people with no memory of who you were. New people who will only see a strong man. A confident man. A man that any son would be proud of."

"It seems so far away," said Herman.

"Oh, it's close, Herman. So close you can touch it. There's three more names on that list and soon there'll be none."

Herman tapped the valve of a gas cylinder with the wrench

he was holding. He checked the pressure gauge as he turned the black, plastic knob and watched with glee as the hose he'd fixed around the room straightened under the pressure of his home-made concoction.

"Are you sure they'll come?" said Herman, touching the nozzle at the end of the hose as if he might somehow make a connection with the instrument that would bring a close to the chapter in his life.

"Oh, they'll come alright," said Lucas. "One by one, they'll come, and when they do, we'll be ready. Their twitching bodies will be the final scene, a sight you'll recollect for years to come. The sound of them choking will be the symphony that carries you through life. A reminder of your strength. A reminder of how wonderful you are. And a reminder that the poor, sick boy with wandering hands and an appetite for the taboo is long gone. In his place stands Herman Hoffman."

"I wish it was all over," said Herman. "I can't stand the waiting."

"But it's the waiting that's important," said Lucas. "It's the patience, the planning and execution that will bring you success. You remember those words, don't you?"

"I remember," said Herman, hanging his head and finding distraction in the grain of the wooden floor.

"You remember what he did to you, don't you?"

"Of course," said Herman. "How could I forget?"

"Don't you want to see him suffer in the same way? Don't you want him to cry out for forgiveness?"

"Yes," said Herman, his breathing heavy with the thought and guilty pleasure of revenge.

"But what do we think about forgiveness, dear brother?"

"It is for the weak," said Herman.

"And?"

"Forgiveness will weigh me down for all my years to come,"

said Herman, reciting the words his brother had committed to his memory.

"So what do we do about it?" asked Lucas. "What do we seek in place of forgiveness?"

"Revenge," said Herman. "We seek revenge."

"And why do we seek revenge?"

"Because revenge will raise our heads up high."

"And?" said Lucas, prompting his little brother to continue on his path.

"Revenge will see us standing tall and proud."

"Very good, dear brother," said Herman. "You're so close now. Can you feel it? Can you feel the strength growing inside your body?"

"Yes," said Herman, watching his hands clench and fingers unfurl with fascination.

"It's electrifying, isn't it?" said Lucas, as he pulled his rucksack onto his back and lifted his hood up to cover his face. He took a deep breath, letting the intense power surge through him, tensing his muscles and breathing hard to push the feeling through his body, prolonging the sensation.

He slammed the flat of his foot against the bedroom door, sending it crashing back into the wall behind. The boy cowered at the noise, still blinded by the hood. Martina tensed, preparing to defend herself.

Lucas watched, marvelling at the effect such a simple action can have on the human psyche. He waited for Martina to stop struggling against her restraints then stepped into the room and, with a deft whip of his hand, he removed the boy's hood.

"It's time," said Lucas.

The flashing blue lights of a single police car danced off the houses at the end of the street. Two uniformed policemen stopped each car as it entered or left the street to question the driver and passengers, while another managed the traffic, stopping them and waving them on when the questioning was over.

Overhead, a helicopter patrolled, shining its bright spotlight along the maze of alleyways and back streets.

Harvey stood in the shadows contemplating his next move, one hundred yards away from the roadblock.

The voice played over and over in Harvey's mind. The spiteful words were spoken with the same timid and monotone voice that accompanied the pale eyes from the restaurant. Familiarity teased at Harvey's memory. But the thought was broken as a car cruised past the alleyway where Harvey waited.

At the end of the alleyway, parked on the side of the road, were four cars. Each of them were large four-door saloons and no more than a year old. Checking both ways, Harvey stepped out onto the road and crouched beside the first car. To his right, about seven hundred yards away, the house raid was clear in the dark night with a riot of spinning blue lights and activity.

The roadblock had been called in almost immediately.

Whoever was in charge was a seasoned policeman and would be hot on Harvey's tail.

He pulled his knife from the sheath on his belt and lay on the cold, tarmac road. The space was tight, but he shuffled underneath the car, fumbling until his fingers found the fuel line. He slid out of the gap and waited for the trail of fuel to reach the roadside and trickle to a safe distance. Then, with a cursory glance left and right to check the police hadn't closed in, he produced the lighter from the stolen car.

A car was being checked by the roadblock police. One of the men was searching in the back of the car, while the other questioned the single occupant who answered in a loud, irritated tone that carried into the night.

The car was released and the driver put his foot down in a weak attempt to demonstrate his frustration at being stopped in his own street. The noise provided cover for Harvey to strike the lighter. But just as he did, the helicopter roared past overhead, banked, and then returned.

In an instant, Harvey dropped to the ground and shuffled under the car once more. The space was heavy with the smell of fuel and he could feel the petrol soak through his already damp clothes. The helicopter seemed to hover for a moment, its searchlight brushing by the ground where he'd been standing a few seconds before. Then it moved off to search the alleyway from where he'd come.

The alley was long and straight. Harvey had run its length in under two minutes and gauged how long the helicopter search party would be occupied for. Sliding out onto the path, Harvey rolled in a patch of grass to remove any surplus fuel from his jacket. Then, with his heart pumping like a steam train, he checked left and right and lit the fuel, stepping back the instant the fumes caught the flame.

The trail of fuel took light with immediate effect and, with a loud rush and whoop, popped into life beneath the car. A single police officer came running from the roadblock, talking into the radio that was fixed to his shoulder. He was joined by the other two uniforms. They spread out to stop any traffic from passing and maintained a safe distance in case the petrol tank ignited and blew.

The distraction allowed Harvey to slip past the unmanned roadblock, out of the side street, across the main road and into Wimbledon Common to lose himself in the mass of trees. He tore a new path in the long grass, stumbling on clumps of vegetation but pushing on, running with everything he had. His heart raced but found rhythm in his steps. His ears, tuned into the sound of the helicopter, were on high alert, and his eyes, accustomed to the dark, sought new ways out.

It was ten minutes later when Harvey stopped beneath a tree on Wimbledon Common with the road far behind him and a vast pocket of dark forest and footpaths before him. He paused for breath, leaning against the trunk and running the words over and over in his mind.

"Find the place where long grass grows, between three trees and then you'll know."

Sliding his back down the tree to a crouch, Harvey closed his eyes and listened to the voice in his head. The monotone taunts. The childish humour.

Those eyes.

He pictured the eyes in the darkness, pushing the voice from his head, quietening his mind until the eyes, only the eyes, existed.

The trees.

The shadows.

The eyes.

No monotone voice.

Harvey stood.

The eyes peered at him from the forest. Clear and pale. As if they called to him.

He ran into the forest, blind to his surroundings, following only the pale gaze that taunted him.

A memory.

He had it.

It was so close.

He glanced left then right, searching for the memory, the recollection.

A break in the trees up ahead.

The place.

Three hundred yards away.

It was a spot he could never forget.

Trees reached down to whip at his face and low bushes linked arms across the path, nearly bringing Harvey down as he stumbled through the trees in the pitch black. But nothing would stop him.

He burst into a clearing. Three trees in a triangle framed the spot, blocking the wind and allowing only the moonlight to touch the grass that covered the place he'd been before during the same cold, winter moon.

Harvey dropped to his knees, memories of a struggle running riot in his mind. He pulled at the clumps of grass, tossing them to one side and leaving a patch of bare earth. He jammed a broken tree branch into the dirt, scouring deep lines in the soil until it was loose enough to dig with his hands then scoop out.

Then, when the loose soil was removed and the ground became too hard, he started again.

Scour. Dig. Scoop. Scour. Dig. Scoop.

He was an arm's length deep when his fingers found the rocks he'd placed inside the hole so many years before. He raised one, pulling it free of the earth and dragging it through the dirt. He reached into the hole, expecting to find those memories, cold, hard and dead.

But he found nothing lying beneath.

Fingers searched the dirt, waiting for the sickening touch of decay. He pushed himself, tearing out the rocks with both hands and tossing them to one side.

But he found nothing.

He pulled more dirt out.

Scour. Dig. Scoop. Widening the grave with frantic jabs of the stick.

But still, beneath the disturbed rocks lay nothing but cold soil and a space where ancient memories had once been.

Dejected, Harvey fell back onto the grass behind, drawing his knees up to his chest and hugging them close with his filthy arms.

Somewhere, far away in the sky, the helicopter banked, widening its search.

But Harvey stared into the hole, reliving the night. The wait in the darkness. The struggle. The guilty cries of the man. But no name came to him.

The muffled screams and begging. Tears that cut through blood.

But no name came to him.

The wild eyes that begged for mercy as the first shovelful of soil covered his wretched body.

No name found the memory.

The smell of the condemned accepting death with one foot in the next life.

Still no name came to him.

And when all that remained was a hose pipe in the ground to feed the man air.

He stared up at the moon, sucked in a lungful of air and

whispered as those pale eyes took form. White skin, as if it had never seen the light of day, emerged and surrounded the eyes, and a breath of thin, blonde hair, parted neither this way nor that, or styled in any way, shape or form, hung across his forehead.

The look of fear took hold as Harvey's memory played the scene over and over. His eyes widening. His mouth parting to scream.

Like a sting to Harvey's heart, the name found his lips.

"Herman Hoffman."

Cold, concrete walls, still damp from the recent hosing down, offered a bleak setting, perfect for breaking the minds of those who opposed the nation. Closing the steel door behind him, Reilly began to pace the circumference of the room, letting the heels of his shoes click on the bare concrete floor.

In the centre of the rear wall, a second door led to the unknown, a place where Reilly had only seen people go, often never to return.

At the table in the centre of the room, Mills sat with her hands cuffed behind her back and a hood pulled down tight over her head.

The hosing down had done little to improve the smell that lingered from years of countless beatings, torture and destruction of souls from the team who ran the operation.

"You're familiar with the process, I assume?" said Reilly.

As ever, Mills said nothing.

"It's just you and me right now, but when I give the word, we'll be joined by others," said Reilly, searching for a twitch, a movement of any kind. But he found none. "You'll know from experience that this place doesn't exist. The men that run the facility, they don't exist either. It's a place of forgetting, kind of like an oubliette. Do you know what an oubliette is, Miss Mills?"

No response.

"Let me enlighten you. Oubliette is a French word. It means a place to forget. The French would build dungeons that were only accessible from a small hole many metres above the space. Once they dropped the prisoner inside, there was no escape. Death would come slowly to the prisoner who would wither and die. Of course, we're not going to drop you into a hole. We're not going to give you time to starve. But you will be forgotten. Nobody knows this place exists. Nobody knows you are here. Nobody can hear you scream."

Reilly stopped his pacing and turned to face Mills, allowing a pause, long enough for her to digest his words.

"Unless, of course, you talk," said Reilly. "I want to explain my perspective. Just so we are clear here and there are no misunderstandings."

He began his pacing again, circling the table while he thought about the best place to begin the story.

"Three days ago," he began, "a gas bomb was detonated in Jubilee Gardens. Many innocent people died on the scene. Many more died a slow, painful death from their injuries."

He stopped opposite Mills and rested his hands on the chair in front of him.

"Have you ever seen a man choke to death on his own blood? Have you ever seen a child suffocating on their own swollen lungs and throat?" asked Reilly. "It's not a pretty sight. The very next day, an identical gas bomb was detonated in Victoria Embankment Park. It was a callous and vicious attack on defenceless people who stood no chance at all. More deaths. More innocent lives lost. But we got a break, a real chance at catching the bomber."

The pacing began once more as Reilly thought back to the footage they'd watched on Cole's tablet.

"Just seconds before the second bomb detonated, we found two people running into the park. A man and a woman. The woman, if you haven't guessed, is yourself, Miss Mills, and she had her face covered by a scarf. The man, who appears not to exist in any records anywhere in the country, is holding a phone and he's making a call."

Her body tensed as he rested his hands on her shoulders. Then she shrugged him off. But Reilly held her in place, his grip tightening.

"So, you see how this looks, Miss Mills," said Reilly, "when we find the homemade device with a detonator rigged to be triggered by a phone call? Is there anything you'd like to say at this point, Miss Mills?"

But Mills remained silent.

Snatching the hood from her head, Reilly watched as Mills' eyes adjusted to the single bright light and searched the room.

"I told you we're alone," said Reilly. "And I told you this is your chance to talk. After this, I can't help you. The men here know far more ways to extract information than I do, and with less accountability. You can imagine how efficient they are."

Mills stared back at him across the table with an almost blank gaze, unfazed by the facility's less than welcoming charm.

"Imagine how intrigued we were when we saw you both run to the train station," said Reilly, keen to progress his side of the story and to start developing hers. "But wait. Two of you entered the train station. And we have a witness who has made a statement that he saw you both in what appeared to be a tense conversation as the train was brought to a stop. He goes on to say that both of you got off the train with the other passengers. But only one of you emerged onto the platform."

As expected, Mills offered no insight. Instead, she held his gaze, waiting for him to continue.

"I'll tell you where he went," said Reilly. "He walked back to Embankment, tied up a member of staff, and killed the lights in the station before escaping in a taxi, which he then switched somewhere near Elephant and Castle. From there, we lost him. He's a very resourceful man, Mills. But not as resourceful as me."

The comment failed to raise an emotion from Mills, who remained unsurprised and unimpressed.

"Then, earlier today, yet another bomb detonates. A restaurant in Fulham. And who do we find running from the scene? Your friend, Miss Mills. And, as if that wasn't bad enough, we chased him and he ran. A guilty man running for his life, prepared to face death in the River Thames rather than face the consequences of his own actions."

Mills' eyes closed, as if she was hearing the story for the first time and couldn't bear to imagine the man she was protecting jumping to his death.

"But he didn't die, did he? He'd have us believe he was dead. But no. He's not as smart as he thinks he is. He came to see you. He came to see you, didn't he? Because you're the only thing he has in his life. Am I right, Miss Mills? We know he came to see you. We know he stole a car to get there because we found it. And we know he escaped because the fire brigade are putting out the fire he started as we speak. He's cunning, Mills. But not as cunning as me."

Reilly let his last words hang in the air, tempting Mills to speak. Anything. The first words were often the opening of floodgates. A monosyllable. A murmur or a whisper. It didn't matter. All he needed was a single sound and he knew he would have her.

The silence was broken by the slamming of a steel door along the long corridor outside.

"You're running out of time," said Reilly. "They're coming and there's absolutely nothing I can do to stop them when they arrive."

Mills remained silent.

"Mills, talk to me. You're one of us. Don't do this. Help me stop him."

Her eyes softened.

"Mills, you know what happens here. I don't need to lie to you. If these men take you, the chances of you getting out alive are slim. They receive their instructions from much higher up the food chain than me. Help me find him. Tell me his name at least. Give me something to go on."

A knock at the door added urgency to Reilly's tone.

"Mills, look at me," said Reilly, meeting her distant stare. "They'll make you disappear and when they find your friend, they'll tear him to bits."

But still, Mills said nothing.

Slamming his hand on the steel-plated desk, Reilly felt his heart rate jump into action, thudding against his chest, and felt his course breathing shallow. It was coming. He knew it was coming.

Another bang on the door.

"Sir, it's time," said a man's voice from outside.

"If you can't do it for me, Mills, do it for the people out there. The innocent people."

Another bang on the door.

Reilly stood, panting for breath. He plunged his shaking hand into his pocket and felt for the bottle of pills.

Mills stared up at him, defiance in her eyes.

"Sir, open the door," said the man in the corridor outside.

"I can't help you anymore," said Reilly softly, and reached for the door handle.

Two guards walked either side of him, strode to Mills' side and tilted the chair back. The second man opened the door at the back of the room for the other to pull Mills into the dark space beyond. He tracked her eyes as they darted from man to man and searched the new space around her.

But just as the door began to shut and Reilly's eyes closed with the failure and potential consequences, a strong female voice called out.

"Harvey Stone."

The men stopped and turned back to Reilly for a decision, whose mind processed the words with individual scrutiny. The name. The slither of hope that appeared like a light in a dark tunnel. His eyes opened and he turned back to face her.

"His name is Harvey Stone," said Mills. "Untie me and I'll help you find him."

CHAPTER THIRTY-THREE

"There's something you need to know," said Mills. "Remove the cuffs and I'll talk. We don't have long."

Gauging her sincerity with practiced eyes, Reilly nodded at the two men in black who removed the cuffs.

"You get one chance," said Reilly. "Mess up and you'll be dragged back there and never seen again."

"I know how it works," said Mills.

"Then you'll know I'm not lying," said Reilly.

"The goons stay out," said Mills, gesturing at the two men.

Reilly waved them forwards and closed the door behind them, leaving him and Mills alone in the room. Then he leaned into the corridor.

"In here, Cole," he called, and listened as Cole's heels clicked along the hallway.

He closed the door when she arrived. Reilly took a seat beside Cole and opposite Mills, and laid his hands flat on the desk.

"What I have to tell you is top secret. It goes against the official secrets act and about a hundred non-disclosures," said Mills.

Out of the corner of his eye, Reilly caught Cole's reaction, glancing at him and then back at Mills.

"The room is not bugged. The room does not exist. The facility does not exist. Any conversations did not happen," said Reilly.

"Good," said Mills. "You know who I am?"

"Melody Mills," said Cole, opening her file. "Fifteen years across various police services with an exemplary record, including several years working with organised crime, under-cover work and several years unassigned."

Mills nodded. "Do you know what unassigned means?"

"It usually indicates that you were assigned to something the agency would prefer not to be accountable for," said Reilly.

"Exactly," said Mills. "It was SO-10."

"And I'm guessing Stone was part of it too? He was also SO-10?"

"How far does your clearance go?" asked Mills, directing the question at Reilly.

"Far enough that I rarely need to ask for permission."

"You're going to need it for this."

"You want me to do some research?" asked Reilly.

"Harvey Stone doesn't exist," said Melody. "He's one of the best operatives SO-10 ever had, but he doesn't exist. He's put his life on the line for this city more times than you can imagine, but he doesn't exist."

"Why is that?" asked Cole. "SO-10 had dozens of operatives. I can pull their files without any clearance at all."

"But they aren't Harvey Stone," said Mills.

"What makes Stone different?" asked Reilly.

"You'll know when you meet him."

"I asked you what makes Stone different, Mills. I told you. You get one chance before that door opens and you cease to exist."

"He's a killer," said Mills, taking a long, slow breath and releasing it through flared nostrils. "I wish I could fluff it up for you, but it's a fact. He was raised by a crime family, trained by a contract killer and has been killing since he was a teenager."

"And you're protecting him?" said Cole. "I don't see how a man like that would be employed by a government agency, officially or unofficially. In fact, he sounds like the type of man that wouldn't lose sleep over a few gas bombs."

"Let's just say his morals are in the right place," said Mills.

"Who did he kill?" asked Cole.

"Bad people," said Mills. "Sex offenders. Rapists. Child molesters. Plus whoever the family needed him to."

"He was a vigilante?" said Cole.

"He had issues," said Mills. "It was his way of dealing with them."

"I'm pretty sure SO-10 don't accept transfer requests from murderers, Mills," said Reilly. "Even if they are cleansing the city. This has all the hallmarks of a plan to buy him time. I don't need to remind you of the position you're in, Mills."

"He was exonerated in return for his services to the City of London. He spent three years saving this city with the threat of prison hanging over him every second of every day."

"So what do we need clearance for?"

"We're going to need access to Harvey's file."

"You just told us he doesn't exist," said Cole. "And now there's a file on him?"

"Harvey Stone exists on paper in one place and one place only," said Mills.

"The director of British Special Forces," said Reilly, falling in with where Mills was going. "That would be the highest level of classification inside any special operations."

Mills nodded.

"And you expect me to call the director of British Special

Operations and ask him for a file on a man that doesn't exist? You understand how long that might take?"

"He's the prime suspect in a national terrorism threat," said Mills. "I'm sure the matter can be expedited."

"Right now, we have every police officer in London hunting for him."

"Right now," said Mills, raising her voice for the first time, "you have every police officer in London hunting for the only man who can save thousands of lives."

"And what makes you think Stone's file is going to help?" asked Cole.

"Because that file contains the names of every person he killed."

"A list of dead people?" said Cole.

"And how is that going to help us?" asked Reilly.

"Because one of those dead people is the gas bomber. You're going after the wrong guy."

CHAPTER THIRTY-FOUR

In the distance, the helicopter had widened its search area. Police cars patrolled the main roads like wild animals on the prowl. Harvey stood in the shadows of the forest while the city prepared for the biggest party of the year.

Groups of people walked along the footpaths in the common. Families walked to see the New Year's fireworks. Teenagers stalked in packs, clutching bottles of cheap alcohol and looking for a park bench or a quiet place to celebrate. Couples walked hand in hand, a civilised bottle of wine in a bag, maybe heading to a friend's house for a dinner party.

But for Harvey, there would be no celebrations. With every police officer in London looking for him, and just the name of a dead man to hunt, there was only one place to begin.

He fell in behind a small group who walked beside the road. It was two couples, each walking hand in hand with their partners, reminiscing about the previous years' celebrations. Traffic had started to build on the main road so, with his hands in his pockets to hide the dirt, Harvey kept pace with the foursome until they crossed the road, stepping between the stationary cars to the other side.

Harvey watched them cross. He considered following them but it was too late. The move would look false and create attention. So he continued straight, aware of the heads turning in the endless line of cars that sat in the evening traffic.

A cold wind whipped at Harvey's jacket and stung his ears. But with each passing step, the vision became clearer and the physical discomfort eased, replaced by hope, leaving only unanswered questions and the unknown to fog his mind.

With his head down low and his hands in his pockets, he passed the slow moving cars, only for them to catch him when the traffic lights turned green. A few minutes later, the same cars passed and Harvey felt the same stares.

A police helicopter flying into the wind caught him by surprise when it appeared above the rooftops of the houses on the far side of the road. The thundering noise of the rotors was sudden and its huge spotlight lit the street with inescapable scrutiny. Harvey glanced up once, watched it pass, but maintained audible contact to gauge its distance as it ran its spotlight in long sweeping arcs across the common. Harvey continued his walk, retracing the journey and racking his mind for details his brain had long since tucked away somewhere cold and dark.

Flashes of newspapers that Harvey had read while researching the kill.

Those eyes.

An image of a brick building buried in the shadows of a dark alleyway. A sliding steel door with two huge, round garbage bins outside. And a smell. He remembered a smell. It hadn't been thick or putrid, just evident, as if it the air was permanently stained or ingrained in the structure of the building. It had clung to the back of his throat.

A row of trees had lined the perimeter fence as if somehow adding some green would counter the industrial look of the place.

The faces of dozens of Harvey's victims rolled through his memory as if they were on a carousel. He saw not the pained expressions moments before their last breaths like the faces that haunted his dreams, but the shocked and fearful faces they'd worn when they realised their dirty games were up and the remaining moments of their life would be unbearable.

Audible gasps of guilt.

Mouths hung open in disbelief and fear.

Postures slumped in self-loathing and cowardice.

And eyes widened when they saw the cold, hard stare that Harvey offered them.

Those eyes.

A car horn beeped in unison with screeching tyres, shaking Harvey from his trance-like state, and the images he'd recalled faded once more. He stopped in the middle of the road his subconscious had steered him to cross.

A man rolled down his car window and leaned out.

"Hey," he called, shrugging off his wife's attempts to stop him. "You want to watch where you're going, mate. I could have killed you."

Slowly, Harvey turned to face him, aware of the approaching helicopter and fighting the urge to retaliate. But the man hadn't finished. Harvey stared back at him, clinging to the memory of the brick building, the trees and the smell.

"Get out of the road," shouted the man, as two more cars pulled up behind him and began to honk their horns.

Harvey didn't reply.

It was coming. The memory. The pieces were there. The route he'd taken when he'd followed Hoffman that night. It was the junction where he stood.

When he'd dragged Hoffman into the common.

The road opposite where he stood seemed so familiar, differing only in age. The common to Harvey's left and behind, and the houses to his right. The journey Harvey had taken, keeping to the shadows as Hoffman had navigated the maze of back streets, played in reverse.

Another car joined in the chorus of horns, all aimed at Harvey, urging him to get out of the road.

"Right, mate," said the man in the lead car, as he pushed open his car door. "It's your bleeding funeral."

He slammed his door on his wife's hysterical objections and walked towards Harvey as more car drivers joined in vocalising their outrage via their horns. He ran his hand across his balding head and rolled the cuffs up his thick arms as he approached.

"You've got three seconds to move out of the way, mate," said the balding man, as he drew closer to Harvey. "One," he said from a few feet away.

Harvey didn't reply. He stared at the road ahead, piecing the puzzle together.

"Two," said the man. A tiny piece of spittle flew from his mouth, his emotions firing on all cylinders.

Harvey turned his head to look at the man, whose rage was distracting him from the memories.

"Funeral?" said Harvey, as a connection was made and the journey in his mind was complete.

"Three," said the man with finality, and drew his arm back to swing a punch at Harvey.

The memory was complete. The fragments of memories came together in a moment of clarity. With lightning-fast reflexes, Harvey's hand shot up and took hold of the bigger man's throat mid-swing. The punch faltered and, as predicted, the man's arm shot to Harvey's hand to release his iron grip.

"You're a genius," said Harvey, then ran across the road and disappeared into the now familiar side street.

CHAPTER THIRTY-FIVE

"We need the names of every person killed or injured in all three attacks," said Mills. She fingered the plastic label on the front of the binder as if she was recalling a memory.

"We don't have time to find a link, Mills," said Reilly. "Are you going to open that or what? You do realise I've committed to this now, don't you? The director will be wanting results and so far all we have is your name and the name of a guy that doesn't exist."

"Actually, sir, the PM wants an update in thirty minutes," said Cole. "The city is on high alert and it's too late to stop the celebrations. It would cause mayhem and panic, which could potentially be as bad as another attack."

"So you see, Mills," said Reilly, "Harvey Stone is all we have. So if you can't piece this together, I'll have no choice but to bring him in."

She stared back at him, still clutching the binder to her chest.

"It won't come to that," she said. Then, as if a switch had been flipped, the emotion disappeared from her face and she slammed the folder onto the desk. "Where's that list of victims?"

Seeking approval, Cole glanced at Reilly, who gave her the nod. Two blue paper folders as thick as a phone book were pulled from Cole's bag and she took the seat opposite Mills. It was as if the fact that Mills was the only suspect in custody had been forgotten and she was now on the team.

"Just remember," said Reilly, "you're still a suspect in a terrorist attack. You're still in the facility and nobody knows you're here."

"I remember," replied Mills, keeping her head down as she flicked through the pages of Stone's file. "I should remind you that we have six and a half hours until the clock strikes twelve. So you can either stand there making idle threats or you can get in here and help us."

Both Cole and Reilly glanced at each other then back at Mills, who felt their stares and looked up at them, flicking from one to the other with her eyebrows raised in question.

"What?" she said.

"What happens when the clock strikes twelve?" said Reilly. "Is there something we should know?"

Keeping her place in the binder with the flat of her hand, Mills let the pages fall closed and sucked in a deep breath.

"The fireworks," she said.

"What about them?" asked Reilly.

"Well, if you were a terrorist planning an attack on New Year's Eve, when would you detonate your bomb?"

"But I'm not a terrorist," said Reilly.

"Well, you need to learn to think like one," said Mills, opening the binder again. "If we're going to catch this guy, you need to be him. You need to live him. You need to breathe him. Right now, he's two steps ahead of us and there's a million people out there who need us to work together. Are you in? Or are you going to continue to disrupt us?"

Reilly digested the outburst. He scratched his chin and stared at the woman who seemed so confident.

"And if you can't stop that hand shaking, just have a drink. It's in your pocket," said Mills.

Cole slowly turned her head to offer Reilly a knowing look. He opened his mouth to speak.

"I can smell it on your breath," said Mills.

"It's medicinal," said Reilly, as he took the seat next to Cole, reddening with both anger and embarrassment.

Flicking through the binder with one hand and making notes with the other, Mills seemed too distracted to hear him. Reilly pulled the second thick, blue binder across the desk and busied himself by flicking past the introductory pages of the report to the details of each victim.

"There's not many ailments out there that can be treated with scotch," said Mills without looking up.

Reilly stopped, aware that Cole hadn't offered him her look again.

"Some things just aren't treatable with medicine," said Reilly. "Some things require a little help just to get through the day."

"Well, how about you find me a connection to one of these guys," said Mills, spinning the sheet of paper on the desk for them both to read.

"Who are these?" asked Cole, looking up from her list of names.

But Mills didn't reply. Her look said it all.

"These are Stone's victims? How did you shortlist the names?" asked Reilly. "It could be any one of those people in that file."

"Correction," said Mills. "It can't be any of them. They're dead."

"So how did you come up with the list?" said Cole.

"You really need me to explain?" said Mills, flicking her eyes between the two of them. She sighed then opened the binder and spun around to face them, moving her list to one side. A polished and manicured nail rested on the name of Stone's first victim, while her other hand held the wad of papers bent and ready to flick through. "This guy was found with his limbs burned off. This guy was found boiled in a bathtub. This guy was found hanging from a crane."

She continued to flick through each sheet, identifying the manner of death and the state of the bodies as they were found.

"And this guy was discovered glued to a bathtub with his entrails in his lap and his testicles in his mouth," finished Mills.

She closed the binder and turned it back towards her to avoid the obscene photos being on show.

"And the list?" said Reilly, covering for Cole, who had fallen silent at the sight of the images and the descriptions Mills had provided.

"That's easy," said Mills. "Their bodies were never found."

The silence was broken by Cole's phone vibrating on the desk. Reilly fixed Mills with a stare then nodded for Cole to answer the call. She stood from the table and stepped into the corridor, but returned before the door had time to close.

"Sir," she said, glancing at Mills then back at Reilly, "Harvey Stone has been spotted in Wimbledon. He attacked a member of the public. All units are on stand-by."

Mills' face dropped like a stone in the sea and her head fell forward in defeat.

Reilly opened his mouth to talk but nausea got the better of him. He swallowed hard, feeling his throat close and his chest tighten.

"Sir?" said Cole. "What do you want us to do?"

He opened his mouth to breath, but found nothing but sharp stabs in his lungs and a pounding heart.

"Sir?" said Cole.

"What's happening?" said Mills, as the sensation eased and Reilly's airways opened up. A burning red covered the skin on his face and a layer of cool sweat formed on his brow.

"Sir, are you okay?" said Cole. "You need to see someone."

"Just go," said Reilly, catching his breath and clearing his throat of phlegm.

"I can't leave you like this," said Cole.

"You'll do as you're damn well told and that's an order," said Reilly, leaning on the table to steady himself. "And you can take her with you. She might be useful. I'll be fine. I'll be right behind you."

CHAPTER THIRTY-SIX

"Are we going to watch the fireworks?" asked the boy, holding the hands of his mum and Herman as they made their way through the crowds of people in London's Parliament Square. He looked up at his mum then across to Herman, who smiled back at him.

"Quiet, Sam," said Martina, offering Herman a warning look.

"Of course, son," said Herman. "Have you ever seen fireworks?"

"Don't you talk to my son," said Martina. Her face screwed up and her voice lowered to avoid causing a scene. "It's bad enough you brought us here. You're sick."

"I think you're forgetting who's in charge," said Lucas. "Do I need to remind you what's in your little backpacks? One wrong move, Martina, and it's game over for you."

Her hand touched the strap across her chest, where a small black padlock fixed it in place. Herman watched as her eyes fell to the boy's backpack, a smaller version of her own but otherwise matching. The same joyful blue. The yellow beading around the edges. And the same black padlock to stop it from being removed.

"I didn't want to do this," said Herman. "I didn't want-"

"Don't talk to me," said Martina. "Or my son."

"If Herman wants to talk to his son, Martina, you should let him. Every boy needs to hear his father's voice once in a while."

"Stay out of this, Lucas."

"I'll stay out of nothing. Let the boy talk if he wants. Let the boy see what a good man his father really is."

"Herman Hoffman is-"

"Misunderstood, Martina. My dear brother is misunderstood. That's all."

They moved to the side of the road to let a group of people dressed as farmyard animals through, and the boy smiled in delight as the giant pig made a show of scratching his back side and trying to straighten his tail.

"Do you like farmyard animals?" said Herman, crouching to be the same level as the boy.

He nodded.

"Do you have a favourite animal?" asked Herman.

The boy thought for a while, biting his lower lip and glancing up to his mum for approval. She feigned a smile and nodded for him to answer.

"Dogs," said Sam.

"Dogs?" replied Herman, with a little too much enthusiasm. "We had a dog when we were your age. Do you want to know his name?"

Sam nodded, not taking his eyes off Herman.

"His name was Conrad and he was black," said Herman, "with a long, furry tail and big droopy ears."

"Was he a good dog?" asked Sam.

"He was the best," replied Herman, and ruffled Sam's hair.

He stood and stared at Martina.

"He likes me," said Herman.

"He's a child. He doesn't know any better," said Martina.

"Let's go," said Lucas. "We don't have time to chit chat." He found a gap in the crowd and pulled the family along until they all walked side by side, bunched together to avoid being separated.

"Don't try anything stupid, Martina," said Lucas. "My brother may be soft, but I have a much firmer hand."

"Where are we going?" asked Martina.

"To see the fireworks, of course," replied Lucas, flicking his eyes down to the boy and back to meet Martina's hate-filled stare. "It'll be a night to remember."

"You know there'll be a thousand police here? You won't get away with anything."

"I won't be needing to get away with anything, Martina," said Lucas, as he pulled them to the side of the road overlooking the river.

"This seems like a nice spot, doesn't it, Sam? What do you think?" said Herman, and leaned down to pick up his son. The move sparked Martina's fears. She cried out and reached to pull Sam away. But Herman held him tight, moving him out of Martina's reach.

"No. Don't," she said, above the din of the crowd.

"What are you doing?" said Herman, and smoothed Sam's hair. "You do trust me with my own flesh and blood, don't you?"

But Martina just stared at him.

"You trust me, don't you, Sam?" said Herman, the tone of his voice as childish as his son's.

The boy nodded and peered down at the water, marvelling at the reflections of the city lights against the inky, black river.

The crowd flowed past in waves of what seemed like thousands at a time, but the spot they had chosen was out of the flow, like the outside of a meandering river bend.

"Are you my daddy?" asked Sam, with the inquisitive confidence of a child.

The question hit Martina hard. In the corner of Herman's watering eye, he saw her turn away, unable to look, as if he was some kind of monster.

Herman thought on his response. He wanted to cry out 'yes'. He wanted the crowd to know. Instead, he just nodded and let Sam wipe the tear from his eye. They shared a smile, father and son, and for the first time for as long as Herman could remember, there was happiness in his world.

"Daddy," said Sam, eliciting a further grimace from Martina, who stood a few feet away.

"Yes, son?" said Herman, then cleared his throat.

"What happened to Conrad?" asked Sam, his head cocked to one side as Herman's often did.

Herman bit his own lower lip. He swallowed hard and was about to speak when Lucas opened his mouth and stole the moment from him.

"The same thing that happens to all of us, Sam," said Lucas, his tone hard and sharp.

"No," said Herman. "No, don't."

"What's that?" asked Sam.

"He was killed."

CHAPTER THIRTY-SEVEN

The smell hit Harvey first. It was a tangy scent of rot and decay, sweetened by the overbearing chemical smell of disinfectant. He stood in the shadows of the trees that lined the fence, opposite the sliding shutter doors he remembered so well.

He touched the tree, finding the V in the trunk where two branches split that he peered through, exactly as he had done close to ten years before. The lights were off in the building. Dark windows offered no clue of the life inside.

He waited a full minute, enough time to pass for anybody who may have seen him to venture out.

But nobody came.

The steel shutter doors were locked, but the small doorway to the right was open, as if it was inviting Harvey in.

He drew his knife from his belt, checked behind him, and stepped inside.

His footsteps echoed in the darkness and the door slammed shut behind him, killing any ambient light.

A drip of water was the only sound, save for the regular thud of Harvey's heart. He breathed slow and long, controlling his desire to leave. Instead, he edged forward, rolling his boot as he stepped to quieten the noise, until his foot found the first stair and his hand touched the rail.

Step by step, listening to every sound made by the old building, Harvey climbed the concrete stairs, blinded by the darkness but guided by a memory of what once was.

A single doorway, its shape darker than the surrounding wall, stood at the top of the stairs. A round door handle offered itself, its shiny finish contrasting with the dull wood and concrete.

It turned in Harvey's hand and the door opened to reveal more of the smell, the odour of death and bad hygiene, but little to see in the dark space except a flashing green light on the far side of the room.

Harvey stepped inside, his senses tuned for movement and sound. He pulled the door closed behind him, working the handle to avoid the click of the mechanism giving his presence away. The more he searched the darkness, the clearer his vision became as his eyes adjusted to the gloom.

A full minute passed. Shapes became clearer. A single chair in front of a computer desk, which was the source of the flashing green. A window with heavy curtains that blocked any ambient light pulled closed.

Stepping further into the room, Harvey found a bedroom door open. The same heavy curtains blocked the light. A small bed had been placed against the centre of the far wall.

The floorboards creaked under his weight, loud in the silence and amplified by the empty, featureless room.

"Hoffman," said Harvey, and waited for a response.

The flashing green light at the top of the computer screen seemed to beckon him, holding his attention like a hypnotist might distract a patient with a swinging pendant.

But something else caught his eye. At the far end of the room, darker than the shadows that surrounded it, was a shape.

The closer Harvey stepped, the clearer the image became, but denial ushered reality away until Harvey's hand touched it, affirming the facts, cold and hard.

Beneath his fingers was the grain of polished wood. He ran his hand from right to left across the surface. Even in the darkness, the craftsmanship was evident. His fingers found the edge of the moulded coffin lid. Every part of him fought to leave it be.

But he had to know.

He had to look.

He lifted the lid and stepped back.

Loving hands had assembled the skeletal remains of the body. Soft, plush material lined the inside of the coffin and was infused with some kind of scent to mask the stale odour of decay.

Harvey dropped the lid, but the image remained as if it had been branded onto his eyes.

Allowing the silence to steady his jumbled flow of thoughts, he stepped back, until the flashing green light once more teased him.

With each flash of the tiny light, Harvey could make out the contents of the small desk. He ran his finger across the pen that lay on top of a large, lined notepad. The lid of the pen was missing and the writing on the pad was neat, far neater even than Melody's methodical and meticulous handwriting.

The light flashed on once more, offering Harvey a short glimpse of the words.

Six names.

Six lines.

Three with hard lines through them as if the culprit had dug the nib of the pen into the paper and dragged through each of the three names with malice and contempt. Harvey ran his finger over the writing, feeling the depth of each line. It was as if each line was deeper than the last.

A growing anger.

But somehow, the angry lines failed to match the timid and weak persona of Hoffman as Harvey remembered him. He was a disturbed man, a victim in the eyes of most who knew him, who found solace and peace working with the dead in the funeral parlour beneath Harvey's feet by day. By night, he would find his prey on Wimbledon common, subjecting his victims to sordid, unthinkable things to mask his own misgivings and weaknesses.

Harvey looked around the room, remembering with new found clarity the images of the children Hoffman had lured there and held captive. While grieving widows arranged the funerals of their loved ones downstairs at the front of the shop, Herman Hoffman would be in the workshop out back, his mind tinkering at the thought of his latest pleasure in the upstairs flat.

Flashes of the newspaper images ran through Harvey's mind, now complete and no longer obscured by the fog of time. The boy in the room that the police had found, starved and hooded. The images on the computer too sick to print. The headline stating that Hoffman had run away and become another man the police would one day stop looking for.

But Hoffman hadn't run away.

Harvey had found him first.

And now the tables were turned.

The green light on the computer stopped flashing, but it stayed lit, casting a green glow across the keyboard. Lowering himself into the chair, Harvey peered at the screen as a window appeared. The word 'connecting' scrolled from right to left at the bottom and a single beep signalled that the connection had been established.

Harvey took a breath, knowing what was to come.

"Harvey Stone," said Hoffman. "I knew you'd find us."

CHAPTER THIRTY-EIGHT

The sound of Cole's heels clicking along the corridor faded to a whisper, then stopped, and the ping of the elevator doors announced their journey up to the ground floor.

Reilly exhaled, loud and deep, emptying his lungs, and spat the blood from his mouth into a tissue. Using the back of a chair to steady himself, he pushed himself to his feet and waited for the head rush to cease.

The smooth corridor wall guided him to a small kitchenette used by the men who ran the facility. Grateful that the room was empty, Reilly fell across the sink, holding onto the draining board with both hands, and let the remaining blood run from his throat. He spat and cleaned the sink then searched for a glass to use to rinse his mouth. Behind him in the centre of the room was a small table with four chairs. A pack of cards, an ashtray and three empty coffee cups had been left for the cleaning contractor.

A small TV had been mounted to the wall to keep the men amused during their breaks and the periods of downtime. The volume was low, barely audible above the noise of the ventilation unit and the thud of Reilly's heart in his ear.

He rinsed his mouth then refilled the glass, certain the attack had passed. Then he turned to lean back on the sink. The ashtray in the centre of the table was overflowing. The remains of the cigarettes seemed so appealing. It couldn't hurt. There was no more damage to be done.

He stepped across to the table, eying the butt with the most cigarette remaining, and picked it up from the piles of ash. Reilly rolled it in his fingers then sniffed in the foul but intoxicating odour.

A small box of Swan Vesta matches had been used as currency for the men's break time card games and several lay sprawled across the table. He placed the glass down and picked up a single match.

He glanced behind him to make sure he was alone and listened for a second for the tell-tale sound of army issue boots on the painted concrete in the corridor.

But he heard nothing.

One strike was all it took for the match to light. He placed the butt in between his lips and raised the flame to the end, raising his head to avoid the heat so close to the two days' growth on his face.

The tobacco crackled like a tiny log fire as the flame grew closer, singeing the end of the butt enough to elicit the foul smell. He gagged as the first tastes of stale tobacco touched the back of his throat and pulled the butt from his mouth, taking deep, painful breaths to hold down the contents of his stomach.

He tried once more.

Raising his face to the ceiling, he lit one more match.

This time he didn't hesitate.

He brought the flame to the butt and inhaled, drawing the heat into the tobacco and feeling the taste as the nicotine found its way to his blood. He closed his eyes and let the smoke crawl from his open mouth, savouring the taste and remembering the days when he'd light a cigarette before even stepping out of bed.

The feeling passed.

He brought the butt up for one last drag, his eyes falling on the TV as he did. A pretty, young news reporter was standing on Westminster Bridge with her hood pulled up and a large microphone held in her gloved hand. Behind her, thousands of people had gathered for the fireworks. A few teenagers vied for a position on camera and waved to their families.

Unable to hear what the reporter was saying, Reilly watched as the camera panned to take in the full view. The thousands turned to millions, a sea of heads as far as the eye could see.

Reilly crushed the cigarette and picked up the glass of water, draining it in one swoop to wash away the foul aftertaste of the tobacco.

The camera continued to pan.

A teenager jumped up from behind a group of people to be seen by the camera. A group of girls waved, giggled then shied, and policemen standing nearby winked at the camera, a proud sign of London's resilience. Even in the midst of a terrorist attack, nothing would stop the city from celebrating as it had done for years.

But standing to one side of the policeman, pressed against the bridge out of harm's way, a family of three caught Reilly's eye. There were no smiles on their faces. The boy looked overwhelmed by the chaos and noise. The mother appeared downtrodden, clinging to her son as if he was everything she had.

And the father.

There was a silence.

A skip of Reilly's heart.

And the glass crashed to the floor.

For a split second, the father's eye met the camera. It was

less than a split second, a nanosecond, and then the camera had moved on.

But it had been enough.

Like two iron fists crushed Reilly's chest, another attack came on, squeezing his lungs with a ferocity like never before. He staggered through the door, slipping on the broken glass and pool of water. Then, clinging to the wall, he made his way back to the interview room.

He'd taken three steps before he dizzied and fell to the floor. Clinging to consciousness by a thread, as his head spun with impossibilities, he half-crawled and half-dragged himself to the door.

"Sir?" said a voice behind him. It was a man's voice. A northerner. Reilly recognised his tone as the security guard. He reached up to the number pad to enter the entry code. "Sir, are you okay?" said the guard. From the corner of Reilly's eye, he saw the man begin to run to help him.

"Open the door," said Reilly, with the flat of his hand ready to push it open.

"Sir, should I call someone?" said the guard.

"I said open the damn door," said Reilly. "Please. Just open the door."

Six beeps of various tones signalled the guard entering the code. Then, as Reilly shoved open the door, two strong arms pulled him up and helped him onto one of the chairs.

"What can I do?" said the guard, stepping in front of Reilly.

"Water," said Reilly, breathless and wheezing. "I just need a minute."

The guard shot from the room, radioing for medical assistance while he walked.

The palm of Reilly's hand slapped onto the table, snatching up Stone's file.

Reilly knew it would be in there.

He didn't need to look.

But he did.

Tearing through the pages of the file, flicking past scenes of devastation, torture and sickening human ability until he found what he was looking for.

He gave a moan and closed his eyes as memories began to inch their way into his conscience.

But they called to him. They begged him to look.

From the open page of the file, taunting him with cold malice, framed by white, deathly skin, was a pair of pale, shining eyes.

CHAPTER THIRTY-NINE

The heaving crowd closed in as people found their places to view the annual spectacle, crushing Martina into Herman, who held Sam up high, resting the boy on his hip.

"Please, Martina. Don't look at me like that," said Herman. "I'm different now."

"So stop this," she hissed in reply. "Get us out of here before Lucas comes back."

"I can't," said Herman, checking behind him. "You don't know what he's capable of. If he finds us-"

"Then why?" said Martina, swallowing to restrain the tears that threatened to burst from her. "Why us? Why now?"

With a quick glance at Sam, who was enthralled by his lofty view of the sea of people standing on the bridge, Herman met Martina's eyes then lowered his head.

"You wouldn't understand," said Herman. "You could never understand. Nobody could."

"Help us," said Martina, her eyes pleading with her ex-husband. "We can run away. The three of us. It'll be like old times."

Herman's mouth fell open, picturing the scene. He gently lowered Sam to the ground.

"We could start over, some place new," said Martina, sensing Herman's interest.

"Like a family?" said Herman.

"Yes," said Martina.

"And Sam would have a father?"

"Yes."

"That was what I always wanted."

"Just you, me and Sam, Herman," said Martina. "We can find somewhere remote. Somewhere he'd never find us."

"In the country. I always wanted to live in the country, away from..." Herman's voice trailed away as he cast his eyes across the smiling families, couples and young children waiting with anticipation for the fireworks.

"Away from the people?" asked Martina.

The question roused Herman from thoughts he'd long since buried. He stared at Martina.

"Temptation," he said, his eyes softening. "I'd treat you so well."

"Oh, Herman," said Martina, working her way under his arm. "These past few days, it's been all I could think about, lying there on that bed. Oh, Herman, you would never treat us like that, would you?"

"No," said Herman. "Never. I'd do anything for you. I'd do anything to make it right."

"We have lots of time to make up for, Herman," said Martina, squeezing his hand. "And Sam would love it too. Wouldn't you, Sam?"

The boy didn't flinch at the sound of his name. A pair of circus clowns entertaining the crowd had captured his attention.

"He would," said Martina. "I know he would."

"I could take him for long walks, show him stuff and-"

"And what?" said Martina.

"And be a father to him," said Herman, smoothing Sam's hair. "I want him to be proud of me. He shouldn't have to know about-"

"He doesn't have to know," said Martina. "We'll never speak of it again. It's my fault anyway. I neglected you. I wasn't there."

"Don't speak of it," said Herman. "That was the old me."

"And you can have it," said Martina. "We can have it all, but-"

"But what?" said Herman, his dejection apparent in his tone.

Martina checked around them to make sure nobody could hear, and then leaned in close.

"You have to help us out of these bags," said Martina, raising her lips to Herman's neck.

Feeling her warm breath on his neck, Herman sighed, offering her more of his skin with a lift of his chin.

"Please, Herman. You have the keys in your pocket. Take the bags off before Lucas comes back. We can throw them in the river. Look at all these people."

She nuzzled in closer, finding the spot behind his ear she used to kiss so many years ago.

"Can I hold him?" asked Herman. "I want to feel him. I want him close."

Martina bent and hoisted Sam into the air. She kissed him on the forehead then held Herman's gaze as she passed her son to him.

Like a natural father, Herman leaned to one side so the boy sat on his hip. He turned to Martina but could only smile at the joy and mumble a thank you through the emotion.

"Just unlock the bags, Herman, and we can be free."

But Herman pulled away. "No," he said. "No. We can't."

"But we'll die," said Martina, closing the gap once more.

"Come on, Herman. You were always the smarter brother. You were always the one with the brains."

"He's my brother," said Herman. "He's done so much for me. He's made me a man. For the first time, I feel like I'm in control."

"But you are in control, Herman. Don't you see? Look at you. He's trusted you to stand here with us because you're in control. And where is he now? When there's danger? Where is he when there's real work to be done?"

"He's not afraid. He's strong. Stronger than me," said Herman.

"No. Don't ever say that. The Herman I married would never say that. The Herman I married knew the difference between right and wrong," said Martina. "Or maybe that's it? Maybe I was wrong about you? All those years I thought you were dead, and really you were just hiding like the coward you are. All those years I was widowed. I carried Sam for nine months thinking you were dead, hoping and praying you were alive, hoping that the Herman I loved was alive somewhere and that one day you would walk through the door and everything would be alright. But I was wrong, wasn't I? Tell me, Herman. Tell me you're really back. Tell me the Herman I once knew is back and he's going to save us from his evil brother."

The information rolled around Herman's emotional mind. The questions, the statements, the accusations all blended to form some wild concoction that pulled Herman away.

"Where's Lucas?" said Herman. "I need Lucas."

"Unlock us, Herman," said Martina. "Before it's too late."

"I don't know who I am," said Herman. "Lucas saved me. He gave me life. I can't abandon him now. Not when we've come so far."

"Oh, Herman," said Martina, her voice in quiet despair. "He's going to kill us all. Don't you see?"

She gripped him by the arms with enough force to rouse

Sam from the excitement around them. Herman pulled away, struggling to find a path between the people around him, trying to get away from Martina, from the incessant questions.

"Herman, listen to me," she said above the noise, and no longer caring for their privacy. "Herman, don't run away."

The crowd shoved him back, defending their positions and the views they'd secured. With his back against the bridge, the angry faces of the neighbouring crowd glared at him and Martina's voice dug deeper into his mind, like ants finding the smallest crevice to get inside. He buried his face into Sam's soft jacket, covering his ear and his eyes with his spare arm.

"No," he said. "No more. Stop."

"Herman, listen to me."

"No. I can't take it."

"Herman, don't do this."

"Leave me alone," he said. His eyes squeezed shut but the wall of sound from all around found its way through any barrier he put up.

"Help us," said Martina.

A surge of emotion rushed from the very pit of Herman's stomach.

He pulled his arm away from his head, raised his head up high and screamed, long and loud. The scream came from inside him. It came from years of pent-up frustration. Of buried secrets. Of hidden truths and lies. Desires that frightened him. Memories that excited him before but sickened him after. And hate. So much hate.

He screamed until all he could hear was his own voice, hoarse, and until the people around him quietened. His eyes squeezed shut, his gut tight from the power the scream pulled from him.

Then he stopped.

He listened to the silence then the murmurs that hummed like a machine.

He opened his eyes to find a space had been made around him. A thousand wondrous eyes. A thousand astonished eyes. A thousand scared eyes.

But as the crowd moved away, huddling closer than before, one man remained where he was with two eyes that bore into him with a malice like no other.

CHAPTER FORTY

"Put the boy down, Hoffman," said Harvey. "There's no way out for you."

He was almost exactly as Harvey remembered him. He had pale skin beyond the paleness of most people. Thin lips framed his imperfect teeth and a small tuft of white blonde hair sat on his chin.

But above all, the feature that identified him more than any other was the pale eyes, unnatural, cold and deathlike.

The woman to Hoffman's side edged away but stayed within reach of her son.

"Stop him," she screamed at Harvey. Her face reddened and the outburst seemed to trigger a burst of tears. She dropped to her knees. "Please, he's got my son."

Harvey took one step closer.

The crowd took a breath.

And Harvey took one more step.

But Hoffman snatched the boy around, holding him over the water.

"I'll do it," said Hoffman. "Get away. One more step and I'll drop him."

The woman to Hoffman's side lunged at him. But Hoffman caught the movement and held the boy further out.

"No, Martina. You can't stop this now. It's gone too far."

The crowd had fallen silent, save for the whispered wonderings of the women, who pulled their own children closer. Phones were pulled from pockets, filming the spectacle like it was some cheap street show.

"Why, Herman?" said Harvey. "Why now? Why these people? It's me you want, not them. Let them go. I'm here."

Harvey raised his arms out to his side to show he was unarmed.

"Take me, Herman. Give the boy back to his mum."

"He's my son," said Herman. "I'm his father. He needs to know his father's a strong man. He needs to see that his father won't be pushed around anymore."

As if on cue, the boy's face crinkled and tears began to roll down his face. He gave off a loud, high-pitched wail and was reaching for his mum, who could do nothing but reach a hand out from where she knelt on the ground, just to let him know she was there. That she was close.

"You want to kill me? Well, here I am," said Harvey. He opened his jacket, raised his shirt and whipped his knife from the sheath on his belt, turning the point to press into his own skin. "You want to see me die? Is that it, Herman? You want to see blood for what I did to you?"

Hoffman's eyes were wide. They flicked from side to side at the crowd then returned to find Harvey.

"Put the boy down, Herman," said Harvey. "And I'll open myself up right here, right now."

The crowd gasped in unison and a small news crew pushed to the front, the camera just three feet from where Harvey stood.

Without warning, Herman brought the boy in from over the

water, more from fatigue than his better judgment. His face lost the scared and bitter snarl, dropping into the defeated, down-trodden look that Harvey remembered from the days he spent following him.

The days before his death.

"Do you honestly think this is all about you, Harvey Stone?" said Hoffman, shaking his head and setting the boy on his hip, smoothing his hair to calm him down. "Are you that egotistical that you think everything we've done was to get at you?"

"So why am I here?" said Harvey. "Why are you trying to frame me?"

"You're just a name on a list, Harvey," said Hoffman.

The words were clear.

The meaning was simple.

Harvey could picture the list.

But there was something different about his voice. It carried the same mechanical, monotonous tone, but there was an anger there, a strength that hadn't been there before.

"They all deserved to die, Harvey Stone," said Hoffman, his voice rising as a fury grew behind his pale eyes. "Every man that ever wronged us. The man that touched us as children and warped our fragile little minds. The man that sullied our family, poisoning her with his seed."

Hoffman raised his finger at the woman, who looked up from where she sat crumpled on the ground.

"And you, Harvey Stone," said Hoffman, lowering his hand to his side. "The man that took it all away from us. The man who buried us alive and all our honour along with it."

A murmur from the crowd behind began to grow as people moved further from Harvey.

"That's right," said Hoffman, addressing his audience. "This man here took our lives. Do you remember, Harvey? Do you remember how you forced us to dig a hole with our own bare hands? Do you remember how we pleaded for our life?"

Harvey didn't reply.

"I do," said Hoffman. "I remember you forcing us to lie down in the hole. I remember the first grains of dirt hitting my face as you buried us, with nothing but a hose pipe to breathe through and the weight of the earth crushing our bones."

Harvey stared at him. There was a difference, so subtle he couldn't place it, but it was there in his posture. It was in his voice.

And it was in his eyes.

But the moment was gone.

In an instant, the whole bridge was lit with a bright searchlight, and the deafening roar of rotor blades filled the air as a helicopter rose from beneath the bridge.

The boy's cries were drowned by the thump of the chopper blades, and with renewed vigour, the woman lunged once more. But she was knocked down with one swipe of Hoffman's back hand. He turned to face the helicopter, threatening to drop the boy.

Harvey took a single step forward.

The sea of people moved further away, squeezing together for safety but lingering in sick curiosity.

One man stepped forward from the crowd, parting the way with confident authority. The hum of the crowd quietened once more as the man raised his gun and aimed at Hoffman's back.

Sensing the change in the atmosphere, Hoffman turned his head as if listening for a clue to the disruption. He smiled as the man spoke, whose words cut through the air like a sharp blade through flesh.

"Lucas Hoffman," the man began, stepping further from the crowd to create a triangle between Hoffman, Harvey and himself. "Bring the boy back. Let him go. It's over."

CHAPTER FORTY-ONE

A sharp kick to the back of Stone's legs dropped him to the ground and two strong armed policemen cuffed his hands behind his back.

Reilly glanced at Stone once, studying his face, unable to remove the images of the details in his file.

But Stone's eyes flicked between Reilly and Hoffman as if he was confused.

"Herman," said Stone from his position on his knees. "You don't need to do this."

Hoffman's snarl dropped, softening into a sorrowful look. His posture followed. First his shoulders slumped then his back hunched forward as if the boy's weight was taking its toll.

"You don't understand, Harvey," said Hoffman. "You don't know what he's like. I owe him so much."

"Who, Herman? Who do you owe?" said Stone.

"Lucas," said Reilly. "Lucas Hoffman. You don't fool me. Show yourself."

At the mention of the name, Hoffman's face hardened. His eyes narrowed and his lips thinned to reveal yellowed, uneven teeth.

"It's over, Lucas," said the man. "You remember me, don't you?"

"I remember you alright," said Hoffman. All weakness from his voice had vanished, leaving nothing but cold malice and contempt. "I've waited, oh, so long to see you."

"Well, I'm here now. So put the boy down, Lucas. Enough people have been hurt. Enough people have lost their lives."

"Five long years, Reilly. Five long years we've waited to see you. Planning. Preparation. Patience," said Hoffman, and cast his eyes across to Stone. "Sound familiar, Stone?"

But Stone didn't reply. He knelt on the ground with the armed policemen either side of him, staring back at the deranged, pale-skinned man.

"We've killed them all," said Hoffman. "Every man that ever wronged us."

"We know about your list," said Reilly. "We know about the other men. And we know why we're here."

"They were all for Herman," said Hoffman. "All except you, DCI Reilly. You were for me. You're the last man on our list, and while I sat in that cell, day after day, night after night, I imagined your face as you breathed your last filthy breath."

"That's funny," said Reilly. "You're the last man on my list. But I can't say I ever gave you much thought. You're just another sick individual who should be locked away."

"You can't win them all, Reilly," said Hoffman. "We've thought about this long and hard. Now put the gun down."

A thousand eyes drilled into Reilly's back. He considered giving Hoffman what he wanted, letting the gun falter a little, which raised a smile on Hoffman's face.

But then he straightened and aimed at Hoffman's head, to one side of the boy. He could never take the shot. The risk of hitting the boy was too great. But there was no way he was letting Hoffman get the better of him.

"The boy, Hoffman," called Reilly, as the helicopter's bright searchlight swept across the bridge, the pilot fighting the strong winter winds that rolled off the Thames. "Set him down. He's done nothing to you."

"Don't you understand, Reilly? You all deserve to die," said Hoffman. He pointed his finger at the woman. "She betrayed Herman. She betrayed us both. Couldn't keep her legs together for five minutes, and for that, she dies along with her spawn."

"No," said the woman, who knelt on the ground to Reilly's right, out of Hoffman's vicious reach but close enough for her son to see her. "No, please. Not my son."

"And him," said Hoffman, pointing at Stone. "You know all about him and what he did?"

"He killed your brother," said Reilly.

"And you," said Hoffman. "You locked me up and took away everything we ever had. And for that, for all your sins, you die."

Reilly stepped forward.

The crowd gasped once more.

"Don't come any closer," said Hoffman.

But Reilly took another step.

"Show me Herman," said Reilly.

"No," said Lucas. "He's weak. You'll manipulate him with your cheap tricks."

"Herman," said Reilly, "I want to talk to you."

"No," said Lucas. His face twisted as if fighting some kind of inner battle with his own mind. "No, you can't."

"Herman, your family needs you," said Reilly. "Herman, only you can save them."

The sharp, venomous voice of Lucas faded and the narrowed eyes widened to reveal a scared looking man holding his son. His breathing quickened. His head flicked from side to side as he took in the crowd and their stares. Fear took him in its firm grip.

"I'm dying, Herman," said Reilly. "You can't save me. And Harvey Stone? He's beyond saving. But you can save your family, Herman. You're stronger than he is. Put the boy down, Herman. We're all here. It's just you, me, Stone and her. That's what you wanted, wasn't it? Well, it's over, Herman. Put the boy down. Nobody needs to get hurt."

With one hand tightly holding the frightened boy, Hoffman backed up against the bridge.

"That's it, Herman," said Reilly. "Just relax. Nobody needs to die here. It's over."

Hoffman's body relaxed once more. He leaned against the balustrade and turned the boy to see his face before lifting him up to kiss his forehead and pull him close.

"You're right about one thing, Reilly," said Hoffman, his face hidden behind the boy. He unzipped the small child's rucksack to reveal the top half of a gas cylinder with a small electrical unit attached to the valve. "This is everything I ever wanted."

He pulled a mobile phone from his jacket pocket and held it high for all to see.

The murmur among the crowd grew to a riot of panicked chatter. Then, as the foremost people identified the contents of the bag and the rumour spread back through them like an ocean wave, the screams started and people began to run.

Children were held high out of harm's way but disappeared from sight as their parents were overcome and trampled. A police horse reared up, kicking out at frantic pedestrians who were forcing a path to safety. It fell to the ground to become another obstacle for the wave of people. One man, seeing no other means of escape, barged past Reilly, knocking the gun from his hands, and hurled himself off the bridge into the river.

Some women screamed somewhere close by, loud and shrill. Reilly turned to find them clutching their children, too scared to run and frozen to the spot as the stampede rushed past in all directions.

As the stampede eased and the bridge emptied of people, groans of pain were all Reilly could hear as he rolled to his side clutching his chest.

A woman screamed for her children who had been swept away by the crowd. She fell to her knees, unable to decide which direction to search for them.

Only the thundering rotors of the helicopter could be heard as Reilly recovered. A knee had scuffed his face and a boot had stamped on his chest as some poor soul had run for their life.

He lay on his back and took in the sounds.

Gone was the hum of the crowd.

Gone was the chatter of the news reporter.

And gone were the cries of the boy.

He sat up and searched around him to find the bridge empty, save for the injured and the swarm of police running towards him.

The spot where Hoffman had stood was empty, and where Stone had been held, now only a pair of handcuffs lay on the ground.

CHAPTER FORTY-TWO

Riding the panicked crowd, Lucas wrenched Martina from the ground and pulled her into the throng, gripping her tight as he found his feet and kept pace with the stampede.

"Don't even think about losing me, Martina," said Lucas.

He held Sam over his shoulder, forcing the slower runners out of their way and dragging Martina along as they tripped over the fallen and bumped their way to freedom.

At the foot of the bridge, the police opened the barriers they'd installed to control the flow of people. Police horses moved to one side and, as far as Lucas could see, a sea of heads parted, making way for the thousands of people that sought escape from the bridge.

A right turn onto Lambeth Palace Road showed itself through a gap in the crowd and with a sharp pull on Martina's arm, Lucas followed hundreds of others to escape the rush into the comparatively empty piece of road.

Whistles blew and fluorescent jacketed police officers attempted to guide the roaring crowd with glowing batons. But the mass soon overcame them, forcing them to one side in time for Lucas to rush past.

The helicopter swooped low, shining its light and searching for Lucas, who diverted into a backstreet. He slowed to a walk, glancing over his shoulder to make sure they hadn't been followed.

"Where are you taking us?" asked Martina, breathless and frightened. "I can't run any further."

"We're going to where all this began," said Lucas. He stopped, pulled her wrist so she crashed into him, and then, with his hand still clutching the mobile phone, he ran his finger along her cheek. "Soon all this will be over."

He glanced over her shoulder at the buildings behind her, remembering a fourteen-floor office block with floor-to-ceiling glazing and an automatic revolving door at ground level that welcomed visitors and workers into a marble clad reception.

In its place was the shell of a building wrapped in scaffolding and green protective netting. In place of the automatic revolving doors was a wooden sign holding the name of a construction company and artistic renders of what the new refurbishment might look like.

"Follow me," said Lucas, pulling on Martina's wrist, offering her little choice in the matter. "And bring the bags."

He pushed a loose panel in the hoarding, holding it open for Martina and Sam to step through. Martina held both bags at arm's length as if they might go off at any second. Lucas followed and entered the construction site with Martina and Sam in tow.

The reception layout was exactly how he remembered it, minus the marble cladding, the long reception desk and the echo of expensive shoes. In their place were bare concrete walls, piles of acoustic insulation, the distant sounds of London and an eerie silence.

"I want to see Herman," said Martina. "I want to see him one last time."

"Well, you can't," said Lucas, as he searched for the stairwell. "Herman is weak. He's not to be trusted. I gave him the chance to finish it all and die a man. But he couldn't, could he?"

Darkness shrouded the concrete stairs. Broken bricks and concrete dust littered them, threatening to break a careless ankle. But with Martina in front and Sam between them, Lucas forced them up, floor after floor, until they reached the top. A hallway offered a choice of left or right. Old carpet still adorned the floor and the gypsum walls still stood, but all possessions and assets had been removed, ready for demolition.

Lucas turned left into the hallway. On his right was the shell of a single corner office where he remembered a large director's desk had stood in front of fine book shelves that were filled with leather-bound books and framed certificates.

To his left was an empty elevator shaft, dark and foreboding like the entrance to hell and from which a cold flow of air rushed, bringing with it the smell of damp and concrete. The void had been blocked with lengths of timber fixed across the opening and a yellow sign warning people of the danger.

Ahead of Lucas, only one office remained. Faint light spilled through the open doorway onto the carpeted floor as if it were welcoming Lucas home.

"In here," he called to Martina, pushing Sam ahead of him.

The room was smaller than he remembered. The smell of the demolition from the floors below and the perpetual city pollution that flowed through the empty window frame had tainted the fragrant sandalwood scent that accompanied Lucas' memories.

But it was the room. Of that he was sure. The two desks may have been removed and the vanity photos of celebrity meetings may have been relocated to a newer, shinier office, but it was the same room.

"Sit in the corner," said Lucas, when Martina stepped

through. She clutched the doorway as if considering running. But with one hand on Sam's shoulder, Lucas eyed her, weakening the threat until she broke and stood in the corner furthest from the door.

"I said sit," said Lucas, as he gazed through the empty window frame.

She dropped into a defensive crouch with her arms around her knees. The bright moon and city lights lit her shiny, scared eyes from the corner of the room.

Lucas shoved Sam towards her.

"Is this it?" said Martina. "Is this where it all ends? In a crummy old office that's about to be torn down?"

"It's significant," said Lucas with a smile, remembering being led from the room in handcuffs.

"It's a construction site," said Martina. "It's hardly the glamorous ending I heard you boasting to Herman about."

"You don't deserve a glamorous ending," said Lucas. "After what you did to my brother, you cheating whore, what do you expect? A brass band? A last request? You'll get nothing but the ending you deserve and you'll be grateful I'm saving you from a lifetime of guilt and regret."

The comment roused Martina from where she slumped in the corner. She rose and stepped forward to put herself between Sam and Lucas.

"I did nothing wrong," said Martina. "We did nothing wrong. Your brother-"

"My brother what?" snapped Lucas, then paused to watch her squirm. "My brother is weak. But not for long. When I'm done everyone will see how strong he is. Nobody will remember him as the weak man that let some old man fiddle around with him and mess with his head. Nobody will remember him as the man whose wife slept around with whomever she wished. But to change people's minds, to alter their perception, takes work. It takes courage. And that's a courage Herman doesn't have."

Lucas made to leave the room, but Martina reached for his arm, digging her heels into the floor. He turned back to face her, outraged.

"He's not weak," said Martina. Then she let her voice trail away and her arms fell to her sides. "Not the man I loved. He was strong."

"Stop it," said Lucas. His face twitched and his eyelids blinked.

"Why should I? He's in there, isn't he?" said Martina. "You're keeping him from us, from his family."

"No," said Lucas, covering his ears. "Don't you talk to him."

"Herman, it's me," said Martina, offering him her softest voice. "Come to me, Herman. You're better than this."

"Stop," said Lucas. But his voice had already begun to weaken. His eyes widened and glistened with tears.

"That's it, Herman. That's it, my Herman. There you are. Oh, Herman. I love you. Come back to me."

"Don't say those-" Lucas began, but his voice weakened mid-sentence and his posture slumped. "Martina," he said, as if seeing her for the first time. He pocketed the phone and pushed a loose strand of hair behind her ear. "Do you mean what you say?"

"Of course I do," said Martina, her soft voice accompanied by a small fog as her breath met the cold and frigid air. "It's always been you. I missed you so much, Herman."

He turned as if he was unsure of his feet then stood before her, prepared for Martina to either attack or fling her arms around him.

"It's over," she whispered, stepping closer and laying her hand on his chest. "We're safe, and it's all thanks to you, Herman. You saved us."

She pulled away, holding him at arm's length to take in his face.

"What?" said Herman. "I didn't-"

"I just want to look at you," said Martina. "You did everything right, Herman. You were so strong."

"I was?" he said, searching through the cloud of memory but finding nothing. He looked around him. "Where are we?"

"We're safe," said Martina. "That's all that matters. Get us out of these bags."

"The bags?" said Herman, and a flicker of light shone across a dark area of his mind, a place he was forbidden to venture. "The bags? But I-"

"Herman, there's no time. We need to get out of here, but I can't run with this bag," said Martina, gripping him by the arms. "It's too heavy."

"No," said Herman. "I mustn't. I-"

"You're strong, Herman," said Martina, waving her hand at Sam. "Look at what you did. You saved us. You saved your son. You're his hero."

Sam, who had climbed to his feet and was clinging to Martina's leg, looked up at Herman, his eyes wide with fear but pale just like his father's.

"My son?" said Herman.

"Yes, Herman. Help us get these off before it's too late."

"But Lucas-"

"Lucas is gone, Herman," said Martina. "You mustn't mention his name or he'll return."

The fog in Herman's mind thickened. The answers were there at the tip of his tongue. So much familiarity but so little clarity.

"The keys are in your pocket. You're in charge now, Herman. We have to stay strong."

He searched his pockets and found a small keyring with two

keys. Holding them up to the moonlight that shone through the empty window, another memory flashed across his mind then vanished as quickly as it had arrived.

The crunch of broken glass on the carpet in the hallway stopped them both.

"Hurry," said Martina in a whisper. "Unlock the padlocks."

"Who's out there?" said Herman.

"It doesn't matter," said Martina. "Just unlock us, Herman. Save us. You're in charge. Remember?"

He snapped back to her then fumbled with the locks as the slow footsteps of a man grew louder in the quiet corridor outside.

"Quickly, Herman," said Martina, offering him the padlock with a frantic glance at the door. "Please."

But the key wouldn't fit the lock. The darkness and his shaking hands prevented him from finding the hole with the key.

"Hurry, Herman. Please," said Martina.

The footsteps stopped.

Herman's eyes narrowed.

"No," said Martina. "No, Herman. Come back."

Lucas straightened, clicking his back as if it ached from slouching. He found Martina staring up at him, aghast.

"Miss me?" he said.

Then he shoved her and the boy back into the corner as the body of a man fell through the open doorway fighting for breath.

CHAPTER FORTY-THREE

The old, worn carpet itched at Reilly's fingertips yet gave the sensation of electricity when his fists curled and unfurled. A string of blood hung from his lips and clogged his throat, barring the airway for clean air to reach his diminished lungs.

He dry-retched and spat the iron taste from his mouth before the first kick slammed into his chest.

"Don't you die yet, Reilly," said Lucas, and rolled Reilly onto his back with a hard shove of his foot. "Don't you spoil my game now, will you?"

The blood collected at the back of Reilly's throat, causing a coughing fit. Bloody, red mist flew from Reilly's mouth but his swollen airways restricted his breathing even more. In a panic, he rolled away from Hoffman onto his side, spat a wad of blood onto the carpet and focused on calming his breathing. Each deep breath allowed more air through than the last, slowing his racing heart.

He sensed rather than saw the layout of the room. A cold snap of wind on his back from the window at the opposite end of the room. The whispered murmurings of the boy. The whimpers of the woman huddled in the corner.

"So this is your big rescue, is it, DCI Reilly?" said Lucas. "I'll be honest with you. I'm less than impressed and I imagine Martina and Sam here are wondering why you bothered at all. Should have stayed at home with your hot chocolate, old man. Counter-terrorism is a young man's game, I'm sure."

"While there's life in these old bones, Hoffman, I'll be stopping people like you. It was what I was born to do."

"You conjure such a romantic image," replied Hoffman. Then he paused and Reilly could almost hear the smile on his pale face. "Do you recognise this place?"

With a final cough to clear his throat, Reilly rolled to a seated position, leaning against the wall to see Hoffman. His silhouette was dark against the bright night sky but his shape was unmistakable, lean and lithe, and almost feminine in the way he stood.

"Of course I remember it," said Reilly. "I have fond memories of walking you through those doors, and even fonder memories of slamming the door to the meat wagon that carried you away. What was it? Five years? We should have fought for a longer sentence."

"Parole is a wonderful thing," said Hoffman. "It's amazing what a little good behaviour will do, coupled with a thirst for knowledge. In fact, I should actually thank you for catching me when you did. If my original plan had succeeded, I would have ripped this floor off the building and taken Jasper Charles with it. But then I would never have learned the things I did, locked up in my little cell with my cell mate, whiling away the hours, listening to him teach me all the things he knows about..."

"About what?" said Reilly.

"Chlorine bombs. Their toxicity. Mobile phone technology. Everything I needed to know, Reilly. And all because you walked me through that door," said Hoffman. He gave a little laugh. "I'd probably still have half of my list."

"I would have caught you," said Reilly. "We would have, the force. One failed assassination plot may have opened doors for a smart lawyer to get you off, but not this time, Hoffman. This time it's for real. You'll never see the light of day again."

"That's interesting," said Hoffman, and he pushed off the window sill, disappearing into the dark corner where the woman sat with her son.

"What is?" said Reilly. "You're not interesting, Hoffman. You're sick."

"Exactly," said Hoffman. "I'm sick. We're sick. Both of us. Herman and me."

"Your brother is dead, Lucas."

"No," said Hoffman, stepping closer, quickening his pace to close the gap. "He's alive. He lives on. In me. I'm resurrecting his memory. I'm cleansing the world of the bad things he did."

"You're killing the reasons he did what he did," asked Reilly. "Isn't that admitting he was sick too?"

"He was weak. He was easily manipulated," said Hoffman. "There's a difference."

"Talk to me about Jasper Charles," said Reilly. "Tell me where he fits into all of this."

"You'd like that, wouldn't you?" said Hoffman, turning his back on Reilly. With his arms behind his back, he paced the room, turning on one heel to begin the return journey. "He's the one that started it all," said Hoffman. "He had the twisted mind of a man even weaker than Herman. A man so devious and evil, he built a small empire to shine the light away from his sick and perverse taste in young boys. Look around you. Do you remember how this place looked, Reilly? Do you remember the glass cabinets with the awards and photographs of him with the stars?"

"I remember," said Reilly. "He was a successful man."

"He was a successful man," said Hoffman, with a tone that conveyed his hidden smile. "Not anymore though, eh?"

"What about Jubilee Gardens?" said Reilly. "The first bomb?"

"Patrick Gervais," said Hoffman. "It was him that sent Herman under really. Jasper Charles may have started the whole thing, but by the time we went to school and Fatty Patty got hold of him, poor Herman didn't stand a chance."

"He bullied Herman?"

"He humiliated him. He distributed photos of Herman and..." He paused, as if unable to say the name again.

"Jasper Charles?"

Hoffman nodded.

"It scarred him for life," said Hoffman. "Can you imagine going to school every day with two hundred kids laughing at you? Opening wounds that you try to bury every night?"

"But you're his brother. Why didn't you help him?"

"I can't be everywhere," said Hoffman. "I spent my entire life looking out for that boy. Can you imagine spending every day worrying if today's the day that your twin brother, the other half of your own being, will kill himself?"

His voice softened and, for the first time, a trace of humanity showed itself like a weak sun behind black thunderheads.

"I've spent half my life keeping him alive," said Hoffman. "And the other half spent correcting his mistakes, erasing his past."

"Do you think it's time?" asked Reilly.

"Time for what?"

Reilly allowed a pause, time for Hoffman to tune into what he was about to say. He waited for Hoffman to stop pacing and turn to look his way.

"Do you think it's time to let him go?"

But Hoffman remained silent as if he was digesting the statement. Fighting the statement. Searching for a reasoned argument.

"You've helped him all you can, Lucas," said Reilly, as he pushed himself to his feet, one hand on his chest, the other steadying himself on the wall. "He must be looking down at you right now, smiling with the love that only a brother can have."

"No," said Hoffman, his voice almost a whisper. "No. Herman lives on. He's right here. He's with me. You can't take him away anymore. Nobody can."

"He's gone, Lucas. You have to let him go," said Reilly. "You've done it. You cleaned his memory. Let him fly. Let his name be remembered with smiles. Don't hold him back. Not now."

"I can't let him go," said Hoffman, snatching away to pace the room. The soft tones Reilly had drawn from him were replaced with bitter, snappy snarls.

"You've done it," said Reilly, raising his voice. He waited for Hoffman to turn away from him, gave the girl and the boy a quick glance and found them huddled together, eyes wide with fear and wonder, then pulled his handgun from beneath his jacket. "You set him free, Lucas. You set him free but you paid the ultimate price."

Reilly armed the weapon. The sound of the metallic slide was clear in the relative silence.

Hoffman stopped beside the door.

His head lifted.

"The ultimate price?" said Hoffman. He turned to face Reilly, testing his resolve.

"Stay where you are," said Reilly, his finger poised over the trigger and, for the first time in months, his hand was as steady as a rock.

"I suppose you'd like to be the one who walks me out of

here?" said Hoffman. "I suppose you'd find some kind of cyclical satisfaction. I can see the newspapers now. The old photo beside the new."

"Take your hands out of your pockets and raise them over your head, Hoffman."

But Hoffman didn't comply. He didn't even acknowledge Reilly's demand.

"You remember what I told you on the bridge, Reilly? The others on the list were all for my dear brother, Herman."

He took a step forward.

"But you were for me."

"Hands, Hoffman," said Reilly. "It doesn't have to end this way."

"No," replied Hoffman, pulling his hands from his pocket. "No, it doesn't."

"Drop the phone," said Reilly, steadying his aim.

But the phone's green screen lit up.

"You're right," said Hoffman. "It doesn't have to end this way."

He hit the green call button.

In the corner of Reilly's eye, a second green screen lit up, somewhere in the corner of the room.

In the split second that Reilly connected the pieces and made a decision, the same split second that Hoffman winked at him and made towards the door, he felt death's presence looming above him like a cloud with long, spiteful fingers teasing at his dying body.

He bound across the room as the phone connected to the woman's backpack gave off its first ring.

An emotionless trill, three seconds long.

"One," said Reilly, as his hands found the padlock. But he couldn't force it open.

The screen flashed green again, accompanied by the same trill sound.

The girl looked up at him, frightened, frozen with terror.

With everything he had, Reilly pulled at the straps. But they wouldn't budge. He jammed his foot against the furthest strap, forcing the bag and the woman against the wall, and pulled on the second strap. There was a tear of fabric.

He pulled harder, his chest closing with the exertion. His airways tightened. He growled, giving every last ounce of oxygen he had inside his body to the muscles that tore at the straps.

And they ripped, sending him staggering backwards.

The green screen flashed on for the third time, lighting the side of the woman's terrified face in emerald hues.

"Get it off," he yelled, and launched himself at the girl. He pulled at the backpack, bending her arms back as the trill sound began its final alarm.

"It's stuck," she said.

Shoving her against the wall, Reilly tore the bag from her body.

But as he stepped away, clutching the bag against his own body, for the tiniest fraction of a moment, he found the boy's wide eyes, inquisitive, wide, and paler than any eyes Reilly had ever seen before.

Time seemed to stop.

The shrill tone stopped.

Somewhere on a digital switchboard far away, a pre-recorded voice message began to play.

Four uncertain eyes stared at the bag then up at Reilly, tears shining in the bright moonlight as the evil grip of his disease stabbed with its steely claws into his chest, closing his airways for good.

And with a silent acknowledgment to the woman, an unspoken passing of the gift of life, Reilly held the bag and launched himself through the empty window, and welcomed the solace and peace that awaited him on the hard concrete below.

CHAPTER FORTY-FOUR

Cold hands found Lucas' neck, hands with a strength fuelled by malice and unconstrained by doubt, fear or trepidation.

He dropped the phone on the old carpeted floor and grasped the cold hands. But instead of fighting, instead of grappling with the man's strength, Lucas held the hands in his own, caressing the hard skin until their fingers interlocked.

"Harvey Stone," said Lucas, through his constricted throat. "I knew you'd come for us."

As predicted, Stone pulled away, stepping back from Lucas but covering the exit.

"What are you going to do, Stone? How are you going to kill us?" said Lucas, taking a single step towards the man who had taken Herman's life, the man that who had haunted Lucas' dreams for five long years.

But Stone didn't reply.

"You could take us to Wimbledon Common? I know this place. You could bury me alive," said Lucas, taking another step forward. "Just like you buried Herman."

Stone took a single step back, keeping his distance, but his ever watchful eyes followed Lucas, reading him, waiting for a move.

"Don't you see?" said Lucas. "Whatever you decide and however you choose to do it, we win."

The words had no reaction on Stone's face. Although it was swathed in shadows and only a faint outline of his hard face could be seen, there was no variation in his expression.

"If you decide to bury us alive, they'll find us, and we'll win. If you decide to crush our skull with those strong hands of yours, we win. They know about you now, Harvey Stone. The whole world saw you on TV. So you can walk us out of here and hand us over to the police. Or you can finish it right here. Squeeze the life from our body. Either way, we win and you lose."

Stone didn't reply.

Lucas stepped forward, forcing Stone back another step.

"You're afraid," said Lucas. "The great Harvey Stone is afraid of losing."

He stepped forward once more. But Stone remained where he was. From his hand, a flash of steel caught Lucas' eye.

Lucas smiled.

"What are you going to do, Stone?" said Lucas, taking another step forward, taunting the man with opportunity. He stopped just two arms' length away. "Are you going to cut my throat? Are you going to cut me open?"

"How did you know where I buried him?" said Stone, his voice dry and cold like the blood that ran through his veins.

"Instinct," said Lucas. "We're twins."

"No," said Stone. "Tell me how you found his body. Tell me how you found Herman."

The mention of his brother's name woke something inside Lucas, a sadness that hung heavy on his heart, tightening his chest. Casting his mind back more than five years was easy. The images he recalled had haunted him day after day, night after night.

"Do you remember the rain, Harvey?" said Lucas, lowering his voice. "That night. Do you remember how it fell in sheets?"

Stone didn't reply.

"I do," said Lucas. "It's all I remember. The reflections on the wet road. Bright car lights and deep shadows, Harvey. Shadows deep enough to hide a grown man."

"You followed me?" asked Harvey.

"Just as you clung to the shadows, stalking my brother as a lion might stalk its prey, I followed you. I could have taken you then. I could have stopped you before you even touched him."

"But you didn't."

"No," said Lucas. "You fascinated me. The way you moved. The silence you never broke."

With his arms hanging at his sides, Lucas offered himself with no suggestion of attack or means of defence. Instead, he rode the ego of the man he'd dreamed about so often, his life on the blade of Stone's knife.

"At first, it was curiosity. I watched Herman leave through the window of our flat. I knew where he was going, of course. I knew what he was going to do."

"And you didn't stop him?" said Harvey.

"You didn't know him. Not like I did. He didn't mean any harm," said Lucas. "He didn't know any different."

Harvey didn't reply.

"That was when I saw you. You stepped from the trees in the car park. You followed him. Always behind. Always out of sight."

Somewhere, behind the eyes of the man, the night was being played out. Lucas wondered if a killer like Stone could recall the details at will, or if he managed to file the night away, compartmentalising the atrocities.

"Do you remember, Harvey?" said Lucas. "Tell me you do."

"I remember."

"Do you remember the Common? How you stepped through the trees, flanking poor Herman?"

"I do," said Harvey.

"And you remember forcing him to dig his own grave?" said Lucas, a taste of bitterness evident in his words.

"I do," said Harvey.

Neither man spoke for a few seconds. The scene played out between them. Memories. Flashbacks.

And for Lucas, tears.

"Can you imagine how it felt to watch you do such a thing?"

Harvey didn't reply.

"Can you imagine how it felt to watch my poor, dear brother's broken body being dropped into a hole? He was alive. Damn you," said Lucas. "He was still alive. There was a chance you could have stopped yourself. There was a chance he'd be alive now, instead of forcing me to carry him, sharing my body with his tainted soul."

"He needed to die," said Harvey.

"He needed a chance," said Lucas. "He needed guidance. You could have stopped."

Harvey didn't reply.

"All night, I sat on his grave," said Lucas, after a pause. "I heard his final cries for help. I felt his final breaths in the hose you forced into his mouth. And I felt the last beat of his heart in my own. I felt him join me, Harvey. I felt him enter me. I can see what he saw. I can feel what you did to him. The earth piling on top of him. The fright. The fear. The terror. Knowing that when that earth covered his face he'd never ever again walk this earth in his own mortal body."

"But you didn't stop me," said Harvey.

The words caught Lucas off guard. He stepped back.

"You didn't try to stop me," said Harvey. "You watched him dig the hole. You watched me break his bones. You heard him screaming. Tell me you heard him screaming, Lucas. Because I can remember it now. Right now. The noise is playing in my head. The tears. The begging. It's all here," said Harvey, tapping his temple with his index finger.

Lucas shook his head, shaking the thoughts from his mind.

But Harvey stepped forward once more, forcing Lucas back further. "You watched your own brother die and you did nothing. You sat on his grave when I'd gone and you did nothing. Tell me you tried, Lucas. Tell me you tried to pull him out of the hole."

"Stop," said Lucas, his voice high. He brought his hands up to his ears to block out the sound.

"None of this is for him, is it?" said Harvey, moving ever closer, rubbing the handle of his blade with a practiced finger. "This is all for you. This is all for your guilt. You watched your brother die. Your twin brother. The only person in this world you were supposed to care for and now you can't live with yourself. Can you?"

Lucas dropped to his knees, burying his head in his hands.

"Stop," he screamed. "Stop it. You don't know. You didn't know him. Not like me. Nobody did. He just needed love. He just needed showing."

"You killed him," said Harvey. "You killed him just as much as I did."

A flood of blood rushed to Lucas' head. A tightness overcame his mind. His thoughts whirled around, teasing him with the fragments of memories of Herman he'd clung to for so long.

But all clarity had gone.

The memories were lost to a wash of guilt.

He sat up on his knees and stared up at Harvey.

"Do it," he said, offering Stone his open throat. "Let me go to him. Let me find him, wherever he is. He needs me."

Harvey stepped forward.

He took a handful of Lucas' hair in his hand and held his head still.

A fierce light shone in Stone's eyes, ice blue and devoid of emotion.

"Do it," said Lucas, as he felt tears fall from his eyes and run across his pale skin. "You win, Harvey Stone."

But Harvey didn't move a muscle.

He waited.

Then he rolled his neck from side to side as if the stretching gave him some kind of relief of tension, allowing him to savour the moment.

Then his faced dropped and his knife hand shot into the air in a flash of light.

"Stop right there," said a voice.

Harvey froze.

It was female. Authoritative.

"Drop the knife, Stone," said the woman from somewhere close to the staircase.

"Harvey, do as she says," said another voice.

The command was supported by the sound of a weapon being armed.

But Harvey didn't reply. He held onto Lucas' head, knife poised to strike while behind those cold eyes, the odds were being weighed.

"Do it," whispered Lucas. "Finish it."

"Harvey, don't listen to him," said the second woman, as if she knew the man, as if she could get to him. "It's a trap, Harvey. If you do that, he wins."

"He needs to die," said Harvey. "They both need to die."

"That's not your call, Stone," said the first woman. "Drop the knife before it's too late."

"Don't come any closer," said Stone.

"Harvey, listen to her," said the second woman. "Please. It's me. Listen to her."

Harvey tensed.

His hand pulled hard on Lucas' hair, pulling his head back further, opening the neck up ready to slice. His face tightened with the power he was summoning for the strike.

Lucas closed his eyes, welcoming the kill. He thought of Herman. He thought of his face. His eyes. His soft touch.

And Stone's hand relaxed, releasing Lucas' hair from his strong grasp.

Lucas opened his eyes.

"Do it," screamed Lucas. "Kill me, you coward."

But Harvey lowered his knife. He took a step back.

Clinging to the thought of death, the chance of escape and the hope of being with Herman one more time, Lucas scampered across the floor on his knees.

Stone backed away and the policewoman stepped into view.

"Kill me, you coward," cried Lucas. "You killed him. Now kill me."

Lucas dropped his hands to the floor, burying his face into the old carpet to wipe away his tears and scratch the frustration from his angered mind.

As Stone stepped away and the policewoman stepped closer, Lucas backed away from her.

"Get away," he screamed, and stood to defend himself.

But the woman aimed her weapon at his chest, her stance strong and her hands unwavering. "Lucas Hoffman," she began. "I am arresting you on suspicion of murder on multiple counts. You do not have to say anything, but anything you do say-"

Her speech was interrupted by a scream to Lucas' left. From

the doorway of the second office, Martina launched herself at Lucas, scratching at his face, tearing his skin with her nails and driving him back further and further towards the elevator shaft.

Teeth found skin.

Fingers pulled at hair.

And sharp claw-like nails found the soft flesh behind Lucas' eyes.

Until the crack of wood snapping stopped the attack.

And, as if the doors of hell opened up and swallowed him whole, he fell.

The slice of moonlight that shone into the corridor faded to a dot.

And Herman's smiling face grew bright and clear in the darkness until Lucas' body hit the bottom of the elevator shaft and the slither of the desperate soul he'd clung to for five long years was released.

CHAPTER FORTY-FIVE

Spinning, blue lights lit the narrow side street. Bright yellow jackets walked to and fro, some urgently, others less so. Uniformed officers had cordoned off the area creating a concentration of bustle and noise.

But there was a sense of relief.

Two paramedics pushed a gurney towards one of the two waiting ambulances. A sheet had been used to cover the body, but from the looks of disdain from each of the uniformed officers they passed, Harvey knew it was Hoffman.

Loading the gurney was unceremonious. The paramedics closed the rear doors, asked the senior officer in charge of the scene to sign a release form, and then pulled out of the crime scene with a police escort front and back. The blue lights flashed but they drove in silence.

Staring from the rear seat of a police car, Martina watched the ambulance leave. She wore neither the bitter look of hatred nor a look of dismay. Her face was blank as if she was coming to terms with a stain on her life being washed away. No matter the consequences, the Hoffmans were gone.

"How are you feeling?" asked Cole.

Harvey nodded, but said nothing.

"You're free to go," she said, and flicked her eyes between Harvey and Melody, who was standing by his side. "We have your statements and we'll be calling you in for further questioning during the enquiry. But as far as I'm concerned, we have everything we need until then."

Harvey opened his mouth to speak, but a clatter of metal to his right caught his attention. From the side of the building, two more paramedics wearing hazmat suits pushed a gurney towards the last ambulance.

Like the first, the body had been covered with a sheet.

But unlike the first, each officer stopped, removed their hats, and offered Reilly their own silent thanks as he passed them for the last time.

The senior officer raised his hand to stop the paramedics then glanced up at Cole as if he was seeking permission to remove the sheet.

Cole let out an audible breath then inhaled, filling her chest. Her eyes moistened as Melody reached out and touched her arm.

"Say goodbye," said Melody, as if the two were friends, connected on some level far deeper than Harvey knew of. "You'll always regret not saying goodbye."

Cole dizzied and closed her eyes.

But as the senior police officer went to push away Reilly's body, Cole spoke. "Connor," she called, then hesitated, finding the strength inside to do what she knew was right. "Wait."

The policeman offered her a look of sympathy and held out his hand for her to hold onto, offering his own strength.

"We should leave them to it," said Melody, and turned to face Harvey.

He glanced back at the construction site, looking up at the

windowless top floor, and then cast his gaze across the rooftops and high-rise buildings that reached into the night.

Harvey nodded.

A uniformed policeman held the red and white tape up for them and they made their way onto the main road.

Cars honked in celebration. Drunken men and women linked arms, their collective mass spanning the footpath. Lights shone in every direction as Melody and Harvey reached the riverside where the ordeal had begun.

They found a spot on the bridge and gazed down at the inky water below, flowing regardless of the night, just as it had done during countless other horrific nights in the city.

"Life goes on," said Melody, as if she was reading Harvey's mind.

Harvey didn't reply. He nodded and met her eyes.

"Do I have to say I told you so?" she asked.

Harvey raised an eyebrow in question.

"I told you to let the police deal with it."

Harvey didn't reply. He stared down at the water.

"But I am proud of you, Harvey," said Melody. "I'm proud that you-"

"That I didn't kill anyone?" said Harvey. "I must be getting old."

"No," said Melody. "Not old. You're in your prime. I wouldn't change a single thing."

Harvey laughed, a single breath that produced a small cloud in the cold air.

"Do you think it's over now?" she asked. "Do you think we can relax now? Put all this behind us and start our new life? A new year. A new beginning."

"I'll try," said Harvey. Then he turned to her and smiled. "I can't promise anything though."

The first chime of Big Ben announced midnight and the new year.

The crowds that lined the riverside erupted into a giant roar. Arms waved, people hugged and the night sky exploded into life as the fireworks display began with a riot of colour and explosions.

But that was somewhere far away, somewhere that right there and then, as Harvey stood with Melody by his side, faded with insignificance.

He reached out for her, pulling her in close and pushed a strand of hair from her face.

"I told you I'd find you, didn't I?"

Melody laughed. "I think you'll find I found-"

But her words were cut short as Harvey leaned in and found her lips. He kissed her with everything he had, everything he wanted to say but couldn't. Everything she needed to know was right there in that kiss.

It was as the last of Big Ben's chimes rang out that he pulled away, hovering close to her and leaning his head on hers.

"It doesn't matter who found who," said Harvey.

"No," said Melody, letting her arms find their way into Harvey's warm jacket. "But it's important to us that things will settle down. We need you around. We need you to be safe."

"We?" said Harvey, pushing her away a little so he could read her expression.

She smiled. For the tiniest of moments, uncertainty flashed across her eyes. But then they eased, and shone with tears of joy as her smile broadened.

"You're going to be a father, Harvey."

Harvey didn't reply.

The End

Also by J.D. Weston

Award-winning author and creator of Harvey Stone and Frankie Black, J.D.Weston was born in London, England, and after more than a decade in the Middle East, now enjoys a tranquil life in Lincolnshire with his wife.

The Harvey Stone series is the prequel series set ten years before The Stone Cold Thriller series.

With more than twenty novels to J.D. Weston's name, the Harvey Stone series is the result of many years of storytelling, and is his finest work to date. You can find more about J.D. Weston at www.jdweston.com.

Turn the page to see his other books.

The Silent Man

To catch the shadow he must break all the rules...

See www.jdweston.com for details.

The Spider's Web

The harder you struggle the tighter his web becomes...

See www.jdweston.com for details.

The Mercy Kill

To light the way, he must burn his past...

See www.jdweston.com for details.

The Savage Few

Coming October 2021

Join the J.D. Weston Reader Group to stay up to date on new releases, receive discounts, and get three free eBooks.

See www.jdweston.com for details.

The Stone Cold Thriller Series

Stone Cold

Stone Fury

Stone Fall

Stone Rage

Stone Free

Stone Rush

Stone Game

Stone Raid

Stone Deep

Stone Fist

Stone Army

Stone Face

The Stone Cold Box Sets

Boxset One

Boxset Two

Boxset Three

Boxset Four

Visit www.jdweston.com for details.

The Frankie Black Files

Torn in Two

Her Only Hope

Black Blood

The Frankie Black Files Boxset

Visit www.jdweston.com for details.

FREE EBOOK

So, you've met Harvey Stone. You know he's a ruthless killer with a heart of gold and morals to suit. Are you looking for more of his stories?

If you'd care to witness his birth, meet his parents and learn how he became the man he is, then perhaps you'd enjoy a free eBook. *The Inside Job* is the story of where it all began.

Visit *www.jdweston.com* to claim your free eBook.

The Stone Cold Thriller series is set in East London and Essex and features places from my own childhood.

The headquarters building was just a few streets away from my first flat in Silvertown. The farm where the girls were kept is fictitious but Pudding Lane was a favorite haunt of mine, a place to park our cars and do all the things that teenagers like to do.

The big house is real. My parents lived there for a while before I was born and I have vague memories of visiting the owner as a child. Sadly, the image of the house and rabbits in the surrounding fields are all I can recall thirty-something years later.

Epping Forest is real as many of you know. I have many memories of long walks with my family in there. When I became old enough to drive, the forest was a cool place to hang out, camp and just escape the urban life.

If you know the area, and recognize places from the stories, please do reach out to me. Theydon Bois will always be a special place to me and I'm sure if you've been there, you'll feel the same.

Thank you for reading.

J.D.Weston

ACKNOWLEDGEMENTS

Authors are often portrayed as having very lonely work lives. There breeds a stereotypical image of reclusive authors talking only to their cat or dog and their editor, and living off cereal and brandy.

I beg to differ.

There is absolutely no way on the planet that this book could have been created to the standard it is without the help and support of Erica Bawden, Paul Weston, Danny Maguire, and Heather Draper. All of whom offered vital feedback during various drafts and supported me while I locked myself away and spoke to my imaginary dog, ate cereal and drank brandy.

The book was painstakingly edited by Ceri Savage, who continues to sit with me on Skype every week as we flesh out the series, and also throws in some amazing ideas.

To those named above, I am truly grateful.

J.D.Weston.